DAWN OF OPPRESSION

Other Books by D.I. Telbat

The COIL Series: Christian Suspense

The COIL Legacy Series: Christian Suspense

COIL Legacy Collection: 3 Books in 1 Volume

The Resolution Series: America's Last Days

The STEADFAST Series: America's Last Days

STEADFAST Collection: 6 Novellas in 1 Volume

Last Dawn Series: America's Last Days

Leeward Set: Where Christians Dare

Never Lost Series: Trafficking Rescue Novels

Arabian Variable

Called To Gobi

God's Colonel

Soldier of Hope

Short Story Collections

DAWN of OPPRESSION
America's Last Days

BOOK TWO OF THE LAST DAWN SERIES

D.I. TELBAT

IN SEASON PUBLICATIONS
USA

Printed in the United States of America

DAWN OF OPPRESSION: America's Last Days
/ D.I. Telbat -- 1st ed.
Categories: Futuristic Christian Fiction;
Christian Suspense

D.I. Telbat / In Season Publications
https://ditelbat.com
https://books2read.com/DITelbat

ISBN 978-1-7371777-7-7

Cover Design by Streetlight Graphics

For Christians, where they suffer;
For the oppressed, where they stand;
For the persecuted, where they perish;
For the hurting in every land . . .

Acknowledgements

Long books may be enjoyable reads, but they require lots more editing and formatting work. I sometimes feel like I have the easy task of just telling the story, but thanks to Dee, she whips each manuscript into shape for you. We also thank our proofreader, Sharon, for her attentive and helpful eye on *Dawn of Oppression*. I thank our beta-readers for their attention to many book details, and for taking time to leave reviews. My thanks to Bob B, who gave me the idea a few years ago to include some young outcasts in a tunnel system as part of a novel. Additionally, I would've stopped writing a long time ago if you, the reader, didn't occasionally let us know that you enjoy what I share with you. We're so thankful for your support. To God be the glory! *—David Telbat*

Character Sketch

Brian Steelman – a Federation Enforcer whose violent past haunts him as he searches for the Serval, the man who showed him kindness long ago.

Bruno – a bear-sized man who has dedicated the last decade to securing safe passage for Christians in the underground movement in New York and New Jersey.

Chen Li – Nathan's wife who now works in Citizen Processing, using her position to help God's people endure the Federation's harsh treatment.

Chloe Azmaveth – COIL's original public relations officer, now in her late sixties, who has used her clandestine wiles to infiltrate the enemy's administration.

Corban Dowler – the founder of COIL. Although he's in his eighties now, his mind is still sharp enough to recognize the dangers of the Federation as they loom against the operatives he trained.

Heather Putelli – Luigi's wife. Although her health is failing from being underground for so many years, she becomes grandmother to many orphans.

Hedgehog – a resistance leader with an aggressive side to him that tries the Bandit's patience.

Jenna Dowler – the blind daughter of Corban Dowler. Now nearly forty, she is COIL's chief strategist who is often underestimated. She has a secret that if discovered, could be the end of her life and of those around her.

Kendrick Obrador – the Federation's chancellor, a domineering man who belittles everyone so he can live the life of luxury he won by sending adversaries to the gallows.

Lena Travers – the older sibling of the Twins, a pair of Enforcers who terrorize all nonconformists in the Federation. Killing means nothing to this vicious woman.

Levi Caspertein – the witty son of the infamous Titus Caspertein, also known as the Serval.

Luigi Putelli – this aged Italian was once Corban's most loyal companion. Now, he has dedicated himself to keeping Radiant Shade and Jenna secure.

Milo Rotham – a colonel in Philadelphia's Citizen Army. He's an ambitious soldier who was raised on video games.

Nathan Isaacson – also known as Eagle Eyes, he's become a prominent official inside the Federation, utilizing his station to secretly help the persecuted.

Owen Travers – the younger brother of Lena, together known as the Twins, a vicious pair of Enforcers who terrify and kill nonconformists.

Radiant Shade – the code name for the woman who covertly encourages and comforts Christians in the underground throughout the Federation. She's willing to sacrifice herself for the people under her protection.

Scooter – one of the original COIL Special Forces team members; he has become the resistance leader, known as the Bandit, to draw the attention of Enforcers away from the Christian underground.

Sean Harris – a gruff sergeant who accompanies Nathan Isaacson in New York City.

Willie – a heavy-set resistance leader, originally from Minnesota.

Glossary

Appalachian Federation – the new nation founded ten years after Pan-Day, along the East Coast of North America, spanning from New Hampshire to Georgia.

Citizen Army – the name of the socialist-style military that operates across the Federation.

COIL – the abbreviation for the **Commission of International Laborers**, a Christian relief organization that helps persecuted and oppressed people.

Nonconformists – those who reject the Federation's laws.

Pan-Day – the general reference to the time when the Meridia Virus began to wipe out one hundred million Americans.

Vags – the nickname of the orphaned vagrants who live underground in New York City's tunnels.

MAP A

Manhattan, NYC, Northern half

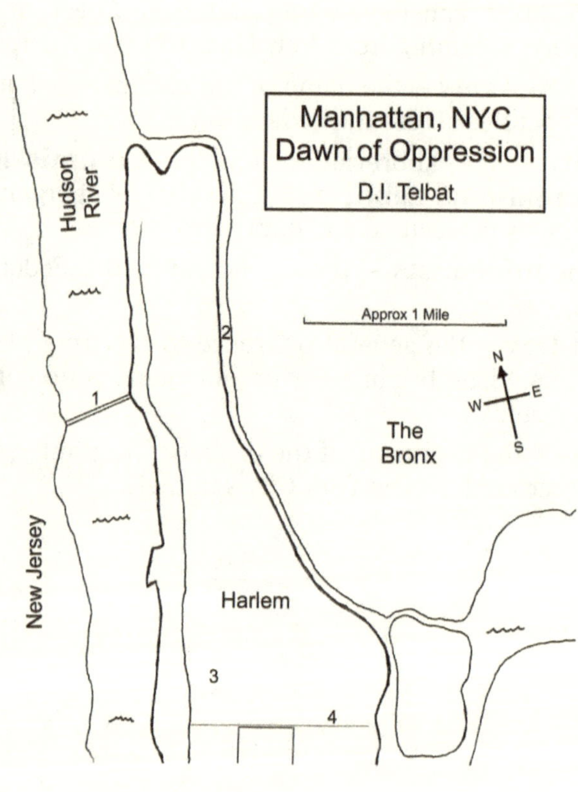

Map B

Manhattan, NYC, Lower half

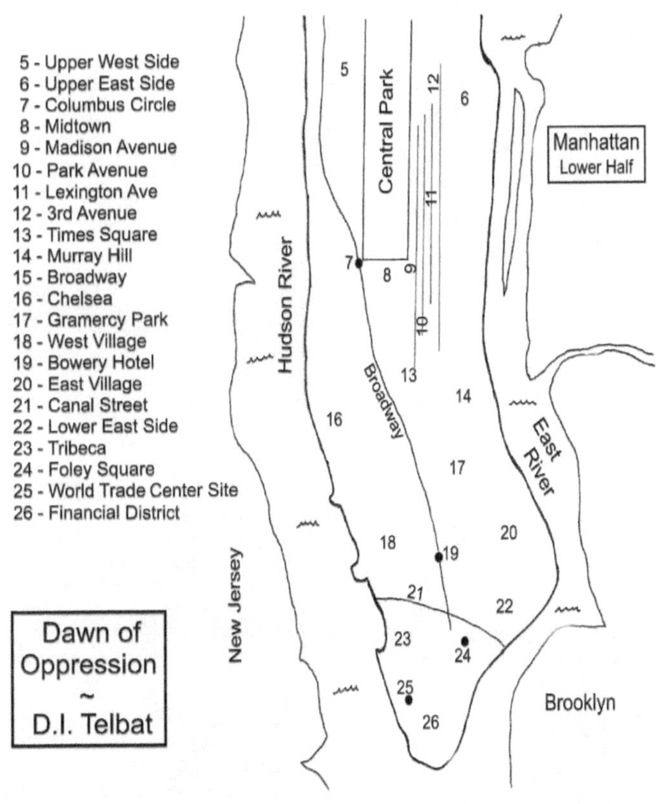

A Note from the Author

Dear Friends,

The *Last Dawn Series* continues with this book about oppression, which involves a return to COIL's beginnings of standing against Christian persecution. Without spoiling the story, I want to offer a few insights to make your read that much more enjoyable.

First, most of this book is based in New York City—Manhattan, to be specific. Although a few scenes are in the subway tunnels, I haven't attempted to label them since there are so many modern, as well as hidden, tunnels. But the surface street names may be of interest to you, so I've included a map with just a few highlights. You may want to note that in Manhattan, avenues run north and south, and streets run east to west. Broadway, which is referenced often, is an avenue, and it runs the length of the island, top to bottom, on the west side of Central Park.

Second, I refer to the "gesture of the cross" in the first few chapters. This signal is used by the underground Christians to secretly identify one another in public. This gesture is fictionalized for this book, but it's based on the real lengths that actual Christians must go through in our world today where they are persecuted and in hiding. Throughout history, Christians behind closed borders have had secret languages, signs, and gestures to communicate.

Third, I've made a point to write a sample of coded poetry within the book. It's an example of the way Christians have shared the Word of God even under strict laws against having Bibles. In this novel, the Bible is coded by counting every third and seventh word in each line of poetry. In real life, in such places as China, Iran, and North Korea, much greater efforts to preserve and share the Bible are exercised. Be sure to check out Back To Jerusalem (backtojerusalem.com) and Vision Beyond Borders (visionbeyondborders.org) to get involved in their covert efforts to share God's Word behind closed borders.

The Bowery Hotel, merely a conveniently-located building for this story, is a real place today, but I've fictionalized all of its interior for the sake of the story.

The Citizen's Entrance Exam *(CEE)* is pronounced *SEE* throughout the book. The Bible indicates that something like it will be required for people to pass prior to receiving legal or financial status in the Antichrist's kingdom.

Finally, although this story is fictional, the reader will notice that I have drawn from some of today's headlines. There are certain situations, attitudes, and movements in America today that contribute to this adventure, but that also line up with Bible prophecy about the Last Days. In the Last Days, only those who conform and unite with the fallen world's government will be legal citizens. Those who do not conform to cultural demands will be hunted down and killed. We are told in Romans 12:2 *not to be conformed to this world, but to be renewed.*

Dawn of Oppression is a book about brave men and women who refuse to conform, and they pay for it with their lives. But their hope is in the resurrection and the life hereafter with their Lord and Savior.

May we likewise follow Jesus Christ and trust in Him, even if it costs us our lives. And may you be blessed in the reading of this book, and may God be honored by the work of my hands.

David Telbat

Prologue

Kim Egan touched her daughter's sleeping face. Alison had never been this sick. The fever refused to break.

"Please, God," she prayed while kneeling on the floor of the cold jail cell, "we're in Your hands . . ."

Her eyes went to the narrow window near the ceiling. Most of the glass was covered by boxes or wood outside, but she could still see a sliver of blue sky somewhere over Philadelphia. Perfect blue. It was a gift—just what she needed from her loving God.

"Thank You, Lord . . ."

Tears fell from her cheeks onto Alison. The girl seemed to be barely breathing. She'd been unconscious for two days. Their jailors hadn't cared when Kim had begged for medicine. They hadn't seen a reason to waste medicine on a condemned child. Any day now, their executioners would come to take them to be hung outside.

To call oneself a Christian was legal in the Appalachian Federation, but to be a Bible-believing Christian was not. Intolerance of sin was illegal. Kim had never hated people who lived in sin, but when the compliance officers had questioned them about right and wrong, they'd both agreed with God's Word regarding specific sins. Their confessions had sealed their fates.

A key rattled in the door, and it opened just wide enough for a woman to toss in two biscuits.

"Last meal!" a female guard snapped, then slammed and locked the door.

The noise hadn't even startled Alison. In her heart, Kim prayed that her daughter would never waken, that she would pass gently into eternity, her dreams sweet and warm. Kim picked up the biscuits and blew them free of lint and dirt.

"Thank You, Lord," she prayed as she nibbled on a biscuit. "Your face is all I seek . . ."

Suddenly, her tooth struck something hard inside the bread. She pulled the item out of the biscuit and blew it free of crumbs. It seemed to be a piece of plastic with strange contours—almost like a . . . *hearing aid?*

Kim smiled. A hearing aid in her biscuit? It probably wasn't something that had dropped into a mixing bowl without notice.

Hesitantly, Kim inserted it into her right ear. It didn't fit. She tried her left ear. Yes, that fit, but it definitely wasn't for hearing better since it plugged her whole ear, blocking all sound.

Examining it in her fingers again, she found a miniature switch on the outside. She flipped the tab and pressed it deep into her ear.

"This is to Kim and Alison Egan," a woman's gentle voice said. It was the voice of an angel! "You are not forgotten. You are loved with eternal love, and your eyes will soon behold your Creator. May both of you stand strong in the faith until that glorious day. Soon, I may also join you. But for now, it is the blessed honor of Radiant Shade to pray for your endurance as you pass from the temporal to the eternal. Kim, your husband and son have been rescued. I am securing their safety beyond the mountains. They love you both. Remember these words as you await your day: *'The Lord is my Shepherd, I shall not want. He maketh me to lie down in green pastures: He leadeth me beside the still waters . . .'*"

Kim wept, but they were tears of joy. She listened to the recording over and over, until its miniature power source ran low and died.

At midnight, she was hung for her faith in Jesus Christ. But Alison never woke.

Chapter One

Eighty-four-year-old Corban Dowler was being followed. Since he could no longer move swiftly as he had during his younger years, he'd been extremely careful during treks into Manhattan's East Village. Nevertheless, the evening light behind him had revealed a tail. If the drizzle of rain had been heavier, Corban wouldn't have seen the man at all, but there was no mistaking the square posture of a fit soldier coming up the street behind him. It was an Enforcer.

For a moment, Corban considered destroying or abandoning the material he was smuggling for the Christian underground. His hollow cane was packed with what the Appalachian Federation would certainly consider to be contraband. Chancellor Obrador's cruel Enforcers wouldn't show mercy to even an old man, especially if he were caught with the recordings from Radiant Shade. She was the underground's voice of compassion in the collapsed country.

Corban coughed violently and fell against the cracked granite siding of a tall building. His health had been worsening, so the day-long venture from Times Square to the Federation headquarters wasn't helping his recovery. But the Christian underground was spread thin as many outspoken Christians had already been rounded up and executed. Christians were nonconformists, and nonconformity was illegal. Now, Chancellor Obrador was sending his Enforcers out to hunt down those still in hiding—some in the subway system, and others in plain sight.

Avoiding a street patrol of four Citizen Army soldiers, Corban moved up an alley at the back of the building, still heading toward the downtown area. His contact was waiting for him not two blocks away, but there could be no exchange with this tail shadowing him. However, there would be no outrunning the stalker, either. After years of subterfuge and caution since Pan-Day, Corban saw no way around a confrontation this time. The material he carried for Radiant Shade simply had to be delivered!

At the end of the alley, Corban heard a footstep of his pursuer when a boot splashed in a puddle. Corban turned the next corner to find the street empty, so he returned to the alley and crouched behind a rusty dumpster. Rats emboldened by their own years of hardship snapped at his boot laces until he kicked them away.

As much as he wanted to have a face-to-face with the enemy, Corban couldn't risk being seen as the aggressor. For a decade, he'd built his reputation as a disabled, aging man of no consequence, operating the Federation's regional identification office out of the old COIL headquarters. Hiding in plain sight? Only by God's grace had he and his old team survived without anyone uncovering their pasts as covert operatives in foreign countries. Their subtlety ensured the safety of Christians where it was illegal even to own a Bible. Now, on the East Coast of the United States, the Appalachian Federation was one of those territories where biblical Christianity was illegal . . . and punishable by death.

Kneeling against the dumpster, Corban removed the rubber tip from his metal cane, and twisted the length clockwise. A half-inch needle extended from the end. It wasn't much, but it was long enough to pierce through a winter coat, and it was laced with a tranquilizer that could incapacitate a foe for up to an hour. If the tranquilizer didn't work, Corban had no backup plan. He was too old to fight an elite killer.

The rats scuttled around Corban's knee, and the stench from the dumpster nauseated him, but he focused on the whisper of movement coming up the alley. A figure rounded the dumpster. Corban let him pass, then rose upright and jabbed the cane into the prowler's back muscle. As the stalker started to turn, Corban hid his face. Then, the man dropped in the mouth of the alley.

Setting his cane aside, Corban took hold of the man's right arm to drag him into the alley. On the other side of the dumpster, he propped the stranger against the building, then fetched his cane. Since his health had been tenuous at best, he was panting and wheezing from the exertion, trying to catch his breath. His mind was sharp, but his lungs, bones, and joints simply weren't firing on all cylinders anymore.

He drew back the hood of the stalker, and gasped in recognition. It was Owen Travers, one of Chancellor Obrador's most feared Enforcers. Owen and his sister, Lena, were nicknamed the Twins—not because they looked alike but because their cruelty was identical to one another's. Corban believed the Twins were responsible for a number of assassinations in the city against non-compliant residents suspected of association with the resistance. Obrador hated Christians, but even more, he despised the nonconformist resistance fighters who lived in his capital city.

Corban wondered what it meant that Owen Travers had been tailing him. Maybe he'd finally been discovered. Maybe someone had talked. Or maybe Obrador merely suspected everyone for how Radiant Shade continued to receive notifications before Christians were arrested or executed. Very little happened on Manhattan Island that Corban didn't covertly monitor through the COIL network, but he knew Obrador had secret informants who were just as sly.

Quickly, he frisked the man and took his sidearm with silencer, identification papers, and a taser on the back of the soldier's belt. Twice, Owen and his sister had come to the regional identification office to pick up citizen papers for the Federation, so Corban recognized the man up close, but he'd also seen the Twins at Obrador's side during Federation parades through the city streets. The underground had also identified the Twins as suspects in an untold number of murders from Chinatown to Harlem.

Corban took Owen's ID, not because Corban needed it, but because without it, Owen's life would be complicated until he acquired a new one. Since Corban hadn't lost his sense of humor with his fleeting youth, he chuckled at the irony of taking the man's papers. To receive new ones, Owen would need to get orders from the chancellor himself to have Corban print and laminate new ones at the identification office. The printing service for the Federation kept Corban subtly involved in the government's happenings, but not so much that he would be noticed as a threatening figure or part of the hierarchy within the Federation. To most, he was just an old printer.

With the killer's possessions inside his coat, Corban left him and crossed to the next street. Several citizens passed him, their heads down. They were probably processors or maintenance workers, ending their shifts for the day at the Citizen Processing Building.

Reaching Delancey Street, Corban rounded a corner, then pulled up a metal panel on a window where glass had once been framed. On one knee, he scooted through the window, then allowed the panel to drop closed behind him. There was a sealed door two yards away, as if the owner of the establishment still hoped to open again one day. The building had once been a quaint, antique clock shop, though all the clocks that had been on the shelves had been stolen by looters. One large clock still remained on the back wall. It was too heavy for even two men to move. Corban had kept it wound over the years.

He peered through a small crack in the front paneling at the gray street outside. The rain was falling harder now, and the light from the sky was gone. There would be no streetlights that night, even though Obrador had been working hard to power the whole grid south of Times Square. The resistance fighters from the Upper West Side continued to sabotage the chancellor's efforts to present himself as a benevolent and resourceful ruler.

At the back of the small store, beyond three empty metal shelves, Corban lightly knocked twice on the wall, paused, then knocked twice again. He had wall-papered the secret passage ten years earlier, so he wasn't surprised when a three-by-three foot section shifted and Nathan "Eagle Eyes" Isaacson's face appeared in the opening.

"Come on in, Boss." Nathan took hold of Corban's elbow to guide him over the ledge and into the carpeted, secret room. "Take off your coat. You're freezing. Huddle around the candle."

Corban submitted to one of his most trusted and faithful operatives. Nathan had been with him from the beginning of COIL, leading covert raids into dangerous countries to rescue Christians marked for death. Although the six-two ex-Marine hadn't stormed a fortress or shot his way out of a prison in twenty years, the man, now clean-shaven and in his late fifties, hadn't been idle. On his green Federation uniform, he wore a lieutenant's insignia, and with his officer status, he'd aided thousands of Christians up and down the East Coast—either to reach safety or to die well for Christ.

Shivering, Corban held his hands over the single source of warmth: a candle in a tin cup. The wick was an old shoelace soaked in pilfered fuel.

After Nathan replaced the wall panel, he sat on the opposite side of the candle in the room large enough to hold ten people, if they squeezed together. Ten had been just right, Corban thought to himself, remembering the Bible studies he'd led in the secret space. Of course, that had been back when Janice was still alive, before the Second Wave—the second Meridia Virus outbreak—had happened and taken his wife to glory. The other Christians who'd once hidden with them in the room had been executed by the Federation, or smuggled to the west, out of Obrador's influence or power.

"Lord, we're here for You and Your people," Nathan whispered, his head nearly touching Corban's. "We're in danger every day, but we know our despair and suffering in this flesh makes our fellowship with You that much stronger. Because of You, we live and breathe. Until Your Son comes, we serve with joy. Comfort the poor souls in the prisons, the cages, and in danger right now, from here to Georgia, Lord. We can't help everyone, but You can, and You do. Give them strength, Father. In Jesus' name, amen."

"Amen." Corban watched the flame, thinking how it brought warmth to his fingers and warmed his blood, which circulated up his arm and touched his whole body. That's what Nathan was—a small flame that circulated warmth beyond what he or anyone else knew. But God knew. "It's time, Nathan."

"Time, Boss?"

"Operation Esther." Corban lifted his eyes to meet Nathan's. "Radiant Shade is ready, she says. I'm officially handing over COIL to her. Operation Esther is her idea as planned. Are you ready to implement it?"

"It's such a sacrifice." Nathan frowned. "She'll be in so much more danger, Corban. I won't be able to protect her. None of us will be able to."

"It's her decision." Corban felt his eyes well with tears. Radiant Shade was all they could whisper—a name so sacred to their work that it had spawned hope across the Federation, as well as wrath from Obrador's office. But Corban couldn't speak her real name, not in the same conversation, even though she was his own daughter. "And the plan is sound. The Lord will protect her."

"Well, the timing couldn't be better, I suppose." Nathan dug into his pocket, then held a spent rifle cartridge in the candlelight. "Look at this. The chancellor's fighting force out west, led by Colonel Tentmaker, returned to Federation territory two days ago. But Tentmaker was killed in front of the unit's very eyes. Shot dead on a street of a little Colorado town. I read the debriefing myself, Boss."

"Colorado? You mean Meeker, Colorado?"

"It sounds like everyone we sent out there made it safe and sound." Nathan gave the cartridge to Corban. "This was all the Federation soldiers returned with—a few of these spent .308 rifle casings. I guess they picked them up as they fled Meeker."

Corban turned the brass in his fingers.

"This is a COIL battle rifle shell."

"Yeah." Nathan grinned. "Radiant Shade sent our people to the right place. Meeker is apparently willing and able to repel Federation troops. Obrador sent an entire convoy with Colonel Tentmaker. Only two vehicles returned. They said the rest deserted on the way back."

"You know what this means?" Corban muffled his laughter. "Titus is alive! The Casperteins are in Colorado! Oh, the Federation is in so much trouble. Titus will come for us!"

"The old Serval himself?" Nathan sighed with a smile. "I'll be honest, Boss. For years, you've told us to hold steady, to stand and be quietly effective. But I doubted there would be any real impact. Sure, we help people here and there to escape execution, but we haven't put any heat on Obrador himself."

"This must be what Radiant Shade has been waiting for." Corban touched the cartridge to his lips, strategizing like in his old CIA days. "Yes, the refugees we sent will tell Titus what pressure we're under here. He'll do something."

"Do something? Obrador has thousands of troops in the Citizen Army, Corban. I know Titus is the Serval, but he's only one man."

"One man who repelled a whole armed convoy in Colorado!" Corban shook the casing in Nathan's face. "No, God has heard our plea. He's heard our cries. And He's sending the Casperteins. I know it! This is it. It's perfect. We need to be ready. Radiant Shade is a step ahead of everyone else. You must initiate Operation Esther immediately so everything is in place for when the Caspterteins arrive. They must have a place in this whole plan . . ."

"Well, you've never steered me wrong yet, Boss." Nathan unwrapped a piece of thick bread. "Want some? Chen Li is always turning our rations into some sort of fancy cuisine food. Who knew apricot bread could be so tasty?"

Corban nibbled on a piece the size of his finger. The whole city was starving, yet they were eating apricot bread. It was a small blessing in a cursed land.

"You've given me your news." He licked his fingers. "I'm afraid my news is much less pleasant."

"You brought the cane." Nathan touched the metal staff. "Radiant Shade completed the messages, I hope?"

"She did. It's not that. On the way here, I ran into Owen Travers."

"What? The Twins?"

"He was alone, tailing me. I tranqed him. I had to. I couldn't shake him."

"Did he know it was you? I mean, can it be traced back to you? It's been years since we tranqed anyone. It could lead back to us, if anyone remembers who occasionally tranqed people back in the days of COIL."

"The days of COIL may have returned, with Titus Caspertein on his way here and Operation Esther unfolding. But no, Owen didn't see who tranqed him, but he was following me, so he'll probably suspect me."

"We can handle suspicions." Nathan growled under his breath. "We don't need you in prison right now, awaiting your own execution, when so much is coming together. Radiant Shade needs you. All these years of hiding have been worth it, haven't they?"

"It will be. Radiant Shade says so, and she's twice the clandestine operator I ever was."

"I'll have to take your word for that, since I haven't seen her since she was in her twenties." Nathan lifted the candle in front of his face. "You've got us so compartmentalized, I don't even have a clue where you've stashed some of my own men. Scooter? Bruno? It's in your blood to keep secrets, isn't it?"

"Believe me, Nathan, I wish we didn't have to do it this way. If it were up to me, we'd be meeting weekly for a few hymns around a burning barrel just to keep up morale."

"But Radiant Shade says otherwise?"

"This is now her operation." Corban smiled, partly with pride for his daughter, and partly in mourning that his body and health were in such decline. "Her rules. And they seem to be working."

With their hands on each other's shoulders, they prayed for God's strength and grace. Corban admitted that this could be their last time together, if they were found out. And Nathan, overcome with emotion, was silent for a time. Although their circumstances were grave, Corban sensed very strongly that God was indeed with them, guiding them forward.

Before they parted ways, they made the exchange. Corban took his cane apart to give Nathan fifteen hearing aids. Nathan rolled up a list of names and fit it into the cane shaft to be smuggled back to Radiant Shade. There, she would decode the list and make arrangements for Christians in danger.

Finally, Corban drew a paperback book from his coat pocket and gave it to Nathan. Nathan held it up to the light. It had a plain, blue cover with simple font titled, *The Relationship, A Love Letter*, by Mora B. Leever.

"Another installment from Radiant Shade?" Nathan flipped through the pages. "The code is the same? Three and seven?"

"Three and seven." Corban chuckled. "I think you'll enjoy this sequel to the last one. The paper's faded, but at least it's legible. We'll keep printing until the press breaks or we're run out of town."

Nathan tucked the book into his uniform, then drew back the carpet to reveal a trapdoor in the floor. When he yanked up on the handle, a waft of cold air nearly blew out the candle. In the shadows below, Corban glimpsed a make-shift ladder descending thirty feet. He held the trapdoor as Nathan climbed down.

"You've got it from here, Boss?" Nathan asked one final time, his face turned upward.

"The Lord does. Be safe, Eagle Eyes."

Corban replaced the trapdoor, then smoothed down the carpet all the way to the wall. For a few more minutes, he held his hands over the candle. He was tempted to spend the night right there, rather than brave the cold rain and danger outside, but Christian lives were at stake. Nathan had risked execution to bring them another list of endangered Christians, and before the people were arrested, Radiant Shade needed to send messages to warn them.

Reluctant but committed, Corban left the small room and walked with his cane across the clock shop. At the front, he peeked through the crack again. Another foot patrol was stomping down the wet street, now in the dark. The curfew was implemented whenever the electricity was out, and it was definitely dark outside. Thirty city blocks? It would take him all night, and it might even kill him, he realized. But now wasn't the time to shrink back. Operation Esther was now in effect, and the Casperteins were on their way!

☦

Brian Steelman sat handcuffed in a crowded Humvee that plowed through the trash-filled streets of a New Jersey town. Next to him on the seat, a mangy German shepherd growled and bared her teeth. He looked away from the killer canine in the hands of her handler, Lena Travers—one-half of Chancellor Obrador's most ruthless Enforcer team called the Twins. Lena was slim, blond, and cold, and she'd hardly said a word to him since she'd captured him in Morristown.

Through the window, Brian watched as they passed by a burned-out Newark neighborhood. He couldn't believe he'd been captured, but he guessed it was part of whatever the cosmic Designer was sculpting for his life to include. After running from the Appalachian Federation two years earlier, he should've kept running.

But no, that wouldn't have worked, either, he thought to himself. He'd hated Obrador and the Federation and all that they'd used him for, but he'd returned for reasons that transcended his own hatred. A man had saved his life, and Brian was both curious and indebted to the stranger. Once his leg wound had healed, he'd started back to the east, hoping to intercept the commanding but gracious traveler who'd kept him alive—a man his friends had called the Serval.

Lena was gazing out her window when Brian looked over at her. He'd seen the forty-six-year-old, ex-army woman murder people and laugh about it later. She was cruel, but Brian thought her younger brother, Owen, was even more dangerous. He was always trying to impress his older sister, to out-do her own savagery. Owen wasn't right in the head, Brian thought, and mixed with expert hunting skills, that made the man especially lethal.

"Yep, I'm going to do it," Lena said suddenly, squinting her already-narrow eyes at him. She was beautiful, except for the rabid, wild look in her face. "I'm going to ask Obrador if I can kill you myself. I've invented some new ways while you've been gone. He'll want to use you as an example. We'll do it in Foley Square in front of other nonconformists. You'll beg me to make it stop, but I'm going to make it last forever. A traitor deserves no better."

"I didn't come back to die in one of your execution circuses, Lena. Play your mind games on someone else. Remember, I taught you and your insane brother half of what you know."

"Oh, you think you know me?" She scoffed and petted her dog, making the animal snarl at Brian even more. She'd named the dog Death, and the fur around the dog's muzzle was stained crimson. "And who taught us the other half?"

"I'd say some demon from hell, but then again, I'd still just be talking about you."

He saw her jaw clench, and he knew he'd gotten under her skin, but she didn't respond.

The Humvee swerved around an abandoned bus on the highway, then climbed the ramp to George Washington Bridge, which spanned the Hudson River. Brian gazed down at the capital city from their height on the bridge—it was gray, broken, and perpetually smoldering even after all those years.

So many millions had died in the last twenty years, and Brian had once thought he was one of the lucky ones. Now, he wasn't so sure. The things he'd done for the chancellor, and now being captured by the Federation— he didn't feel too lucky. If only he'd found the stranger from Arizona. Though the man's traveling companions had called him the Serval, a lot of people had assumed nicknames after Pan-Day, but he'd never heard of the Serval until that day. Then, of course, he'd heard it a lot since Arizona. The Serval had followers all over the West. And they were thriving, unlike the polluted, oppressed Appalachian Federation in the East.

The Humvee surged off the bridge and swerved right, then left onto Broadway, and continued south, after avoiding a forced labor crew. As they passed the streets, Brian watched for any changes from the last two years. But the same trash was piled everywhere, rubble from destroyed buildings was still heaped on the sidewalks, and collapsed cranes lay strewn across whole streets. And then there were the civilians in their drab clothing, with their heads hanging, too broken to resist the fierce stranglehold Obrador held over the city especially, but also over the whole coastline.

When they reached the East Village, the Humvee was parked in front of the Bowery Hotel, Chancellor Obrador's headquarters. Cement barriers and armed sentries stood before the front doors, now reinforced with steel bars where glass had once been. A suicide bomber's attempt to reach the lobby had left its mark on the outside awning. Ball bearings were still visibly embedded in the cement outside, another sign to Brian that little had changed while he'd been gone.

"Try anything," Lena warned, "and she'll tear you to pieces before I do."

Brian glanced at the growling guard dog.

"If you sic Death on me, she'll be the one who limps away, and it'll be your fault."

Again, she fumed without responding. Brian guessed he could be executed that evening, but not before he thoroughly irritated at least this half of the Twins.

The driver and front passenger drew their sidearms as Brian climbed out of the back seat. The handcuffs behind his back were cutting into his wrists, but he wouldn't allow anyone to hear him complain.

Lena put her dog on a leash and exited the Humvee holding Brian's silver Bushmaster .45 rifle in her arm. He'd been careful to keep the intimidating rifle clean, but it had jammed that very morning, and they'd closed in on him where he'd been camping against a crumbled wall. They'd destroyed his tent and torn his backpack apart, then left everything else behind. If he could only get his hands free and hold his rifle once more, they'd regret ever stumbling upon him like that!

They marched him through the entrance, and several uniformed guards gasped at the sight of him, obviously surprised at who'd been captured. Brian didn't appreciate their gawking or admiration. He'd only gained their acknowledgement years earlier by teaming up with the Twins to put down all of Obrador's enemies. But something in him had changed. He was no longer proud of those years. For a strange reason, he felt that his shift had something to do with the Serval and his kindness in a brutal land.

Inside the once-grand hotel, the lights flickered—a testament that the electrical grid was still not as secure as Obrador wanted. No wonder the whole Federation was a mess of insurrection, starvation, and disunity. Obrador couldn't even keep the power on in his own capital.

Climbing the stairs flight after flight, their boots echoed in the cold stairwell. Water dripped down the wall and mold caked one corner, but Brian seemed to be the only one who noticed. The stairwell probably hadn't been cleaned since he'd been gone.

On the twelfth story, they emerged from the stairwell. Male and female guards with automatic weapons snapped to attention as the party neared a set of double doors at the end of the corridor. Lena knocked loudly, waited for a summons, then entered a spacious suite with wall-to-wall windows that looked down on the East Village.

Chancellor Kendrick Obrador waved several aides away from his polished desk in the middle of the room and rose to his feet. Obrador may have gained a few pounds around his midsection, but his tall frame hadn't stooped an inch. Brian was over six feet, but he'd always been forced to look up at the sixty-five-year-old man. He was balding and his skin was pale, but his beady eyes were like blue ice that could stare down the fiercest killer—and he'd employed dozens.

"Well!" Obrador smiled, making his high cheekbones seem more prominent than his small mouth and thin lips. "This is a delight! Brian Steelman! Come. Come here."

Brian stiffened as Obrador drew him into a gentle embrace, then held him at arm's length.

"We found him camping in Morristown," Lena said. "He was alone. We delivered your orders to Pennsylvania and were on our way back when we saw—"

"Yes, yes." Obrador waved his hand, silencing her without taking his eyes off Brian. "Get him out of these ridiculous cuffs. Right now. This is no way to treat a prodigal son! He's come home. Look at him, everyone. One of our own has returned!"

Obrador clasped his hands together, and several aides voiced their quiet approval.

"Sir, he tried to kill us!" Lena held up the rifle. "It misfired or something. He didn't come back voluntarily."

"Lena, don't you need to feed your mutt or something?" Obrador shook his head at her. "Don't you understand human nature? People always return to where they belong. Listen, Lena, your brother had a bad night for some reason. Why don't you go cheer him up and leave the real decisions to people who can understand these things? You did well. Now, go."

Brian smirked at her, and her face reddened from the rebuff. She thrust Brian's rifle into the hands of one of the other escorts then retreated out the door. A guard unlocked the cuffs, and Brian rubbed at the impression of metal on his skin. He was tempted to reach for his rifle, but decided patience was necessary. This certainly wasn't the reception he'd expected!

"Lena's a mutt herself." Obrador smiled slyly at Brian and picked up a bottle of hard liquor to pour into a glass. "You have to kick her once in a while to keep her vicious. She scares me a little, you know that? But she gets the job done. That's all that matters."

"Some mutts should be put down." Brian eyed the guards in the room. Six armed men and a couple bodyguards, besides the male and female aides who weren't armed. "Believe it or not, I was on my way back to the Federation."

"I believe you, Brian. Sit." Obrador waved his hand at the guards, and they withdrew to the vicinity of the door. "There were reports that you made it to the Mississippi. The Plains Zone isn't as prosperous as you thought it'd be?"

"Something like that." Brian sat on a white sofa covered with some animal skin. A wine stain blemished one arm, but it was still the softest thing he'd touched in months. "You could say I've struggled with a little disillusionment."

"I don't doubt that." Obrador leaned forward and signaled Brian to join him to speak privately, their heads closer together. "I want to be honest with you, Brian. I was hurt when you left. Truly, I was. You killed a lot of people as you departed. I thought we were family."

"If you wouldn't have tried to stop me, those soldiers would still be alive."

"Oh, the people you killed weren't good people, so I didn't mourn them. But I took it personally, you understand. What happened? I thought we shared the same heart. Forget the Twins. It was you. You put me where I am today—that and my irresistible charm. I guess what I'm saying is that I feel the need to tell you that I'm going to require something from you now."

Brian did his best not to react. There was always a catch with Obrador. A smile and a dagger went together.

"I didn't return to go back to doing what I used to do."

"You're a killer, Steelman. The Twins do the job, sure, but they relish it too much. What makes you so special is that you have instinct. It's the detective in you. And that's what I need you to do now. Sure, we'll let the Twins keep handling raids and executions. I'll spare you from that stuff, even though it's necessary. The Federation demands perfect loyalty. But I need you for something else. One job. Only one. It could save the Federation as we know it. Then, I'll forgive the past. All will be history. But you have to do this one thing. It's really just one person. You must do this. No one else has the wits for it. Then, you can write your own ticket. Anything you want to do, it's yours."

Sitting back on the sofa, Brian studied Obrador's deceptive face. How many lives had this one man alone snuffed from the earth? Thirty thousand? Forty? Such a thought wouldn't have bothered Brian years earlier, but now, he felt himself changing inside, softening, and he wasn't altogether resistant to the change. However, refusing the chancellor's conditions could be met with a death sentence. It was just one more life he was asking him to take . . .

"Who is it?"

Obrador snapped his fingers and pointed behind one of his aides. The aide turned and picked up a tray of appetizers—vegetables and fruits, cheeses, and meats. Toothpicks had been jabbed unevenly into the bite-sized pieces, but Brian thought it was an honest attempt at luxury. The nation was starving, but Obrador was feasting on snacks no one else had seen in twenty years.

"Did you hear that a caravan of nonconformists made it west?" Obrador received the tray and held it on his lap, offering none to Brian. "I sent Colonel Tentmaker after them. He was like a son to me. You two were friendly, weren't you?"

"We got along." Brian tried to ignore his own hunger, but his stomach rumbled loudly.

"Reports show that Tentmaker died in Colorado. Morale among the troops is low. Sure, they're doing the work, and they're forcing the people to rebuild this wonderful country, but we have enemies, as you know."

"The resistance?"

"A plague on my city. They're worse than the rats, I swear. Along the coast, noncompliants simply shoot at us. But here in the city? No, I'm not talking about the resistance exactly. Sure, they harass our power grid, hijack food shipments, and stir up rumors. They breed like rabbits down there, Brian, so I'm trying to crush the life out of them. Forced abortions have increased. Forced labor is up. Indoctrination classes are packed every night. But there's one thing, one voice, that seems to urge them all against me—*Radiant Shade*."

"She's still around?" Brian crossed his legs, not unsatisfied to witness the chancellor's agitation. "I thought you would've put her down by now."

"No, regrettably not. She's crafty. Secretive. The Twins are useless at this sort of hunting. This is going to require stealth. Tact. Maybe even trickery."

"You want me to kill Radiant Shade." Brian stood, which made the bodyguards tense, but he walked slowly to the windows and gazed out at the city. For a moment, he thought about the kill order Obrador was placing before him. He'd heard some of Radiant Shade's recordings, which she'd smuggled in to nonconformists about to die. She was also suspected of warning others that they were about to be arrested, but no one could find the informants within the Federation. "I'll want to hunt her alone."

Obrador joined him at the window and offered him food from his platter. Brian selected a single piece of square cheese, although he was tempted to take the whole tray.

"Of course."

"I don't want the Twins anywhere near me."

"I'll put them exclusively on chasing down resistance activists and tunnel rats."

"Radiant Shade isn't part of the resistance?"

"She might inspire them, but we've made some of her people talk under interrogation. She's one of those

Christians, spreading her hate speech all over the Federation. Repent and turn, she says. Pray or burn. Her idea of life wouldn't let any of us truly live. According to what I've deduced, there's every indication she's right here in the city."

Brian felt his disappointment rise. He'd been hoping to get out of the city, and maybe search for the Serval while Obrador thought he was hunting for Radiant Shade.

"If she's really here, I'll find her." Brian selected a piece of meat, hoping it wasn't dog or horse. "But it'll take some time. Like you said, she's slippery. We know she's connected, if she's stayed alive this long."

"Do whatever you have to do. You have the rest of the winter." Obrador left the window, taking the platter with him. "Move into your old room downstairs. If someone's in it, kick them out. Go up to the ID office and get yourself an all-access pass. See that old man with the cane. He always puts a rush on my administration orders."

"Just like that?" Brian turned to face Obrador. "I'm reinstated?"

"Like I said, you have the winter. Find Radiant Shade. Do whatever you have to do but kill her before spring. That's the condition of my forgiveness."

Chapter Two

For years, Trenton native Patrick Wolcott had worked as a welder for the Appalachian Federation labor union. The specialty jobs had come to him, and the pay kept his wife and daughter fed through the summers and clothed through the winters.

Then the compliance officers had questioned him. Enforcers. It hadn't been a surprise. The entire Federation had been blaming the Christians for everything for months. Not enough coal? The Christians were hoarding it for themselves, out of spite for nonbelievers. Not enough drinking water? The Christians were wasting it on their ritual bathings called baptisms. The police were too harsh? Blame it on the Christians and their intolerant beliefs that had to be snuffed out. Patrick had expected to confess Christ during the interview, but he hadn't expected to be taken into custody immediately afterward.

"Do you believe adultery is evil?" the Enforcer had asked. His partner had stood nearby, a sidearm on his hip.

"Well . . ." Patrick had looked from officer to officer. "Define evil."

"The opposite of good. Do your current beliefs lead you to think ill of men or women who sleep with partners outside of your definition of marriage?"

"Yes, my beliefs in the Bible's truths do frown on adultery."

"You realize the consequence for such a belief?"

"I know I'm thought of as evil, yes." Patrick had smiled then.

"Are your intolerant beliefs subject to change? Will you comply with Federation laws?"

"And tolerate or approve of sin? No. I can't imagine God will change His mind about sin, so I won't change my mind, either."

"Who determines a Federation citizen's sexual identity?"

"I'm with God and biology on that one."

"Are your intolerant beliefs subject to change?"

"Probably not, since reality can't be altered by personal determination."

"Do you believe the God of your religion is the only God?"

"I do."

"Are your intolerant beliefs subject to change?"

"I'm sensitive to the beliefs of others, but, no, I can't be convinced there are multiple gods in existence."

"Do you believe . . .?"

The questions went on for hours, clarifying and repeating, until Patrick felt he couldn't possibly be mistaken for anything but a Bible-believing Christian. Of course, their conclusions meant to paint him in the worst light possible, but he couldn't deny his confidence or his conscience. The truth was the truth.

His sentencing happened a week later. It had been one month since his interview, and there'd been no word from his wife or daughter. Had they been wise enough to run when he hadn't come home? Or had Chancellor Obrador and his Enforcers picked them up during his interview?

Maybe he didn't want to know what had happened to them, he decided. Enforcers were merciless to those who were condemned.

The cell door opened, and an apple was tossed onto the floor. Patrick tried to see who the officer was, to glimpse his face so he would have an image in his mind when he prayed for the guards over him, but the man slammed the door too quickly.

Patrick scooped up the apple before it stopped rolling. His thumb sank through the rotten skin.

"Last meal." Patrick closed his eyes. "Lord, I'm not real grateful for this last meal, but maybe this'll make me appreciate even more the supper I'll be having with Your Son."

Peeling away the skin, he dug for the seeds. He'd been collecting the seeds from other rotten fruits and drying them in the corner. Whoever the next resident of the cell might be, maybe they could collect some dirt and grow a little plant.

His hunt for seeds was interrupted by a plastic . . . *hearing aid?* He sucked it clean of tart apple juice and held it up to the light of the window.

"What in the world?"

With his fingernail, he flipped a little tab on the device, then shoved it into his ear.

"Brother Patrick," a woman's gentle voice said, "my name is Radiant Shade. I am a member of the Christian underground. I don't consider myself an enemy of the Federation, only a friend of God's redeemed ones."

Patrick sat on the floor of the cell, careful not to move or tilt his head too much, lest the recording cease.

"Since so many believers live quietly already, I don't discover them as believers until they are arrested. I can't help you any more than encourage you at this late stage of your life. You have stood for Christ this far. I know you are an overcomer. Please know that the moment I heard about your arrest, we smuggled your family to a safe location. We'll send them west with other refugees when it's time. They won't live in terror. Rest assured there is a strong Christian presence in the West who will protect and nurture your family. I know this will give you some peace as you face the noose that awaits you. And now, let me leave you with some words from the Psalms: *'The Lord is my Shepherd, I shall not want . . .'*"

Patrick leaned his head against the cell wall. His whole body was consumed by a wave of warmth and peace. He would die tomorrow, but it wouldn't be a death of sadness. Whoever Radiant Shade was—he prayed for her safety, that her dangerous but comforting work would continue. *His family was safe!*

The next morning, Patrick was executed. As the hangman fit the noose over his head, Patrick was whispering Psalm 23.

Jenna Dowler was blind, so she didn't mind the utter darkness of the sub-basement under the old COIL headquarters in Times Square. The cold cramped her fingers sometimes, and occasionally a new leak in the basement roof dripped on her, but otherwise, she'd grown accustomed to her life, working in hiding, praying in hiding, even singing in hiding.

She lived in absolute secrecy, although she did venture above ground to live a semi-normal life, to move about in the building her father maintained for the Federation. No one but trusted COIL operatives were allowed to come to her in the basement. Those were her rules, adopted from her legendary father, whose own tactics had kept countless Christians alive for twenty years. But so many more had died, she thought, and that had been on her watch. Although she knew she wasn't directly responsible for their gruesome deaths, she felt every passing of God's people, and remembered every name.

Of course, she'd never seen any of their faces, but her informants knew to communicate every possible detail of their lives to her, so she knew how best to comfort them in their hour of greatest need. If she couldn't save their lives, then she was committed to loving them, as Christ did, in their moment of death. Rescuing and comforting the condemned required intel. That was another lesson she'd learned as a youth from her father's tradecraft lessons.

As she moved from her chair at a desk by the wall, she habitually clicked her tongue on the roof of her mouth. As a child, she'd learned to use echolocation to navigate the world around her, but when above ground, she still carried a cane. It was part of her plan—Operation Esther—to present herself as a true invalid. Everyone needed to see her as the poor, blind woman who lived with the old man at the identification office. The old man and the blind woman were harmless.

She chuckled to herself as she reached one of ten expansive tables organized with recording equipment, hearing aids, and stacks of paper. If Obrador only knew who had kept his Federation from ruling effectively . . .

At the table, she fit a computer chip from the recording machine into the hearing aid. This one was for a family in North Carolina, warning them that Federation Enforcers had been ordered to surveille their residence for two weeks, to gain evidence before arresting and executing the parents. Their children would be placed in a conformist family, where indoctrination classes would begin. Obrador wanted all Christians wiped out. The man worked tirelessly to spread his brand of socialism across the states under his reign, so Jenna worked tirelessly to encourage those believers who remained.

A coded tapping sound reached her ears. The sound was heard in the water pipes over her head, but the tapper was probably still ten minutes from arriving. It was Luigi Putelli, right on time. She had another dozen messages for him to smuggle out. Her father's old confidant had become her private and reliable counselor and ambassador to the outside world, lurking where only Luigi could lurk.

She stowed the hearing aids in a waterproof bag, in case it was raining above, then seated herself at her desk chair to wait for him. As an afterthought, she reached for the lantern on the shelf and primed the oil, then pressed the flint switch to spark it to life. A few seconds passed before she felt the heat on her fingertips against the glass. Now, Luigi would be able to see in the wide, long room, and avoid bumping into her tables that were so meticulously arranged.

Luigi's coarse breathing reached her ears before his footsteps could be heard. Jenna still remembered the first night she'd met Luigi, when she'd been just a little girl. Death had come for her and her mother, but Luigi had arrived in their home, fighting the bad guys and whisking them to safety. Little did Jenna know at the time, but her father had only just recruited the Italian assassin as a guardian of the family—a task which Luigi had taken seriously all those years. Now married, Luigi's wife, Heather, had also been brought in to share in the same work, where confidence and faithfulness were required.

"Hello, Luigi. It's good to see you again, brother."

She stood as he came to her, and those who knew her best knew she didn't like to be embraced, unless for comfort. In greeting, she clutched the bony hands of Luigi, who was in his late seventies now.

"Your humor never tires me, Jenna," he said, but he didn't laugh at her joke. Luigi wasn't one to laugh or show much emotion. His stoic consistency was what she most appreciated about him, but she didn't mind testing his resolve occasionally. "I have reports."

"Good." She seated herself and gestured with her hand toward a chair she knew was cleared for her few visitors. "Tell me everything."

He smelled of onions and sweat, rain and something sweet. Perfume. Yes, it was the kind that Heather wore. Subtle, like honey. Some people had preserved a remnant of the past, or maybe Luigi had kept her supplied from an old stash.

"The Bandit left you a message in Uptown. It read, *W-O-K*."

Jenna sat very still, not writing anything down in braille, or commenting on the message at all. And Luigi didn't ask what it meant or offer any interpretation. The Christian underground depended upon secrecy and compartmentalization, and sometimes that meant not speaking about things where curiosity usually caused accidental errors. Luigi couldn't tell Enforcers what he didn't know, if he were ever caught, which did seem inevitable.

But Jenna understood perfectly the response from the Bandit. The Bandit was the public name that the leader of the resistance went by. But he was far from an actual resistance leader. Jenna and her father had foreseen the Federation's crackdown against Christians, and a subversive group was organized to attract and split the government's attention. Scooter, a Hispanic COIL operative, had birthed the resistance years earlier, and in a subway tunnel on the West Side, a community of sorts—fugitives and resistance fighters—had gathered with their families. Some children had even been born in the tunnels, playing in the dark, avoiding rats from the sewer and Enforcers above on the streets.

Luigi had gathered and brought her the *W-O-K* message. The three letters would have appeared in braille lettering, disguised on a city wall amidst graffiti art, which had been purposely maintained across the city to throw off the Enforcers to its actual usefulness. But Luigi knew where to look for codes on the walls of certain buildings.

The "*W*" Jenna understood to refer to water. The "*O-K*" simply meant that Scooter had received her message to sabotage the Federation's water supply with red food coloring. It was harmless, but definitely psychologically annoying. She was always showing Chancellor Obrador that the resistance could access his most vital systems—and yet he and his men were never really harmed. The resistance pestered Obrador so the Enforcers focused more of their resources on the resistance rather than on the Christian workers and their families. She played offense constantly, so she didn't have to play defense as much. It seemed to work, since she'd never been found out.

Of course, she guessed Obrador thought that the resistance didn't have the backbone to follow through with an actual violent attack, but Jenna saw it as Christian grace. Scooter, as the Bandit, kept his fighters unarmed and wise to the streets, sometimes equipping them with identifications from her father's shop above. Their violence was kept in check, as they sought reform rather than actual bloodshed. Nevertheless, the resistance was vilified since isolated civilians sometimes attacked Obrador's Enforcers. The resistance was always blamed. But this was war. Light was flickering in darkness, and the darkness would use every method possible to eradicate the light.

"What else?" Jenna asked Luigi.

"I delivered the books you printed last week."

"The families understood the code?"

"They do. As you instructed, I gave them only to those who publicly show the greetings."

"Good." Jenna smiled at the thought of another creation that she and her father had implemented. In public, Christians identified themselves by brushing imaginary lint off their left shoulder—two swipes vertically, two swipes horizontally. Some had begun to call it the Christian salute, and others called it the greeting of the cross. "What else?"

"There's a rumor that—"

"Rumor? Facts, Luigi. Give me context."

"I was visiting with two Enforcers, sharing some trail mix with them on the streets. They were talking about Steelman being back in the city."

"Steelman? Obrador's Enforcer?"

"Yes. He arrived in handcuffs with one of the Twins, but he left alone from the Bowery with his rifle. The gun he carries is a silver rifle, a Bushmaster. The other Enforcers and the Citizen Army are on edge about him being back after two years. You remember."

"I remember." Jenna prayed through her dread, her anger. "He's slaughtered many of our brothers and sisters."

"Butchered is the word, Jenna. I've seen his trail of death. Many times."

"Well, it doesn't matter." She lifted her chin, remembering that her father had taught her that a confident force of people could only be led by a confident leader. "Everything moves forward. Especially Operation Esther. Whatever Steelman's purpose is back in the city, we'll leave it in God's able hands."

"It can only mean trouble for us. You want me to put someone on him?"

"No, he's too dangerous. He'll know he's being watched. Just report sightings to me. I want to know where he's seen but don't follow him. Too much is at stake now. No one must be arrested who can reveal anything."

"The resistance could kidnap him, like a civilian arrest. A jail could be constructed by the Bandit to keep him underground."

"It's a possibility, Luigi, but I don't want to develop such an aggressive offensive, or set a precedent for others to do those things. We're not kidnappers. What else?"

"Now that your father has confirmation that our first wave of Christians safely reached Colorado, Bruno's ready across the river to stage a second exodus."

"Very good." She smiled. "Let's begin to siphon refugees to the warehouse in New Jersey. By early spring, another group should be ready. Bruno will take care of the details."

Bruno was the handle of another COIL operative, a bear-sized man, as Jenna recalled, whose wife had died during the First Wave of the virus. Now, he was in charge of security outside the city, and protecting and relocating endangered Christians. Like Scooter and Luigi, Bruno's self-sacrifice to remain in service for so many years without complaint was a testament to his love and loyalty to Christ.

Luigi left with new orders for servants beyond New York, especially for those in the South, and he carried the bag of repurposed hearing aids for distribution to endangered believers. Jenna prayed her comfort and instructions reached people in time. There were highways to travel, thieves to avoid, and Enforcers to elude. One misstep, and the whole network could fall apart.

Jenna climbed halfway up a ladder, then fit the earpiece of a stethoscope into her ears. The other end had been fastened permanently to the floor above. For a few moments, she listened to the instrumental music playing in her father's print shop. Music was their code for caution. Corban always turned on the stereo when Federation customers or city residents came to the office for identification pick-ups. She could hear indistinguishable voices above—one belonging to her father and the deep voice of another man.

They were visiting, not walking around too much. Her father usually appeared frail and old, and his years of practice at making people feel comfortable naturally drew intel out of some. The simplest of information could be used to intercept a Federation food shipment or sabotage a transport. The Bandit was always willing to employ his eager soldiers toward some nighttime scheme.

Then, she heard footsteps and a door closing. The music was turned off. Corban tapped his foot twice, then twice more on the floor—their signal—in case she was listening, to indicate that he'd indeed been the one to turn off the music. Sometimes, she merely listened, but this time, she knocked back, signaling that she was finished for the day and ready to come up.

From the ladder, she walked across a platform, of which she'd been told was at a dizzying height above an abandoned shaft, to reach another ladder. She climbed this second ladder only three rungs to reach the ceiling of the basement. An instant after her head bumped the ceiling, the door opened wide, and warm air with fresh scents poured into the hole. The walls still held the smell of toner.

She reached upward with one hand to find her father's hand, and then she used her other hand to guide herself through the square trapdoor. Corban directed her to stand aside and placed her cane in her hand. Then she clicked her tongue, sensing his movements as the hole was closed and covered with linoleum flooring that could be rolled up or unrolled in place. They did all this without speaking, and she guessed her father took care of the flooring right then as he had for years—in the dark of the back supply room.

Her father opened the door, and she took his elbow as they left the room. They lived one flight up, but Corban had kept the entire COIL complex under his control, even reclaiming adjacent and lower offices to house the printing equipment. The street level had been converted into the identification office, while the second level contained their living quarters. The third was a COIL furniture storeroom, where Corban's old office sat under dusty sheets, though Jenna doubted the building would ever again see COIL's days of glory.

She placed her foot on the bottom stair to ascend with her father to their living quarters when someone knocked loudly on the front door.

"Who is it?" Jenna asked her father in a hushed whisper, her heart beating faster. Since she'd just emerged from the basement, she was particularly suspicious of visitors at that late hour.

"Just one man," Corban answered. "Plain clothes. He's carrying a rifle over his shoulder."

"Do you recognize him?"

"He seems familiar. Maybe. From a long time ago. Let me see what he wants."

She heard Corban cross the office and step down two stairs to the landing for the front door. He unlocked and opened the door.

"I need an identification prepared tonight," a man stated. Papers rustled. "Look. The chancellor's own signature this afternoon. It can't wait for morning. He told me to see you personally."

Jenna moved from the stairs and used her cane to maneuver to the front counter, which she knew overlooked a small waiting room where citizens sometimes waited for their papers to be printed and laminated.

"Everything seems to be in order," Corban said. "We already closed, but since it's you, I'll see what I have on file. It'll take a few minutes. Have a seat."

Corban passed her and went to a back room where the cabinets, laminating machines, and printers were. She heard the visitor seat himself roughly in one of the metal chairs.

"Have you been here before?" Jenna asked, realizing some people didn't immediately realize she couldn't see. "Please excuse me. I'm blind. I was just trying to recollect your voice."

"I remember you. I was here a few times years ago. I've been gone for a couple years, but I came back." His voice was tired, reserved. And he still hadn't said his name. "I'm looking for someone."

"Someone? Sounds mysterious. You work for the chancellor?"

He didn't answer right away. Jenna didn't need to see to recognize reluctance.

"For now. I'm doing a job for him."

"Then you're an Enforcer?" She leaned over the counter a little more. "You live in the city?"

"What is this, the Citizen's Entrance Exam?" He scoffed. "Yes, I live at the Bowery, all right? It's not exactly my choice. It's just what was available."

Jenna listened carefully, sensing so much more than what he said. It was how he said it, shifting, even apologetically, that he was who he was, or that he was doing what he was doing.

With more boldness than she usually expressed in public, she tapped her way past the counter, then down the two steps to the waiting chairs.

"What are you doing?" he asked as she bumped into him.

Knowing now where he was, she sat in the chair beside him and leaned her cane against her leg. With both hands, she reached for him. One hand went to his neck as the other touched his face. His body was rigid, resistant, as if he wasn't used to being touched by other people, especially by a woman.

"You're a soldier?" She felt his jawline and the way he turned away, then slowly turned back to her, swallowing hard. "Yes. You've been gone a long time. In the weather. On the road?"

"Yeah. I said I was."

"Where?"

"Out west."

"How far?"

"Arizona. I made it to a little town called Oatman."

"You were scouting for Obrador? You work for him. He's trying to expand west?"

Jenna titled her head, aware that many saw her just as she wanted to be seen—as a harmless blind woman with whom secrets were safe. She could pry where others couldn't.

"I ran away, you could say," he said, speaking past the hand touching his face. "I didn't like who I'd become. Yes, I used to work for the chancellor. Then I came back."

"And now you search for someone?"

"A man. He helped me in Arizona. He saved my life. He asked me questions about the Federation, the conditions over here, so I know he was coming here. There was just something about him and the people he was with that let me know he was a good man."

"Who was he with?"

"Simple people. An Indian woman. A one-armed black woman. And a baby. I was shot up, dying from an infected wound. Nobody cares for people these days, not the way he and his people took care of me, even for a few hours. I've traveled enough to know that people are cutthroats, selfish."

"He sounds like an angel." She had his face committed to memory, and withdrew her hands to his shoulder and arm, keeping her presence close. "And you want to thank him for saving your life?"

"Thank him. Or warn him. Help him. I don't know." He swore under his breath. "I'll probably never see him again. I came back here for nothing."

"I don't believe in accidents. What is it Obrador wants from you? Whatever it is, you're uncomfortable about it. I'm blind, but I can see that much is true."

"I'm a hunter. It's what I do. Your father remembers me. I saw it in his face. It's in my file, if he still has it."

"He's a careful record keeper." She withdrew her hands from him completely. "Why are you ashamed?"

"Ashamed?" He stood briskly and walked across the waiting room. "I'm just here for my papers. Will this take much longer?"

"I didn't mean to offend you."

"Well, you were touching my face. I haven't bathed in weeks. You're asking me personal questions. Nobody asks questions like you do."

"I'm sorry. I'm alone most of the day." Jenna dipped her head. "I guess I'm not sociable the way people expect me to be."

A silent moment passed.

"Look, I'm just not a nice person, okay? You're a likeable enough woman, and definitely too pretty for anyone like me. Just let me get my papers and leave."

"I'm not trying to pick you up." Jenna shook her head. "I'm trying to let you see that there are those who can see more deeply than others."

"Yeah? And what do you see?" His voice was sarcastic, but Jenna guessed he regretted it immediately. But she wasn't so sensitive that she would take offense.

"I see your loneliness."

"Me and everyone else in the world."

"No, not everyone else. Some are held in a peace that passes all understanding, a joy that transcends suffering, and a love that bears all things. You could use a little of that."

"Lady, you have no idea." He laughed aloud. "I'm the poster child for the opposite of love, joy, and peace. If you only knew what I was hired to do . . . No, if you knew what my life hinges on doing, you would spit on me. That's who I am."

"You're being forced to do something?" She stood and walked back to the platform behind the counter. "Then, you're not that unique. Since the beginning, people have been trying to make others do things. But we all have a choice."

"Here you are, Mr. Steelman." Corban returned. "A new identification and fresh compliance papers. I used your old photo. I hope that's okay."

"This looks good. Thanks. You guys are on the payroll, right?"

"Payroll?" Corban asked.

"Federation ration pay. You receive extra rations for your work? Loyalty pay? You obviously have electricity. I'm just making sure you're taken care of."

"We're adequately compensated, sir," Corban said. "Thank you for asking."

"No problem." There was a lull, and Jenna sensed the man wanted to say more, but now that Corban was there, he was hesitant. "Well, thanks. You, too."

Jenna guessed he meant that for her, so she lifted her hand. The door opened, then closed, and he was gone.

"Did you say Steelman?" she asked Corban as he locked the door again. *"Brian Steelman? I've heard of him!"*

Corban moved up to her and took her firmly by the arm. They never spoke openly downstairs, not where the public and Federation loyalists sometimes frequented. Listening devices could be planted. Jenna regretted her question, but it had slipped out. *Foolish!* She chastised herself all the way upstairs, where Corban left her standing in the middle of the room as he went into their kitchen area, then returned to her side.

"We're clear." Corban said, and she knew that he meant a frequency device usually stored in a cereal box was registering on green—no transmissions detected within ten feet. "Caution, Jenna, at all times. Even a harmless question can create suspicions."

"I know, Dad. I've just heard his name recently. What do you know about him?"

"He's Brian Steelman. He's been working with Obrador since Pan-Day. He used to be some hotshot detective from Boston."

"I heard his accent."

"Between him and the Twins, they've probably killed over a thousand people, and more than a few of those have been our people. What's wrong?"

Jenna lifted her hands, realizing she was trembling.

"I touched him. I spoke to him like he was a little, lost orphan. I thought he needed guidance. I believed he was in pain. How could I so thoroughly misread someone like that?"

"Or, you read him rightly." He took her shaking hands into his own. "If he has really done all those things, then he is lost, orphaned, and in need of guidance. You didn't say anything to him, did you? Nothing serious?"

"No, I—" She replayed their conversation. "No, I was just trying to feel him out, give him reassurance that there is still hope in this fallen world."

"Luigi was once a killer. And there have been others, many others, who've turned from their evil ways. Even myself, of course. There were lives I took during the Cold War, but your mother led me to Christ in spite of all that."

"Oh, I still miss her."

"Me, too. Every day. But the moral of the story is, that man who just left is one of the most brutal Enforcers this city has ever known, but his brutality shrinks before the compassion of Christ. His sins carry no clout against the cross. Christ's resurrection proved that redemption was a success for all people—because an infinite Life was given, and an infinite Life was raised up again. Not all will receive that offer, but it is available. Maybe you planted a little seed of hope in his young heart, and we can pray about him."

"He's young? He felt to be about fifty."

"Okay, old to you, young to me." He chuckled and squeezed her hands again. "Can we eat now? Cabbage, beans, and rice. Doesn't that sound delicious?"

"I know people who are eating worse," she said, meaning to add to the lightheartedness, but it was just a reminder of how awful conditions were across the Federation.

That night, on the second floor of the old COIL office suites, Jenna sat in a flannel nightgown in a soft chair, her Bible in braille on her lap. The cover of her Bible had been removed and replaced with a hardback encyclopedia cover, since Bibles had been outlawed for being "hate speech." Her fingers moved over the raised dots on the page through a portion of the First Epistle of Peter. Beside her, she could hear her father breathing steadily, having drifted to sleep while he waited for her next instructions.

"Dad? I have a few more lines."

Corban cleared his throat and rustled the papers on his lap.

"Okay. Go ahead. I'm ready."

"Write this:

'I am but a bird, for even hearts fall,
Call me if you can, for you are tall.
If you should see me, or suffer to find me,
Then try for me, my love, the heart to free.'"

"Jenna, this is pure nonsense!" He laughed.

"Stop it, Dad!" She faked a pout. "It doesn't have to be good poetry, as long as the words are placed correctly and it rhymes. Three and seven. That's all I care about."

"Okay, okay." He sighed, and she imagined him shaking his head. "Keep going."

"'For my sake, don't leave; feel of my touch;

Fly with righteousness in the clouds; you have so much.

The eagles are beside me, the blessed predators high;

Swans below and storks aside; how do I say goodbye?'"

"Let me see here . . ." Corban counted the words, using the code Jenna had embedded, ensuring each line contained the right words from the Bible. "Okay, this all works. We'll print these pages tomorrow. In another week, we'll be able to bind another book for the series. It's a lot of paper for so few words but at least the Scriptures are getting out there."

"What's that?" Jenna closed her Braille Bible and leaned forward. "Dad, you hear that?"

She sensed Corban rush from his chair to the windows, which they kept curtained at night when their small lamp was on. The building had bulletproof, glass windows and an alarm system armed with electric current, but they still tried to keep a meager presence in the community.

Outside, there was shouting and gunshots, which made Jenna whisper a prayer.

"Who is it?" she asked after a few minutes.

"It's the Cantons. Both of them."

"God, please help them . . ." Jenna gasped. "Are they getting away?"

"No. They didn't make it. Two vehicles stopped next to their bodies about thirty yards up the street. In the headlights, I can see they're not moving. They may have been trying to reach us."

"They were warned to leave the city weeks ago!" Jenna clenched her fists. "Why didn't they run when they had the chance?"

"Why doesn't anyone?" Corban returned to her side and clicked off the lamp. "Change is difficult, even when it's change that will save their lives. And the rest of us stay because we're too stubborn. Why do you stay?"

"You know why. The people. Esther did it for her people. I do it for ours. How long until we hear about the operation?"

"Leave it to Nathan and Chen Li. It'll take time for word to spread."

In the privacy of her own bed, partitioned off from her father's bed in the corner, Jenna wept softly into her pillow. During the days in the basement, God had blessed her with so much determination and care for the suffering people across the Federation that she was willing to face a firing squad rather than stop serving fellow Christians. But at times like these, when loss of life was close and danger loomed ahead, she felt the overwhelming weight of loneliness, hopelessness, and fear. Except for her father, she felt she had no one, and although Corban was kind and gentle, his stamina was fading slowly. His energy waned every evening, and he was beginning to forget details that were important. She dreaded losing him to aging, and she was terrified of losing him to enemies within the administration. Without him, how could she endure? She would be so utterly alone!

Suddenly, like a whisper from God, she realized that her father had built the new COIL network around her, knowing that he would indeed be gone one day. But she wouldn't be alone. He had secured everyone around her, making her the center of COIL, using her keen memory and creativity to continue the work. Maybe he knew his mental sharpness and physical stamina were fading. Yes, he knew, and that reality broke her heart afresh. He'd designed the network just so he wouldn't encumber God's efforts as he passed on quietly. Everything was in place, so that Operation Esther could happen, with or without Corban Dowler. *Oh, it was too horrible to think of existence without him!*

And yet, she'd been the one who'd volunteered to enter the lion's den, to abandon what little safety she knew, and to step into the valley of the shadow of death. What loneliness would there be then?

Reaching out with all her heart, Jenna sought the God of all comfort. Her eyes were wet as she inhaled sharply at the beauty of her Lord. An instant later, she smiled. Although she'd been blind since a child, when an explosion had taken her eyes and her birth parents, the Lord nevertheless revealed His incomprehensible beauty to her. Seeing nothing, she saw so much! It wasn't a particular thing that she saw, but the essence of God's presence—His love, His strength. As if she could see beautiful music or hear a wonderful story, her heart was touched, and the comfort she desperately needed swept over her soul.

Sometime in the night, long after her eyes had dried and confidence had been restored, she slept peacefully. The danger she was about to face—which she'd planned herself—didn't trouble her further. God was beside her.

Chapter Three

Eli Anders did his best not to look back as he walked home from the shoe factory that winter day. He knew he was being followed. The danger to himself wasn't his concern. His wife, Sylvia, wasn't even his greatest worry. They were both nearing their eighties and had resigned themselves to dying soon in the service of their Lord and Savior Jesus Christ.

Rather, the aging couple was concerned about being a liability for the Christian underground network in Virginia. No one wanted to be the cause of someone else's arrest or execution.

Climbing a set of stairs, Eli reached his door and knocked rapidly. Sylvia opened it an instant later, and Eli chanced a look back. The man who'd been following him was gone.

Inside the apartment, Eli held up a loaf of bread he'd gotten from their contact at the market. He hung his jacket by the door as Sylvia plucked a knife from a drawer. She sliced thinly, until the knife edge stopped against something hard.

"Radiant Shade?" Sylvia asked. The Christian underground sent messages in various ways, but Radiant Shade was the only one who used a recorded message in an ear device. "Why does she go to these extremes to record these when a coded, written message would be easier?"

"Who knows?" Eli held up the ear piece. "Maybe she can't write?"

"Go ahead. You first."

Eli fingered the tab to activate it, then pressed the device into his ear.

"Hello, Mr. and Mrs. Anders. This is Radiant Shade. Your arrest is imminent, but we need you alive for the cause of Christ. We have gathered many others to be escorted west to where you once lived. It's time for both of you to lead, now, but you must get to the safe house up north. Be careful to lose your shadows. Word has it, you're being watched. When you get here, a man named Bruno will find you. Thank you for your loving service. Someday, I hope to meet you both. If not here, then in the Lord's presence."

"It's finished." Eli pulled out the device. "We have to leave right away. Tonight."

"That's it?"

"We're meeting Radiant Shade's people up north, a man named Bruno."

"She would only relocate us if we're in danger."

"That, yes, and it sounds like she needs people who are familiar with where we used to live."

"Colorado?"

"And we're taking other Christians with us."

Sylvia laughed for joy at the prospect and inserted the device into her own ear as the recording began again.

"Her voice—the voice of an angel." Sylvia closed her eyes. "This Radiant Shade is one of God's special ones. I know it."

✝

Lieutenant Nathan "Eagle Eyes" Isaacson walked with his squeaky leg brace across Canal Street toward Broadway with Sergeant Sean Harris at his side. Harris had been a construction worker before Pan-Day. Nathan had picked the quiet, older man to be his aide for whatever odd jobs the chancellor's administration gave him to do. The last few years, it had been to oversee eight different forced labor crews, comprised of men, women, and children.

Although more of his time than he preferred was spent at a desk in the Bowery, Nathan appreciated the position he felt was orchestrated by God Himself. It allowed him to watch over Christians who'd been arrested and were forced into work details.

"The street hasn't been this clean since before Pan-Day," Sergeant Harris commented as they stopped on the sidewalk. "We're a little ahead of schedule. The chancellor should be pleased. Canal Street wasn't due to be cleared until Christmas Day."

Nathan grunted in response, often finding it difficult to hide his emotions when he observed such hardship forced upon the citizens. He'd received his Federation commission ten years earlier when he'd shown himself to be committed to rebuilding the country, and as an ex-Marine, the chancellor's people had given him a sergeant's rank to start with. Since then, he'd risen as an aide under several captains.

In front of him, men and women clothed in rags were carrying or dragging the last of the rubble off the street. Behind these laborers, weaker women and children followed, using brooms to sweep or dustpans to pick up the last of the glass or garbage. None of the people lifted their heads to look at Nathan or the other uniformed men. Every Federation service member had committed shocking acts to instill dread into the hearts of civilians. Nathan was no exception.

Years earlier, Nathan had found a subtle way to prove his loyalty to the Federation. In Murray Hill, he'd caught a civilian man who'd been hoarding food in violation of the ration system. Nathan had marched the man into an abandoned building, leaving his men and other prisoners outside. Inside the building, Nathan had begun to thrash about the walls and remaining furniture. The man had been convinced to scream with every blow. It had been a risky attempt to create a terrifying reputation, but it had worked. He knew he still carried the whispered name of Lieutenant Leather.

Now, Nathan had to implement Operation Esther. It was in his hands to hasten the beginning of the end of the Federation as they knew it. No longer would COIL live quietly in hiding. But it all began with one more act that would surely boost Nathan's ratings among the treacherous, and it would terrify the prisoners under his heavy hand.

"Sergeant Harris," Nathan said, "line up all the workers. Three rows. Children in front, women second, men third. Quickly. It's too cold to be standing out here like this."

Harris immediately snapped orders to the other officers and workers. In less than a minute, the prisoners on Canal Street had dropped their burdens and brooms and lined up. The Citizen Army soldiers hissed to silence their cries for mercy and gasps for rest.

"That's all of them, sir," Harris informed in his gravelly voice.

Nathan didn't particularly like the sour-faced man with eyebrows about as unruly as Nathan's own. But he wanted Harris' bad attitude against prisoners kept in check, and that meant he needed to remain under Nathan's charge. A few of his other men had been caught abusing workers or prisoners, but there was only so much Nathan could do to limit their evil, since he himself was rumored to be the worst of them all.

Stepping from the sidewalk, Nathan walked first in front of the line of children. Youths under thirteen were sent to him if they were unruly in their assigned boarding homes—or if they were caught with hate literature, or using hate speech. Obrador didn't want orphans running around the streets, so they were given homes and schools to attend, or worked until they either died or conformed. Nonconformists of that age were given forced labor beside their parents until they conformed, or until they fulfilled their allotted sentence. At night, nonconformist workers were housed in cages behind the Bowery.

The cages for the workers were divided by age rather than gender, and every evening, the cages at headquarters were filled with the crackling sound of speakers that indoctrinated the workers with Federation standards. Little hope was offered in those cages, Nathan had recognized—no individuality and no personal care was allowed.

Simultaneously, Obrador pushed for a conformity in society that allowed individuals to blur gender lines, depending on preference, and opposition to this lack of gender distinction was to be harshly punished. A gender-neutral society was the epitome of civilization, Obrador had stated. Otherwise, citizens were required to submit all beliefs and education to the Federation's regulators, who Obrador said knew best.

This strange, amoral system that was so rigidly enforced created a void where immorality had risen to fill. Venereal diseases among citizens had spiked, and recreational drugs among the soldiers was at an all-time high. But as long as Obrador maintained everyone's freedom to choose anything but God, he seemed happy with the conditions.

Nathan knew that the blurring of natural gender realism, while restricting personal freedoms to choose beliefs, had been rising in popularity before Pan-Day. But now, believers could see it for what it was—the making of a self-empowered populace who ignored their Creator and the Creator's order. The nonconformists were primarily Christians, but they were being systematically oppressed into extinction. Drastic action needed to be taken and soon, since faith in the Bible's truths was close to disappearing from the land altogether. Thankfully, God had given them Radiant Shade, who was able to envision a path toward restoration.

After inspecting the two rows of adults, Nathan returned to the front and surveyed the workers' faces. They were a weary lot, underfed and forced to work hard. And sleeping in the cages every night had broken many of them. Nathan usually managed to bribe the cooks to feed his crews a little extra, but even the Citizen Army was hungry. Chen Li, Nathan's wife, kept a community garden on the roof of a nearby apartment building, and grew tomatoes indoors, but no one was overweight.

The faces of the children were filthy, their clothes torn, and their hands too small for the adult-sized gloves Nathan had given them for protection. Their faces had lost the spark of life, joy, or purpose, which seemed to be the Federation's goal, but it wasn't Nathan's goal. He wanted to see the kids set free, running and laughing, riding bicycles on the streets, attending school, and if they wanted, attending church services. But all of that had been forced out of them. Very few had any light at all left in their eyes.

The adults were no different—haggard, depressed, defeated. They stared straight ahead as he walked past them, their eyelids half-closed, some of them wavering in their dust-caked shoes.

They were all nonconformists, but they weren't all Christians. Some were guilty of excess food violations, or fighting, or fishing without a license. For punishment, everything they owned had been confiscated and dispersed among the arresting officers, and the citizens had been sent for reeducation, which was a nice word for the horrible forced labor and cage life. In the cages at night, the workers were forced to listen to indoctrination recordings about socialism.

Nathan's eyes lingered on those he knew had been arrested for their first offenses as Christians. Either they'd been found with a Bible, which the Federation had outlawed, or during their Citizen's Entrance Exam, or *CEE*, they had opposed the Federation's policies.

But on that day, Nathan counted the Christians in that clean-up crew. Eighteen of the thirty-six had been documented as first-time offenders for belief in Jesus Christ, or for loyalty to God's moral absolutes, which amounted to a hate crime.

His gaze settled on one woman named Rachel Mason, in her sixties, just a few years older than Nathan. But Rachel was in worse health than the other laborers. She moved as if in terrible joint pain, and the cold, wet weather wasn't helping in that. It was just a matter of time before Rachel was identified as a burden to the Federation. Then, she would be left behind in the cages when the rest went out to work. When no one was looking, she'd be taken from the cages and strangled quietly, and burned in the refuse pile a few blocks south of the Bowery.

Thus, Nathan had chosen her for removal from the labor crews, before she met a cruel fate at the hand of the Enforcers. More specifically, he needed to make an example of someone, to get Obrador's attention, and Rachel best fit his plans. He'd learned from Chen Li that Rachel had been caught distributing Bibles, and her sentence was nine months hard labor and reeducation. Under those conditions, she wouldn't last the winter.

"You've made the Federation proud!" Nathan announced to the workers. He was too young to have been involved in the Cold War, but he'd learned socialist jargon from its rise in America, well enough to speak it when he had to. "You've used your attention and energy to help this capital city recover from the disasters of the past. Together, with hard work and dedication, we will see more clean streets where rubble once lay. Our new lives are lived in dedication to the preeminence of the Federation!"

Several officers clapped, but Nathan wanted to vomit. His own words sickened him. By the looks on the faces of the laborers, they were just as weary of the Federation's nonsense, but he had to play the part.

"You've made the Federation proud," he continued, "but not all of you. *You!* Take a step forward."

He pointed at Rachel Mason. She tried to stand up straighter when she noticed she'd been singled out. Her face was pale in the cold air. With effort and a grimace, she shuffled forward.

Nathan rushed forward, grabbed her roughly by the arm, and forced her several yards to the side of the gathering.

"You and you!" He pointed to two male laborers, strong men who'd been sentenced for hoarding more than their family's share of food, selling it, and extorting other families. "Open the manhole. Remove the cover. Do it quickly!"

He held Rachel by the arm as everyone watched the two men use hammers to pry up the manhole cover.

Pausing, Nathan considered the distance between Rachel, the other laborers, and the officers. When he stepped up close in front of her and made a show of searching her clothes, he believed most of what he did with his hands could be seen by no one, and what he said quietly to her couldn't be heard by the closest laborers.

"Don't be afraid," he whispered firmly, and ripped a half-eaten piece of stale bread from one of her pockets, then threw it on the ground. "Jesus Christ is with you. He will never leave you nor forsake you. Trust in Him. And pray for me."

In his hand, he palmed a folded piece of paper, and pushed it into her coat pocket. Then, he turned her so all could see as he pulled the paper out of her pocket, glanced at it, then threw it on the pavement as well.

Nathan noticed that her face was filled with bewilderment, and he hoped she didn't smile and give them both away.

Finally, he shoved her toward the gaping, dark manhole. Many of the subterranean tunnels of the city had been flooded permanently, or they flooded daily with the tide. This one was no exception. Below, black, filthy water reflected the overcast sky. But something else was moving down there on the water, at the edge of the light that poured in. Nathan glanced up and affirmed he was indeed at the intersection of Canal and Lafayette. Then he prayed the resistance was in place.

Overpowering Rachel, he tripped the older woman by sweeping her feet from under her, forcing her to tip forward headfirst into the manhole. She screamed in fright an instant before she hit the water. But even as Nathan watched, the bow of a narrow boat, maybe a canoe, appeared in the light. An upturned face stared up at him, but Nathan hid his own face by quickly backing away. He didn't want to be identified by anyone below as a collaborator with the resistance.

From a few feet away, he dragged the manhole cover, and with a loud metallic clank, it settled into place. He straightened upright and brushed off his hands.

"Disloyalty leads to discipline!" he shouted like the maniac he wanted to project. "Now, get back to work!"

The people scattered to pick up their tools.

Sergeant Harris approached Nathan as he stooped to pick up the folded piece of paper which he'd thrown on the street.

"I don't want to hear it, Sergeant." Nathan unfolded the paper. "Federation resources are too valuable to be wasted on citizens who refuse to contribute."

"She was old." The officer stomped on the manhole cover to ensure it was in place. "It was better this way than dying later in the cages. I've heard the tunnels down there are filled with freezing water this time of year. She'll be dead in minutes, if she didn't already drown."

"I'm glad you approve." Nathan held up the paper. "Look at this. It's typed. I took it from her pocket. It's some sort of letter."

"Look!" The sergeant pointed to the middle of a single paragraph. "It's about the chancellor. Is this for real? How could she get her hands on something like this?"

"I don't know, but something's up. Maybe we should keep it to ourselves." Nathan folded up the paper, then handed it to Harris. "Keep this safe. We may have uncovered something. Maybe it's resistance intel that could set us up for a promotion. Let me take it to the chancellor. I'll bring you into it when it's time."

"You'd do that?" Harris frowned and tucked the note into his coat. "Thank you, sir. A lesser man would keep the glory to himself."

"A man who stands alone can't lift himself up, but two men together can reach higher. Remember? It's in the Federation handbook, *Always Caring, Forever Strong.* Come on. This crew won't be giving us any problems. Let's go across Broome Street and see how the next crew is doing."

They walked north together.

"You really think this note is a bit of intel?" Harris asked.

"You read it. It looks sinister. Chancellor Obrador will know what to do about it. And if we play our cards right, we can ride the wave. Let's stick together, Harris. We're going places."

✝

Scooter, also known as the Bandit, climbed into the brackish water himself, and hoisted the limp woman into the inflatable canoe. Willie, his closest confidant among the resistance fighters, remained in the boat and pulled the woman onto his lap.

The water only reached up to Scooter's chest, but he was thoroughly chilled in seconds. He wasn't a tall man, and he struggled to hop and kick back into the bow of their craft.

"Quit fidgeting, would you?" Scooter joked as he wiggled to right himself in the boat. "Hang on."

With a pounding heart, Scooter shivered violently as he paddled vigorously away from the manhole above. For just an instant, he'd glimpsed Nathan Isaacson's face up in the cloudy daylight. It was his old friend! They'd once served in the Marines together, found Christ together, and later joined COIL together. For years, they'd served beside one another under Corban Dowler and Chloe Azmaveth.

But for several years now, Scooter had seen his old operative friends only from a distance, or in passing. Radiant Shade had spread COIL operatives across the city, some even working inside the chancellor's rancid administration, like Nathan was. He guessed that meant Chen Li was somewhere around Nathan, living well, while Scooter slummed it with the rats in the sewer.

However, there was no real animosity in his heart toward his assignment for the COIL team and the cause for Christ. He'd rather be living in the cold tunnels under semi-freedom than in the sunshine under a brutal ruler. But Scooter knew Nathan could handle it. Both Nathan and Chen Li had pulled undercover jobs in the past for COIL, but living for years in oppression were probably a strain on them.

"Come on, lady!" Willie called in his Minnesota accent, as he slapped the woman's cheek. "I think she's coming around."

Scooter glanced back to see the woman in her sixties fully embraced in Willie's monstrous arms. The burly Mid-Westerner had worked at Scooter's side ever since Scooter had proposed a plan to the tunnel refugees to start a resistance fight against the Appalachian Federation above. Willie had been the first to call him the Bandit, on account of Scooter's ability to lead ambushes and raids against the Federation transports or warehouses.

The rubber craft bumped against a subway platform where four other resistance members stood ready to receive them. Battery-powered lamps lit the damp cement tunnel as Scooter held the boat in place, and Willie shifted the startled and mumbling woman into the arms of the others.

"Come on." Heather Putelli helped the woman to her feet. "Let's get you into some dry clothes. That water is freezing!"

Heather and another woman from the resistance stepped to the side of the platform to help the woman into fresh clothes. Scooter and Willie crawled out to the edge of the landing to help the two other men drag the rubber canoe out of the water and deflated it.

"So, this is part of some bigger plan above ground?" Willie asked. "You still can't tell us?"

"In time, I will." Scooter slapped the shoulder of his much larger companion. "Secrecy is safety."

"The only safe thing I'm waiting for is the demise of the Federation." He sniffed at his clothing. "Phew! We're gonna need to hijack some lemons to soak our clothes in if we're ever gonna get this smell out!"

Scooter climbed to his feet, then strained to help Willie to his feet to stand nearly a foot taller than himself. He relied on several resistance fighters in the tunnels, but none of them knew his real identity or true purpose to work in unison with the Christian underground. Only those from his COIL past, like Heather Putelli, Luigi's wife, knew what was really happening, and they were just as tight-lipped about it as he was.

"Her name is Rachel." Heather led the recovered woman from the platform shadows, now wearing a stocking cap and winter parka.

"Thank you so much!" The woman wept. Her knees buckled, but Heather steadied her. "That man, I thought he was going to—"

"Stop." Scooter held up his hand, then lifted a lamp so the woman could see the seriousness in his face. "Don't ever speak about what just happened or who did it for you.

Do you understand? Carry it in your heart. The one who just pretended to kill you risked his life to save you. Now, you must protect him by your silence. Are you a Christian?"

"A Christian?" Rachel studied their faces. "Yes, I am. Does that matter to you guys?"

"There are other Christians living in the tunnels. Pray for the man above, for his safety, but never speak of this day again. Tell me you understand."

"I understand. Are you all Christians?"

"Let's get moving." Scooter nodded to Willie. "Lead the way. It's a long walk back to the Park."

Willie led them out, but Scooter caught Heather's arm and held her back from the procession. The others were ahead of them before he started to walk alongside her, speaking in low tones.

"This means Operation Esther has begun," Scooter said. Heather was in her late sixties, but had remained sharp and active since Pan-Day so that she was useful in the work. "This changes everything now."

"I don't like not knowing where everyone else is." Heather linked her arm in Scooter's, although she was a couple inches taller. "But soon, the Lord may unite us all."

"In the clouds or in the sunshine."

"Can you imagine?" She sighed happily. "A Federation where Christians are no longer persecuted?"

"Only if we don't blow it."

"Don't think negatively. You sound like Luigi."

"When will we see your lesser half again?"

"Tonight. He'll have orders for us."

Hours later, after skirting flooded subway tunnels and wading through rat-infested darkness, the recovery team reached a subway tunnel fork under the West Side streets. Willie led the party to the right, branching under Central Park, where they came upon a side tunnel that had collapsed onto the tracks.

"It's a dead end," Rachel said, despair in her voice.

But Willie reached into the metal, cement, and trash heap that spanned from wall to wall and all the way to the ceiling, and yanked hard on a lever. Rachel stepped back, bumping into Scooter, as the loud sound of gears clicked and counterweights fell. Gradually, a whole section of the rubble inched forward on the tracks, and opened a gap wide enough for the travelers to walk through.

"Another secret to keep to yourself," Scooter said to Rachel as they moved through the barrier, "like Rahab in Jericho."

"Do you guys have Bibles?" she asked. "I haven't seen one in years."

"They're around. Go with Heather. She'll get you settled."

Scooter moved through the tunnel section that had become his resistance headquarters. Two armed resistance fighters stood directly inside the barrier. Their chief duty was to keep the barrier closed and the people inside secure. The inhabitants were two hundred in number, counting men, women, and children. Light bulbs powered by battery banks from hidden solar panels above were strung across the ceiling. A dog barked as children born in the tunnels ran around him.

A woman crouched outside her tent over a smoky fire, and touched her shoulder in the city-wide gesture of the cross. Subtly, Scooter returned the signal, although he wasn't as outspoken about his faith as he wanted to be in the tunnel. Radiant Shade had instructed him to be a fake resistance leader first and foremost, and remain distant from connecting himself with the Christian underground until it was time to reveal his full intentions.

As he walked past other makeshift shelters, people stood out of respect or nodded from their doorways. He was the Bandit, the great resistance leader, who'd saved their lives or improved their existence in hiding. His name was spoken with awe, but Scooter knew it was all just for show. He wasn't really who they thought he was, and as soon as their circumstances changed for the worse, he would be their enemy.

For years, the habitat below ground had been constructed using wood and metal scavenged from the city above. It was a squatter's community, but it was home. And it was away from the control of the Federation—though not outside their reach. Federation Enforcers had dropped chlorine bombs into the tunnels to root out the resistance, but the tunnels had better ventilation than the chancellor realized, and he'd ended up poisoning parts of his own city above. Other attempts by Enforcers to enter the tunnels on foot had ended in failure. They'd wandered through hundreds of miles of tunnels in search of the Bandit—the infamous leader who harassed Federation personnel and resources—but they'd never found him.

Regardless of Obrador's failed attempts to shut down the resistance, Scooter knew there were still informants in the tunnels, either in his community, or in one of the other tunnels.

He climbed a ladder to a loft with a slanted, wooden floor. Here, he had a twelve-by-seven room with a cot and a little floor space to pace and kneel to pray. With a curtain drawn, he had privacy. A chest against one wall held over thirty recovered Bibles he was waiting to reintroduce to the populace, but for now, he handed out the Mora B. Leever poetry books, coded with Bible verses, if people knew the combination.

In his own tunnel, some people read the poetry books and didn't even know they were the Words of Life from God embedded into the silly lines of romance. Whenever Luigi brought new books to the tunnel, Heather distributed them. The code to unlocking the books was strictly guarded, since it was the last of God's Word in the Federation—until the Federation itself could be turned and Bibles were legalized again.

Laying on his cot, Scooter gazed past his partly-opened, curtained door. The kids had a new rope swing down below, hanging from the steel rafters. Some orphaned teens, called the Vags, for vagrants or vagabonds, who most often participated in supply raids, had rolled some tractor tires from somewhere above, and had created a hangout against the outside barrier, distancing themselves from the supervision of the adults.

An access door on the left led to a community garden, complete with artificial lighting and irrigation. It wasn't much, but it supplemented their diet alongside whatever scavengers were able to provide.

At the back of the tunnel was a medical clinic and school. Sometimes people from the surface needed medical care that the Federation wouldn't provide, so they would be willingly blindfolded and brought inside the barrier. Since the Federation used forced abortions as a method of population control, as well as punishment for noncompliant citizens, several families had been added to the community based solely on the fact that there were midwives living within the resistance population.

Others had been wounded in shootouts with Enforcers, and they'd survived with the aid of the resistance medical aid, and afterward joined the fight. Or, depending on a family's situation, Scooter sometimes organized a night escape off Manhattan Island altogether, smuggling them into the able hands of COIL workers in New Jersey and beyond.

Scooter drifted to sleep, but woke sometime later when a hand touched his shoulder. He opened his eyes to see Heather, her weary but kind face illuminated by a blue lantern. The community was quiet, so she only gestured for him to follow her down the ladder. After tugging on his boots and grabbing a bag of gear, he slid down the ladder to the tunnel floor. Immediately, resistance fighters stirred and lifted their heads. He saw eagerness in their faces. They were ready. Hiding wasn't in their blood any longer, since they'd tasted the thrill of raiding with him on the surface.

He held up his hand for them to wait for his word. They knew, of course, that his word was inevitable when he was up and about at this hour. The whole tunnel would know in minutes.

At the outer barrier, the two armed guards stood with tall, slender Luigi Putelli, whose gaunt face appeared more like a skull than a face with skin on it. The old spook hadn't aged well over the years, living hard and dangerously, and the underground air wasn't helping him, either. Although he lived with Heather in the habitat most nights, he was rarely there during the days, choosing rather to be out scouting the city, watching the Federation, and moving between COIL operatives for Radiant Shade.

Luigi drew Scooter away from the guards, even leaving Heather at a distance. Many eyes in the tunnel were on them, but what needed to be said about the resistance was limited always and only for ears that needed to hear it.

"Urgent orders from Radiant Shade." Luigi passed him a bogus, decoy list of supposed interests, full of empty warehouse addresses and abandoned houses, in case he was ever caught. Instead, he recited the orders from his memory, which Scooter had found was as sharp as it ever had been. "One rescue, one raid, one distraction. You ready?"

"I'm ready." Scooter turned and gave his resistance army the thumbs-up. A hushed cheer erupted as the Vags readied themselves. "Go. I'm listening."

Repeating the instructions twice, Luigi listed three addresses and Radiant Shade's precise orders for each location.

"Sounds simple enough." Scooter leaned closer. "What's the catch?"

"It needs to be done before dawn. Right now." Luigi checked the guards nearby, to make sure they hadn't inched closer to listen. "Enforcers will be at the first address at dawn. Maybe before, if they get anxious."

"No, that's too far for us. Half of the tunnels are flooded between here and there. We'll need more time to scout a route above ground."

"It's this family's second offense with Christian material. They'll be executed right away this time." Luigi wasn't one to touch other people, but he rested his hand on Scooter's shoulder. "You have to make it. You'll need to travel above ground."

"Okay, that's easy enough going down there, while it's still dark. But what about coming back? We'll be in the spotlight of the sun, and I don't like standing on that kind of stage, Luigi."

"Well, I wouldn't try to travel above ground in the daylight." Luigi unwrapped a plastic bag and held it out to Scooter. "Pretzel? They got rained on, so all the salt is gone, but they're still good."

"Thanks." Scooter drew out a couple pretzels. *Pretzels!* In a city where most residents had eyed the millions of rats as a food source. "I guess we'll just have to hole up for the day, find somewhere safe until we can get back."

"Sorry it couldn't be easier." Luigi rolled up his bag and stuck it into his coat. "I have another errand to run before daylight. Any messages from you?"

"For whom?" Scooter scoffed. "I don't know where anyone is or what anyone's doing. Where's Corban? I have no clue. Nathan is topside, I know, but where's Chloe, Bruno, and Chen Li? Are they even alive? It's been years, Luigi."

"I meant," Luigi lowered his voice, his patience sounding as if it were wearing thin, "do you have any messages for Radiant Shade?"

"No." Scooter tilted his head. "I'll leave a marker if I do. Thanks, Luigi."

Luigi left through the barrier door as soon as the sentries opened it. Scooter wasn't alone long before he was joined by an eager crowd of Vags—the twenty young men and women who were the resistance fighters. Since the Bandit's resistance goals in the city didn't include violence, most adults had left the tunnels to fight outside the city, but Scooter was glad he still had a small force willing to harass rather than murder. They carried tools rather than guns—the Bandit's rules.

Together, the fighters knelt with Scooter and gave him their attention. He always struggled with these pre-mission briefings. Some of them could be caught and executed. Although he didn't have any children of his own, he still had many children. These were all his kids, most of them barely in their twenties.

"Seek good and not evil," he called loudly.

"That you may live," the fighters said together.

It didn't matter that they weren't quiet now. The whole tunnel had been alerted that there was a topside mission underway. Friends and children had crept as close as they dared, lest the Bandit chastise them for being too near to hear his orders. Being a Vag fighter required the Bandit's personal training, and not everyone in the tunnel was a fighter.

The call and response that Scooter used as a resistance mantra was from Amos 5:14, and this was recited as a slogan everywhere they went, but Scooter also meant it to be a reminder that would be instilled into their young hearts. And although he needed to maintain his cover as the resistance leader rather than a Christian, he also tried to leave an example of a father figure who encouraged them toward good paths and not evil roads, even though they were active revolutionaries.

"We leave immediately," he stated. "Three teams. I'll lead the rescue. Willie will lead the raid. And Hedgehog will lead the diversion. Everyone knows their teams?"

They all nodded. Hedgehog was one of the older Vags, tall and lanky, with an abrupt wave on the top of his reddish hair. Since he liked exploring collapsed tunnels, Scooter had called him Hedgehog ever since he was thirteen, and the name had stuck. Although Hedgehog was obedient, he was the most vocal about his desire to kill the enemy, which tested Scooter's tolerance just about weekly, but the man had a following.

"Don't get too excited. We're going downtown, and we're going to be stuck out there. We'll all need to find somewhere to hide once the sun rises. And every Enforcer will be looking for us on the surface, until we're under the cover of darkness again and able to come Uptown."

That news subdued their excitement. The resistance loved the tunnels, where they thrived and the darkness kept Federation Enforcers at bay. But topside? That was Federation territory.

Scooter explained their individual missions. He briefed Willie on the raid he would make for a recently uncovered Federation cache of canned food. And Hedgehog was to create a diversion by using a pair of potato guns to detonate an ammunition depot near the East River.

"None of you are beginners," Scooter concluded. "Rely on each other and watch over one another. If it's your turn to die, die well, and remember what Doc has taught us about trusting in Jesus Christ. Seek good and not evil."

"That you may live," they all said solemnly.

"Good." Scooter rose to his feet. "Move out in two minutes. If you want to hear from Doc, join me."

Doc Joss was the best electrician in the tunnels of Manhattan. Everyone needed him, but he wasn't too popular since he was an outspoken preacher. Scooter didn't allow anyone to disrespect the muscled Austrian, but not many attended the zealous man's Sunday services. Nevertheless, Doc's prayer before a mission was tradition, and although Scooter never required his fighters to submit to the preacher's words, he hoped they would. Unfortunately, many seemed to view the pre-mission prayer as a superstition, but Scooter was glad they were at least hearing the gospel.

Scooter shook Doc's meaty paw, then rested his hands on his hips, and bowed his head. The Vags crowded around, their arms over their friends' shoulders. Doc needed no prodding, and others in the tunnels who weren't fighters knew they could join this part, and they moved in.

"God Almighty!" Doc's voice thundered in a rich accent. If anyone hadn't been awake in the tunnel, they were now. "Give Your children feet like the wind as they do Your work against the terrible ones on the surface. Convict our own hearts over the sin that remains, and show us how to come humbly to Your loving cross. And those who strike against Your chosen ones, Lord—strike them down! In Jesus' name, amen."

"Amen!" everyone said, then dispersed.

Doc grabbed Scooter by the arm.

"I wish you wouldn't do this, Bandit." The Austrian shook his big head. "They're so young."

"No one older wants to go," Scooter said. "Besides, half these kids know the streets better than any Enforcer. There's work to be done, Doc. We need to go."

"When will you finally trust in Jesus and give Him your soul, Bandit? Stop playing at this religion, and come fully into God's embrace!"

"Just keep praying for me, Doc." Scooter slugged the man's shoulder, hoping there would be a day soon when he could tell the preacher that he had much more than passive support for Christianity. He'd been a believer for nearly thirty years, since his last years in the Marines with

Nathan. "We're on the same side, Doc. Both of us are searching for useful recruits."

At the outside barrier, Scooter fit a headlamp over his head. His team of rescuers consisted of three young men in their twenties, and three single women of the same age, all natives to the island. Since so many rescues involved women and children, Scooter made sure all of his team were the eldest of the Vags, willing and strong enough to help others over their own safety.

"No one leaves until you return, Bandit," a middle-aged guard confirmed as he opened the barrier on the tunnel tracks.

Scooter gave the man a thumbs-up, then led the way out of the habitat. For security purposes, once a mission began, no one in the community was allowed to leave.

At a jog, Scooter moved southward in the tunnel, leaping over debris that littered the old subway shaft. Where the tracks forked, Willie led his raiding party down another tunnel. Some distance later, Hedgehog led his team away. Scooter was left with his six, which he'd led into danger more than fifty times over the last couple of years.

But everything was different now, even if he was the only one who knew it. Operation Esther was unfolding. For the first time in years, Radiant Shade would be placing herself center stage to change the tide of the Federation. Other COIL operatives were suddenly using their deep cover positions in heightened, riskier ways. One slip could unravel everything, and the years of careful planning would be for nothing.

An hour later, he slowed to a walk, his ears tuning out the squeaking of rats and dripping water. For years, he'd lived in the tunnels, so he knew what sounds belonged and what didn't. His eyes also studied the shadows ahead, watching for anything that would suggest an approaching light. It was around three in the morning, so no one from the surface would be awake and in the tunnels unless they were Federation Enforcers trying to root out the resistance, or block off tunnel access. Fortunately for Scooter, the surface city couldn't completely cut off the tunnels from the surface since Chancellor Obrador was trying to resurrect the city's infrastructure and utilities, all which required tunnel access.

"We're there." Scooter held up a fist and shined his headlamp at the wall below the trapdoor in the ceiling. It blended in perfectly with the rest of the tunnel ceiling, barely distinguishable in the grime and mold. Set against the wall, there was a makeshift ladder, made from a heavy pipe with large bolts fastened along its length. "I'll go up first. We're about a mile away from the target house. No talking from here on."

He tightened his pack strap of gear on his back, then climbed the pole as his teammates steadied the ladder. When he could reach the street level above, he tested the metal plate that rested in place. It was a handmade manhole, one he'd dug himself, since the original manholes on streets were usually too exposed to Enforcer eyes.

Scooter used the top of his head and one forearm to lift the cover a few inches. His headlamp shined into the dark basement of a street shop in Gramercy Park. The floor appeared dusty, undisturbed, no visible footprints in the small room. Years earlier, the resistance had removed everything from the room, so in passing, looters or scavengers could merely glance in, see there was nothing of value, and leave without investigating the floor.

Careful to make no noise, Scooter lifted the cover completely out of the way, and climbed onto the floor of the room. Before he signaled the others to ascend, he stepped lightly to the door and slowly turned the handle. Since he hadn't used that tunnel access in years, there was no telling what was on the other side of the door now. He turned off his headlamp.

Opening the door a crack, he used one eye pressed to the small opening to study the broken shelves and empty floor where groceries and goods had once been stacked in the old establishment. Half the shelves had been removed, and the cashier's counter must've been combustible, because only pieces of it remained. But the store seemed quiet in the eerie darkness. It was hard to imagine that twenty years earlier, hundreds of people had streamed in and out of that very place every day, buying milk, lottery tickets, and microwaveable burritos.

"A burrito sounds good about now," Scooter mumbled, then returned to the hole in the floor.

"It's safe. Let's go."

He turned on his headlamp to guide the three young women up the ladder first, then the three young men. In the tight space, they huddled together against the door. Again, Scooter turned off his lamp, and everyone followed suit. When he opened the door wide on its rusty hinges, he crouched low, leaving an example for the others to remain small, quiet, and wary.

They were now in enemy territory.

Chapter Four

Enforcer Owen Travers was still aggravated about being jumped several evenings earlier. His ego was insulted. He hadn't told anyone he'd been incapacitated while following Corban Dowler on foot, and he'd kept it a secret that his identification and firearm had been stolen as well. There was no doubt in his mind that the old man in charge of Manhattan's identification printing office had somehow bested him, but he had too much pride to admit it to anyone. *Dowler was in his eighties!*

That early morning, he rode in the passenger seat of a van repurposed for Federation raids. The rear of the vehicle had been reinforced with a steel cage wherein nonconformists could be transported to Citizen Processing down at the Bowery Hotel. The van tore up the street and swerved around burnt car wreckage that labor crews hadn't yet removed. Only one of the van's headlights worked, so Owen hoped the driver next to him was paying attention.

"Don't park in front," Owen told the driver, a recent Citizen Army recruit. They were getting them in their teens nowadays. "Park in the alley. I want to catch them sleeping."

Owen drew his sidearm and mentally tried to force Corban Dowler out of his thoughts, but it wasn't easy. The old man printed everything the chancellor had signed off, but the problem with Federation security was that no one knew who anyone had been before Pan-Day. Millions had died and all digital databases had collapsed. Therefore, Owen suspected everyone to have a stolen identity or to be an enemy of the Federation. As an Enforcer, it was his job to systematically investigate every Federation citizen, and that had included the man who printed for the chancellor. With the resistance gaining influence in the city, it was reasonable to suspect the old man responsible for citizen identifications. Little had he known that following the old man would result in being mugged and robbed!

The driver turned off the van's headlights as they turned into the alley in Gramercy Park. Using the rearview mirror, Owen noticed the Enforcer transport vehicle behind them went dark as well. Ten Enforcers had been roused from their bunks to aid in this arrest of a nonconformist family of four. Owen looked forward to executing them that weekend.

When the van engine was shut off, Owen's door window was open, so he listened to the city. So quiet. He recalled the bustling night life of the borough, even at that early hour, not long before sunup. No one had guessed back then that a food-borne and fluid-transmitted virus was tearing through the nation from the west. The Meridia Virus had hit Manhattan last, even after it had decimated Florida and much of the South. Before anyone had figured out how it was spreading, thousands had been infected. Quarantines had merely isolated communities where victims were already contagious. The virus had spread by touch, turning every neighborhood into a petri dish of disease.

Twenty years earlier, Owen had been only twenty years old, and his older sister, Lena, had shut them both up in his apartment in Midtown. For two months, she'd insisted they not leave, and no matter who banged on their door for help, they couldn't open the door for anyone. His neighbors had died or fled the city. They'd survived, but the experience had soured him. His sister was cold-hearted, so intent on survival that she'd ignored the suffering of others. Now, she kept them on the survival path the same way—by being the city's fiercest Enforcers. Although he told no one, Owen had lived a role he could barely tolerate. As Lena always said, do what you have to, to survive. But he hated her for what she'd made him do. However, to change now would mean losing the privileges he'd grown to enjoy from Obrador. Obrador always favored the cruelest Enforcers.

Owen waited behind the van for the Enforcers to gather around him. He was the only one who wore civilian clothes, with a rain-proofed trench coat over his khakis.

"You five, take the back entrance." Owen used his drawn sidearm to point at the men. "We'll take the front. Handcuffs, gags, and hoods for everyone, children included. I want them interrogated separately before they have a chance to talk to one another. We can't question them if they're dead, so only shoot to wound, if you have to. Sync your watches and get into position. We make our entry in five minutes."

Four minutes later, Owen stood with his shoulder against a brick column in front of the townhouse. The others crouched below the front of the porch, perfectly silent, giving the rear entrance team time to get into position.

With the best view of the street, Owen studied the quiet neighborhood. It had rained around midnight, so the pavement was wet, the air fresh, and there was no breeze. The only electricity restored to this neighborhood was a few blocks south and west, closer to the chancellor's headquarters, where Citizen Army troops were housed. Some creative civilians had rigged up solar or wind for power, but Owen didn't see any lights down the moon-shadowed street.

Suddenly, down the block, the whisper of movement followed a string of people who darted across the street. They had to be resistance fighters! No one else would dare to break curfew. Owen raised his firearm to shoot as many as he could, when the pressure of a blunt object pressed into his back next to his spine. He froze. In the next instant, the people who'd hustled across the street were gone, disappearing between houses fifty yards away.

"You're up early," a man's soft voice said behind him. "Lower your gun."

Owen clenched his teeth and lowered his pistol. As soon as it was at his side, the man twisted the pistol from his hand. Up on the porch, the Enforcers broke a window, unlocked the front door, and made entry into the house. None of them even looked back to see that Owen was being held captive.

"Who are you?" Owen asked, and started to turn around.

"Not so fast." The unseen man shoved Owen against the brick, bruising his cheek against the rough surface. "I'll tell you who I am, but we're not at the face-to-face stage in our relationship quite yet."

From the angle of his voice, Owen thought his assailant was a little shorter than himself. If that gun weren't in his ribs, maybe he could've fought back . . .

"You already got the family out," Owen concluded. "You were tipped off?"

"Or, you're just easy to predict, Owen Travers."

"So, you know who I am. In about twenty seconds, my men will come back out here. Do you want to tell me the name of the man they're about to shoot? I can't promise you I'll put it on a gravestone, but I'll certainly curse your name as I shove your body into the furnace."

"You already know me, Owen." The gun in his back suddenly shifted up to the back of his neck as the man pressed closer. "Stay away from Houston Street!"

The weapon against his neck was withdrawn, and there was a clatter on the sidewalk. Owen swung with his elbow as he turned, but the assailant was already fleeing through the alley. Looking down, Owen swore and picked up a salt shaker, which had obviously been the weapon used to press against his neck. But his gun hadn't been returned. For the second time that week, he'd had his sidearm stolen!

"Mr. Travers?" An Enforcer stood on the porch. "The house is empty. I think we just missed them. The beds are still warm."

"Collect all the papers you can find. Search everything!" Owen growled. "Anything significant, bag it. They had to leave some intel behind. Bring it all."

"There's food in the pantry. Can we . . . you know, can we eat it?"

"Just hurry, would you?"

Owen returned to the alley and approached the van. All four tires had been slashed, as well as those of the rear transport. No one had stayed with the vehicles, so they'd been sabotaged. He punched the side of the van and cursed again. *The Bandit!* It had to have been the Bandit!

As if things weren't bad enough, he heard the approaching purr of a motorcycle. Lena rolled up next to the sidewalk on the street bike she often used to get around town, with her German shepherd, Death, on the seat in front of her. The dog leaped down to the pavement and growled at him, restrained only by a thin leash in Lena's grip.

"It's sunrise," she said, "and I don't see any prisoners in cuffs. Where's your weapon, Owen?"

"The Bandit just came and left." He looked away as the sun touched his face. "He said to stay away from Houston Street. We might want to check it out."

"Probably just misdirection." She scoffed at him, making him feel small. "Obrador won't be happy. It's your problem this time."

"How is it my problem if we have a leak at the Bowery? Why don't you find the mole in our own offices, Lena!"

"Don't blame me for your incompetence, Owen." She signaled for the canine to climb back onto her lap. The dog was taller than she was where it sat in front of her. "You never could do anything right unless I held your hand. You'd better bring Obrador a peace offering, or he's liable to think you're doing this on purpose. This is your third failed arrest in three weeks. What's really going on with you?"

She sped away, and Owen was doubly glad she didn't know about his failed stalking of Corban Dowler, or she'd laugh at him over that as well.

But as usual, she was right, he thought to himself as he and his men readied themselves for the dawn march back to headquarters. Though he'd never been disciplined, Owen was likely to receive Obrador's discipline over this failure. A peace offering was indeed necessary, but what would Obrador want? Owen realized he didn't know the man that way—his dreams and goals. But something needed to be arranged to honor Chancellor Obrador, or Owen would pay for it.

Brian Steelman sat in his open-topped Jeep in Foley Square, Chinatown. Since he was originally from Boston, he didn't know how green the Square had once been, but people had told him. Now, it was gray. The ground was swept clean by forced laborers, and in the center of the trapezoidal space, ten gallows stood, the ropes frayed, the wood weathered, and the platform soiled.

Three humble citizens were marched onto the platform as a regiment of Citizen Army soldiers surrounded the site. Brian was too far away to hear the weeping of one of the condemned men, but he could see he wasn't facing the noose with courage. A captain below the platform read the charges, shouting over the ruckus made by the unrestrained man.

The hangman was a broad-shouldered brute, someone new. He ordered the three condemned citizens to remove their shoes, which they did without force. The crying man was defeated, and he angrily tossed his boots onto a pile of other footwear behind the gallows. The other two were more dignified, and Brian admired them as they tucked the laces and tongues back into their boots, so someone else could wear them without the rats getting inside them.

Surveying the Square, Brian looked for Chancellor Obrador. In the early days of the Federation, Obrador had attended the executions of noncompliant citizens. Now, a junior officer presided. And Owen Travers was there, his steady, piercing eyes staring straight ahead. The man was normally a pillar of viciousness, Brian recalled, but lately, the chief Enforcer had seemed distracted. He'd yelled at men in the hotel who hadn't saluted him, and he'd belted one of the chefs across the mouth for giving him scrambled eggs instead of hard boiled.

The city was tipping away from Obrador, Brian realized. Starvation had weakened the people's resolve to grasp Obrador's vision of a strong empire. Maybe too many citizens still remembered Old America, when the city had been lit up by zipping traffic, neon lights, and bustling parties. No one was buying into the Federation's forced motto: *Always Caring, Forever Strong.*

The captain finished reading the charges, and the hangman wasted no time. He yanked on a metal lever and the three fell a short distance. Brian looked away, disgusted. Obrador had made a rule that criminals were no longer to be hooded while hung, so the soldiers below leered and mocked the three as they died slowly. The drop wasn't long enough to break their necks—another device of Obrador. Instead, they kicked and wiggled as they choked to death. Sickened, Brian started the Jeep, then noticed Owen walking across the Square to him. Sighing, he turned off the engine to conserve fuel.

"I remember when this place had two sets of gallows," Owen said as he reached the Jeep, "and you and I kept them filled every Sunday."

"The noncompliant have all been arrested." Brian rubbed his hands together against the cold. "Now, you're just executing people who have different opinions. Did you come all the way over here to reminisce? You really aren't yourself, are you, Owen?"

"Yeah, well, I don't like being made a fool of. I'm sure you heard about yesterday morning."

"The Bandit?"

"The noncompliants aren't rooted out as much as you think. They're just hiding better than when you used to be here. And they have help. That's why I came over here. You just got a new citizen ID, right? You saw that Corban Dowler guy?"

"Yeah, so? Obrador trusts him. He does his job."

"I don't like him. I have reason to believe there's something going on with him."

Brian looked past Owen at the troops who were taking down the dead. They were loaded onto a cart that was pulled by a pair of horses whose ribs were showing.

For a moment, Brian reflected on the blind woman at the printer's office. She had touched more than just his face; she'd touched his heart, speaking of peace and hope. How could she and her old father be dangerous?

"If you haven't heard already, Owen," Brian said, "Obrador has me on the hunt for Radiant Shade. You're on resistance patrol, not me. Have fun with that."

"I'm asking for your help." Owen cringed as he turned his head away. "You and I have never really gotten along, Steelman. I know that. It's because of my sister, right? Listen. Citizens on the island know me too well for me to secretly investigate the old man. You're more low-profile, and you have a nose like no one else for noncompliance. I'm not asking you to stop searching for Radiant Shade. Just look into Corban Dowler for me. Something about him is off."

"Give me a reason to question the old guy for you. Obrador won't like his printer being harassed. The guy's always busy filling orders for the Bowery."

"You're Brian Steelman. You don't need a reason for anything you do. I'm asking you to do this."

"Next, you'll have me interrogating the blind woman who lives with him, too, to see if she's seen anything fishy lately."

"Just do it for me, would you?" Owen backed away. "I'll owe you one."

"And I'll collect!" Brian started the Jeep. "I'll see you in a few days."

Brian drove away, heading north. He had no leads on Radiant Shade, but then again, he hadn't been searching for her the last four days since he'd been tasked with the mission. Deep down, he could care less about her, and he secretly hoped that she would somehow drive Obrador insane with her religious rantings. Obrador hated her sweet, caring voice. They had confiscated hundreds of her hearing aid recordings from the cells of noncompliant citizens, arrested and executed for their second offenses against the Federation's regulations. Brian had listened to many of the recent recordings, but they were the same as the ones he'd heard years earlier. Whoever she was, she must've been a mastermind to elude capture for so many years. It meant she remained isolated, probably sending the hearing aids through trusted couriers no one had ever discovered.

The Jeep roared up Broadway and through Times Square, where Brian glanced at the identification building. The old man's offices were built like a glass fortress, and the surveillance camera system at the front door had always kept Obrador from stationing an armed guard at the office, but maybe there was more going on at the workplace than anyone knew. There was probably a back door that wasn't under surveillance.

But Brian quickly dismissed the suspicions that Owen had presented. Manhattan didn't have a counterfeit identification problem. Dowler's IDs were too sophisticated to counterfeit. Every ID that had ever been checked had matched the list at the chancellor's office of records and Citizen Processing. It was too much of a stretch to think the man was producing genuine IDs for citizens and simultaneously updating the Citizen Processing roster in the administration office. Dowler had no access to the hotel, and it was unthinkable that the Federation's security screenings had allowed an actual infiltrator into its Citizen Processing Department.

Parking his Jeep on the off-ramp of the George Washington Bridge, Brian slung his rifle over his shoulder, and walked up to the checkpoint manned by two Citizen Army soldiers. They were young men, both appearing to have been born after Pan-Day. It was depressing for Brian to consider that there were youngsters like these who would only know an America that looked like it did now. They knew nothing about the grandeur, the entertainment, the splendor, and the vices available at the touch of a smart phone.

The two men emerged from the warmth of a small station hut and sloppily saluted Brian, which meant they'd probably recognized him. It was possible they'd heard rumors that he was back in the city, or they had merely guessed that only a Federation official would be driving a vehicle and carrying a firearm in the city. Whatever the case, Brian didn't recognize either of them, and they were too young to know him from his early days with Chancellor Obrador.

"Any immigrants today?" Brian shook their hands rather than saluting them back. He gazed across the Hudson over the narrowest span between Manhattan and New Jersey. The Little Red Lighthouse was visible, but it wasn't red any longer. It appeared blackened as if by fire. Or it was just covered in grime, like the rest of the city. The water level was low, and the distant shore's dark rocks protruded far out into the Hudson, endangering vessels, if any happened upon the river.

"A couple this morning," one of the young men said. He had freckles on his cheeks. "They had a baby. We sent them with a temporary pass to Processing."

Brian grunted, remembering a time when the bridge had been filled with hopeful people streaming into the newly established capital city of the Appalachian Federation. Those had been years of promise under Obrador. A socialist utopia had been prophesied, and Obrador had assured the people of a new society delivered from bigotry, regulated by the Federation, void of crime, hate speech, and unfair policies. Health care for everyone! And Brian had believed it all as well.

A few years later, the ration lines had grown long, the gallows had swung every Sunday, and few travelers made the trek into the cold, starving city. Now, the limited rations in the city weren't enough for people to travel on, so they were kept from leaving. But Brian believed they would leave, if they could get their hands on enough provisions to escape.

"I'm expecting a few travelers." Brian shifted his rifle on his shoulder, reflecting briefly on his own two years traveling on the open highway. "A large, blond man who's with a one-armed woman."

"A one-armed woman?" the other snickered. He had an ugly scab on his upper lip, like he'd been in a brawl while drunk. Either way, he smelled of the island's production of the underground potato still. "We might miss the blond guy, but we won't miss a woman with one arm."

"They might be traveling with a small band. I want to be notified when they come through."

"You want us to hold them?" Freckles asked. "We can arrest them if you want to question them."

"Arrest them? No." Brian remembered the way the blond man, called the Serval by his friends, had handled his short assault rifle and moved with a grace that signaled his skill in that violent land. "No, he's not the kind of man you'd want to try to arrest. Just stick to procedure by sending them with a pass to register. But let me, Brian Steelman, know when they cross the bridge."

Brian walked back to the Jeep, feeling trapped on the island, wondering if the Serval would want to leave the capital as soon as he found whoever he was looking for. He'd been worried about someone in Federation land. Maybe the person was in one of the internment camps outside the city, where noncompliants were rounded up and crews were forced to farm and harvest wood. But the Serval had to come to Manhattan, Brian guessed, to check the central records that were kept at the hotel. Chances were, he was looking for someone who'd died of the virus years earlier, or they'd been arrested as noncompliant. So many were still failing the Citizen's Entrance Exam.

He drove the Jeep back down to Central Park and climbed out of the vehicle to admire a wall sprayed with graffiti on West 110th Street. The graffiti was fresh and bright, with swirls and jagged letters of words he couldn't quite decipher. The Federation knew that the resistance was using graffiti to communicate something to someone, but they'd never figured out what. Brian doubted it had anything to do with Radiant Shade, but there were so many unknowns beneath the surface of the city—maybe there was a connection between Radiant Shade and the resistance ... Figuring out what the city's secret citizens had been up to while he'd been gone would take Brian more time than Obrador was allowing him.

Several civilians were moving to and fro along the sidewalk, their heads down, coats zipped up, and carrying canvas bags of rations. How was he supposed to find Radiant Shade unless he connected with the people? He had to earn their trust, and that could take weeks. But it could be weeks until the Serval arrived, so why not make peace with Owen and look into Corban Dowler? Who knew? He might stumble upon Radiant Shade along the way.

Suddenly, two boys ran out of an alley and darted across the street. In seconds, they had disappeared down an avenue. Just boys playing? Brian wasn't so sure. Children that age were to be in the state-mandated schools, being taught a curriculum ordered by Obrador himself. It was basic socialism, Brian thought, with Obrador's unique twist of amorality and panpsychism— the belief that all objects in the world had a conscience and deserved a voice. Although Brian had never objected to the chancellor's ideas, the long-term effects of that dogma was showing itself across the Federation. Hope had died. While teaching amorality, the Federation was rotting internally. Disease and drug use had never been so rampant, even without Meridia Virus outbreaks. Taking from citizens who'd had much, to give equally to those who didn't want to apply themselves, had diminished the Federation to a people who expected handouts. The city's food ration system was a prime example. The wealthy had lost what they'd worked for, and the poor didn't have to work since the government had promised everyone an equal share. Entitlement ensued.

Instead of pursuing the boys, who were certainly skipping school, Brian walked toward the alley from which they'd run, and looked in. Apparently, Morningside Heights hadn't been one of Obrador's priorities when it came to trash disposal. Garbage bags and refuse were piled two stories high, a mountain crammed between two buildings that someone would need to climb over to pass through the alley. Civilians in the upper apartments had probably been tossing their garbage out their windows for years, creating this rotting mess, which apparently fed a population of rats that made the garbage heap seem alive.

The boys couldn't have come out of that alley, Brian realized, unless they'd been playing in the smelly trash with the rats.

Brian took a step into the alley, then glanced back at the Jeep in the street. The resistance was rumored to be in the area, but would they really do something to a Federation vehicle in the middle of the day? He guessed they had no qualms about sabotage, no matter the time of day or night—remembering what had happened to Owen and his convoy's tires. And none of these citizens would probably report on the mischief of the resistance, either. Years earlier, Brian had interrogated a civilian who'd informed him that the resistance looked out for some of the citizens in the city, giving them food and medicine, thereby undermining the Federation's control on equal ration management. And from where was the resistance getting food to feed others? From their raids on Federation depots, no less!

Leaving the Jeep behind, Brian walked deeper into the alley. If the boys hadn't been picking through the horrendous mountain of debris, what else could they have been doing?

He was halfway along the left wall of the alley when he noticed a metal grate leaning against the wall. But looking closer, he found that behind the grate, there was no wall, but darkness.

Immediately, Brian knew what he'd stumbled across—a hidden entrance to the tunnel system below the city! Most of the subway entrances had been sealed off to discourage access, but there was no policing the hundreds of miles below ground. Manholes still existed, though some covers had been sealed. Obrador had resigned to tolerating the occasional power outages, though he'd always made a "tunnel rat" resistance fighter suffer before execution when one was caught.

He lifted the grate aside and peered inside. Cement rubble acted as a rough ramp down into the inky blackness. *And the smell!* Brian had heard of families who lived below, children who'd never been to the surface. What a life, to live in the sewer! But standing in the rotten-smelling alley, Brian guessed the infested city had become no better.

After crawling through the entrance, he turned around and dragged the grate back into place. Inside, he could stand upright. The basement of the apartment building was tall enough to accommodate even his rifle barrel, which extended a few inches above his head. For a few seconds, he waited for his eyes to adjust to the darkness, but there was no adjusting. Human eyes couldn't adjust to this blackness. There had to be light ahead somewhere, he decided, and he inched his way down the rubble, feeling the ground with his feet and the air with his hands.

The sound of rats and dripping water echoed against a wall ahead. His hand touched the slimy wall. He flinched away from the grime for an instant, but touching it at least gave him a sense of direction. As he continued ahead, following the wall, he heard running water somewhere to the right. Whatever cavern he was in sounded broad, and since he was directly under the apartment building, he guessed there was structural damage from the running water after so many years. But Obrador had no engineers for repairs in the city. His efforts were focused on population control and keeping himself living in luxury.

Suddenly, Brian's foot felt a ledge, and when he reached with his other foot for another step, he felt nothing below. Imagining that he was on the edge of a great precipice, he backed off, panting from anxiety and fear, close to panic, dreading the worst. Light. *He needed light, now!*

Gasping for relief, he stumbled back the way he'd come, tracing his fingers along the wall, catching the unseen grime under his fingernails. He tripped over the rubble that was piled up to the grate. *Daylight!* He climbed hand over foot up the pile, eyes focused on the sliver of light peeking around an edge of the framework. Reaching the grille, he shoved it flat and rolled onto the alley floor. A rat scurried over his leg, but in his relief at being back to the surface, he simply shook the creature aside instead of hurting it.

Blinking in the sunlight, he noticed he and the rats weren't alone. A tall, gaunt man, his face wrinkled and bony, stood against the wall next to the tunnel entrance. His posture was peculiar, Brian thought. The man's right thumb was hooked into the top of his leather belt next to a sparkling belt buckle.

"I heard you coming all the way out here," the gaunt man said. He had an olive complexion, but his features appeared more European than Hispanic. "You need to emerge a little more carefully next time. There are Enforcers and their informants everywhere. People will rat you out for a piece of bread these days."

"Rat? Funny." Brian grimaced at the green and purple ooze clinging to his fingers. "You're going down there?"

Rising to his feet, Brian realized he was looking at a potential resistance fighter. No one else would hang out in such a gag-worthy alley. Yet, the man had said nothing about the Jeep on the street, or the Bushmaster rifle on his back.

"Close up after me," the man said, then climbed into the opening with surprising agility.

Brian leaned down to see how the gaunt man managed without a light, but all he saw was darkness. Yet, it wasn't a wasted day. He just needed to come back with a flashlight. The tunnel would give him something to explore while he waited for the Serval to reach the city. And if he could get a lead on Radiant Shade in the meantime, it would keep Obrador off his back.

As Brian approached his Jeep, two suspicious men wearing parkas stepped back into the shadows of a doorway, but they'd been eyeing the unattended vehicle.

No common citizen was allowed to own or carry a firearm, so even if they didn't know exactly who he was, Brian guessed they had a good idea that he was an Enforcer in plain clothes. However, in that neighborhood, Enforcer or not, Brian figured he'd better watch his back.

Driving down Broadway, he arrived in Times Square and pulled over on the street in front of the identification office. Twenty years earlier, parking on that block would've been difficult, but traffic was different nowadays, with only twenty operating vehicles on the whole island. Obrador's fuel trucks brought in fuel monthly from New Jersey's refinery, but sometimes the trucks were hijacked by the resistance in other states. They needed to run vehicles and generators sparingly.

The identification office was a building seemingly untouched by Pan-Day—the riots and fires, and all the strife that had led to the founding of the Federation. Brian climbed out of the Jeep and leaned against the door, admiring the building. With his arms crossed, he studied it with a critical eye, with instinct he'd originally hoped to use as a detective in Boston. Pan-Day had changed his career pursuits, but he still had his instincts. Besides, hunting down noncompliants had taught him to notice what was missing, or what was hidden in plain sight. If Owen was right about Corban Dowler being a threat to the Federation, Brian decided it was a worthy challenge to sniff out some clues. Again, if he could throw Obrador a bone, maybe he'd get some relief from the pressure to find Radiant Shade.

The most interesting part of the building above him was that all its windows were in place. As far as Brian knew, no buildings within a mile had first floor windows. Years earlier, Brian remembered Obrador vetting Corban Dowler for printing authority. Dowler had been one of the first people to take the Citizen's Entrance Exam, and passed with no red flags. And all the equipment for printing and laminating identifications for the budding nation had already been inside this building. How very convenient, Brian thought. It was almost as if the old man had made arrangements to become the Federation's identification expert—even before the Federation had assumed control and enacted its Citizen Processing regulations. What kind of a person was in the right place at such a time? No one could've planned for all that would happen, or what the Federation would require. *Could they?*

Brian took his rifle from the Jeep and crossed the street. The door to the office was locked. The glass doors were heavy, but obviously not just glass. They were bullet-proof, like the plated windows above the ground level. He knocked on the glass, and noticed Dowler peer out from the back room, wave, and start toward him.

Since Brian had found the tunnel entrance on 110th Street, he was feeling particularly lucky that late morning. Maybe he'd catch himself a resistance sympathizer or disrupt their network with an arrest—and be back at the hotel by dinner. It was time to question Corban Dowler.

But in the back of his mind was the blind woman who lived there. She'd been an angel of gentleness and care toward him. What would happen to someone like her in a city full of citizens who only looked out for themselves?

Chapter Five

When Corban looked out and noticed the Enforcer known as Brian Steelman outside, he immediately switched on the stereo to play classical piano music. Jenna was below ground, and she would know the warning was from him to her. Steelman had no reason to return to the office. Something was wrong. For several days after Corban had incapacitated Owen Travers, he'd expected a police raid, but nothing had happened, and he'd started to believe he was in the clear. And now this second visit. Operation Esther was so close to unfolding!

Using his cane, he descended the stairs to the front door and unlocked it.

"Mr. Steelman." Corban opened the door wide, smiling. "This is a pleasant surprise. Is your ID in order? Your papers? Did I misprint something?"

"Everything's fine." Steelman pointed up at the front room's camera. "Is that camera working? I'd like to see your surveillance system and video storage."

"Of course. Just let me lock up while we're in the back room."

With his heart beating slowly but loudly in his ears, Corban intentionally struggled with the lock as he studied the street outside. No Citizen Army soldiers were in sight, so this didn't seem to be a raid. But he had a hard time believing this was a routine visit—not by the infamous Steelman. If he arrested him right then, with Jenna below ground, she'd be left to fend for herself, not knowing what had happened. She could even emerge from the basement into the hands of investigators, and all of her important work would be exposed—the poetry books, the hearing aids . . .

"The woman I was speaking to here the other day, your daughter?" Steelman asked.

"Jenna? Yes, my wife and I adopted her as a child. She's not in the house right now. Come back here with me."

Corban led him into the print room where multiple copies of current printing projects lay spread out on a number of tables. Three monstrous safes stood against the wall, and he turned the dial on the middle safe.

"No security concerns here?" Steelman asked.

"Not that I've noticed." Corban swung open the safe to reveal a digital system, recording on a one-month loop for four cameras. "You're looking for someone specific? We can replay from any of four views of the front using this screen here. The resolution is phenomenal."

"Very state of the art." Steelman studied the equipment, reading the labels on the machines.

"I was taking classes on surveillance before Pan-Day. I was getting my investigator's license."

"Then you know a camera system even like this can't catch as much as an alert human eye. Tell me what you're looking for, and maybe it's something I've seen and didn't realize meant something. There are people coming and going all day, every day. If they entered this office, or even if they were on the street outside, they're on this system. I might know something about them."

Steelman turned his back and walked around the table, peering at the identifications laid out on the table. Corban closed the safe door and walked to an electric water heater. Now he knew what Steelman was doing there. He wasn't looking for anyone; he was looking for clues, testing him. Something about him or the office had raised suspicion.

"Cup of tea, Mr. Steelman?"

"No, I won't be here long." Steelman plucked up an ID card from one table. "Why are these ration cards a different color than the one you gave me?"

"Last year, the chancellor implemented the Loyal Citizen Program to encourage citizen cooperation. You were given a loyal citizen ration card. Those are for citizens who've never been charged with loyalty breaches or civil crimes."

"Huh. Obrador's always thinking of new incentives, isn't he?" Steelman looked up into Corban's face, eyes piercing. "Ever heard of Radiant Shade?"

"Yes, I have. The security alerts I receive from the Bowery have mentioned that name." Corban leaned on his cane and tilted his head. He'd spent too much time undercover in Russia and the Middle East to crack under the pressure of a single Federation Enforcer, but he could still crack if he didn't think ahead and choose his words carefully. "Do we know yet if it's a man or a woman?"

"I've heard recordings of her voice. She's definitely a woman. Has anyone from the resistance ever approached you to print IDs for them?"

"No, no one involved in the resistance, as far as I know, has ever been here to ask for an ID." Corban was forceful with his words, but he was also particular in his answer, careful not to lie. "Besides, all of my identifications come straight from the Bowery. I wouldn't print anything that didn't originate from headquarters. No ID or papers would be worth anything, even as flawless as I try to make them, unless they're ordered from the Bowery."

"What was this building before Pan-Day? I mean, bulletproof glass? This place is a fortress."

"The two floors upstairs were used by a small aid organization called the Commission of International Laborers—COIL, for short."

"COIL? That's a unique name."

"The people who once worked here . . ." Corban smiled, remembering the gifted and loving Christians who'd filled the offices upstairs. "They gave their lives, not just their time, for others. Most of them died around Pan-Day."

"From the virus or other ways?"

"Some from the virus. They cared for the sick and dying, so, yes, they caught the Meridia. Others were killed, caught in the riots, or died in the fires. The ones who survived made it back here eventually, but I sent them away. There's nothing international about COIL anymore. They now focus on other things these days."

"And public servants needed reinforced glass?"

"These did. Because they often made enemies for whisking the condemned out of harm's way."

"Give me an example." Steelman raised his head and crossed his arms. "How would they do it?"

"I can think of one time there was sectarian violence in Yemen. Women and children were kidnapped and held for ransom. Or for slavery. We went in, found them all massacred, except for one boy. We got him out of the country, but the Yeminis knew it was us. Yemen had agents all over the world back then. Hence, the bulletproof glass."

"So, you worked for the US government? The attention to detail in these IDs and your papers—Obrador has used your prototypes all over the Federation. They're the best I've ever seen, even before Pan-Day."

"I don't have much to offer, but I do want what's best for the Federation."

"Of course. I would expect you to say that. You're modest, Mr. Dowler. Or you're being careful."

Corban saw the Enforcer narrow his eyes, perhaps trying to read through his answers in his mind.

"I just want to be helpful, Mr. Steelman."

"When was your last *CEE?*"

"My Citizen's Entrance Exam?" Corban acted as if he were considering the date. "Well, let me think. They're administered yearly now . . .

"I want you to take it again. Immediately. There's something about you that makes me wonder if you're trustworthy. I don't know what it is, but something is going on here. Everything is too perfect. Or careful. I want your daughter to retake the test as well."

"I don't mind. But you'll need to clear it with the chancellor. He's always told me that I answer to him."

"Don't tell me who I need to clear it with." Steelman's shoulders stiffened. "I could arrest you on my own authority without anyone's say-so."

"I'd be glad to take the *CEE* again." Corban shrugged. "But can we do it here? Otherwise, I'd have to shut down the office, and it'll be easier for Jenna if we didn't have to leave. Will you administer it yourself?"

Steelman turned his head and seemed to study the room before answering.

"That seems reasonable. Yes, I'll administer it myself."

"I look forward to it."

Corban smiled, but his gut was in knots. He'd always had Nathan Isaacson fabricate his *CEE* results, like they did for all of the Christians since they would never be able to pass the *CEE* otherwise.

It was time to deal directly with Brian Steelman. There was no getting around taking the exam now. Operation Esther was in jeopardy!

Nathan Isaacson stood stiffly on his braced leg in a side room of the Bowery Hotel. Beside him, Sergeant Sean Harris kept smoothing down his wrinkled uniform and checking to make sure he still had the evidence folded in his pocket. The aged sergeant hadn't been upstairs to see the chancellor before, so Nathan understood his nervousness. Obrador ruled like a dictator. His word was law, and he could rain death down upon a man's career, life, or family, so Nathan would expect any non-believer to worry about such a man.

But Nathan saw the chancellor much differently. Since he knew the intimate details of Operation Esther, he knew Obrador himself was just a character playing a part on a much larger stage than even Obrador knew. God was the real mover behind the scenes—guiding Christians like Radiant Shade to use what was in place, even if it was the Appalachian Federation that was in place. COIL's job as a group of Christians wasn't to conform to the world, but to apply what they knew to be true, no matter the seeming invincibility of the worldly system.

As cruel as Obrador had been, Nathan saw potential, and because he saw potential, he didn't hate the ruler of the land. But that didn't mean he wouldn't try to sway the man with clandestine efforts. After all, Corban had been helping Radiant Shade move people into place for years, trusting God to protect them from compromising their faith, all for this very purpose. COIL had trained for this, prayed for it, and practiced at it for decades. And with Radiant Shade taking the greatest risks, they'd agreed to follow her strategies even if she was blind.

One of Obrador's executive aides entered the side room. She was a woman in her sixties, still beautiful, with dark, natural, gray-streaked curls. Her face was well-sculpted with high cheekbones, and her eyes, framed by dark lashes, held a firm gaze. In her manicured hands, she carried a clipboard, which she held close against her suited frame. Nathan thought the suit was a man's Armani suit, but she wore it well.

"The chancellor will see you now," the woman stated crisply. "Answer his questions directly. Don't ask for favors. You're here on a confidential intelligence matter, is that correct? Did you fill out Form 1824?"

Nathan nudged Harris with his elbow, indicating he wanted his sergeant to speak for them both. From years of training, Nathan knew that a good spy kept a proxy between himself and exposure as often as possible. Why risk the operation when someone else could be put forward?

"Uh, yes." Harris patted his uniform's breast pocket. "I have the item right here."

"And you?" The woman checked her clipboard. "You're Lieutenant Isaacson?"

"Yes, ma'am."

"The chancellor has been asking about the man who executed the noncompliant by throwing her into the flooded tunnels. That was you?"

"It saved a bullet." Nathan cleared his throat, maintaining his cover as Lieutenant Leather. "Or a hanging spectacle. My methods get the attention of the workers."

"Indeed." The woman raised her chin. "And the chancellor's attention as well. He may ask you about it. Keep your words brief, respectful, and stand at attention until he tells you to stand at ease. Follow me."

Nathan gestured for Harris to enter the next room first. Although Nathan had known for years what his precise part would be in Operation Esther, he was only now seeing how Radiant Shade had placed Chloe Azmaveth to play a role as well. It was hard to calm his pounding heart while thinking of this exact moment being played out. It was a play, after all. *And Chloe was Chancellor Obrador's executive assistant!*

The last time Nathan had spoken to the former COIL public relations liaison had been at her husband's funeral over ten years earlier. Zvi had died, and Radiant Shade had given all remaining COIL operatives their assignments, utilizing Pan-Day's loss of records and identities to blur anyone's detection of the coming infiltration.

Although Nathan had occasionally seen Chloe from a distance, and he'd known the brilliant Syrian-Jewish woman had worked her way into the Federation's administration, he'd had no idea she'd actually become the king's cupbearer, so to speak!

Harris stopped where Chloe indicated in the next room, on thick carpet in front of a glass table, behind which Chancellor Obrador's frame was bent over a task. Nathan stood next to Harris and did his best not to flex his knee in the brace. Climbing all those stairs had gotten the fire in his thigh burning again, and simple anti-inflammatory meds were no longer available in the Federation.

Obrador was occupied with writing a note on notebook paper. Nathan and Harris waited together at attention. Behind Obrador was a wide window, and through it, Nathan could see the northern skyline of New York City toward Central Park. He knew other activities were unfolding over there as well that were related to Operation Esther.

"Yes? What is it now?" Obrador set his pen down and sat back in his padded chair. "Who is this?"

"Lieutenant Isaacson and Sergeant Harris," Chloe introduced. "They have an 1824—um, confidential information—for you privately."

"I hope it's real this time." Obrador rolled his eyes. "How many ridiculous claims do we get, Chloe? People are always looking for something from me without offering anything credible."

"It's real, sir." Harris plucked the folded paper from his pocket and held it up. "What I have here may change the tide of public opinion in this Federation. We took this off a woman before her execution last week. Lieutenant Isaacson here is to be credited, sir, but we were there together, and he's given me the honor of giving it to you."

Nathan's eyes moved from Obrador to Chloe, reading their response to Harris' statement. He was, after all, saying everything that they'd planned.

"Public opinion?" Obrador scoffed and wagged his head. "What do I care about public opinion? Chloe, what does it say? Is it even worth my time?"

Chloe took the paper from Harris and unfolded it.

"It's some sort of letter, or memo, maybe from within the resistance." She turned the paper sideways. "Oh, wait. Here's something interesting."

"If it's about the resistance," Obrador said, waving his hand, "give it to the Twins so we can get back to work. The Enforcers deal with the resistance without me getting involved."

"There's something here about a beauty pageant." Chloe squinted at the paper. "The ink is a little smudged and faded, but it looks like plans for a beauty pageant followed by a wedding. Yes, here it is. It's a proposal to infiltrate this office in an effort to force the Federation to reclaim the hearts of the people with a beauty pageant and a wedding. Strange idea."

"That's a ridiculous idea!" Obrador reached for the glass of cognac. "How would a wedding be worthy of Federation attention?"

"Sir, if I may? I'm Lieutenant Isaacson." Nathan remained at attention as Obrador studied him.

"Yes, Isaacson. I've heard about you. This noncompliant, lazy worker you executed recently—very creative. Spontaneous. It gave me chills to think there's someone out there who thinks like I do. Well, what do you have to say?"

"I take pride in what the forced labor details are able to complete, Mr. Chancellor. I'm always looking for ways to strengthen morale in the Citizen Army and in the city. Weddings have brought peace to estranged parties for hundreds of years. When I—we—found that note, we recognized it as a resistance plot."

"It could be," Chloe said.

"But we could give it our own twist," Nathan offered. "In a single ceremony, we could bring this city together. Absolve the resistance, unite the people, build morale, and become a beacon of unification up and down the coast. Everyone needs this. The Federation could use this."

"You're on thin ice, Lieutenant." Obrador glared. "You're implying that the Federation is weak and vulnerable, and in need of anything. I've put people into your labor details for such claims. You're talking about using a half-baked idea the resistance thought up!"

"Sir, my efforts for all these years show my loyalties." Nathan broke from his posture and placed his hand over his heart. "We've risked ourselves in coming up here, proposing this, but we knew to come to you privately, confidentially, so you could get ahead of it, make it your own idea before it becomes anyone else's fabrication."

"Just whose marriage is the Federation supposed to support?" Obrador shrugged. "Who would the people care about like this?"

"Your marriage, sir," Harris said, glancing at Nathan, who nodded for him to continue. "If you held a beauty pageant, and then picked a woman of the people, someone the people could love beside you, it could, well, you know, help . . ."

"My image?" Obrador chuckled. "I'm an aging man, Sergeant. I'm not worried about my image. Besides, everyone knows I have women on standby, if you know what I mean. No one would believe that I would marry anyone like who you're proposing. I take what I want. I don't like the idea. It's too soft. The Federation needs to project strength, and that's not something that a beauty pageant exactly offers."

Nathan felt the plan faltering. He leveled his eyes at Chloe, communicating to her with his gaze.

"Chancellor," Chloe said softly, "symbols can have remarkable strength. With the right symbol? The resistance would fall apart if more of the people were won over to support the government."

"We rule the people by regulation, not popularity," Obrador stated. "I'd look weak marrying someone below this office."

"You'd look like royalty," Nathan said. "In complete uniform, a symbol of the Federation, uniting with its people. Every family in the Federation would swell with pride. You'd be the ruler they'd want to back with renewed loyalty and devotion. You care about the Federation. Your care through an arranged marriage would transfer to their hearts."

"Moving, Lieutenant, but who am I supposed to marry? If I had my pick, it would be one of the women downstairs who already know what pleases me."

"It needs to be someone from outside, if we do this," Chloe said. "Someone with devotion to the Federation."

"You're an enigma, Lieutenant." Obrador laughed, shaking his finger at him. "You kill an old woman for not working hard enough, and then the next day, you're speaking about romancing the Federation."

"There's a little romance in all of us, sir." Nathan feigned a blush. "I'm married myself to a devoted woman who works in Citizen Processing. We're stronger as a team for the Federation because we're married."

"Again, who am I supposed to marry?"

"The beauty pageant decides that," Harris said. "You alone decide the winner. You'd be both pageant judge and wedding groom."

"A beauty pageant." Obrador rose to his feet, eyed each of them, then turned to the window. "A public announcement could be made. Invite everyone from every state to compete in local then regional pageants, then have the finalists come here to be judged by me alone."

"Chancellor, that's good, but it doesn't guarantee that we'll win the people." Chloe stepped closer to Obrador. "We'd need to make sure, personally, that the right woman is chosen. It can't be a random contest. Hold the pageant, but let me do my homework on the finalists. Some candidates will be better than others, for the Federation."

"They'll all need to be compliant citizens," Obrador said. "I don't want anyone sneaking into our pageant. This could backfire on us, if I choose a noncompliant pageant winner who rallies noncompliant citizens. After all, that was the plan of the resistance. I do like the idea of taking it from them completely."

"We'll find the perfect wife for you and for the Federation." Chloe took notes on her clipboard, as if she were making it up as she went along. "The final contest could be in the spring. We could make it a holiday."

Nathan barely breathed as he stared at Obrador's back. *This was it.* Chloe had played her part perfectly! He wanted to scoop up his old friend and embrace her for her years of commitment, but they each had a persona to maintain. He even wanted to hug Harris, who'd played his part without knowing it had all been staged.

"You'll put it together?" Obrador asked Chloe. "It might liven things up around here. We could have another parade, too."

"I'll look at the calendar and put it all together." Chloe nodded, her seriousness unflinching. "I'll assign a special security advocate to protect your interests, maybe even one of these two, since they're familiar with the specifics already."

"Yes." Obrador turned and pointed at Nathan. "Isaacson, I want you to stay on top of this. Don't let this pageant make me look like a fool. This is your idea, so you're responsible. You do everything Chloe here says. Plan it all. Get all the final contestants into the city, and tell me which one to pick, for the sake of the Federation. Be sure about this, you two. This could get messy if the resistance uses this moment to sabotage or raid us."

"Mr. Chancellor," Nathan said, "Sergeant Harris has been my right hand for several years. I trust him. Please grant him special placement with me on this project."

"Yeah, yeah." Obrador sat down at his desk. "Chloe, make it all happen. But just because it's a symbolic marriage doesn't mean I want some mutt to smooch in the ceremony, you hear?"

"She'll be the appropriate woman for you and for the Federation, Chancellor." Chloe bowed her head slightly in subservience. "Think nothing more of it. Gentlemen, you'll hear from me soon. You're dismissed."

Nathan and Harris thanked the chancellor, then left the room.

In the stairwell, when they were alone, Nathan and Harris clapped each other on the back.

"You kept your word," Harris said, his gravelly voice breaking. "No one's ever stuck their neck out for me like that. You found a way to get us off winter labor duty! You did this, Lieutenant. I won't forget it! You're going places, and you're doing me a favor by taking me with you. I owe you!"

They descended the stairs together, Nathan's brace squeaking at the knee joint. He couldn't believe how much he'd been sweating!

"There's no reason why officers loyal to the Federation can't benefit alongside the Federation's prosperity."

"I can't figure you out, Lieutenant. Sometimes you seem like a cold-hearted coyote, and the next minute you're talking about romance and prosperity. I see why the chancellor called you an enigma. You must be a handful for your wife."

"She keeps me in line." Nathan laughed, but his nerves didn't relax. "Come on. Let's make the most of our last couple days on the streets, before our new assignment papers are processed."

Although his mouth spoke smoothly about the Federation, it was God Almighty who received the honor from Nathan's heart. Operation Esther was happening. His role had been to propose the pageant idea, but he'd walked out with even more. Chloe had gotten him the security responsibility over the event all on her own, which was both risky and providential for the operation.

It was a new beginning, but also a return to something familiar. After so many years apart, he was about to be reunited with his old COIL teammates! Ironically, instead of bringing the Federation to destruction, they hoped to reform it from the inside out— if they didn't get caught and hung in the process!

Heather Putelli hadn't been above ground in years, but she never complained about it. Between living in the resistance community with Luigi under the Upper West Side streets of Manhattan, and delivering Christian underground packages for Radiant Shade, her life was complete.

At the soft chime of a bell ringing its warning to the community, everyone in the entire tunnel hushed themselves, per Scooter's long-standing orders. The outer barrier door opened, then closed. Silence was necessary when the door was open, since noise traveled down the tunnel so easily. An Enforcer a couple miles away might hear laughter or a ruckus, then hunt farther than they had before. The maze of tunnels and hidden habitat behind the barrier was safe only if it wasn't searched out.

She saw her husband, Luigi, walk in from the barrier. The families who lived in the resistance stronghold maintained their silence, watching eagerly as he moved through the shelters. He was a legend within the resistance, and Heather was proud of him for the honor he'd earned over the years. Everyone knew the Bandit was the leader of the resistance, but the Bandit listened to

Luigi, responded when Luigi came into the tunnel, and often discussed things with him in their shelters without anyone else privy to their conversations.

But this time, Luigi wasn't coming with orders for Scooter. He made his way straight to her, where she was cooking rice and beans over a propane stove, so everyone returned to their activities. Luigi obviously had no news. Scooter wasn't even in the tunnel right then. He was out on a scavenger hunt with his rescue party of Vags.

"You're safe," Heather said softly as she embraced her husband, whose health had worried her more of late. She felt his bony arms pull her close, and she wondered how he had any strength at all since he was bone-thin. "Do you have time to eat? Or do you have to leave?"

"I can eat." He squatted on the floor of their curtained shelter, on the edge of the low shelf that was their narrow bed. At that moment, two grown house cats, fat and sleepy, had claimed the top quilt as their own, but Luigi didn't appear to mind sharing with them. The cats kept the rats at bay in the habitat. "I have news."

Tapping her stirring spoon on the side of the pot, Heather then poked her head past the curtain that separated their shelter from the next. The neighbors, a young couple with two children, were gone down to the playground, or were scrounging in the tunnels. Since Heather had gained enough weight for her husband and herself put together—blaming the gain on the lack of exercise outside—it took her some effort to lower herself to the bed. Of course, rising would be much more difficult, but Luigi, when he was there, never minded helping her.

"What is it?" Heather asked. "Jenna's okay?"

"Operation Esther is under way. A date is being set for the spring. There's to be a beauty pageant."

"It's like in the Bible!" Heather covered her mouth and squealed. "It's official then? The announcement's been made?"

"Within a couple of days, the whole Federation will be buzzing with the news." Luigi crawled over to the pot to sniff at the beans and rice. He used the spoon to taste the blend. "The Bandit needs to know so he can discontinue the raids. Nothing can interfere or set the pageant back. Or the wedding."

"How will we keep supplied, Luigi?" Heather felt her heart ache. "We have so many children to feed. I'm like a grandmother to a dozen of them."

"Jenna planned for everything. Scooter put something aside from every raid."

"What? You never told me that!" She swatted his leg. "You're so secretive, Luigi. It's one of your best traits. I love the mystery, ever since the day we met. Remember?"

"How could I not? Franklinville. I remember. You tried to arrest me on our first lunch date."

"Instead, I married you." She picked up one of the lazy cats and held it on her lap. "So, we'll be okay for a few more months down here?"

"We'll be okay. We have stashes all over the city, pantries in the tunnels. The Bandit's most trusted Vags know where they are."

"I wish we could stop calling him the Bandit."

"Soon."

"Do you have a house in the city picked out for us, once we can safely return to the surface?"

"You know I do."

Heather saw a rare smile creep across his face. She set the cat on his lap, then kissed him on the cheek. With a grunt and his support, she climbed to her knees to fetch another spoon for the pot of beans and rice. With a little cilantro, celery, and tomato slices, it was seasoned just the way they liked it.

"Jenna will need your help preparing herself for the pageant." Luigi ate slowly. "There's to be a preliminary interview soon for all contestants, then a final presentation this spring here in the city, where Obrador will be the judge. What's the matter? You were just celebrating."

"I know. But it's so sad. We can really work it out so she'll win the pageant?"

"Everyone is in place."

"People we know?"

"People we know. All COIL."

"And how long after the wedding until we're able to surface and reunite?"

"Jenna hasn't shared that with me." Luigi set down his spoon. "She's implied it will come after some hardships."

"So, it really is just like the Bible story. We may still have to fight for our lives."

"None of this was a guarantee. It's given us all a purpose to work toward through the years, helping many. But yes, we may still need to fight for our lives. Everything could collapse around us."

"We're too old to flee the city, Luigi. What's wrong with just staying in the tunnels if things get worse?"

"The rats."

"The cats will keep them away."

"The air."

"The vents and fans help with that."

"The lack of sun."

"We all take vitamins."

"The water."

"We take tablets for that, too."

"Don't you miss the sky?"

"Of course, I do, but I know why I can't go out there, and it's okay. It's too dangerous for me. Police officers from New Jersey are part of Obrador's Citizen Army. They'd remember me as a Christian, and maybe you, too. Living down here with you, staying together, is worth giving up even the stars and the moon."

"You are my star, Heather."

"Don't get poetic on me now, Luigi. Just keep everyone safe, and tell me when I need to go see Jenna. What does she need? Help with her dress or makeup?"

"Both. Corban can only do so much—no better than I could."

"Well, Jenna needs a woman's touch, that's for sure. I'd be happy to go. It's not that far through the tunnels."

He took her hand and kissed it. She leaned her head against his own. So much of their world and their future was unknown, but their love wasn't. What they could do, they were doing. The unknown things were in God's hands.

✝

Chancellor Kendrick Obrador smiled at himself in the mirror of his private suite in the Bowery Hotel. He knew he wasn't especially handsome, but he felt power had given him a confident glow that made him desirable. At least, women weren't ashamed to be seen with him. Of course, the extra ration cards he gave to his lovers did help.

He laughed at his private joke and turned to the left and right, trying to see himself from every possible angle from which a young woman might view him. *A beauty pageant and a marriage?* It was ingenious! He hadn't thought of it himself, but maybe that would just add to his legacy, he hoped. Instead of devising the scheme himself, the people had arranged a contest and marriage for him. And he had merely submitted to the demands of the people.

"Maybe caring for them will become a trend of mine?" he mumbled and checked his teeth, which needed a cleaning. Killing the last dentist for slipping and cutting his gum might've been an overreaction. Now he was about to marry, and his teeth weren't in the best oral condition.

He moved to his bed, which remained unmade from the company he'd kept, and picked up a digital calendar.

A technician on his staff of technicians had found him a tablet to use for which a lithium battery could be recharged from the generator's power supply on the roof. On the organizer app, he'd begun to keep careful records for himself, basically a journal of each day. So much was happening! The Federation had squashed the armed resistance in Georgia, and scouting reports were due in from the West, where he was hoping to expand the borders of the Federation past the Appalachian Mountains.

That Lieutenant Isaacson was something special, he thought as he donned his suit jacket. He wanted men like that surrounding him—men of honor, principle, and grace. The leeches who usually clung to him had no vision. They were yes-men who gave him nothing original. But Isaacson? He genuinely sought the Federation's well-being. Obrador sometimes wondered if he was as hungry to rebuild America as he'd once been, but then he met men like Isaacson, and he felt reborn, revived. The Federation would remain strong as long as it remained in the hands of men like Isaacson and himself.

Wedding security was below the lieutenant's qualifications, no doubt, but Obrador hadn't felt inclined to say no to Chloe's request to put Isaacson on the task. Chloe had been an unabashed supporter of the Federation since the early days. He still remembered the day she'd approached him, after the battle at Marcus Garvey Park. It had been his first real victory for control of the island, and she'd walked out of the smoke, carrying a rifle over her shoulder.

"I just buried my husband," she'd told him, but there'd been no tears, only fury in her eyes. "I'm a fighter, and you need fighters beside you. Don't ever ask me to sleep with you, but you can ask me to do what's best for this government you're building. You can count on me."

The dark-haired beauty had stolen his heart that day, and he'd never asked her for more than she gave, which was more than anyone else on his staff. She was his voice of reason and calm when there was strife in the Federation. When he wanted to massacre captured insurrectionists in Philadelphia, she'd proposed a forced labor program across the land. It was Chloe who'd helped him strengthen the nation through farming and ration incentives, and she'd even proposed to send security personnel to secretly infiltrate anti-Federation groups in other states. She ran it all, with his supervision of course, but he'd never had to wonder if she were loyal. Daily, they discussed opportunities to build his empire, his name, and his legacy.

Some had whispered accusations about his assistant's motives, but Obrador had removed such busybodies. He'd seen Chloe's true heart. More than a dozen times, when she could've taken advantage of situations for self-promotion, she'd remained out of the spotlight, given credit to others, and always offered a gracious front for his administration.

Since she'd been behind the pageant proposal and wedding, he knew he was in good hands. He could already feel the people swaying to support him like never before!

Chapter Six

Chloe Azmaveth held the Mora B. Leever poetry book in her hands while sitting in her comfortable hotel room two rooms away from the chancellor's suite. Her eyes skipped from line to line and from word to word, the pattern of Bible Scripture so natural to her after years that she hardly noticed the extra words that filled the coded book. Instead, her soul was nourished by God's personal message, lifting her spirit in the midst of pressure and tension that had only grown over the years.

She bowed her head as tears fell on the pages of the open book. Only God could've arranged all this. Only God could've orchestrated a peaceful takeover of a government through the eyes of a blind woman. Chloe knew Jenna was Radiant Shade. *Jenna?* The little adopted girl Corban and Janice had brought into their family? Knowing the woman's history made the poetry books that much more special. Jenna had written all the words—well, almost all. The embedded, coded Scripture was all from God, of course. And Corban had typed and printed the books himself.

What foresight, Chloe thought, thanking her Lord for His provision of the coded books. Jenna had known God's people would need His comforting truth while undercover. So, even in the Bowery Hotel, the capital building of the Federation, Chloe kept on her shelf the entire set of books that Corban had printed for his daughter. They included the *Psalms*, the *Gospel of John*, and many of the New Testament Epistles. The poetry itself rhymed, but it had never interested Chloe. Many on the

Federation staff enjoyed the poetry, totally unaware of the Bible coded throughout its pages, line upon line.

Closing the book, Chloe set it on the shelf with the others. Once, Obrador had called on her in the night for some Federation figures, and he'd asked to see what she'd been reading.

"Just an old reprint," she'd told him, offering the book to him.

He'd read a few lines, wrinkled his nose, clearly not impressed, then given it back to her without further comment. Of course, the poetry was weak, but in a city where every other book had been burned to heat rooms through frigid winters, the Leever Collection was read now by dreamers, just happy to distract themselves with something that didn't remind them of their hunger and insignificance in the Federation. As far as Chloe knew, they were the only books in print in the city, distributed Federation-wide.

Since the books were so often found in the hands of noncompliant citizens, Enforcer Lena Travers had once filed an inquiry into the location of the printer, but that had been three years earlier, and Chloe had "refiled" the inquiry into a burn box.

She pulled on a blazer instead of a winter coat since she was only going down to the Citizen Army mess hall across the street. The winter had been mild, with rain and snow flurries rather than blizzards, but there would probably be a snowstorm in the next month, she guessed. That would bring the Federation to a halt. The army and Bowery staff would be fine, and the citizens surviving in the city knew how to make do. But Chloe would need to appeal to Obrador personally about the noncompliant forced labor workers in the open-air cages next to the Citizen Processing building. They needed to be given more clothing, blankets, and sleeping bags. Although she'd arranged for a few of them to work rather than be executed, the crews lived under horrible conditions, and some executions still happened weekly. Even operating undercover so close to Obrador, she still hadn't been able to help in some ways, and that bothered her heart. It was a pain she had to keep hidden, at the risk of her life and position, as well as Operation Esther. She hoped that with Jenna soon in the Bowery, they could make more of a difference together.

Christmas was two days away, so Chloe wasn't surprised to pass a couple drunk soldiers in the stairwell. In their stupor, the soldiers recognized her and tried to hide their bottles from her sight, but their behavior was obvious enough. Yet, she wouldn't report them. There were more pressing issues in the Federation.

Across the cold street and under a dark sky, Chloe entered the mess hall. The gutted building was packed with chairs and tables around a forgotten restaurant kitchen. Since it was late, the kitchen was closed, but the hall was open. Young people in fatigues gathered in small groups here and there at the tables.

On the far right, a tall, dark-haired man waved at her. It was Lieutenant Nathan Isaacson, minus the mustache he'd worn throughout his youth. He sat with his wife, Chen Li, another undercover COIL agent, placed by Chloe personally as a supervisor in the Citizen Processing Department. But Chloe hadn't socialized with anyone from COIL for ten years, not since they'd all gone to their assigned posts. Direct communication was prohibited by Jenna as a rule. Instead, Chloe received coded messages now and then, smuggled to her through whom she guessed was Luigi Putelli, or someone else on the COIL team.

"Nice to see you again, Lieutenant," Chloe greeted officially, loud enough for someone across the hall to hear if the soldiers were listening. She shook Nathan's hand, then Chen Li's hand. "Mrs. Isaacson, your reputation as a supervisor in Citizen Processing precedes you."

"Thank you for meeting with us." Chen Li gestured to a plastic cup. "It's just a lemonade mix, nothing like you're probably used to upstairs, but it's actually pretty good."

Chloe sat down across the table from the couple and took a gulp of the beverage. Chen Li was an old friend and Chloe knew she'd meant nothing by her upstairs comment, but Chloe was sensitive about talking of her privileged position, while so many others were starving, filthy, and sick.

"The acoustics in this place . . ." Nathan nodded his head at a rumbling metal box across the hall. "That heater's loud enough to cover our conversation, if we keep our voices low."

"I let Obrador know I'd be meeting with you two off and on," Chloe said. "He knows it'll be about the pageant. Since I keep him updated on all of my activities, I'll be the last one he suspects of anything. This is a good, public place to meet again in a few days—in plain sight. Where's Sergeant Harris?"

"His girlfriend wanted to have a dinner date with friends." Nathan leaned back in his chair, but he didn't appear relaxed. "People are trying to pretend like it's before Pan-Day and the holidays are the same as they ever were. Harris isn't a believer, so I didn't want him here for this first meeting, but I'll keep him informed. He's just happy he's included in the wedding plans at all. We'll be careful with him. He knows nothing more than what's been discussed with Obrador."

"How long have we waited to meet like this?" Chen Li bit her lip, disguising her smile. Chloe remembered when the Hong Kong native had been rescued by Nathan during a COIL operation in the South Pacific. "All these years, Chloe—I can't imagine what you've been through with you-know-who!"

"Obrador's not that bad." Chloe laughed a little, hoping their play-acting appeared harmless to observers. "Undercover work is uncomfortable for us all. We've all witnessed things that make us sick, I'm sure. Let's hope it's almost over. A few more months. Has anyone even seen Jenna? Is she in the city?"

"She's been living with Corban since coming into the city about three years ago." Chen Li sipped her own lemonade. "I've kept her file updated at Citizen Processing, so I've kept track of her. It's Corban I'm worried about. He's drawn some heat recently."

"Now what?" Chloe rolled her eyes. "How is he still kicking? The guy's like a hundred years old, and he's still causing problems?"

They laughed together, all aware that Corban wasn't actually causing problems, but that his interactions with people tended to reveal his underlying stand for truth and justice.

"We think Owen Travers is on to Corban," Nathan said, glancing at Chen Li. "He and Brian Steelman have been showing interest in the boss. Maybe it was just routine surveillance, but last week, Corban was making a delivery to me, and he couldn't shake Owen."

"Oh, no." Chloe crossed her arms. "What'd he do?"

"He tranquilized Owen. He was smooth and wasn't identified, but now they're looking closer at Corban."

"Steelman wants to administer another *CEE* on Corban tomorrow," Chen Li said. "He picked up the polygraph machine today. It's so sudden, we can't get word to Corban in time."

"Corban will sacrifice himself to save the operation." Chloe growled under her breath. "It could jeopardize the op. What can we do? Anything? Steelman's heart isn't even in the Enforcer program any longer. Obrador's forcing him to hunt down Radiant Shade, but as far as I can tell, he has no leads."

"Unless he and Owen have put things together to look into Corban and Jenna," Nathan said.

"Can Corban pass a poly on his own?" Chen Li asked. "He's not exactly in his prime anymore."

"Steelman may not be completely into his job," Nathan said, "but he's always been good at what he does. The poly will expose Corban. I don't think that's even a question at this point. The question should be, what's Corban going to do with Steelman once he's exposed?"

"What do you mean?" Chen Li scoffed. "You think Corban might do something to Steelman?"

"Well, he can't just let the Enforcer walk away, knowing what he'll find out from the polygraph." Nathan rested his forearms on the edge of the table. "Corban will have a contingency plan. He won't just sacrifice himself if he's exposed. That would lead to more problems for Jenna. And Corban won't risk our lives, either, by allowing Steelman to walk away."

"One thing for sure," Chloe said, "none of us three can lift a finger. Can the resistance cause a distraction? Maybe Corban can fake-kill himself off, and go live in the tunnels."

"No, we still need him in the ID office." Chen Li looked worried. "What'll we do? This is the worst timing for one of us to be investigated!"

"It's better him than one of us."

"Nathan!" Chloe scolded. "How could you say that? None of us is expendable."

"The op still has a chance if he's arrested," Nathan said. "I'm not being cold, just honest. If one of us three were arrested, the op is off. I'm just saying that if one of us has to be investigated, it's better off being Corban. He's more experienced at dealing with this kind of pressure."

"Well, it's too dangerous to do anything for Corban now." Chen Li folded her hands, which were visibly shaking. "We'll have to trust that God is completely in control."

"Let's hope Titus Caspertein doesn't show up and make a worse mess for us!" Nathan chuckled. "Can you imagine him anywhere around the Federation? He'd take on the whole Citizen Army."

"Obrador gets in a sour mood whenever anyone brings up the failed Colorado mission," Chloe said. "Titus is in his sixties now. I sure hope he's aged better than me."

"Yeah, right!" Chen Li guffawed. "Chloe, you don't look like you've aged five years since the North Korea job! If Titus is able to make it this far east, God will use him, no matter how old he is. I sure miss his sarcasm."

They were silent for a little while, until Chloe glanced up.

"A two-page Federation newspaper in the Bronx is starting up. Their first cover story will be about the pageant. They'll get Operation Esther moving right along. We have our stories straight about Jenna?"

"If we can weather this *CEE* with Corban," Nathan said, "I'll steer Sergeant Harris toward her as the best candidate. Then you and I will agree with him, Chloe."

"Meanwhile," Chen Li said, "we'll try not to get polygraphed by Steelman, arrested and hung by Owen, or suspected by Obrador. Piece of cake."

"This has been nice." Chloe sighed sadly. "I'd better get back upstairs. We're close to the end. Let's stay on our knees, you two."

"If all this starts to implode and fall apart," Chen Li said, "I don't remember hearing of Jenna's escape plan."

"Every man or woman for him or herself." Chloe shrugged. "Get out of the city, then find your way to Meeker, Colorado. Federation forces were defeated once out there. Maybe they'll think twice about following us that far."

"Caspertein's out there somewhere," Nathan said, almost as if he wished he were beyond the Federation's grasp as well. "Let's pray we don't need him, and this wedding thing works out."

"It worked in the Bible!" Chen Li muffled her laughter again. "Could it be that easy?"

"If it is," Nathan said, "we wouldn't need to rely on God like we are. All this is for Him. He's working on each of us, getting us ready for glory with Him. There may be hard times ahead, but we won't be alone, and it won't be a waste."

"For what it's worth," Chloe said, then drank the remainder of her lemonade, "I'd be honored to die with you two any time. But I'm ready to bring this business to a close. I want to read a regular Bible. I want to pray openly in the sunlight. I want to sing *Amazing Grace* on the rooftop without getting sent to a forced labor detail!"

"If that happens," Nathan said with a wink, "I'll put in a good word for you. We'll get you a street-sweeper job."

As Chloe left the mess hall, she felt tears in her eyes. How desperately she yearned to leave her assistant job to Obrador, and live freely as a normal Christian! Hopefully, a little while longer, and they'd be free. Unless Corban blew it for them all!

✝

Brian Steelman hadn't given a polygraph test to anyone in over two years, but the setup was easy, and Corban Dowler hadn't fought him. According to the Citizen Processing file, Corban had been *CEE* tested nine other times, and he'd always passed without any questionable results.

In the main printing room of the ID office, Brian had folded up one of the tables himself to make space for his equipment for the test. Jenna sat against the far wall, her hands folded in her lap, and Corban sat in a chair in front of him, the heart rate strap on his chest and the blood pressure cuff on his arm. Next to another table behind Corban, Brian had lain his silver Bushmaster rifle, where he could grab it quickly if need be. But honestly, he didn't foresee much happening between the old man and the blind woman, even if they did need to be arrested.

Brian turned on the machine and the needles began to trace Corban's vitals.

"Okay, we're ready," he said, barely containing himself. Something was off at the shop, and he was certain a few precise questions would pry out the answers he was looking for. And then Owen Travers would really owe him!

"Are you comfortable?" Brian asked. He already knew the answer. The polygraph machine was hard to fool.

"I'm comfortable."

"Yes or no answers, please."

"Yes, I'm comfortable."

"Is your name Corban Dowler?"

"Yes."

"Are you in New York City?"

"Yes."

Brian used a pen to mark the paper where the needles indicated his control questions. Now, he was ready to get down to business! He glanced up at Jenna, but her calm, blank face revealed nothing, as if she'd been through this a hundred times.

"Are you a printing specialist for the Appalachian Federation?"

"Yes."

"Do you consider yourself to be a loyal citizen of the Federation?"

"I don't understand the question."

"You don't understand the—" Brian looked up. "Are you for or against the Federation? Are you against the Federation?"

"No, I'm not against the Federation."

"Okay. That wasn't so hard. Were you part of a relief organization called COIL before Pan-Day?"

"Yes."

"Were you an office worker?"

"No."

"Were you a field agent?"

"Yes."

"What did you do in the— I mean, you were an aide worker?"

"Yes."

"Were you overseas like you said a couple days ago?"

"Yes."

"Did you work for the government?"

"Yes."

"Do you support Chancellor Kendrick Obrador's administration?"

"No."

Brian's breath caught. Maybe the man hadn't heard the question properly.

"Are you currently supporting Chancellor Obrador's administration?"

"No."

Brian checked Jenna's face, but she hadn't reacted strangely to her father's confession. He'd found a crack in the identification specialist's story, but oddly, Brian felt his victory was bittersweet. He actually didn't support Obrador's administration, either, and he was leaving Federation territory as soon as he got what he'd come for. But he had to stay alive while in the city, and that meant making Obrador and people like Owen happy.

"Have you ever worked against the chancellor's administration?"

"Yes."

Brian studied the poly. He was telling the truth.

"Have you plotted against the current chancellor's administration?"

"Yes."

"Are you part of the resistance?"

"No."

"Do you know the Bandit?"

"Yes."

"Have you communicated with the resistance?"

"Yes."

"Have you worked for the resistance?"

"No."

Brian wiped his sweating palms on his pants. Some of Corban's answers made little sense, but he wasn't lying.

"You know the Bandit, but you're in no way working for or with the resistance?"

"No."

"Do you know others who are against the chancellor's administration?"

"Yes."

"Is your daughter, Jenna, to the best of your knowledge, against the chancellor's administration?"

"Yes."

Brian glared at Jenna. He was angry with them both, but he wasn't sure why. Did they expect him to go easy on them? Nothing inside him wanted to arrest Jenna and see her suffer at the hands of the Twins. This was horrible—much worse than he'd ever wanted!

"Are you part of a network?"

"Yes."

"Were you recruited by someone?"

"No."

"Are you . . .?" Brian frowned. Something was wrong. Corban should've been trying to lie at least a little bit, but he wasn't hiding anything. No one was this honest. "Are you the leader of the network?"

"No."

"Do you know the leader of the network?"

"Yes."

"Is it the Bandit?"

"No."

"Is there a network besides the resistance that is working against the chancellor's administration?"

"Yes."

Brian reached over and turned off the polygraph machine. His anger was boiling hotter. If he didn't know any better, someone was pulling a prank on him. What was happening?

After a couple deep breaths, he turned the machine back on.

"Is the chancellor in danger?"

"No."

"Is your network politically motivated?"

"No."

"What? I mean, is it . . . survival motivated?"

"No."

"Is your network somehow . . . materialistically motivated? You're just trying to collect enough supplies to stay alive?"

"No."

Brian stared at the back of Corban's head. He was just an old man. Maybe his mind was going. No one who belonged to a secret network like this would be this honest, unless . . .

"Did you plan ahead of time to tell me the truth?"

"Yes."

"Did you discuss your plan with your daughter, Jenna?"

"Yes."

"Do you have ulterior motives by telling me the truth today?"

"Yes."

Brian's anger was checked by fear. Now he understood.

"Does your network know I'm questioning you today?"

"Yes."

"Are we three . . . alone in the house?"

Corban paused.

"No."

Brian measured the distance from his seat to his rifle halfway up the table. He'd need to lunge for it, but he didn't know who the aggressor was, or from where to expect the attack. Someone else was watching or listening!

"Am I in danger?"

"No."

"Do you, uh, think that you're going to recruit me into your network?"

"Yes."

"You obviously don't know who I am." Brian's hand clenched. He wanted to dive for his weapon. But, no. Someone was behind him. He could feel it now. "I'm not someone you can manipulate."

"Is that a question you want me to answer?" Corban asked.

"I think the *CEE* is finished, don't you?" Brian turned off the machine and the recorder. "My Jeep is parked out front. Everyone at the Bowery knows I'm here."

"Your Jeep has been removed. The polygraph equipment will be returned to Citizen Processing as scheduled. No one will ask questions. There'll be no trace of your whereabouts."

Still, Corban remained in his chair, his back to him, completely calm. And Jenna hadn't moved an inch.

"You said I wasn't in any danger."

"You're not, Brian." Corban unstrapped the cuff and the chest strap, then rose to his feet and faced him. "But you can't leave the way you came."

"Yeah?" He snorted. "What's stopping me? You? Or her?"

"Me? No." Corban reached into his pocket and withdrew a quarter. "This will stop you."

"A quarter? A quarter is supposed to stop me?"

Corban flicked the quarter onto the floor to Brian's left. He watched it spin, wobble, then topple over. Heads. Brian reached down and picked it up. It was just a common quarter, completely useless in the Federation's ration and barter system where old money had no value.

When he sat upright, he flinched at the figure suddenly standing next to the table. Whoever had been behind him was now hovering over his Bushmaster rifle.

"That's just mean," Brian said, looking up at the new arrival. He was startled that he recognized him. It was the gaunt, older man from the tunnel opening! "If you guys aren't resistance, then why did I see this guy at the resistance tunnel entrance two days ago?"

"There is no resistance, Brian," Corban said. "Well, technically there's not. It seems you were in the process of stumbling onto that intel, so we had to step in."

Brian watched as Corban expertly dismantled the Bushmaster and put all the parts into a garbage bag, barrel and all, and left it on the table.

"Next, you're going to take off your masks, and reveal that neither of you are wrinkled, old men," Brian said.

"Who's old?" the olive-skinned man asked with a straight face.

"This was all a setup." Brian knew he should've still been angry, but he struggled to feel anything past irritation. He tossed the quarter across the room. "A dirty trick."

The gaunt one moved behind Brian as Corban turned his chair around and sat down in front of him. Brian felt cornered, but with Jenna there, he didn't think they'd do anything too rough to him.

"Tell us where you've been for the last two years, Brian," Corban asked, "and why you've returned now."

Brian looked down at his hands.

"It's a strange story."

"Naturally." Dowler smiled patiently. "We live strange lives."

"I ran away from the chancellor two years ago. I sort of told Jenna all this already. I was tired of the killing."

"But you were the best executioner of noncompliants, if I recall correctly." Corban frowned. "Where did you go when you left Federation territory?"

"Just west. I was thinking about Oregon or California. I got as far as Arizona. A little town named Oatman."

"We're listening."

"My travel companion shot me—the little jerk. Monty Ashlaw. Got me in the thigh, and it wasn't healing. I was nursing an infection when I met a man."

"A man?"

"Just a traveler. He had an Indian woman from the desert with him, and an infant just a year or two old, and a one-armed, black woman."

"A one-armed woman?" Corban raised his eyebrows. "That's curious."

"I tried to scare them off, but the leader—a big, blond guy—wasn't having it. He needed water, and he had a way about him, I'm telling you. He carried me closer to the water source, and that Indian woman fixed my leg. She wasn't too gentle about it, but they saved my life. I'd never met people like that in the Federation. They didn't steal from me or anything."

"Maybe you're too used to hanging around with the wrong crowd," Corban said.

"Or maybe you keep killing all the good people," said the gaunt man behind him.

"Whatever." Brian shrugged and tried to brush off their accusations, but they weren't wrong, he figured. He'd killed hundreds. "That traveler didn't know me. He didn't care who I was or what I'd done to survive all those years. He just took care of me, we visited, and he left. But I knew he was coming here, to the Federation. He was looking for someone. And now I'm looking for him."

"Who was he looking for?"

"I don't remember who he was asking about. It was strange. He asked how the Federation would treat noncompliants, and I told him that most noncompliants had already been rounded up, imprisoned, or killed. I knew because I'm the one who'd been doing the majority of it, at least here in this region of the Federation."

"That doesn't explain why you came back east." Corban folded his hands and crossed his legs, completely too calm, Brian thought, for someone who was kidnapping a Federation Enforcer. "Explain."

"I don't know." Brian suddenly felt embarrassed for the reason. "It doesn't make any sense. Nobody in their right mind would have returned, not after I'd just spent two years running away."

"There are no accidents in life, Brian," Corban said. "Whether it makes sense to you or not, there's a reason."

"That guy took care of me, saved my life. I couldn't let him walk into the dangers of the Federation without warning him. Or helping him. Not that he wasn't the kind of guy who could take care of himself. I just wanted to know more about him. But I was found by Obrador's Enforcers before I could find the Serval. That's all I know him by. The one-armed woman with him called him the Serval."

"*The Serval?*" Corban rose to his feet abruptly. "You're sure he was the Serval?"

"Uh, yeah. Why?"

"In Arizona?"

"Yeah."

"How long ago? When?"

"Early summer. I don't know. Maybe late spring."

Corban looked past Brian at his companion, then spoke fluently in another language, which sounded like French. Then Jenna spoke French with them, and they ignored him for several minutes as they went back and forth.

"He was a tall, blond man?" Corban asked. "About six-three? In his sixties?"

"No, more like a tall blond in his late thirties. And I'm six-two. This guy was a couple inches taller than me. And stronger. He carried me down a flight of stairs like it was nothing."

"It's not Titus," the gaunt man said. "There's only one other person who would use the Serval's name and fits that description."

"It's Levi." Corban chuckled and looked at Jenna. "The son has become like the father. Brian, you said you talked to him about him coming east. Please remember. Who was he coming east for? Think, man!"

"I've tried. Maybe he didn't say, exactly. It was someone he assumed would be noncompliant."

Corban and his friend spoke in French again, their voices and posture animated. Something was afoot, Brian could read—something much bigger than a couple of old men running an identification hustle against the chancellor's administration.

They studied him, their voices softer now, and Brian suddenly felt like a young man in the presence of adults who were discussing his future, as if he weren't mature enough to decide it for himself.

"The Serval is our friend," Corban stated in English. "He's coming here for us, either to rescue us, or help us somehow. He must've been held up somewhere if you beat him here."

"He was going up to Colorado after he saw me," Brian said. "The winter weather would've been tougher to the north."

"We'll need him here if Obrador doesn't cooperate," Corban said to his gaunt friend. "If Levi's anything like the rest of his family, and a believer, then he'll cause a scene just by his presence."

"Look," Brian stated, "we're obviously looking for the same guy. I'm not with Obrador exactly. I'm just killing time, hunting for Radiant Shade while I'm—"

"*Radiant Shade?*" Corban took a step closer. "What's she got to do with you being here?"

Brian held up his hands.

"Whoa! Easy, Dowler, I'm just a government man, trying to stay alive like everyone else. I don't care about the Federation anymore, so I don't really care what you guys are doing against Obrador. Look, let me go, and I'll leave the city. I got away from Obrador once. I can do it again, easy, especially if you tell me what you did with my Jeep. I can cross the bridge and be halfway across Pennsylvania before I run out of gas. I might even run into the Serval before that, and I can direct him to you."

"We need him here," said the gaunt one, nodding at Brian. "He's not central to the operation, Corban, but holding him would destabilize Obrador. He has intel, and we can use him as a pawn."

"Hello?" Brian scoffed. "What am I, deaf? No one's using me as a pawn!"

"Quiet," Corban said. "We're doing you the favor of speaking in English so you can listen, but that doesn't mean you have an opinion to offer."

Brian opened his mouth to protest, but they continued to talk past him.

"Heather could watch him," Corban's friend said. "Doc won't allow anything to happen in the tunnel. Half of the Bandit's Vags are always around. Put a hood on him, and take him there. From what I saw two days ago, he's not exactly comfortable in the tunnels, so he won't be moving around too much."

"The Jeep is taken care of?"

The man answered Corban in French.

"Brian?" Corban sat in front of him again. "For your safety and ours, we're sending you down into the tunnels."

"With the resistance? I thought you said they weren't real."

"They think they are, but we're just using them to get things done. When you figure it out, keep it to yourself, like everything else."

"I'm never figuring this out." Brian felt his anger rising again. "And you're not making me a prisoner for no reason! I swear, if you try to put a hood on me, I'll—"

"Brian?" Jenna's sweet voice shocked him to silence.

She moved to his side, gently touching his shoulder with her small hand. Her face was close like it was the other day, beautiful even without any makeup. Her hand shifted and squeezed his shoulder, communicating volumes through her touch. This wasn't right, ambushing him like this!

"Go with them," she said, in almost a whisper. "We may need you to help others. I was listening the whole time. I believe you. The Serval's kindness toward you in Arizona changed something inside of you, right?"

"Yes. Yes, it did."

"Then trust me when I tell you that the Serval would want you to do this kindness for us. Remove yourself as Obrador's hound. Let him worry about what's become of you. We want him destabilized to help him lead in the right direction. Can you do this for me?"

Brian fought tears that whelmed his eyes. His throat constricted with emotion. *What was happening to him?* He'd never been thrust into something with so much gentleness! How could a couple of old men and a blind woman restrain him and upset him so much? He hadn't even been bound or handcuffed, yet he felt he couldn't say no.

"I'll do what you want me to do," he said to Corban. "But whatever you're up to, now I feel like I should be involved. I only came back for the Serval. I can help you with Obrador."

"The Serval is coming back for me," Jenna said. "As soon as we know he's in the city, we'll tell him you're here, and that you want to meet with him. If I know him, and I really do, then I know he'd want to meet with you as soon as possible as well. Is that okay?"

"Yes." Brian lowered his head, ashamed for insisting to have his own way. "That's fine. What about my rifle?"

"You won't need it where you're going," Jenna said. "And if you leave the city, we'll give it back to you, or give you a better rifle."

"All right." Brian sighed. "Now what?"

"I'm Luigi." The gaunt man offered his hand without a smile, but his eyes weren't unkind. "I'll take you where you need to go. You'll be living with the Bandit."

Brian followed Luigi into another room, small and cramped, and Luigi rolled back the linoleum flooring to reveal a trapdoor. When the door was opened, the smell of mildew and rain reached his nose. It was dark down there, but he was learning to trust these strange people, the Serval's friends.

He stepped down the ladder, then paused before he ducked his head below the floor level. Corban stood there with his daughter, Jenna. And Luigi held the trapdoor, obviously about to follow him into the sublevel. They were involved in something so much bigger than Brian could grasp, even though he realized he already knew more than they were comfortable with him knowing.

"Bye," he said.

"Goodbye, Brian," Jenna said.

He wondered if he'd ever see the Dowlers again.

Below the floor, he reached a platform. From the light of the open door above, he tried to see what awaited him farther below. There was a floor down there, and now he smelled oil, and maybe paper. Was that a printing press? Tables laid out with small objects were positioned in rows and columns, as wide and as long as he could see to the edge of the light.

Then Luigi was beside him, and the trapdoor was closed. Perfect darkness choked him, and Brian fought the same panic he'd felt two days earlier. But Luigi took his forearm and placed his hand on his shoulder.

"Move with me," Luigi said in his frank voice. "There's another ladder here. Get your feet on it and go down."

"There are no lights?" Brian felt below.

"We'll use light when we need light. Kids have lived their whole lives down here with very little light. You can make it a little ways before I turn on a flashlight."

Then Brian understood. Luigi wanted him blind to hide what the basement held. More secrets.

But Brian was free from the chancellor's grip. And now he was sure to meet the Serval. It was almost as if his whole life had been arranged, and Someone was moving him toward something he hadn't quite imagined yet.

They reached the bottom floor, and Luigi led him out of the wide room, past a leaking pipe, and into an echoing tunnel.

Chapter Seven

Lena Travers, Chancellor Obrador's chief Federation Enforcer, hated the idea of the beauty pageant and wedding. Where was the strength, respect, and honor in a superficial ceremony? It was weak, she thought, and made the whole Federation seem soft. She blamed Chloe Azmaveth, whom she'd heard had backed the whole proposal to Obrador. Long ago, Obrador had wanted Lena's counsel, to find out her perspective before moving on an idea, but that time was long gone. Chloe had pushed her out, replaced her, silenced her input that could've contributed to the strength of the Federation.

On a rooftop of a high-rise apartment building on the East Side, Lena lay on her belly, a sniper rifle tucked against her shoulder. Death, her German shepherd, panted not ten feet away, on her belly as well. Lena had sighted the rifle herself. The army had prepared her for everything Pan-Day had thrown at her, and though most people saw her as an equal partner with her brother, she felt Owen was really just holding her back. He questioned her methods more often, and he used a soft hand when she was certain a heavy hand could accomplish a better result.

And yet, Owen was family. They were known as the Twins, even though they'd been born six years apart, so everything he did or didn't do reflected on her, which reflected on the Federation. Like it or not, she had to take Owen with her, and that meant sacrifice and extra work on her part.

But on that day, she was just after revenge. Three days earlier, she'd ridden her motorcycle past the target building below her, and citizens on the roof had thrown rocks at her! Now, she'd parked her bike inside the stairwell, and climbed with Death to the roof of a much taller building.

"Go ahead and bring rocks to a gunfight, huh, girl?" Lena joked to Death as her cheek rested against the gun stock.

However, no one was on the roof of the nearby building that day. She had no qualms killing one of them to set them all straight, even if it were a child who'd thrown the rocks. It was improper for a compliant citizen to do such a thing. On behalf of the Federation, sometimes one young life needed to be sacrificed so the many could learn a lesson. Socialism demanded such adjustments for the good of the whole. It was ruthless, she knew, but the Federation would be stronger because of it. And people wouldn't dare throw rocks at her again when she was speeding up the city streets!

For a few minutes, Lena swung her scope far to the west to see Brian Steelman's Jeep swerve around a corner. Years earlier, when Brian had been a stoic, ruthless Enforcer, she had loved him. But he'd run away for two years, and he'd come back changed. Now, she saw him as a coward. The West was lawless, unmanaged, and wild. How could he prefer that over this? The Enforcers were at the top of the food chain. Who would leave all this? The Federation was theirs!

She wouldn't trust him ever again, and it angered her that Obrador did. Obrador had been making all kinds of sentimental decisions lately, choices she would never make if she were head of the Federation. If his behavior continued, she felt she'd need to gather the support of others who agreed—and do something about him.

Steelman's Jeep moved out of sight, and Lena focused her scope back on the building rooftop below. Where were the little brats? She blew at a strand of hair that fell across her face. It was time to shave her head again. Even if it made her look less lady-like, she didn't care. Being an Enforcer was about self-sacrifice, and the Federation was worth it. Besides, anyone who had a problem with her looks would find themselves charged with a hate crime. At least Obrador would back her up on that. He hated traditional gender conventions as much as she did.

There was movement to the right! A person. They weren't on the roof, but Lena didn't care. She was there to shoot someone, so she sighted on an aging woman who hustled down the street toward her. Her face wasn't familiar, but her rags were. The woman wore the same drab clothing as thousands of others in the city. Only loyalists received new clothing from the Federation stores, clothes that weren't faded from washing and wearing for years. A textile factory down in Raleigh was running again, but no one received those clothing shipments except for Federation heads of state. Or the resistance, if they hijacked a truck, which sometimes happened.

The woman carried a bulky purse in her arms. Lena wondered why she was in such a hurry, but then she remembered. The pageant officials were beginning their preliminary rounds, interviewing the locals who wanted to enter the contest. Lena guessed it did give people an essence of hope to better their lives, but such a distraction wasn't healthy for the Federation. If people would focus their hopes on the Federation, then the Federation wouldn't need such silly contests to boost morale!

Lena studied the woman's face a little closer, using her high-powered scope. This woman was pale, and her eyes blinked and squinted as if extremely uncomfortable being outside. The sun was too bright for her on an overcast day? Then it all made sense. *She was a tunnel rat!*

Wanting her alive for questioning, Lena aimed at the woman's right shoulder and fired. The woman sprawled across the pavement, and her bulky purse spilled onto the street next to her.

Smiling, Lena ejected the spent cartridge, climbed to her feet, and fit the rifle sling over her head. Although she'd meant to teach the locals not to harass her, catching a resistance fighter was even better for the Federation!

"Come on, Death. You want to chew on a tunnel rat? Yes, you do! Come on, girl."

Heather Putelli caught her breath where she lay bleeding on the pavement, and blinked up at the bright, winter day. Although it was overcast, the sky was still much brighter than she was used to down in the tunnel. She struggled to sit up, but her body felt pinned to the street. Something was wrong. Maybe she'd had a seizure?

She turned her head and gasped. The contents from her purse lay scattered across the street. *All the hearing aids!* With her left hand, she tried to sweep them toward her. They'd recently been altered by Doc Joss, the tunnel electrician, for Jenna to record a message of hope for the persecuted Christians. Every hearing aid was important. Each one needed to reach its destination!

"Stay down!" a woman screeched at her.

Looking past her feet, Heather saw a blond woman in Federation fatigues, aiming an assault rifle at her. *No, she couldn't be taken!* She'd heard the horror stories of the Federation's interrogations. They used chemicals and torture during questioning, and everyone talked at some point, especially when sleep deprivation was added to the routine. The mind simply lost track of reality.

"I said, stay down!" The woman stood over her and lifted her rifle. The soldier used the gun like a club to batter Heather on the head. "Lay still! Don't move again."

Heather's head lolled to one side. *This didn't seem real.* Besides her head pounding in her ears, her right shoulder was throbbing with pain. Her body wasn't cooperating. She couldn't move!

"What do we have here?" The woman knelt and picked up a couple of hearing aids. "Let me guess. You have a hearing problem?"

"No, I . . ." Heather reached for the woman's hand.

"Keep your grimy hands off me!" The blond smacked Heather's hand away.

Hyperventilating, Heather felt blood trickling across her forehead from the battering. A dog growled inches from her ear. *This was it*, she thought to herself. For years, she'd pitied those who'd fallen victim to Obrador's regime. Now, it was her turn. Her husband had prepared her for this. Corban had warned her when she'd joined COIL that the Bible spoke of persecution entering the lives of all of God's people. It was the nature of their work. The darkness hated the light. Those who belonged to the Kingdom of the Son would suffer where they didn't belong: in the kingdom of the world and of Satan.

All that was left now was to die with honor, loyalty, and loving Christ to the end. She reached out for the Savior's presence right then. Since before Pan-Day, she'd been a faithful, Bible-reading Christian, never being discouraged from the oppressive circumstances of daily life. It was from those years of consistent trusting in God that she naturally trusted in Him now, and found His grace sufficient indeed. He loved her. And she was about to suffer for His name's sake by giving her life for Him.

Heather gasped from the pain in her shoulder as the woman rolled her onto her stomach, then pressed her knee on the back of her neck. She thought the Enforcer was trying to break her spine, but instead, the woman twisted her arms behind her to be handcuffed.

"I'm ready to die," Heather heard herself saying over and over again, clinging to Jesus. "I'm ready to die, Lord Jesus . . ."

"That's good, tunnel rat, because I just caught you with executable evidence. You will die, and no Jesus is going to save you from that. Now, just lay there!"

As the Enforcer returned to her feet, she pressed Heather's cheek into the street. The growling dog remained snarling next to her head, as if daring Heather to move.

"This is Lena," the woman said on a small handheld. "Is anybody there? I need a pickup. Send my brother out here alone. I have a present for him."

Closing her eyes, Heather started to pray for Lena. Everyone in the city knew Lena Travers's reputation for killing Christians and other noncompliants. But that didn't disqualify her from God's grace. No, Lena's sinfulness is what qualified her for God's grace, if she would only repent from her unbelief. This could be Lena's moment, Heather hoped.

"You're not wearing makeup yourself. What is this stuff for?"

Heather opened her eyes to see Lena picking through her purse. Sure enough, there was a little lip gloss and eye liner she'd been taking to Jenna at Times Square. It had been Heather's job to prepare Jenna for the beauty pageant's preliminary appearance on Christmas Day. Jenna had trusted no one else, and no other woman in the underground knew where Radiant Shade lived, to prep her for Operation Esther.

"Don't you have any papers?" Lena asked. "No papers at all? You really are a tunnel rat. How long have you been down there?"

Anything Heather said might give some detail away, so she didn't answer. She couldn't. Operation Esther was already unfolding, and now she was its greatest threat. Maybe they would kill her quickly and not make her say anything. Earnestly praying, she asked that God would hold her tongue even if she were drugged. Luigi and all of the others undercover needed to remain hidden!

Minutes later, a vehicle arrived, and a man in boots walked up and stood next to her head. Lena's brother, Heather remembered from Luigi's intel, was named

Owen. The Travers Twins were deadly, vicious, and had run the streets red with blood for years.

"Look what she had on her, Owen," Lena said. "Hearing aids. Thirty of them. Who carries hearing aids all over the city? See? They're altered. They're ready to record something."

"This is Radiant Shade?" A rough hand yanked on Heather's hair, turning her face toward him. "Say something. Speak. I'll recognize your voice. Speak!"

"She was praying a minute ago," Lena said. "She's definitely a noncompliant. No papers. I thought Radiant Shade would be younger, but who can tell from a voice?"

"Wait a minute!" Owen cursed. "Are you letting me take this in? You know I need this, sis! This would square me with Obrador!"

"Why do you think I called you, you idiot? We're a team, remember?"

"*Radiant Shade!* You shot her? She's going to die before we even get her to the Bowery."

"She's your problem now." Lena nudge her with her boot. "You take care of it. I'm outta here. Come on, Death. There'll be other tunnel rats you can chew on."

Lena walked away. A moment later, the whine of a motorcycle engine raced away.

Owen picked up all the contents from the street and returned them to the purse.

"Sorry to break it to you, but Chancellor Obrador is going to make you miserable before killing you." Owen used his finger to poke Heather's cheek. "Come on, missy. Spare yourself the trouble. I'm the only one who can make it quick for you. You got anything to say to me?"

Heather's mind raced. *He thought she was Radiant Shade!* She tried to think through her pain about the risk of claiming to be Radiant Shade. From what she knew of Jenna's operation, it was possible that all this was providential. If she died as Radiant Shade, Jenna would be that much safer! Was Radiant Shade even necessary anymore? Not if Jenna was going to become the chancellor's wife!

For a moment, she pictured the situation as an opportunity to love not only Jenna but her Lord. Yes, such a death, to help the cause of Christ, was no great loss.

"I'm almost glad you finally caught me," Heather said, speaking higher than she normally did, to more closely match Jenna's voice. "I've used a voice synthesizer for years. I've been so lonely. I . . . surrender to you."

"It *is* you!" Owen laughed. "Come on now. Don't die on me out here. You'll miss the parade Obrador's going to throw for me!"

Feeling weak, she closed her eyes. Blood had soaked into her clothes. Maybe she would die right there. That would spare someone the horror of having to kill her, and the mercy of not having to suffer further.

Owen dragged her closer to the Humvee and roughly loaded her into the back.

Heather played dead rather than fight him. She was ready to die. It was for Jenna, her sister in the faith. It was time to meet her Savior face to face. Luigi would understand why this was best. She would see him again in glory. She would never see Jenna crowned queen, or the Casperteins' arrival to the city, but death no longer carried a sting for her. She was going home.

✝

Chloe Azmaveth was in Chancellor Obrador's office when Owen Travers burst into the room. He had blood on his clothes, and the security officers who'd been outside mumbled their apologies to Obrador as they arrived an instant later.

"Do you mind, Owen?" Chloe snapped. "We're in a bit of a crisis here! The coal miners in Virginia are protesting again."

Obrador stood and put his hands on his hips. With the window and morning light behind him, his whole body was in shadow, which reflected his mood most days.

"Wait!" Owen held up both hands, his eyes alive. "I'm going to fix your whole day—both of you. Say goodbye to your crisis! Are you ready?"

"Owen!" Obrador boomed. "I'll physically remove you myself! What little patience I do have, is coming . . ."

"*I caught Radiant Shade!*" Owen held out his arms as if he were ready to be embraced. "On the East Side. Look! This is her blood on my clothes. *Radiant Shade!* Can you believe it?"

Chloe instantly felt sick to her stomach, and she was having a hard time breathing.

"It's really her?" Obrador stepped past Chloe. "You're sure? How do you know?"

"I caught her in the act. She had a bag of hearing aids on her—all of them rigged to record. And she admitted it was her after I shot her. She sounded like she was glad she was caught, finally."

"Radiant Shade!" Obrador took Owen by the shoulders. "You've done it, boy! Chloe! *Radiant Shade!*"

"Yes, I heard. Wow." Chloe raised a triumphant fist. "Congrats, Owen."

But inside, Chloe was quaking. *Not Jenna. Not here.* Chloe had seen what Obrador did to his enemies. The executions themselves were merciful compared to what the Federation did to noncompliant citizens beforehand. It all seemed so much worse to mistreat a blind woman who had merely cared for persecuted Christians her entire adult life. Yet, these men didn't care if she was disabled or not. Jenna had been a thorn in the Federation's side for years.

". . . Then I loaded her up in the Humvee and brought her here." Owen took a breath from telling his story. "Yeah, she's downstairs right now. The boys are watching her. Honestly, she's not what you'd expect, but like I said, she didn't even put up a fight."

"I want to see her." Chloe cleared her throat. She walked across the room to Obrador. "We should both see her. Look into her eyes. We've been waiting for this moment for a long time."

"Let's go." Obrador led the way out, his two bodyguards hustling to keep up.

Trailing behind, Chloe fought the urge to vomit. They'd be merciless to Jenna, questioning her, roughing her up, even drugging her to make her talk. But at some point, they'd take a break. Or Jenna would pass out. And that would be COIL's window to get her out. Assuming Jenna was healthy enough to travel. Nathan and Chen Li needed to be put on alert. Together, the three of them could find their way into the tunnels, and as long as Jenna was conscious, she could tell them all about her contacts to escape the city. All their covers would be blown, but all their covers had been for Operation Esther, and if Esther was missing, then there was no more operation.

On the ground floor, the lobby was filled with Citizen Army soldiers, all of them veterans of hundreds of raids and arrests across the city.

"Clear a path!" Owen announced their arrival, and pushed his way to the center. "Here she is!"

Chloe inhaled sharply. Heather Putelli, in her mid-sixties, was tied to a chair, her head bowed, her arms cuffed behind her, and blood was leaking from her right shoulder. Her clothing was soaked with blood, making Chloe wonder if she'd been injured further.

Obrador took Heather's chin in his hand and lifted her head. Chloe knew already it wasn't Jenna, who was a slender woman barely forty, but she wasn't prepared to look into Heather's battered face. The older woman's clothes were torn, and her face showed proof of her mistreatment. Owen had obviously abused her before they'd arrived.

"You're Radiant Shade?" Obrador asked.

The whole lobby fell silent. Part of Chloe wished Heather would claim she was indeed Radiant Shade, and another part wished the woman confessed that she wasn't, so she'd be spared the terrible treatment Obrador certainly had in mind.

Heather's eyes ran over with tears, and her gaze seemed to take in the many who'd gathered. She was alone, a lamb in the midst of wolves. Their hatred was apparent to Chloe. Radiant Shade was responsible for embarrassing them all numerous times.

"She had these with her." Owen opened a leather purse to show Obrador, then the rest of the room. "Hearing aids, everyone! She had thirty of them on her."

"We'll get everything out of you!" Obrador shook his finger in Heather's face. "Take her to interrogation, Owen. I'm right behind you. I want to hear from her own mouth who she's been using in this administration to get intel! And someone find Steelman! He was supposed to be looking for Radiant Shade himself!"

For just an instant, before she was untied and yanked away, Chloe saw Heather's eyes fall on her, and recognition swept across her face. Chloe's heart seemed to stop, because Heather's eyes widened, possibly revealing their connection. They hadn't seen each other in years, but they'd been close sisters in Christ before and right after Pan-Day. But no one seemed to notice Heather's expression. The crowd roared and surged out of the lobby with their captive.

Chloe almost screamed as her arm was jerked to the left. Her body was whiplashed backward instead of being allowed to join the procession outside. Thinking she was being attacked in the confusion, she reached with her other arm for her attacker, intending to fight back. But then she realized it was Nathan.

By the stairwell, he shoved her into a maintenance room and entered behind her. But he didn't close the door all the way. Keeping it cracked, he peered back into the lobby.

"That was Heather!" Nathan stated sharply, though quietly.

"I know." Chloe rubbed her arm, knowing his treatment of her was only out of urgency. "They think she's Radiant Shade." Chloe pressed herself against the wall next to him, hiding behind him in case the door was opened. She couldn't be seen collaborating with anyone! "He'll make her talk, Nathan. Obrador has drugs. Remember the early days? Whether she means to or not, she'll give up something, either about us or the tunnels. *And she saw me!*"

"I've got some NL battle rifles in a tunnel on First Avenue. I can get there and back in thirty minutes. This craze will be thinned out by then. Chen Li can help. We can all go on the run."

"Wait, Nathan!" Chloe pushed her hair out of her face. "Let's think about this. What would Jenna want? If they think Heather's Radiant Shade, it solves a problem. They'll stop hunting for her."

"Chloe, it's Heather, Luigi's wife! She knows more about Radiant Shade than you and I put together. We have to get her out before she talks."

"There's two thousand men awake right now, all ready to fight. Dozens alone are taking her to Processing. It's a maze down there. You know it is! You want more of us to get caught? Chen Li could be next. Think, Nathan!"

"Jenna wouldn't want Heather to be tortured! We're not standing by. Even if it blows everything. Jenna wouldn't want this! I won't allow it. Don't ask me to!"

"Fine." Chloe shuddered, trying not to think of Heather at that instant. "Oh, Lord, please intervene! Nathan, we need a plan. Can we get in and out of interrogation without a shot being fired? You know the building over there better than me."

Nathan kept his eye glued to the crack of the open door. He didn't answer right away. When he did, his voice was quieter.

"Maybe in a few days, we could find a way, and we could ask Corban to send us a silencer for a smaller caliber. All I have are the battle rifles right now. They're for war, not stealth. One shot from that rifle, and the whole Bowery would come down on our heads."

"We don't have a few days, Nathan. Heather doesn't have a few days. Before morning, they'll have her talking. She'll be delirious from exhaustion. If they give her any truth serum, she's done. We're all done. We need to move now, get into place, or just walk away from it all."

"Can you get to her? You could get to her, Chloe. No one would oppose you. People know you, and they know you and I are working together. Maybe we could get down there together, then take Obrador hostage. Yes! We'll force our way out. No one knows we won't really shoot him. We could stage a bluff."

"Our covers would be blown. We'd need to get out of the city immediately. We have no resources, Nathan. Things have been so fluid beyond the capital. Luigi and Jenna, maybe even Corban, might know where some safe houses are, but we've been in the wolf's lair, so we've been kept in the dark about things. We can't risk contacting anyone now, or signaling anyone. We wouldn't last a day on the streets without knowing where to go. We'd never reach the Plains Zone like this."

"I'd rather die trying than sit by and let them torture her! How would we live with ourselves, Chloe? How could we ever look Luigi in the face, assuming we see him again?"

"We could go to the tunnels!" Chloe slapped his arm. "That's it! We take Obrador hostage in interrogation, then we go straight to the tunnels."

"The only tunnel openings I know about are too far away." Nathan shook his head. "I mean, there are tunnels this far south, but they're collapsed or flooded to the north. We can't get to the resistance from this point. And the subway tunnel to Brooklyn is flooded, too."

"But we could hide somewhere," Chloe pressed, now as the optimist. "We have places to go to in the city, right?"

"With Obrador as captive? With Heather in her condition? I saw her when she came in. Without medical care, she'll bleed out if we move her too much, and there's no way we won't move a lot if we're on the run. If Obrador thinks she's Radiant Shade, and we go without him, he'll send everyone he can into the tunnels or whatever neighborhood we enter. Many more would die."

"Then what do we do, Nathan?" Chloe cried.

"I don't know."

Chloe leaned her head against the wall.

"We pray. Oh, Lord, we beg You, help Heather!"

Deep, deep underground, Brian Steelman sat in the semi-darkness of the tunnel that was occupied by the resistance. He'd been given his own shelter two days earlier, but he was far from being free. It was now Christmas Day, and the resistance was still holding him prisoner.

From his third level shelter, he could see the outer barrier where armed resistance guards stood sentry over the families in the tunnel. The guards kept the barrier closed, and their presence kept him from getting out. For two days, ever since Luigi had left him there, he'd been watching that barrier. The counter-weight system required two grown men to open the door, a door which was really just a heavy chunk of concrete with garbage piled on it. The door opened to a subway track when the concrete was rolled back. No less than two guards manned the barrier day and night, so there was no escape. But even if he could escape, what would he escape to?

Teenagers lived in the shelters next to Brian's. They introduced themselves as Vags, which he guessed stood for Vagrants or Vagabonds. They were a special class of youngsters who'd been born and orphaned since Pan-Day, and had lived their whole lives in the tunnels. Only two Vags were older, born before Pan-Day. In total, they numbered about twenty, and they seemed to worship the Bandit and the two older Vags who led them. Listening to their conversations through the curtained walls, Brian had heard them speak of memorable raids on Federation storehouses, and exciting missions to sabotage equipment depots. They hated the Federation, Obrador, and especially Enforcers, so Brian kept his own identity a secret. Luigi Putelli hadn't revealed his true past to anyone except maybe the Bandit.

The older Vags had free reign of the tunnels, Brian had noticed. They came and went through the barrier at will. But when the Bandit was in the tunnel, the Vags gathered on the discarded tires heaped near the barrier wall, where they hung out and watched the Bandit from a distance. Even when the Bandit was sleeping in his private shelter, they stared in his direction, waiting for him to wake and lead them.

Brian hadn't met the Bandit personally, but he'd seen Luigi speaking to him privately on the floor level, and the Bandit had looked directly at him. Although Brian had suspected Luigi of being the Bandit, now he knew that the short, Hispanic man around sixty years old was the real Bandit. The Vags had spoken of him with awe. He was a legend, a savior of sorts, like a Robin Hood and King Arthur combined. Luigi, it turned out, was unfriendly with everyone except his wife, Heather, who'd fed Brian the night before. Or maybe it was the day before. It was hard to tell if the dim lights on the ceiling were lowered on schedule, or from periodic power shortages.

"What bothers you?" asked a muscled man with a crewcut. From the level below, the man could look directly up into Brian's shelter. The man, whose accent was European, huddled over a low desk of electronic parts. "You're safe here, friend."

"And what makes you think I'm worried?" Brian asked, his tone sounding sharper than he meant it to be.

"You look at the door as if you're afraid of who may enter. Come on down here."

Brian hesitated. He hadn't yet decided how to take his abduction and housing with the resistance. He'd returned to the Federation to find the Serval, but now people who claimed to be friends of the Serval had imprisoned him. To make matters worse, it wouldn't take much for someone to recognize him from his past. Some of the Vags were probably orphans from Brian's executions years earlier. How could he relax where he could be killed? He was a man without a people or refuge.

He climbed down a three-rung ladder to arrive at the second level where the man was seated. Brian knelt next to the work bench to study his neighbor's project. Although he expected the electrician to be building a bomb to be used in the resistance effort, instead he found a hot pot flipped upside down and wires trailing from it.

"I'm rigging it to boil water," the man said, then extended his hand. "Doc Joss. They call me Doc."

Brian had felt the grip of strong men over the years, but nothing like the rock-solid firmness of this foreigner.

"Call me Brian," he offered, guessing not many knew his first name. "I'm not scared. I'm just trying to find my place."

"Sounds like the journey of life for everyone," Doc said. "Here, hold this wire up like that. We're all trying to find our place, where we belong, even who we are. Not many realize what God made us to be—citizens of heaven."

"You're a noncompliant," Brian said dismissively.

"Noncompliant?" Doc frowned, as if patiently tolerating a child. "None of us live down here because we're compliant. And if you're down here with us, you're in the same pot, as they say."

"I meant, you're a Christian. I'm not."

"There's time for that still," Doc said, "at least until you die. Then you'll face the judgement. There's no getting around that."

"I don't believe any of that."

"No one would expect you to believe something you don't know to be true."

Brian blinked at Doc, trying to process his words. He realized he'd underestimated the intelligence of this man.

"I don't know what you mean."

"You'll learn what is true, Brian, and then you'll believe it. I'm confident of this. Hand me that battery there, and then tell me your life story."

"My story is my own business." Brian handed him a battery the size of his fist. "You tell me yours."

"Okay." Doc smiled, as if he'd planned to all along.

Of course, as soon as the man started talking, Brian realized he was in for a long story, but there was nothing else to do. Doc shared about his past in Austria, then coming to Christ and becoming a preacher. Two Vags from above joined them to listen to Doc tell his story, and Brian started to feel privileged to hear the tale, as well as to feel ashamed that he hadn't been so forthcoming with his own history. But really, he couldn't speak to them about his years as Obrador's lead Enforcer. Maybe Doc was a forgiving Christian, but the walls of the shelters were thin and others could hear what was said.

In his third hour, Doc finally reached the part of his life when the Bandit had asked him to join the resistance in the tunnels, rather than get arrested as a noncompliant Christian on the surface. As a preacher and an electrician, he'd become both chaplain and tech for the resistance, to improve the lives of the outcasts.

It didn't take much deducing to realize Doc was the one who'd altered the hearing aids for Radiant Shade.

Brian was just piecing the relationship together—between the facade of the resistance and the Christian underground—when someone below called his name. He leaned over the edge of Doc's floor. It was the Bandit. Brian hadn't even noticed that the barrier had opened and shut to allow entry for the notorious leader.

"You called me?" Brian asked.

"You're Brian, aren't you?" The Bandit waved him down. "Do you want me to yell out your last name, too?"

Brian felt the blood drain from his face, realizing that many of the Vags were listening, as they'd gathered around the Bandit. The secret ex-Enforcer was at the Bandit's mercy.

He climbed down and stood in front of the leader, looking down at him a moment, before the Bandit thrust out his hand, a look of amusement on his face.

"I heard you met the Serval a few months back." The Bandit's grip was firm, but not as strong as Doc's. "The Serval has saved my life before, too, so that sort of makes you and me family."

"Okay." Brian glanced at the others standing around them now—two grown men along with the Vags. "None of this was exactly expected, but I guess if the Serval is our common ground, I'll take it."

"We're running a resupply mission on the surface," the Bandit said. "We need strong people to carry supplies. If you want to get out of here for a while, we leave in about five minutes. Seek good and not evil."

"That you may live!" the crowd shouted as one.

They dispersed, and Brian stood alone until Doc climbed down and joined him.

"Don't be bothered by the way we do things down here." Doc set a heavy hand on Brian's shoulder as they watched the Bandit give a mission briefing to the Vags near the outer barrier. "We've had to balance survival with remembering we're on earth for a purpose. The Bandit is a little brisk with people, but he's soft inside. He, Luigi,

Heather, and I have kept all these people alive ourselves. It's changed us, and not in a bad way. But we're different. We know that. You'll see our hearts in time."

The Bandit and the Vags returned to Doc, and Doc prayed over them, as if they were fighting a holy war, light against darkness. But the Bandit wasn't easy to read, Brian thought as he watched him shrug on a backpack. The man led like a father and a resistance fighter simultaneously, but it was a far cry from the resistance army that Brian had imagined living in the tunnels. These were families and misplaced orphans mostly—Federation outcasts. They certainly weren't dangerous. They didn't even carry firearms, except for the two barrier guards. Yet, they were all noncompliants, condemned to death if they were ever caught by Enforcers.

A bell rang, and every occupant in the tunnel went silent. The barrier opened as the concrete was rolled out on the rails. The Bandit turned on a headlamp, then led the way outside. Many of the Vags didn't have lamps or flashlights, and they seemed perfectly comfortable walking into the darkness. But one of the two men present, with wavy blondish hair, carried a flashlight so Brian chose to stick with him.

The air outside the resistance tunnel was considerably more foul smelling, but Brian couldn't take time to stop and gag with disgust if he wanted to keep up with the man with the light. They stomped at a jog through running water, then climbed into a smaller tunnel that opened up in a subway tunnel. Brian was thoroughly lost within five minutes. Though the Vags were just teens, they didn't seem concerned about the Bandit's zigzag route.

An hour later, they slowed to a walk and stopped. Brian struggled to catch his breath against the horrible smell of sewage. The city's waste removal system was based on draining into the tunnels. The waste then relied on rain to flush it out to sea via one of the rivers, or for the tide to flood in and carry the waste out.

The Bandit lifted a Vag boy up into one of the drainage ducts. A few minutes later, the boy's head emerged after he'd pushed a manhole cover up and out of the ceiling. A knotted rope was dangled from the street and the ten Vags and two men started to ascend. Brian stood next to the Bandit, who held the rope as the Vags climbed it to the street. Finally, only the Bandit and Brian remained in the tunnel. The Bandit signaled to Brian to go up next, so he reached for the rope.

"Hold it! Someone's coming!" the Bandit warned, and waved the Vags away.

In an instant, the rope was withdrawn from the hole and the cover replaced. The Bandit turned off his headlamp, and the tunnel seemed to collapse in darkness. It felt like a heavy weight to Brian. Totally blind now, Brian was led by the arm down the tunnel a short distance, then forced against a wall by the Bandit's body.

"Don't move," the Bandit whispered.

Brian wouldn't think of moving. Besides, they had handicapped him by not giving him a flashlight. He was again at their mercy, which was foreign to him, since he'd dominated those around him his whole life—especially as an elite Enforcer. Submitted now, he wasn't fighting against his new placement in life. It had started in Arizona, trusting the Serval, then he'd been put on probation by Obrador, and now he was following orders from the Bandit—a man he'd previously hunted. There was still a Federation reward for the Bandit to be taken— dead or alive. And somehow, Brian's life had become entangled with these people through these events. His life was not his own.

The sound of running feet, and boots splashing through water, filled the tunnel. Brian didn't know which was worse—the suffocating darkness or the dread of Enforcers finding him in the company of the resistance.

The approaching noise sounded like one person, and Brian felt the Bandit ease away from their place against the wall. The light of the approaching person wobbled off a perpendicular tunnel wall. Brian stared at the little bit of illumination, realizing he was clinging to the Bandit's coat, even as the Bandit was pulling away to peer around the nearest corner.

"Luigi!" the Bandit called, and shook Brian's grip loose completely. "It's okay. It's just Luigi."

Brian sighed with relief. Facing an armed Enforcer in these tunnels would be suicide, since he hadn't seen even the Bandit carrying a weapon.

Eager to be nearest the light, Brian joined the Bandit's side as he turned on his headlamp and walked up to Luigi, who was winded from running.

"They captured Heather!" Luigi stated. "She was on her way to Jenna's when she had to go to the surface. She had to go around the tunnel on the East Side that had collapsed. One of the Twins got her."

Flinching at the mention of the Twins, Brian knew better than anyone who the Twins were and of what they were capable.

"We can rescue her," the Bandit said. "Before they figure out who she is, we can break her out!"

"No." Luigi's shoulders drooped. "The news is all over the street. Obrador thinks she's Radiant Shade. She's already in interrogation at Citizen Processing."

"We have . . . people there, Luigi." The Bandit glanced at Brian, and Brian realized he'd heard many underground secrets already, but there was much he didn't yet know. "She's not alone. We have people."

"She had the hearing aids with her. It's over."

"It's not over, Luigi!" The Bandit reached a hand out to the older man. "Keep hope. Brian, what will Obrador do to her if he thinks she's Radiant Shade?"

"Interrogate her. Try to get her secrets. Try to find out what she knows about all of you."

"We could exchange him." Luigi pointed at Brian. "He's one of theirs. They'll give her back in an exchange, and we can tell them she's not Radiant Shade."

"Luigi," the Bandit said, "Brian's with us now."

"I'm nothing to them, anymore," Brian said, now willing to resist anything that might put him back into the hands of Obrador. "I've been missing for days. They'll suspect me. Besides, if they've convinced themselves that your wife is Radiant Shade, they won't believe us that she isn't."

Luigi turned his back to them, and Brian reflected on his direct words. *Us?* Had he really joined the resistance to the point that he considered himself with them? It meant something to him that Heather had been arrested. She'd fed him the night before. And he knew how cruel the Twins could be in interrogation sessions.

"They'll make her talk, Luigi," the Bandit said softly.

"She'd never talk!" Luigi roared. "How dare you, Scooter!"

"She won't talk intentionally, Luigi," the Bandit pressed. "But you know they have methods. We need to finish out here, and get back to the tunnel to prepare for evacuation. We'll need to leave the island, or at least relocate to one of our other sites. Remember Operation Esther, Luigi! Think, my brother. What would Heather want you to do?"

Brian listened, aware that he didn't know Luigi well enough to comfort him at a time like this. Besides, there was no comfort in such a moment. Heather was lost. Whatever Operation Esther was, Obrador would have Heather drugged and talking within a day or two. He'd also noted that Luigi had called the Bandit Scooter. *Scooter?* Another handle of some sort? These men had more history, Brian guessed, than whatever resistance they were pretending. The Bandit was just a cover, but an effective one, since the whole Federation was convinced he was their greatest enemy.

"What about Jenna and Corban Dowler?" Brian asked. "I'm all for getting off this island, but it won't be easy. We'll need to go north first."

"Everything okay down there?" One of the Vags peered down on them from the hole in the ceiling.

Brian wondered where in the city they actually were. He was anxious to get back to the surface.

"Grandma Heather was caught by Enforcers," the Bandit said to the youth. "Willie, you and Hedgehog take the others for supplies. Luigi's going back to the tunnel to begin evacuations. We may need to relocate to Site B. Go now."

"Where's Site B?" Brian asked.

Luigi glared at Brian, making him feel awkward for even asking a need-to-know question.

"Go, Luigi," the Bandit said. "Brian and I will go check in with Corban. If there's some way we can connect with the others at the Bowery, we'll get to Heather. You know we'll try our best. Otherwise, we need to leave this in God's hands. Heather's trusting God right now. You know that."

"She's my wife!" Luigi shook his head. "I should've been at her side. I should've been escorting her!"

"No, because then we'd be losing both of you." The Bandit raised his hand. "I'm sorry. That came out wrong. She's not lost yet. Go to the tunnel and let Doc know everything. As a precaution, let's prepare to relocate everyone. Go with God, Luigi."

Luigi walked away, his normal gait no longer brisk.

"It's you and me," the Bandit said to Brian. He handed him a spare flashlight. "This is no longer a supply run. This is now a rescue mission. Are you game?"

Brian clutched the flashlight hungrily and turned it on.

"I came for the Serval. I have no problem helping his friends. Forget my past, which you obviously know about. I'm with you. If Heather talks, we're all finished."

"Somehow, we have to get to her before that."

Chapter Eight

Chancellor Kendrick Obrador watched through the one-way glass as a doctor administered aid to the woman called Radiant Shade. She was past her prime, Obrador thought, but she'd caused havoc for his government for years, almost as much as the Bandit had inside the city. Her mind, not her body, was what he was interested in. Radiant Shade could be the key to revealing numerous adversaries within the Federation.

At the other end of the hall of the basement level of Citizen Processing, Obrador listened to Lena Travers give orders to several captains and lieutenants, sending them on missions Obrador himself hadn't ordered. He'd always given her free reign to command, but only because he thought she was perfectly submitted to him. Now, he was beginning to doubt her. Even as he watched, he noticed the men and women in command gave her their attention much more than Obrador's own aides gave him. How long had this been going on? Had Lena really become more influential over his own troops than he was? Was he no longer their inspiration? Maybe he'd been upstairs in his comfortable suite too long, while Lena had been on the streets gaining the hearts of the men and women in uniform. But had she become a threat to his office?

Obrador had been careful not to promote anyone higher than the rank of colonel, just to keep control over the Citizen Army and its Enforcers. Everyone knew that the Federation Enforcers were a special class of hunter-killers within the army, and that Obrador himself was Commander-in-Chief. But the Twins may have risen up to command more respect than he realized. And catching

Radiant Shade would only boost the confidence of the military in the Twins. Unless Obrador did something drastic, the Twins could become a liability to his office. Perhaps his harsh treatment of them hadn't spurred them to new heights as he'd expected, but had turned them against him.

With the exception of himself, Obrador regularly preached that there was no room for individuality in socialism. Self-promotion, self-determination, and self-ambition was encouraged, except and unless others were discriminated against in the process. That kept everyone in check, since discrimination could happen on any front from anyone.

Two Enforcers were in the room with the doctor, who was checking Radiant Shade's vitals. She was strapped to a table, but she was lying still and her eyes were closed. Instead of the doctor focusing on Radiant Shade, though, he kept looking up at the glass. Obrador recognized fear when he saw it. *Radiant Shade wasn't responding!* The doctor had failed to keep her alive! That ignited Obrador's fear as well, and it spread to his heart. How could he show himself as the omnipotent ruler, mightier than even the Twins, if he kept meeting with failure?

On top of it all, Steelman was missing—with one of the few vehicles still functioning in the city! The prodigal's return had given Obrador hope, but he'd secretly suspected Steelman had returned for a reason much different than merely missing the privileges of being the Federation's top authoritarian. Lena had been against giving Steelman his freedom as well, and it seemed she'd been right about that now as well.

The doctor stepped out of the room, lowered his head, and approached the chancellor.

"She, um, died, sir." The doctor pushed glasses farther up his nose. "It may have been an allergic reaction to the serum. Without her medical file—"

"No one has a medical file anymore! Is that really your excuse?"

"It seems this woman hasn't been healthy for years."

"You had one job, Doctor—to keep her alive for me!"

"She'd lost a lot of blood, Mr. Chancellor. She was weak. She was barely conscious when I arrived."

"We didn't get anything out of her. *Nothing!*"

"She wasn't like the others." The doctor shook his head. "They were healthy enough to question, and younger. I just don't—"

"Get out of my sight."

"Do you want me to go back in to her, or . . ."

"Leave! Before I have you executed for negligence of duty!"

Obrador noticed that his raised voice had drawn the attention of others down the hall. And Chloe was coming now, too. Where had she been? Lena Travers was right behind her. Chloe, he knew, would have something helpful to settle his concerns, but Lena, on the other hand, would only provoke him.

"Was that the doctor who just left?" Chloe asked, reaching him first. She stepped up to the window. "What's going on?"

Failure made him look weak, Obrador knew, and he felt his blood pressure rising. Dead or not, Radiant Shade had been captured on his watch. It was to his credit. Somehow, he needed to exploit this over his adversaries. Was he already thinking of Lena as his adversary? She was indeed an enemy if she was beginning to exert control over elements of his administration. She was pulling strings, and unless he acted decisively against her, one of the women he had trusted to build the Federation with him would be the very woman to tear it from him.

"Radiant Shade just died," he said to Chloe, ignoring Lena who stood next to her, with Death on her leash. "But we got her. *We got her, Chloe!* Remember this moment."

He watched her from the side as she looked in at the deceased woman, bloodied and still bound. What he saw on Chloe's face was emotion, and he realized this was why he preferred counsel from Chloe over someone like Lena, who killed and tortured and maimed without regard. Yes, both were strong women, and he'd used Lena's viciousness before, but Chloe had warmth, while Lena had only ice. And Owen didn't seem much different from his sister, evidenced by his treatment of Radiant Shade.

"It's the end of an era," Chloe said, touching her cheek. "Sorry. There's just been so much happening lately."

Lena joined her at the window.

"If she's dead, I say good riddance. I suggest we take full advantage of this moment, Chancellor." Lena raised her head defiantly. "We should put her on display. Let the resistance see who's more powerful. No one can stand against us."

"What do you mean, put her on display?" Chloe turned, her tone sharp. "We're not barbarians, Lena!"

Obrador crossed his arms, studying both women, each from a different generation. Chloe had had a whole life. She'd shared with him that before Pan-Day, she'd served in the Israeli military. But Lena had only been in her twenties, and as an army nuisance, she'd been reprimanded numerous times for excessive force as an MP.

"I say we still hold a public execution." Lena squared off in front of Chloe. "Behead Radiant Shade in Foley Square. Take pictures. Make banners. Parade her corpse up Fifth Avenue. We won!"

"We are the Appalachian Federation!" Chloe thundered back. "We need to think strategically, not like animals!"

"Oh, now I'm an animal?" Lena stuck her finger in Chloe's face. "I've had about enough of your self-righteousness, Chloe. You're always holding us back, making us look weak!"

"What's weak about conquering our enemies instead of inciting them?" Chloe was angry, but she was in total control, calculative. Obrador wondered if the two women had had such a rivalry for long. How could he have missed this before?

"Chloe?" He held up his hand, halting Lena's response. "I've heard Lena's proposal. I like the strong approach. What's the strategic approach? How do you suggest we deal with Radiant Shade? This really could be a moment in which we could boast our supremacy."

"Exactly!" Lena scowled. "No more weakness! We need to make a power move!"

"Whoever's out there and involved in the underground," Chloe said, "isn't defeated because we have Radiant Shade. We have a marriage ceremony this spring. Our goal is to win the people, all of them, even our adversaries, so that we are one, unified country. I say we keep silent about Radiant Shade's death, and pass the word that she's broken and talking to us, telling us everything, even seeing things our way. The resistance might bend to our will if she's rumored to be a guest at the Bowery. What can they do to respond? They'll think we're holding her hostage, or that she's really our guest. If she's really our guest, then maybe they'll follow her lead and fall in line."

"Yeah, right!" Lena snapped. "Chancellor, are you buying this nonsense? We need to get loud and proud about this, not hide it!"

"A captive is more powerful than a corpse," Chloe continued, ignoring Lena as she spoke directly to Obrador. "Think strategically. Win the people. Keep her death a secret, and we'll see what the resistance does to free her. We can stretch it out."

"We'll need to reveal her death sooner or later," Obrador said. "Won't we?"

"No." Chloe smiled. "Think of it. We can even say something like, we're releasing her, or turning her loose to her people, during the week of the pageant. Use her death to win, not just to gloat. Everyone will be on their best behavior, on their knees before you, Kendrick. The Federation will honor you for catching her, and the resistance will scratch their heads about your intentions for her. And we can use the newspaper now in print. We could even put it in the paper that the wedding will be a sacred ceremony, between you and the people. And Radiant Shade will be a guest of honor, as part of the ceremony. We can say it, even if we don't do it. No one will know or say otherwise. It's what we print. You control the press."

"She's our honored guest . . ." Obrador smiled, ignoring Lena's expletives at the same moment. "I can use this. I really can!"

"We can quietly bury her in secret. I'll use someone we already trust to remain confidential. Like Lieutenant Isaacson. He's loyal and experienced at protecting Federation interests. Bury her quietly, privately, while publicly we talk about her as our guest, even our friend. Even if the resistance doesn't buy it, the rest of the nation will get a sense that there's no real conflict. The temperature across the country will go way down. It'll be harder for the resistance to recruit people if the Federation presents a benevolent front."

"No!" Lena fumed. "Chancellor, you have a chance to be lord of this domain, and you're choosing this action instead? We can't hide this. Radiant Shade has been removed by force, not by smiling!"

Obrador stood up straighter, loving the fact that he was taller than everyone.

"Lena, I'm giving you an order. I've decided what I'm going to do. You and your brother brought in Radiant Shade, so I want you two in charge of keeping this quiet. As far as anyone knows, Radiant Shade is a guest in one of the Bowery's suites. Make that happen. No one is to say otherwise."

"*What?* Make *her* do that stuff!" Lena pointed at Chloe. "It's her idea. I'm not your lap dog, Kendrick. I'm an Enforcer. I'm not playing house with some corpse!"

"Arrange it, Lena!" Obrador raised his fist. "Do it for the Federation's triumph, or you'll meet with the might you claim to want to see so badly. I'm tired of your insolence and subtle betrayal behind my back! I'm this close to putting you down—you and your dog! Now, I'm giving you another chance to show you're willing to do the little things your Federation asks of you, and not just the big things, to prove yourself. This is it, Lena!"

Obrador took a breath, appreciating the look of shock on Lena's face. Maybe her disloyalty was even worse than he was suspecting, but he'd brought it up and embarrassed her all at once, devastating her attitude.

Her feud with Chloe was no more. Now, he saw her processing the ultimatum he'd given her. She was on thin ice, and he had the power, not her.

"I'm . . . sorry." She bowed her head, more submissive than she'd been in years. "I'll do as you say. You'll see that the Federation really is the only thing that matters to me. I promise you."

"Good. Thank you." Obrador felt cheerful once again. "Include your brother. Now, carry on. This is an opportunity we may not get again."

"Yes, sir." She turned and walked down the hall, her dog wagging her tail, until Lena jerked on her leash and hissed at her.

"That was simple enough." Obrador rocked onto his toes. "Wouldn't you say?"

"Not quite, sir." Chloe sighed. "Whatever bad attitude she's had, she'll now just keep it more hidden. You pulled her covers. She's not the kind of woman to abandon her mindset through shaming. She has pull with the troops."

"She's always pushed for stronger responses in these situations, but she's never done anything but obey. I'm sure she'll obey now, too."

"Even insurrection is founded in patience." Chloe shook her head. "I'd keep an eye on her. She wants to use a hammer, but you're learning to use your heart, sir."

"I had no idea you were so sentimental, Chloe." Obrador raised his hand to her face and brushed the back of his fingers against her cheek. He surprised himself in his own sincerity.

"Why haven't I seen this side of you before?"

"I need to get a body in the ground, and quietly, sir." She blushed. "And we have a wedding to plan. I'll be upstairs when I'm finished. I'll go get Lieutenant Isaacson to help me."

Obrador watched her walk away, a whole new feeling rising in his chest for Chloe Azmaveth. She'd been at his side so long, and knew all his secrets and vices, so of course he would eventually be attracted to her, despite their arrangement. But this was more than physical attraction. He wondered if she had feelings for him. It had always been business between them, and he'd had any woman he chose on the side. Yet, here she'd been all along. How could she stay with him through so much, unless she had strong feelings for him?

He chuckled to himself as he signaled his security personnel. Chloe might've been arranging his wedding, but it was she who was beginning to steal his heart. And what a Christmas! Radiant Shade was captured and he was falling in love, all in one day!

✝

Chen Li wept quietly as Nathan, from inside the grave, gently lowered Heather Putelli's body into the earth. That early dawn, Chloe was there, her hands folded, her face grim. And Chen Li wished she could be as stoic as the COIL veteran. For years, Chloe had maintained her deep cover, alone, in danger every day, and she still seemed as strong as the first day.

Nathan climbed out of the hole, which was only about four feet deep on account of water seeping in as he'd dug behind a shop on the Lower East Side. The yard had been chosen at random, but Chen Li knew she'd never forget where her Christian sister was being laid to rest. Even if it had to be an unmarked grave, she'd never forget her sister's sacrifice.

Using the shovel, Nathan covered the body with dirt. Soon, Chen Li could see Heather no more.

Chloe had shared about her dangerous maneuverings with the chancellor to get the body, making Lena Travers a worse enemy in the process. The three of them had survived many violent acts committed by the Federation, but this was the first time they'd buried one of their own from their COIL family. With Lena full of treachery now, Chen Li wondered which of them would be the next one to be laid to rest beside Heather.

"Her husband can't even be here." Chen Li moved closer to Chloe, and the two held each other as if desperate to keep the other from leaving. "Luigi must be heartbroken."

"He doesn't even know she's dead," Chloe said, "but he probably knows she was taken. We need to get word to Radiant Shade, so she can calm everyone down before they attempt a rescue. If I know Corban and Luigi, they'll try to rescue Heather from danger, even knowing it would create a mess."

"I'll signal Luigi," Nathan said, resting on the shovel. "I'll do it as soon as we're finished here."

Chen Li knew he meant he'd take a can of spray paint a few blocks northward, to streets not often frequented by the Federation, where the resistance sometimes tagged the walls of the buildings. There, Nathan knew to leave a code in braille, a system of communication taught to them all by Jenna in the early years. The boxed dots blended perfectly with the colorful murals the graffiti artists displayed around the city. By nightfall, someone would get the word to Jenna, Chen Li guessed, and Luigi would be notified. His wife was dead, martyred for Christ while serving the Christian underground network.

Nathan led them in prayer, and did his best to lift their spirits using Scripture that spoke of the resurrection, but Chen Li felt the weight of the years growing heavier. It was hard in that moment to imagine anything but more despair, death, and gloom as their efforts against evil continued. Would Jenna flinch away after such a loss as Heather? Would they finally give up the fight before more were killed? Would the fear of death be their downfall?

"Is God any less loving?" Nathan suddenly asked.

Lifting her head, Chen Li thought about her husband's rhetorical question. But as she gazed at his drawn, bold face, she realized it wasn't a rhetorical question. He was feeling what they were all feeling. And they all needed to be reminded of the truth when something other than truth was beginning to press in upon them.

"No, He's still loving," Chen Li said, a smile emerging through her tears.

"Is He less powerful in light of this?" Nathan challenged them. "Chloe?"

Chloe wiped her nose.

"No, our God is still in control." Chloe squeezed Chen Li's arm. "He's still sovereign."

"And He's not ignorant of tragedy, or of our loss today." Nathan raised his arms to the sky. "Our hearts are hurting, Lord, but our faith is not founded in shakable things. Our trust is in an unshakable Person who loves us. You're invincible, and You favor us even now. We serve You. You'll use this. We just have to wait. And if I know Jenna, she'll use this, too."

"Poor Luigi." Chen Li frowned. "We'll be exploiting his wife like this. So, Radiant Shade is no more?"

"Jenna will see the wisdom of it," Chloe said. "The wedding is next on the calendar. I mean, after the beauty pageant. We can continue to move Christians, just not in the name of Radiant Shade any longer."

"You're sure about getting Jenna in?" Nathan asked. "Obrador's behavior is less and less predictable from what you've said."

Chloe didn't answer, but she didn't have to. Chen Li had worked in Citizen Processing so long that she'd witnessed one man gradually dismantle an entire civilization, compelling citizens to submit to his socialist agenda or risk arrest and execution. Millions had migrated west. Millions more had been persecuted, worked to death in labor camps, or forced underground. Under such oppression, it was just a matter of time until Obrador's own people, who were just as wicked as he was, turned on him with ambitions of their own. The Christians were simply leaping before someone else did.

Chen Li hoped they would all survive until the spring to see the wedding become a reality. Operation Esther had to succeed!

Corban Dowler could hear Jenna still crying upstairs. It was morning now, and she'd been awake all night. They'd had some hard Christmases over the years under Federation rule, but the day before had been one of the worst. A city-wide bulletin had been brought straight to the print office. Radiant Shade had been captured. Within minutes of sharing the news with Jenna, they'd both deduced that Heather's absence the day before was now explained. They'd captured Heather, thinking she was Radiant Shade. Somewhere, Heather was being held, tortured, questioned . . .

In the print room, Corban leaned over one of the tables, and prayed while he worked. Jenna had heard stories and she knew all the rules he'd taught her of espionage, but real life was different. In real life, people who you loved actually died. In real life, the risks you took were actually gambles with people's lives. He'd warned her this day would come. During his own COIL years abroad, he'd lost many field agents, so he knew her heartache now. She felt the pain very deeply. She'd had to decide between rescuing Heather, which would expose a dozen people—or continue with Operation Esther, which would potentially help millions.

Jenna had chosen to continue with the operation, for the sake of the underground, but it meant turning their backs on Heather, who was in Federation custody. Although Corban had told her she'd made the right decision to save lives, she hadn't stopped crying.

Corban cut excess plastic off one laminated document that Obrador's administration had requested, and held it up to the light. Occasionally, the Bowery asked for duplicates of something to be printed and laminated. In those cases, when Chloe's signature was on the request, Corban knew to make one document the actual document, but he was to make the duplicate different. He'd learned to iron flat an entire coded sheet sandwiched inside laminated cards. Even holding the identifications up to the light, he could see nothing strange—no shadow or lumpiness. But on the back of the duplicate, he left a subtle smudge of toner as indication to Chloe which of the two she was to take for herself.

Chloe had been receiving coded papers from Jenna for years this way, where she would need to cut through the lamination and pull out the inner message. Afterward, she could dispose of the duplicate item, and no one would know.

In this way, Corban had remained briefed on Jenna's braille orders to Chloe, keeping her apprised of underground efforts to infiltrate the government, or safely move fugitives in or out of the city. From Chloe's perspective, she could leave Nathan orders to direct patrols in one neighborhood rather than another, so when Christians were being moved somewhere, they weren't discovered.

Of course, Chloe needed another system to communicate back to Corban, so he sent her unsealed 9x12 envelopes on which Chloe could fit two, tiny lines of braille text in the seal, then fasten and send it.

Since Corban supplied the Bowery with its paper and envelope materials, he intentionally left some new requisition envelopes unsealed just for Chloe to seal herself, when communiques were necessary.

The ID in his hand was just such a transfer of intel. It contained an order from Jenna not to pursue a rescue of Heather, unless a rescue could be orchestrated without endangering anyone's cover. That would be unlikely. Since only Nathan, Chen Li, and Chloe had access to Bowery facilities, Jenna was essentially ordering the three of them to stand down. They simply had to remain in place for Operation Esther, and any potential needs the Christian underground might require of them later.

Suddenly, Corban looked up and noticed the red light in the fire alarm on the ceiling was blinking. For how long, he didn't know, but he set down the laminated item and immediately walked to the outer room. No one was at the front door, so he locked it, then moved into the storage room and listened. Someone was in the basement, but it wasn't Jenna. She was upstairs. The fire alarm had been connected to a switch under the house for just this reason, but he wasn't expecting anyone.

He knelt and rolled back the linoleum, then lifted the trap door.

"Corban, thank God!" Scooter said, and quickly climbed out. "I've been flashing you for an hour. Is everything okay?"

"I only just noticed the light." Corban stood back as Brian Steelman also climbed out. "I made the light so discreet, even I forget to notice it sometimes."

He felt foolish for missing an obvious signal, but the men made no complaint for the delay, or they were too weary to protest. Their clothes were soiled and wet from wading in chest-deep water. Scooter's graying crewcut was grimy and flat, and Brian's cheek had a slight cut from something sharp.

"You two already know each other, right?" Scooter asked Corban, gesturing to Brian. "We need to get right to business, Boss. Where can we talk?"

Scooter and Brian stripped down to their shorts, and Corban gave them bathrobes from a wall hook. They weren't the first filthy visitors he'd had. They left their clothes in a deep sink, and followed Corban upstairs to the living quarters.

"We have guests," Corban announced to Jenna, who sat upright from where she'd been leaning on her reading desk against the wall. "It's Scooter and Brian Steelman."

"How many names do you have?" Brian nudged the Hispanic man. "Scooter?"

Jenna used a handkerchief to dry her face and compose herself. Corban offered soft chairs to the two visitors. For years, Corban's health had been in decline, and he was acquainted with not taking the lead when the younger generations were able. He seated himself next to Jenna, touched her shoulder briefly to let her know he was there, then waited on those who'd taken on more active roles within COIL to begin the discussion.

"How are your people, Scooter?" Jenna asked first.

"They're okay, but Luigi's preparing to evacuate them to Site B. Heather was arrested, I'm sure you know, but we've received a recent update in the last couple of hours."

"Yes, we'd heard about Heather." Jenna folded her hands around her handkerchief. "It's wise to relocate. Heather may be forced to disclose something. She's being held inside the Citizen Processing Building, in the basement. We don't see how we can safely rescue her. That's been my decision."

"It won't be necessary," Scooter said. "Heather died. On the way here, we came upon a new tunnel collapse. We had to backtrack and wade through a different tunnel just to find a new route here. It must've been the reason why Heather was above ground in the first place, and exposed enough to be captured."

"Yes." Jenna's face was grim and serious. "Normally, she remained in the tunnels all the way here. She was making a delivery. But—*she's dead?* You're sure?"

"Brian and I had to go to the surface ourselves eventually this morning," Scooter said. "While in the daylight, we saw a message. I'm guessing it was from Eagle Eyes. The paint was still fresh on the wall. It said, 'Heather graduated.'"

"Graduated," Jenna repeated, nodding slowly.

"In braille," Brian added, seemingly fascinated, but then realized he'd spoken out of turn, and looked down at the carpet.

"I understand, Mr. Steelman." Jenna angled her head toward him. "Have you found your way with the resistance?"

"Found my way?" Brian glanced at Scooter. "I don't understand."

"Do you know where you belong?" Corban asked. "Where your loyalties lie?"

"My loyalties are with the Serval," Brian said. "He's the only one who makes any sense to me nowadays. And you've said you're friends of the Serval, so then I'm among friends."

"Well, the Serval seems to have been delayed." Jenna reached for Corban. "Dad, our guests might need something to eat or drink?"

Corban immediately went to the closet where he'd stashed several cases of energy drinks, confiscated by Scooter's own forces.

"I recognize these." Scooter smiled and twisted the top. "I hate to say it, but Heather's death simplifies things for everyone."

"You won't have to move to Site B," Jenna said. "Does Luigi know yet?"

"Not yet. We'll head back there and stop the relocation."

"Good." Jenna nodded. "Please give Luigi our love. We'll all miss Heather. I'm sure our friends at the Bowery took care of her body. My father will simply have to be the one to get me ready for the pageant without her."

"That's a terrible idea!" Corban said. "Unless you let me put makeup on you like we put graffiti on the walls in the alleys."

"Do I really need that much decoration, Dad?"

"Actually," Scooter said, "I think he just called you a wall."

Corban joined them in laughter, appreciating that even Brian was there to witness what was happening. Scooter seemed to be exposing him to the right elements of the Christian life. It wouldn't be the first time a COIL operative had included a ruthless killer on a dangerous mission—all to show him Christ.

"Then, everything moves forward." Jenna paused. "The pageant will be set for March 7, and the wedding will be one week later. Can the resistance make do at least that long?"

"We'll keep quiet." Scooter gave Corban a thumbs-up. "You guys have a plan to get everyone from underground back to the surface without getting arrested?"

"The Lord's on that detail," Jenna said. "Something will need to happen that'll cause the chancellor to legalize everyone living in the city, above or below ground, compliant and noncompliant."

"Can you tell us what that something will be?" Scooter asked. "Is it a signal or something we can watch for?"

"I don't know what it'll be." Jenna smiled. "Sorry. Like I said, we're trusting God with that detail. Some sort of catalyst. All we know is that it needs to happen, and I'll be in place with the others in the Bowery to push forward new legislation to legalize everyone."

"Obrador will never legalize noncompliant citizens," Brian said. "All his Federation policies are based on compliance. I know this. I'm the one who helped him establish those laws."

"Mr. Steelman?" Jenna asked.

Corban recognized the patient authority in her voice. He'd taught her that.

"Yes?"

"Obrador is the ruler, but he's not in control."

"He's . . . not?"

"You'll see." Jenna turned to Corban. "Dad, is there anything else to say?"

"No more visits here," he said, "not if you have to travel above ground to get here. Send Luigi by night if it's something urgent. I'll drop bottled messages through the Fifth Avenue grate on schedule to keep you posted."

"Sounds good," Scooter clasped his hands. "Two weeks and two months until the big day, huh?"

"A lot can happen in two months and two weeks," Corban said. "Look how much has happened in just one week here. Before you go, I'd like to pray."

Corban held one of his daughter's hands, and as he bowed his head, he noticed Scooter throw his arm around Brian's broad shoulders. The outsider stiffened at the touch, but Corban knew love would break through such discomfort.

He prayed for God to have His way in Manhattan and across the Federation, to touch the hearts of the enemy, for the Serval's safety, and for God to be glorified through the faithfulness of His saints, no matter the circumstances. And he prayed for Luigi.

When finished, all but Jenna rose to their feet.

"What's the Serval's role in all this?" Brian asked. "Since he's my whole objective, I'm really waiting more for him than I am being a part of whatever you guys are planning at the Bowery."

"The Serval thinks I'm in danger," Jenna said. "If he arrives before March 7, he could jeopardize the operation. Whoever sees him first needs to tell him to stand down. Understand?"

"We'll pray to God about the Serval's timing," Corban said. "I know the Serval well enough, and I know God, so I'd say the Serval will make his presence known no sooner or later than is necessary."

"Be safe, Scooter." Jenna remained seated, but raised her hand to the operative. "We'll be in touch."

Corban led the two visitors downstairs to the trapdoor. He embraced both men, then they changed back into their dirty clothes to leave.

"You sure you've got this pageant thing under control?" Scooter asked Corban as he descended the ladder into the basement.

"Absolutely not," Corban said. "I look terrible with makeup on!"

Scooter laughed.

"At a time like this?" Brian asked. "Joking? You guys don't realize how much danger we're in. If you did, you wouldn't be laughing."

"And if you knew how much God loves us puny people," Corban said, "you'd realize why the threat of death doesn't frighten us like it does you. Scooter will explain it to you."

With that, Corban closed the trapdoor.

Federation Enforcer Lena Travers climbed off her motorcycle and slowly took off her racing gloves as she watched three men walk toward her. This once, she hadn't brought Death. She stood in the middle of the highway outside Princeton, New Jersey, about halfway between New York and Philadelphia, as agreed. Behind the three men sat two parked trucks and five riflemen in Federation fatigues.

The three men stopped about ten feet in front of her. Lena acknowledged the two young, unshaven men on either side, then focused on Milo Rotham, the tall, lean soldier in the middle with a shotgun in one hand. He had a sour face with hard eyes. The rising sun seemed to make his dark skin shine. She'd met him a couple times in Philadelphia to coordinate the arrests of noncompliant citizens, but that morning, they were there for a much different reason.

"Your offer intrigued me," Rotham said, his voice rough and low. He leaned the shotgun over his right shoulder. "Your radio message was cryptic. What are you proposing exactly?"

"I'm proposing Rendezvous New Castle to strengthen the Federation." Lena rested her right hand on the sidearm on her hip. "With you as the muscle and me as the head. Obrador's gone soft. It's time someone replaced him."

"Why do we need you if we're the muscle?"

"Someone needs to run the government," she said, not liking his challenge so early in their relationship. "I can hold the Federation together and manage the population, while you expand her borders, capture resources, and establish law in lawless towns."

"Will Manhattan go quietly?" Rotham asked. "What about Obrador?"

"I'll remove Obrador myself." She tapped her fingers on the butt of her pistol. "And I'll take care of his cabinet. The Enforcers will follow me. The rest of the staff at the Bowery will fall in line."

"And your brother? I thought he was loyal to the chancellor."

"Owen will do whatever I say. He's with me."

"We heard Radiant Shade was caught. She's with you, too?"

"Obrador killed her in secret. Don't believe what you read in the paper. She's out of the picture now, and any inspiration she brought the resistance has died with her. It's a perfect time for a regime change."

"I don't like meeting like this," Rotham said. "Tell me when you want us in Manhattan, and we'll be there. But first, I need to round up more vehicles for transportation."

"Obrador has his symbolic wedding planned for March 14. I want you rolling down Broadway the day before, on the thirteenth."

"That's over two months away. Okay. That gives us enough time. You're going to kill Obrador the day before he gets married?" Rotham whistled. "You're one cold queen, Lena Travers."

"That's exactly what I intend to be." She smiled. "You do your part, and I'll do mine. I'll see you at the Bowery on the thirteenth. Shall we say noon?"

"Noon it is." He grinned. "Long live Queen Lena."

Rotham laughed and turned away with his men. Lena liked the strength he exhibited, but she didn't trust him. He'd governed Eastern Pennsylvania for the Federation for years, so maybe trusting him didn't matter if he did his job from Manhattan instead of Philadelphia. With him at her side instead of her brother, no one on the coast would stand against the Federation. The resistance should've been destroyed years earlier.

Lena had no qualms about killing Obrador, but she would relish removing Chloe's head. She was still sore about the way Obrador was choosing Chloe's counsel over her own. Obrador had become a weaker ruler with the older woman at his side, poisoning his decisions.

Yes, long live Queen Lena. She liked the sound of that!

✝

Luigi stood alone in the dark behind the shop on the Lower East Side. Heather's grave lay before him. For a moment, he took in the scene by the light of the moon as it had been described to him from a communication from Chen Li. The yard was small, inconsequential, and neglected. Weeds had sprung up where there'd probably once been a lawn. An apartment building, now charred from a fire, sat vacant on the other end of the yard.

When Luigi had thought of the end of their lives, he hadn't imagined he'd lose Heather before he'd finally be taken home himself. And he certainly didn't like her being laid to rest in Manhattan rather than in the countryside somewhere outside the city. He knew it was just her outer shell, but this place both angered him and saddened him. And it broke something inside his heart that she'd died alone, in captivity, without him. His rationale told him that he hadn't let her down, but his heart told him that he'd not cared for his own wife in her hour of greatest need.

He knelt on the ground and felt in the darkness the raised earth that Nathan had covered over her body. From inside his coat, he drew Heather's favorite Leever book, one with the Psalms, and placed it on the ground where he imagined her head might be resting.

She was with the Lord now. The thought brought him to tears. Alone now, without her, he was the one to be pitied in this fallen world.

"All that separates us is my own death," he mumbled and wept.

Sometime later, he dried his eyes and rose to his feet, but he didn't leave quite yet. Heather's passing changed his life. Without her, he was a nomad again—to wander and lurk as he had as a younger man. It was true, he had his loyalties to Corban and to Jenna still, but without family, he had no roots any longer. There would be no need to return to the resistance tunnel to see Heather every night, or to tend to her needs. Now, he had only his

COIL obligations for Corban and Jenna. Otherwise, he was independent for God again. It was a liberating thought, but also a weighty one. He really was just waiting to die.

For hours, he stood there, thinking and praying about the future. He wanted to leave Manhattan. How could he remain so near those who'd killed Heather? Retirement wasn't on his mind, but he sensed the Lord had one great task left for him, perhaps for Corban. And then he would join Heather.

When the sun finally rose upon the small burial plot, Luigi had gone.

Chapter Nine

Two months later . . .

Chancellor Kendrick Obrador held up two different suits in the full-sized mirror in his Bowery Hotel suite. Before Pan-Day, the suits would've each cost hundreds of dollars, but now, his coffers were expansive, his warehouses were packed, and his storerooms were filled. That was, at least, as long as the resistance didn't find his stashes.

The resistance had been quiet for over two months, though—ever since the beauty pageant and wedding had been announced in the paper to the nation. Chloe had been right. The people were rallying behind him. Arrests were fewer. Morale on the city streets was up. He'd even seen some green and white Federation flags around the city. The country was proud again, excited about the pending ceremony. And that made him excited. *Always caring, always strong.* The Federation's motto had never been truer!

He tossed one suit onto his bed and tried on the first. Chloe had picked out both of them. Faithful Chloe. And Lieutenant Isaacson! Both had kept him updated daily on the wedding arrangements, as well as the security involved. After all, the pageant and wedding was all staged, and the perfect woman would be pre-chosen—one who would represent the people but bring the most support for their chancellor and the Federation. It was a stroke of genius, he thought, that the idea had been brought to him. If he didn't know better, he would've thought that Chloe had some ulterior motive for boosting his popularity, the nation's unity, and the Federation's resolve. But at every turn, Chloe still showed only joy that she was able to serve in such a worthy cause.

Although Obrador's awe of Chloe had only grown over the past two months, he had come to face the truth that they would never be together as a couple. Not only did she withhold herself from opening up to him, he knew that soon he would be married to another, and he would need to express his husbandly favor upon his new bride. Chloe wasn't going anywhere, however, and that gave him comfort.

But not all was pleasant in his empire, even though Chloe seemed to highlight daily all that was going well. He scowled at himself in the mirror as he thought of Lena Travers and her brother, Owen. They'd sat through that week's security briefings without even making eye contact with him. Something was definitely off with those two, but Obrador didn't know how to rid himself of the Twins without upsetting the whole Citizen Army. Chloe didn't seem to know what they were up to, although she'd agreed that they were doing their jobs as Enforcers, so he couldn't justly hold that against them. Yet, the noncompliant citizens they'd arrested recently had been particularly brutalized. The two executions Owen had performed that month—a record low—had been swift, merciless, and without emotion.

To add to Obrador's uneasiness about the Twins, Owen was also seeking to advance his reputation in new ways. He had started a new trend, requiring common citizens to bow their heads when he entered a room or when he passed by. And where Lena was concerned, the state newspaper had written a feature article about Lena, approved by Lena, stating how she was leading the Enforcers to new heights as Obrador focused on hosting the pageant. It was true, Obrador thought, but she was becoming bolder in her disloyalty. Publicly, the Twins were impacting the Federation, and not for his own honor!

Simply removing the Twins wasn't that easy, Obrador thought, as he changed into the other suit. Brother and sister had each gained much respect within the Citizen Army—so much so that Obrador wasn't sure who obeyed him for his own authority when he gave an order, and who obeyed the Twins. With Brian Steelman assumed dead, or perhaps escaped to the West again, Obrador didn't know who he could trust to offset the power the Twins seemed to wield over the Bowery.

"This is the one," he said, turning in the mirror, admiring the suit he decided to wear to the pageant in three days. And the other suit would be perfect for his wedding, one week after the pageant.

Maybe, just maybe, all this ceremony business would reestablish him before the people in ways the army couldn't do through its fierceness. Suddenly, he chuckled to himself. It was ridiculous how sentimental he'd become over the years. He blamed Chloe, but he had welcomed the change. He'd learned to care for the Federation with new eyes, gaining respect from citizens who appreciated his patience and mercy, rather than ruling by a hard line. It made him look weak with the army, but he didn't know how else to balance a ruthless reputation with a benevolent presence. Strangely, benevolence seemed to be winning out naturally. Maybe it was his old age, but he wasn't regretting the shift. After all, the Federation had never entertained as much peace as they had the last two months, inside and outside the city. That was to his credit, not of the Twins.

Obrador changed back into his casual clothes he wore around the Bowery, and walked out to his office. Chloe and the rest of his cabinet acknowledged him, but continued their discussion over pictures and files of pageant candidates. Lieutenant Isaacson was there, his muscular frame and predator-like eyes missing nothing. After the wedding, Obrador had plans for the security officer to become much more than a mere wedding planner. Since he was already an officer in the Citizen Army, Isaacson was a perfect fit for promotion, to replace the authority the Twins had usurped over time by their brutality. Maybe it was time to promote someone above colonel. General Isaacson had a ring to it.

"We've got finalists from Baltimore and Rhode Island in this column," an aide said to Chloe, pointing at a marker board. "Both come from loyal Federation families."

"I like them both," Chloe said, "but put them in that other column because neither has confirmed they'll be here in three days."

"There's this West Virginia possibility," another aide said. "She's already part of the Citizen Army, so we know she's loyal."

Obrador observed the strategy session for several minutes, trusting Chloe and Isaacson to narrow the possibilities down to one woman. He could single her out during the pageant—not because she was the most beautiful, or the most accomplished, but because she would be the best for the Federation. But maybe she would be both beautiful and accomplished. That would be icing on the cake, Obrador mused.

"Who's this one?" Obrador interrupted by pointing at one photo in the midst of candidates. "You have a red mark on her photo. Did she die or something since the regional screenings took place?"

"No, sir. She's, uh . . ." Isaacson sorted through several forms, then handed Obrador her application. "Her name's Jenna Dowler."

"She's blind, sir." An aide scoffed. "We had to open up the pageant to everyone, so she entered as well. She's one of the older candidates. Pretty, sure, but she's blind."

"Dowler?" Obrador read over Jenna's form. She played the piano, sang, and spoke several foreign languages fluently. "Wait. *Corban Dowler's daughter?* This is her, all grown up?"

"That's her, sir." Chloe shrugged. "We wanted to give her a shot at the contest, so she's been invited. I mean, she'll be at the finals, since she's a local, but we marked her picture because we weren't sure you'd want to be married to a disabled woman."

"Right." Obrador tilted his head. "But isn't that the point? She's beautiful in a natural, plain sort of way, and she's one of the common people. She's blind, so she wouldn't be a threat to my administration. She's simple, right? The people could relate to her."

"Her *CEE* results are really good," Isaacson said, checking a chart. "She's not a risk as far as compliance is concerned."

"Yeah, and we've used her father for years." Obrador imagined that face lying beside him in bed. She was a mature woman, older than the other candidates in their twenties, but she was no less attractive. "I'm not looking for a sex object, am I?"

"From a public relations perspective," Chloe said, "that candidate could be very powerful. People might at first look upon her with pity, but she's an accomplished, confident woman in her own way. Since she's well-read and educated, she could be the perfect spokesman on your behalf, Mr. Chancellor. Maybe we shouldn't have been so quick to set her aside."

"Yes, well . . ." He handed the bio back to Isaacson. "Keep looking. But put her name in the column of possibilities. Just because we now euthanize disabled babies who would be a burden on the Federation's resources doesn't mean we can't show some tolerance for those who've proven themselves to be an asset. Carry on."

Obrador felt their eyes on him as he went to his desk and sat down. He couldn't believe those words had come out of his own mouth, either! *A blind woman?* It was intriguing. He'd never need to worry about trusting her, or how he looked in front of her. She was blind, so she'd be inconsequential to his day-to-day business. She'd be like a statue. Someone so harmless appealed to him!

He decided right then that Jenna Dowler would become his wife, the winner of the pageant, but he'd allow his staff to continue doing their jobs. It was exciting to have everyone working on something so purposeful and positive! Of course, his office was only pleasant because the Twins had made themselves scarce.

But, whatever inner glow Obrador had had, disappeared at the thought of the Twins.

Owen Travers knew his life had changed for the better, and it had all started with his sister giving him Radiant Shade to turn in. He would never forget that Radiant Shade had redeemed his reputation. One minute, he was Obrador's object of scoffing among the Enforcers, and the next minute, Obrador's belittling comments had ceased. Now, everyone in the Army took him more seriously. To say he'd monopolized his newfound prestige would be an understatement.

He walked from the barracks building below the Bowery to the roadblock on Broadway. As he passed on or off-duty Federation personnel, everyone either saluted or bowed their head to him. Bounty hunters and Enforcers on special assignments weren't regular army, so to receive recognition from all classes was a serious boost to his status in the capital city.

The respect had started a month earlier, not just with the Radiant Shade capture. He'd caught a noncompliant trying to cross the Hudson by raft in the night. The man had had no identification, but he'd had plenty of Bibles in the raft with him. Since Bibles were considered Federation contraband due to the prejudice in its pages against other people's gods, Owen knew he could treat the criminal any way he chose. None of the soldiers with him that night would interfere if he wanted to have a little fun.

Owen had tied the man at the waist to a light pole, and began to mock the smuggler about his beliefs.

"If your God is better than my god," Owen had challenged, "don't bow down to me and my god."

Then, Owen had begun to beat the man.

"If our gods are the same," Owen had yelled, "then bow down to me. Bow, bow to me! Come on! At least, just bow your head to me."

The men with him that night had laughed for the first few minutes as Owen had punched the man in the gut, trying to get him to bend at the waist. But after an hour, the laughter had stopped, and Owen had become frustrated. The man was resilient, and Owen commenced to breaking the criminal's legs. Still, the man persisted in standing up straight, though he wept openly in his misery. Finally, Owen had shot him with his sidearm, and the man had finally bowed in death against the binds that held him to the pole.

Although Owen had only been flexing his Enforcer muscle that night, word had gotten around, and within a couple of days, civilians and soldiers alike were bowing their heads to him.

The city was his, he thought as he reached the gate outside the Bowery. Foot traffic was moving past or into the capital building's perimeter. It took a small army to keep those in the barracks and the Bowery fed and supplied.

Owen considered the changes his sister had assured him were coming in a few days. Lena was planning something big. Maybe the Bowery itself was to be removed, and Chancellor Obrador with it. They had enough explosives in the armory to topple the whole block. But Owen guessed Lena was after something more sinister than a mere assassination. She'd taken it personally that Obrador was carrying on about the wedding so much—and dragging the whole Federation along for the pitiful ceremony.

But Owen wasn't complaining about his sister or the wedding. He was enjoying himself too much to contradict his sister's plans. He was doing just fine riding on her coattails for now, although he wasn't going to miss a slice of wedding cake if he could get a piece. The chancellor had never been particularly nice to him, but Owen didn't have anything truly against the man. How could he? Obrador had built the Federation from the ground up, fighting and winning control against coastal factions until he could establish himself as chancellor. Governors, mayors, and military commanders had fallen into line, thankful for some peace and order across the land, so Owen couldn't fault the guy for all he'd done. But he wasn't going to stand up for him as long as his sister was around. In fact, he didn't know anyone who would stand against his sister. It simply wasn't profitable for one's health to stand against Lena Travers!

A crowd of infantry soldiers saluted and acknowledged Owen, causing him to stand taller. The snow had melted across the city, and the spring warmth was on its way. Whatever Lena was planning, at least none of it would be in the cold of winter.

Then he saw him. Corban Dowler was walking toward him, leaning heavily on his cane. Owen hadn't seen the old printer in weeks, and he hadn't forgotten what had happened to him when he'd routinely followed Dowler over two months earlier. The man had to have been responsible! And now that he thought about it, Steelman had disappeared not long after Owen had asked him to look into Dowler's printing operation.

The people in front of Dowler saluted or bowed their head to Owen, and then Dowler was standing in front of him.

"Good morning, Mr. Travers." Dowler patted the satchel on his hip. "Administrative delivery."

Owen wasn't much taller than Dowler, but he felt several feet taller now. This man was nothing, so weak, needing a cane to walk. Such people were a burden on society, and they were being considered by the legislatures for special "housing" to spare relatives and the city from rationing obligations. Doing away with the elderly was beginning to be considered a mercy, since they lacked a quality of life. They contributed little to society, it was argued. Men like Dowler needed to be replaced by stronger, more productive citizens.

And more respectful. Dowler still hadn't bowed to him!

"Are you too old or too stupid to know who I am, Dowler?" Owen glanced around him, wondering who was about to witness him making an example of someone else. "I'm Owen Travers."

"Yes, good morning." Dowler smiled and tapped his cane on the asphalt. "I called you Mr. Travers a moment ago, remember? You're one of the Enforcers who keeps me constantly updating my citizen ledgers. Every time you kill someone, young man, it gives us all more paperwork to do."

"Is that so, old man?" Owen raised his voice, drawing more people. "If the work is too hard for you, why don't you pass it off to someone younger? What are you complaining for, anyway? Would you rather let noncompliant citizens rot the Federation from the inside?"

"What rots the Federation isn't noncompliance but arrogance, particularly yours."

"Is that so?" Owen stepped up to Dowler, close enough to notice that Dowler didn't reek like most of the unwashed men in the city. "I could have you arrested for that kind of talk. Look here, everyone. Old Man Dowler thinks he knows what's best for the Federation."

Citizens within hearing range hustled away from the gate, but the soldiers nearby moved closer, surrounding the two men, just the way Owen wanted it. Except Owen was disappointed to see amusement on the aged fool's face rather than fear from intimidation. Sure, Dowler was Obrador's pet, but Owen had worked for years to gain the respect he deserved, and no one was going to take that away from him!

"What do you hope to achieve by this, young man?" Dowler asked. "I'm no one important."

"That's right. You're nothing, Dowler. That's why you acknowledge your superiors. Do you know what I did to the last fool who disrespected the Federation?"

"First, you'd have to prove how I have disrespected the Federation when I've simply acknowledged you as the arrogant, young man that you are. We all know the story of how you tortured someone, Mr. Travers." Corban waved one of his arms, clearly familiar with speaking to a crowd. "But I heard another story about you. I heard that you faint at the sight of your own blood."

"*What?*" Travers was so shocked by the ridiculous idea, he laughed in Dowler's face. "I've seen my own blood before. Trust me, I've never fainted at the sight of it!"

"Prove it." Dowler's eyes were bright, full of motive, but Owen couldn't figure out what motive that was.

"I don't have to prove anything to you. I don't faint at the sight of my blood, or of anyone else's blood."

"Then stand there without fainting," Dowler dared. "Someone give Mr. Travers here a sharp knife. Just a little cut, my friend. There, on your arm. And hold it up high so we can all see how and why you faint."

"Oh, I've got to see this!" one soldier said, and offered his blade from his belt.

"I have my own!" Owen slapped the soldier's hand away. He noticed that more than fifty people had gathered now, and somehow, the whole situation had been removed from his control. "I don't want to catch any diseases from your knife!"

Owen slid his own blade from its sheath, and tested its edge on his thumb. He'd sharpened it recently, and contemplated drawing some of Dowler's blood first.

Dowler was smiling, thinking he had him cornered, but Owen didn't understand Dowler's angle. If Lena had been there, she may have been able to tell him what Dowler was up to, but Owen felt like he had to see the challenge through. What was the harm? It was just a little blood.

"Lift it up high, Mr. Travers," Dowler said, helping Owen lift his arm above his head. The press of bodies alone kept Owen and Dowler close together. "We all want to see you faint at the sight of your own blood. This is it."

"This is stupid!" Owen cursed and used his knife edge to cut a thin line on the back of his forearm. "I don't know what the point of all this is."

Owen held his knife aside as a trickle of blood oozed from the cut. At that instant, when everyone leaned closer to see his arm, Owen felt a sharp jab on the top of his boot. He looked down to see that Dowler had just jammed the end of his cane onto his foot.

An instant later, Owen blacked out.

Corban moved out of the crowd as it roared with laughter. This was the second time he'd tranquilized Owen Travers. The aggressive Enforcer was bound to be furious when he woke, as soon as his Citizen Army companions told him what had happened. He would need to be told since Corban had been mixing a cocktail with the cane tranquilizer, and that blurred a subject's short-term memory.

From inside the gated complex of the Bowery, Corban stopped and looked back at the crowd at the gate. Owen had fallen too easily into the trap, but he'd asked for it, spoiling for a fight. While everyone, including Owen himself, had been focused on Owen's raised arm and bleeding cut, Corban had used his cane to tranq the brute in his foot. There would be repercussions, Corban guessed, but he wasn't counting on Owen's response to be greater than what God was doing in the city. God would somehow prevail, regardless of Owen's forthcoming anger about what had happened.

At the shift desk in the lobby of the hotel, Corban was met by Chen Li, her uniform perfectly pressed, and her face as stern as her reputation demanded. She opened the satchel Corban handed her and drew out several departmental envelopes. One was for Chen Li's Citizen Processing, and another for Chloe in the upstairs administration rooms.

"This is it?" she asked, making no eye contact. A clerk sat at a desk nearby, reading a Mora B. Leever poetry book, but he could have been listening. "Did you get the ID renovations after last week's executions?"

"It's in the file." Corban's heart felt particularly heavy that day for Chen Li. They'd lost Heather Putelli, and they couldn't even talk about it. "The list is marked and dated."

With Chen Li, it was Federation business as usual, which was important for their cover. But Corban yearned for a time when he could speak openly with the operatives who'd been just junior agents when they'd joined COIL. They'd been willing to follow his lead into the jaws of death, if necessary. Yes, they were his children, and he was proud of their sacrifices. He wanted to embrace them and give them the credit they deserved.

"I'll get this one upstairs." Chen Li tucked Chloe's envelope under her arm. Suddenly, she looked up into his face. "I heard your daughter is one of the finalists in the pageant."

"Yes, she's grateful for the opportunity." Corban turned his back a little to the nearby clerk. "I have three days to figure out how to put makeup on her face, since the woman who was doing it has graduated to other things."

They both smiled. He'd said that for her, knowing she'd know he meant Heather had gone on to heaven. And he was indeed joking since he'd been applying makeup and disguises to his and others' faces for years.

"Less is more, in this case," Chen Li said. "Not too much. Don't take from her natural beauty."

"Noted."

"In fact, I can have a car sent for her the morning of the event, and I can help her get ready. Would that be okay?"

"That would be wonderful." Corban tapped his cane on the lobby carpet, which desperately needed a cleaning. "We'll be watching for that car, ma'am. Thank you for your time. Have a nice day."

"You, too. We're all pulling for your daughter."

Corban understood the veiled message. Operation Esther only succeeded if Jenna indeed won the pageant. With Chloe and Nathan in charge of Obrador's "best interests," the fix was set.

On his way out of the hotel, several soldiers in discussion passed by him.

"I'm telling you," one was saying, "he fainted the instant he saw his own blood!"

"But, it was Owen Travers," the other said. "He's seen more blood than ten of us combined!"

"Some people just have weak stomachs, I guess, but I know what I saw!"

Now Corban wondered if perhaps he should've handled Owen in a different way since he'd clearly demoralized the man among his own troops. But maybe that was the whole point. Even for Owen, there was hope—as Corban was holding out hope and praying for Brian Steelman. Some men needed to be humbled so they would realize their need for a Savior.

As Corban hobbled slowly back toward Times Square and his old COIL offices, he prayed for Owen, for a spiritual breakthrough in a city where so little of Christ even existed. Corban prayed for a miracle where Owen's heart was concerned. And that prayer included Lena.

Brian Steelman heard the ceiling crack like thunder an instant before the tunnel collapsed on him and Willie. Chunks of cement, lengths of rebar, and icy water cascaded down on their heads and shoulders. Being knocked down, Brian held his breath as he waited for death. The dust settled, and blood from his head ran into his face. The echo of the tunnel collapse continued to bounce off distant cement walls. It seemed the whole underground system was imploding. Somehow, his headlamp was still shining.

The weight on his back and legs felt too heavy to throw off, but as soon as he was able to breathe again, he forcibly rolled to his side, and the hundred pounds of debris that had settled on him slid off. If he would've been crushed, he would've died just now, he reasoned, and that terror brought to mind all the discussions he'd had with Doc Joss and Scooter about life after death. Brian had often dismissed what Doc said since he was an outspoken preacher in the resistance tunnel. But Scooter was no less knowledgeable of the Scriptures, though he didn't seem to let people know of his faithfulness to God. Since Scooter was intent on keeping up his "Bandit" facade, Brian had respected his cover, but they'd still spoken of spiritual matters when alone.

Until that very moment, when death seemed so close, Brian hadn't grasped the necessity, or even the urgency, to place his faith in the God of the Bible, to enter by God's grace into the kingdom of heaven, and have all of his sins forgiven. The idea of "being saved" had seemed like a philosophical topic he'd discussed with the others to pass the time in the tunnels. Merely recognizing that God was real seemed to be enough to give him a pleasant pass into eternity. However, lying in the rubble of a subway tunnel under 145th Street, he realized he still feared death, judgement, and a certain eternity. He knew such fear meant he hadn't yet placed his confidence in a just God who was merciful to those who trusted in His Son for forgiveness. And Brian knew he needed to take God's side against sin and Satan, as Doc had talked about.

"Please save me, God!" Brian cried out, though it was no more than a gasp as he choked on the dust in the air.

From what Scooter had told him, sincere and desperate faith for Jesus Christ to save was the simple entrance into God's loving arms. At that moment, Brian thought he still might not make it alive out of the collapsed tunnel, so his prayer of faith was for both his physical as well as his spiritual condition. He needed God, and he'd heard enough from the Bible the last two months to know how God viewed him as a lost sinner without any hope of new life except through Jesus Christ. Hell terrified him more than dying in that tunnel, though he still didn't want to die in the tunnel!

When Brian shook his head, pieces of earth, asbestos, and concrete tumbled out of his hair. New York's infrastructure was falling apart. Its roads and buildings above, now decades old, were crumbling at their foundations.

"I'm okay." He coughed, then laughed at himself, realizing he meant it again both physically and spiritually. According to the truth he knew from hearing God's Scriptures, he really was okay with God now! He'd trusted in His forgiveness from sins to be made righteous. And he was okay physically. Though bruised, he felt no broken bones. "Willie? Willie? You still alive?"

He shoved on a leaning concrete slab, and it tumbled and cracked. The ceiling groaned. Brian held his hands over his head, expecting more rubble from above, but there was only more dust and water, then all was still again. Several minutes passed before he figured out where Willie was, even though Brian knew the veteran tunnel man had been behind him only a few paces. The man had been allowing Brian a chance to lead through the maze of tunnels, shafts, and corridors that the resistance had been utilizing.

After uncovering Willie, he felt for a pulse, but there was none. Willie was a burly man, but a chunk of concrete had crushed his skull. If that wasn't enough to kill the man, his torso had been pierced by twisted rebar connected to pieces of cement. The backpack Willie had worn had been torn, protecting him very little in the tragedy. It had been Willie's time to go.

Brian shined his headlamp up at the ceiling, then up and down the tunnel. After two months living below ground, he wasn't as afraid of being trapped without light as he'd been that first day. He didn't have the Vags' confidence in the tunnels, but he'd learned a few measures of how to reach safety if he did lose his flashlight. For one, he knew to always carry a second battery as well as a backup flashlight or headlamp. And two, with no light whatsoever, he knew he could follow the left or right wall of a respective tunnel to continue moving, eventually finding a haven.

But there was no use in continuing his journey north, Brian thought. Their supply run for a stash of light bulbs in Harlem for Doc was now cut short.

With care, Brian freed Willie's heavy body from the concrete, then dragged him down the tunnel where the ceiling was still intact. He kicked several rats aside, then sat down to rest. Touching his jaw, he felt like he'd been punched by a night club bouncer. Maybe a piece of debris had struck his face during the collapse, but it didn't seem to be broken, just sore.

To conserve battery power, he turned off his headlamp. He was no more than a half-mile from the resistance habitat, so he wasn't too worried about finding his way back. Exploring the tunnels with the Vags or Willie or Scooter had consumed much of his time the last few weeks, but this was the first time he'd been alone down there. He sensed that Scooter didn't quite trust his loyalties yet, because Scooter had always made sure Brian had someone with him when he went out.

Now alone, though, Brian thought about the surface, where he could see the sky and stars, where he could breathe fresh air, where his skin wouldn't feel the nibble of rats or the trickle of filthy water. And what of the Federation those days? All resistance efforts had been suspended. The Vags would've been complaining to Scooter about their inactivity, except he kept them busy with other missions: coded graffiti missions on the surface, and supply runs. A couple older Vags, with Hedgehog, had even ventured into Brooklyn to explore habitable tunnels for possible relocation or expansion for future needs.

Two months had passed, and there was still no sign of the Serval. The way Luigi and Scooter spoke of him, he was like some sort of legendary phantom who'd traveled the world and defied authorities. It was told that he had a mouthy wit, and when heard, no matter the situation, it was difficult to keep a straight face. Having met the Serval, Brian recalled the man's confidence, but he also knew the person Scooter and Luigi remembered was the father of the man Brian had met in Arizona. Maybe the younger Serval wasn't all that they hoped he was. Maybe Enforcers outside the city had already captured and killed him, along with his one-armed companion.

It was possible the Serval would never reach New York City. The thought caused him to revisit his original plans to head west on his own. Especially now that he'd gotten Willie killed! The resistance wouldn't be happy with him about this. Willie was one of the most beloved Vags, one of the originals.

He swept his hand in the dark, scattering rats already sniffing at Willie's lifeless body. Willie had been his friend as well, a good companion and jokester. But Brian knew that since he was still the new guy in the tunnels, the Vags' loyalties to Willie would be stronger than their tolerance of Brian being with Willie when he'd died.

Leaving the tunnels and fleeing the city wouldn't be hard. He'd done it once, though he'd had a rifle then. There weren't many rifles within the resistance, but Brian guessed he could jump a soldier on the surface and steal a rifle and supplies, then start west on foot.

But oddly, such a thought didn't appeal to him. Even at the expense of himself, he realized he couldn't leave Willie there, and he couldn't leave the resistance in the dark about what had happened. Something inside him had changed, and it wasn't the tunnel collapse, either. It was his moment of faith after the collapse. That moment had changed everything, and it concerned him that he wanted to tell Doc and Scooter about it more than he wanted to run away from facing the Vags. How could his spiritual joy be greater than his concern for his physical safety? It fascinated him. He was a new man. He'd been reborn. Was this what made Scooter different? Like the Serval had been different?

Although he'd served Obrador for years, he'd never felt the chancellor actually cared for him. Not like Scooter and Corban Dowler did. They wanted what was best for him, but he wasn't sure the Vags would care for him after learning of the death of one of their own. But he couldn't run. At least, not yet. He had to take Willie back to his people, and if that meant facing the disdain of the Vags, then so be it. There would be time to run, if necessary. Could he trust God to direct him through all of that as well?

Chapter Ten

Owen Travers flinched at the sting of his sister's slap. She'd just barged into his room in the Bowery.

"You're an embarrassment to us both!" she hissed, shaking her head at him.

He was afraid others could hear her voice through the walls, but Lena didn't seem to care.

"I've never fainted from the sight of my own blood." Owen studied his arm, trying to piece together what he could remember along with what others had told him had happened—while they'd laughed at him. "I raised my arm up like this, then I guess I passed out. It had to have been a trick. Dowler must have—"

"Dowler's an old man!" she spat, raising her hand to slap him again. "How could you? He's nothing! What are you, a child?"

Owen turned away from her, not because he was afraid of her hand, but because he didn't want her to tease him further for the tears forming in his eyes. He was so angry. So ashamed. So humiliated. Intimidating people to bow down to him seemed so ridiculous in retrospect, especially now that he was the laughingstock of the Bowery.

"You're ruining everything," Lena said more quietly. "We're a week away from the greatest moment of our lives, and you're out cutting yourself and passing out because people won't bow to you on the streets? Seriously—*cutting yourself?*"

Owen wiped his eyes and spun toward her.

"Maybe if you told me what you're planning, I'd be able to live up to your expectations!"

"Keep your voice down." She touched his face gently where she'd struck him. "We've been through so much together, surviving. Look at us now. Not even Obrador has the influence in the city that we do. Just promise me you'll stay around the Bowery for the next week."

"No, I'm going to kill Dowler!" He held up his arm. There was a piece of medical tape covering where he'd cut himself. "He's responsible for this! I owe it to myself to put him down!"

"No! Not now. Not like this. Don't do anything for a week. Just stay in the hotel, go to briefings, and let Obrador and Chloe think everything is just fine."

"But it's not?" He smiled, feeling the devil rise inside him. "You're really making a move?"

"Oh, I'm definitely making a move." She stepped back and crossed her arms. "So, can you promise me? You'll stay around here until the wedding? Make nice with the help? Just stay off the streets."

"Fine. I promise." He thrust his finger toward her. "But when it's time, Dowler is mine."

"Yes, Dowler's all yours, Owen, along with all the other pets Obrador has kept in the city—if Dowler doesn't die first of old age."

When Lena left, Owen took a hot shower, trying to wash away the embarrassment. He'd been unconscious, he'd been told, when everyone had been laughing at him. But he could imagine their laughter, so it was as if he could remember it himself—just lying there defenseless on the street as everyone mocked him. What cruelty! *How humiliating!*

How could he ever come back from this? He wanted to strike back. Everything was made worse by the way Lena treated him, not believing he'd been tricked. A week inside the hotel? Everyone would think he was hiding! How he loathed their snickers even now, thinking about what it would be like at the next security briefing. Obrador might even say something.

When he stepped out of the shower, he felt somewhat refreshed. That was the difference between living as an officer in the Bowery, and living in the barracks. He had hot water and they didn't. They were nothing!

As he got dressed, he noticed someone had slid an envelope under his door. He opened and read it. Obrador was inviting him to a banquet in the ballroom downstairs. Of course, it was Chloe who'd probably put him on the list, and Corban had surely printed the invitations, but still— he was invited to a state dinner! How many of those who'd laughed at him that day could say they were invited to the banquet being held after the pageant in three days?

Maybe he was being too sensitive about the fainting. Maybe he had diabetes and he had nothing to be ashamed of. If he was important enough to be invited to a state dinner, then he was important enough to shut the mouths of anyone who laughed at him from now on. Hadn't he always exerted force against noncompliant citizens? Obrador had never held him back from that. Maybe the chancellor would also approve of him punishing anyone who laughed at or bullied him. After all, he was an important state official. And state officials couldn't be laughed at!

Regardless of what Lena was planning, Owen took pride in the banquet invitation. Obrador had first recognized his talent as an Enforcer. It couldn't hurt to enjoy this occasion held in the man's honor. Killing Corban Dowler could wait. He'd find a way, with or without his sister's approval.

✝

Luigi Putelli stared up at the tunnel ceiling of pockmarked cement. Dusty light bulbs and wires spanned the distance from side to side and the whole length of the habitat, but he'd purposely unscrewed two light bulbs directly above his shelter. He preferred dim lighting.

Weariness had settled in his body, exhaustion like he'd never known. No, it was deeper than just his body—his soul was tired. Heather had been gone for two months. The only woman he'd ever loved was gone, and she'd taken something of him with her. They'd had a pleasant marriage, exciting and filled with adventure working together within COIL. He tried to focus on those years of abundance rather than the void he now felt.

For so many years, he'd loved the isolation in the shadows—lurking, guarding, protecting. Now, when he needed the company of another to comfort him, there was no one. Heather was gone. Corban was out of reach. Nathan was off-limits. And Scooter, although nearby in the tunnel, had a reputation as the Bandit to maintain.

He rolled onto his side and gazed down at the tunnel the resistance had nearly abandoned two months earlier. Heather would never have voluntarily revealed the location of the habitat, but Luigi had heard the people's mumbled disdain for her regardless. Those who'd been born in the tunnel, who'd been raised by Heather inside those very oval walls, had spoken of her as a traitor, simply because she'd been captured. It was hard for him to forget their sighs of relief when word had come down that she'd died. But he understood they were safer without one of their own in the hands of the Federation, even though the Federation was still claiming that she, as Radiant Shade, was a guest at the hotel.

Below, on the tunnel floor near the barrier, the Vags hung out on the tires, waiting for the Bandit to announce another supply run or surface mission. There was anticipation in the air. The Bandit had explained just enough of their plans against the Federation that those zealous against Obrador understood why they couldn't make additional raids or sabotage missions just now. A plan was unfolding above, and it might mean they could all return to the surface!

Luigi had heard the complaining of the Vags about such a prospect. Hedgehog, who preferred the anarchy of America's collapse, had led the complaining. Most of the Vags had been born below, so a life in the city was no pleasant prospect. In the tunnels, the weather never changed, and there was no evil dictator with an army of killers. The surface spelled danger, whereas the tunnels suggested safety. But even with all its drawbacks, Luigi thought, the surface for him was many times better than living underground. Heather had been patient, trusting him to one day lead them all back to the surface. She'd died just weeks before it had become a more serious possibility.

Sitting upright, Luigi felt aches all over his body from years of hard living. But he wouldn't trade a single scar, not if it meant giving up the memory of serving God under Corban Dowler. That's what was missing in the resistance, Luigi thought—true love under a benevolent leadership. Scooter, of course, had tried to establish just enough camaraderie within the resistance. He wasn't trying to build up the force, only maintain what Jenna believed needed to be in place to draw Federation attention away from the Christians. A distracted, desperate Federation had created holes in its administration, and COIL had inserted itself accordingly.

But a Christian leader's presence had been missing in the tunnel. Luigi knew if Scooter could've lived his faith more openly, he could've actively complimented Doc Joss's preaching efforts, which fell largely on deaf ears. Doc was tolerated, but was seen more as a superstitious nut who kept their batteries powered and their hot pots wired.

The bell at the barrier chimed, and everyone inside the tunnel hushed themselves. All eyes turned toward the door. A few small teams were outside, making normal scrounging runs, or spraying misinformation graffiti words to keep the surface Enforcers scratching their heads. Every time the barrier door opened, someone could be returning with news of danger, or with new riches with which to offer the community a better life. No day was ever the same in the tunnels.

Instead, Brian Steelman shuffled in, carrying the limp form of Willie over his shoulder. Cries erupted all over the tunnel, even though silence was usually enforced when the barrier door was open. They cried out in dismay because Willie's body was obviously bloodied and hanging as only a corpse would hang.

Several older Vags rushed forward with Hedgehog and took Willie in their arms, then lowered him gently to the tunnel floor. Luigi watched as people crowded around Willie, kneeling next to him. Brian was intentionally pushed away by two Vags, as if they didn't want him near one of their family members. With Hedgehog, Willie had led the Vags for the Bandit for more years than some of the Vags had been alive. In their eyes, Brian was still an outsider, and some rumors had circulated about Brian being a Federation spy. Only Luigi and Scooter knew the truth of those assumptions, although they'd all utilized Brian for various tunnel missions.

But everything was changing, Luigi realized. If the resistance was no longer necessary to protect the Christian underground that was already close to success on the surface, then the caution the COIL operatives took to keep their faith quiet was no longer necessary, either. He and Scooter could live their Christianity in a more visible sense, not holding to a cover meant to disrupt the Federation's current agenda.

As Luigi climbed out of his shelter, he heard the Vags, and Hedgehog himself, shouting at Brian. Their frustration was escalating because one of their own had died.

"What did you do to him? How could you return him like this? This is your fault!"

Luigi walked up the tunnel to the gathering crowd as Brian was further ridiculed. There was shoving, and someone threw a punch, which landed on the big man's ear. Scooter was there, but he didn't seem to know how to settle the mob and find out what had happened. Although Scooter was a reliable operative, Luigi knew he was no Corban Dowler or Nathan Isaacson, Steve Brookshire or Titus Caspertein. After years of living in the shadows, Luigi saw his moment, this moment, to use his reputation for God's purposes. Corban had done this type of thing, and Titus would've used his wit to calm everyone. Now Luigi had to think of something!

He pushed his way through the jostling to reach Willie's body. Seen up close, the injuries and remnants of dust on the dead man's body showed that the two men had been in a tunnel collapse. Even Brian's appearance told the same story—he was torn and bloodied. Although the ex-Enforcer hadn't needed to return Willie to the resistance, he'd brought him back anyway.

"Settle down!" Scooter yelled.

But the mob pressed forward until Brian was pinned against the outer barrier. Angry curses flew, and gnarled fists struck. Luigi reached Brian as he was pummeled to the ground. Several booted feet were kicking at the newcomer, and twice, Luigi himself was struck, but he further shielded Brian with his own body as he knelt over him. He contemplated drawing his belt and swinging it, with its tranquilizer shards to incapacitate some in the crowd. Instead, he more fully embraced Brian, holding him close, while he gave the crowd his back to be bruised. Although Brian was one of the largest men in the tunnel, he was no match for the dozens who wished to brutalize him. And yet, those dozens were no match against the embrace that sheltered Brian. After all, no one really wanted to harm Luigi, the Bandit's closest confidant.

Slowly, Luigi eased off Brian as the crowd and blows settled down. He rose to stand above the ex-Enforcer, and faced the crowd as they stilled themselves. Their faces were no longer full of fury, but of shock. They'd never before seen him insert himself into tunnel meetings, politics, or controversies. Usually, he was the one who came to the tunnel and spoke privately to the Bandit, never publicly, and then Luigi had made himself scarce from the resistance operations, staying back with Heather. But Heather was gone, and Luigi couldn't make himself scarce any longer.

"Bandit," Luigi called to the shorter man, who was closer to where Willie lay, "call an assembly right now, and instruct everyone to sit down where they stand."

Eyebrows raised and heads turned to Scooter. *Did the Bandit take orders from Luigi?*

Luigi didn't care if anyone thought he was acting out of place by telling the Bandit what to do. Since Luigi had known Scooter for many years, and as a brother in Christ, Luigi knew Scooter would do what was right when asked. Besides, it was Luigi's responsibility to ask, since he alone had brought Brian to the tunnel, in agreement with Corban. He was his brother's keeper.

"Everyone, sit down," Scooter stated, his voice calm, though authoritative. "Go ahead, Luigi. It's okay. Speak. We're all listening."

Luigi took his stand on one side of the gathering, and placed his hands on his hips, as he'd seen Titus do in similar situations. Then, he considered what Corban would say for God.

"I've lived among you for many years," he stated, "but very few of you know me. I'm old now, but I can still race you through any tunnel or survive on the surface without difficulty. Many of you left the world above, and some of you have known only this tunnel environment. But I've known many environments, and I've traveled to many countries of the world. And I can tell you that the world is much bigger than the subway system you know here. What God intends for you is much more important than you living from day to day off a stockpile of food supplies and clothes from another era.

"Today, you've lost a friend. Willie has been with us for a generation, and he had a way of talking that made some of us wonder what kind of place Minnesota must be. Every time Willie went on raids, the team with him, they always heard stories about the lakes of Minnesota. Willie was a friend to us all."

He paused as a murmur of agreement rippled through the crowd. Even Brian was sitting up now, battered but alert.

"Many of you have complained about the unjust treatment the Federation gives people on the surface. What's unjust treatment? It's drawing hasty conclusions before the matter is seen from both sides. Just treatment means weighing the situation and praying for God's wisdom to discern an answer that builds instead of tears down. And what you've hated about the Federation in the past, you yourselves have done today against Brian—a man I've brought into this place for safety and protection from hostility. Who dares assault a man who's come here for protection?"

"He killed Willie!" Hedgehog yelled out, and others agreed.

"Don't be ridiculous!" Luigi glared at the Vag elder. "Willie and Brian were friends. A quick look at them shows they've been through a tunnel collapse. If Brian had killed Willie, he wouldn't have brought Willie back here, where he knew he could be accused of something nefarious. But he did bring him back, because he knew you loved Willie. So, how will we honor Willie's good name? By injuring the man who was with Willie when he died? Willie trusted Brian to be at his side. Who here won't listen to Brian's explanation right now?"

"He's one of them!" another Vag shouted. "I can smell an Enforcer from two tunnels away, Luigi!"

"Brian?" Luigi called. "Are you able to stand? Tell us what happened."

With Doc's support, Brian stood in the midst of the gathering. Luigi knew the newcomer to be a man of great physical strength, but in that moment, so weakened by both physical assaults and the tunnel collapse, he appeared frail and humble.

"Willie and I were running north about a half-mile from here, on a mission for Doc, when the tunnel collapsed on us both. I was in the lead, since Willie wanted me to practice scouting ahead. Then the ceiling fell on us. As soon as I freed myself, I went and found Willie, but he'd already died. You can see that his body was torn and his skull was smashed in. So, I carried him back here to you."

"There you have it." Luigi pointed at Brian. "It was all an accident."

"But he's an Enforcer!" Hedgehog stated, his blond hair greasy and his teeth bared. "I remember him from a surface parade. I never forget a face. It's him. Obrador used to call him Steelman!"

Luigi met Scooter's eyes, and by the resistance leader's expression, Scooter clearly wasn't comfortable about where this was going. People who weren't Christians couldn't be expected to grasp the compassion of Christ necessary to love a man who'd done so much wrong, as Brian had done.

"I was an Enforcer." Brian admitted. He seemed to be standing taller. "I've never lied to you about my past, but I've kept it quiet because I left the Federation two years ago. The chancellor is looking for me because I've refused to do what he wants. I'm not proud of what I did back then. But I'm a changed man now. I really am. And I want to tell you what happened when—"

"You don't belong here!" Hedgehog shouted, and others cheered their approval. "We should do to you what the Enforcers did to our families!"

Reading the crowd's rising unrest, Luigi made a calculation. In a few days, the pageant would take place. In another week, the wedding would occur. The resistance had served its purpose. If the consensus was against Brian, then Luigi preferred to side with a minority who asked for grace rather than a mob who demanded an irrational response.

"Quiet now. Quiet!" Luigi called. "You've spoken your outrage clearly enough. But hear this: we've fought to change the hearts of evil men for so long, now that you have before you someone who's changed, you want to keep fighting? I don't want to be a part of a resistance that has no vision for an end to the struggle. If Brian Steelman leaves, I leave!"

"Bandit!" a Vag yelled. "We don't need either of them, do we? Away with Luigi! Away with Brian!"

Scooter raised his hand for calm, and the crowd responded and silenced itself. This was their great leader about to speak, and Luigi hoped he chose his words wisely.

"We have worked together for many years, my friends," Scooter said. "In this moment of testing, are you choosing hatred over mercy? Brian Steelman has run with us for the last two months, showing his heart isn't with the Federation's evil ways any longer. Like him, you all have your own sordid pasts. We can give him a chance, can't we? Doc, what do you say?"

But Doc couldn't speak over the shouts for justice, and their desires to do to Brian Steelman what he'd done to others.

An open can of liquid was hurled over the heads of the resistance congregation, and struck Luigi on the side of the head, cutting his temple and soaking his shoulder. It had come from Hedgehog's direction. After that, the crowd was back on their feet, moving once again to assault Brian. Rage twisted their faces. Fury blinded them as they balled their fists and gnashed their teeth.

Noticing that Scooter shoved Brian toward the barrier gate, Luigi knew what he had to do. He whipped off his belt and swung the buckle end at the surging mass of rage. Two Vags were slashed across their upper arms by the shards on the buckle, which were coated with falaco, a tranquilizing toxin Luigi had used since his early days as a spy in Italy.

Knives were drawn and pointed at Luigi as he swung the belt overhead, whipping it at them. He didn't mind the shift of their anger toward him, since it gave Scooter and Brian a chance to push through the fray toward the door.

Luigi tranquilized three more as he backed up toward the barrier door. The two who actually held firearms had retreated from the crowd as well, since their job was to guard against outside enemies, not civil issues inside the tunnel. But Luigi knew it was just a matter of time before one of the Vags got their hands on a gun. Then, Brian would be finished—along with whoever stood with him.

Scooter reached the first counterweight for the barrier to be levered open, and Brian lunged for the other. Luigi tried to protect them as the door rolled open, but now he was wading through the press of bodies that were unsuccessfully trying to punch and kick him. Their own numbers hindered their intentions, and only by some miracle was he not stabbed, since he could no longer openly swing his belt at them. By their force and not his own, he was moved backward toward the door.

"Save yourselves!" Luigi managed to order Scooter.

The next moment, the back of his shirt was tugged so violently toward the barrier door that Luigi gagged against his collar. Instantly, he was in the channel of the door, being dragged backwards by Brian's superior strength. The crowd tried to fit through the bottleneck of the narrow door, but their offensive was checked as they trampled one another.

Clinging to one another, Luigi, Scooter, and Brian staggered into the darkness of the tunnel, through trash and puddles, stumbling in their departure as they put distance between them and the mob. But no one had lights or headlamps—neither Luigi nor the horde—so the chase was cut short, and Scooter called a halt against a damp cement wall as they caught their breaths.

Far back down the corridor, the resistance fighters backed into the barrier door, and the door was closed. Any light was cut off. Rats squeaked around Luigi's feet. Brian fidgeted next to him, but Luigi was too busy fitting his belt back onto his waist, and thinking about Corban and Jenna, to care about Brian's dread of the dark.

"They've completely lost it!" Scooter said. "We left everything back there. We have nothing—no clothes, no light. Luigi?"

"We need nothing from them." Luigi steadied his voice, putting the past moments into perspective. "God has always provided for us in this city. Right now, we need to move away from the resistance. The Vags are angry enough to come after us, but I'm not interested in permanently hurting them to save ourselves."

"We can't just leave them," Scooter said softly. "Their anger isn't even rational."

"Yet it's no less real." Luigi realized that Scooter had been a good soldier for so many years because he'd always followed careful orders. Being the Bandit had simply been one of those orders. But in this moment, when there were no orders, he was left unguided. "We used the resistance to disrupt the Federation long enough. We channeled the Vags' unrest against Obrador in a useful way. Now, we need to let them run their own course."

"There are Christians still back there, Luigi!" Scooter pressed. "Doc is still in there!"

"And he'll take care of them. We can't stay any longer. We're needed elsewhere."

"How can we outrun the Vags without light?" Brian asked. "I've heard the Vags who were born down here learned to make their way in these tunnels without any light, but how will we know where we're going?"

"Who do you think taught the Vags?" Luigi took Brian's hand and placed it on his own shoulder. "Scooter, you ready to move? We're headed to Midtown."

"Lead away, Luigi." Scooter's voice sounded gentle, though defeated. His days as the Bandit were finally over.

Luigi stepped carefully ahead, recalling the map of the tunnels he'd used for nearly twenty years to evade Enforcers and to tend to Jenna's schemes for COIL. The Lord had brought them so far. The darkness of the tunnels couldn't be the obstacle that made them stumble now!

At the first intersection, Luigi tore off a piece of his shirt and threw it to the right, then led his two companions to the left. To lose their trail to the Vags, they would need to zigzag their way gradually southward, but it would take them hours. He prayed Brian had the stamina to continue after all he'd been through.

Whatever had happened within the resistance that day, Luigi was determined not to let it interfere with Operation Esther. The resistance was much smaller than even the Enforcers had realized, but without disciplined, mature leadership, it was likely the Vags would create plenty of upheaval on their own. If Scooter hadn't kept his life as the Bandit completely separate, then Jenna would've been endangered from the falling out with the resistance now. But Luigi believed that very few of them even knew their connection to Radiant Shade, and none but Brian and the COIL operatives now knew that Radiant Shade was Jenna, and where she lived. However, some of the Vags might've been putting the pieces together.

Voices and sounds echoed up the tunnel behind them, making Luigi guess they were being hunted, but he walked steadily on, with Brian's hand on his shoulder. Because of Scooter, the resistance team hadn't carried firearms, but that was likely to change now. Even Doc, with his caring heart, wouldn't be able to restrain them.

Hedgehog was the only adult left with the Vags, and for some time Luigi had thought the man was a loose cannon.

The resistance was now as much of a danger to them as was the Federation.

The morning of the pageant, Corban walked Jenna out to the curb of Times Square. Other pageant contestants were being driven in from as far away as Georgia, with Obrador sparing no fuel, to make the pageant seem as a legitimate rally cry to unite the Federation. Corban opened the door to a limo, which had come to take Jenna only a few blocks to the Bowery Hotel. Chen Li had come through with the car.

Instead of climbing into the vehicle—a startling sight even with chipped paint—Jenna turned and lifted her face to the building she'd visited as a child, and lived in as a grown woman.

"The sun?" she asked, smiling. "I feel the sun."

"It's a beautiful morning," Corban said, still holding the door. "A few light clouds to the south, but a blue sky."

"How does our building look?"

"Dark glass. Up close, it's a little dirty, but it's still in one piece, which is more than can be said about the rest of the buildings around the Square."

"I just want to remember this moment." She sighed. "This is it, Dad."

"You're not alone," he said, hoping she understood he was referring to God's presence. He couldn't speak openly since the limo driver could hear them through his open window. "It's a beautiful day to start a new life somewhere else."

"With other people," she said sadly. And he understood that she meant his part was mostly finished. Now, she would depend on Chloe, Nathan, and Chen Li in the company of a much different crowd. "You'll be okay?"

"I won't be alone, either."

She felt for his shoulder and leaned toward him. He turned his cheek to her for a kiss.

"I love you, Dad. Maybe I'll be home tonight, because they just won't want an old, blind hag."

"In that case," he chuckled, "I won't rent your side of the room out to anyone right away. I'll wait a few hours."

"How gracious of you!" She laughed and climbed into the car, then held out her hand.

He gave her a medium-sized tote bag, which contained her pageant gown, another change of clothes, and a few personal items.

"You know where I am if you need me," he said, but hesitated to close the door. She was still his little girl, the child he'd encouraged to learn to read braille, to play the piano, to speak foreign languages, to think like a spy, to live as a Christian in a fallen world, to pray to the God of the Bible, to trust . . . No, she wasn't his little girl, anymore. She may have been blind, but she wasn't weak, alone, or naïve.

"I'll be okay, Dad."

He closed the door, then patted the car's roof to signal the driver. Just six years earlier, he'd lost Janice to the virus. Now, he was losing Jenna. Of course, her presence at the Bowery was meant to sway the Federation in a particular direction, but he wasn't delusional. He knew he was old and the Lord could take him home at any time. His work was finished, and he was no longer necessary. Being obsolete, he could gradually back out of the work he'd faithfully done for the Federation. The nation was finally in the hands of people closer to the chancellor—younger people.

Corban had thought he would've been dead by now, killed somewhere overseas while smuggling Christians across closed borders. But no, the Lord had chosen to allow him to grow old, to see two more generations of COIL operatives rise in prominence—to the point that they were staging the peaceful takeover of a struggling, corrupt nation!

Oh, how he wished he could witness two of his finest operatives in action—Chloe and Nathan. They were in the thick of it now. Jenna had had the foresight to put the best trained in the most dangerous place. One wrong move, and they could all be implicated, Jenna as well.

But Corban had his memories, and he could die quietly and peacefully now, remembering how God had used him, and all he'd been allowed to witness. For many years, he'd lived for himself—violent and worldly-minded, serving the intelligence community. Yet, after coming to Christ, everything had shifted. He'd reapplied his skills, and the Source of his life had determined the path. He was grateful for God's directing, even though many had perished along the way.

And Satan was certainly not willing to give up the fight. Although COIL intended to establish a government that was neutral concerning Christian freedoms, darkness was trying every conceivable measure, behind the scenes, to foil the advance of Christ's light.

"More prayer," Corban mumbled to himself, guessing he'd become an old goat who talked to himself now that Jenna was gone and he didn't have anyone else to speak to. "You didn't want to take me in my prime while on my feet, Lord, so maybe You'll take me while I'm all washed up and on my knees."

He turned toward the front door of the print shop when he paused and looked back. The sun's reflection shimmered off glass on the second story of the abandoned electronics store across the street. *A signal!* Someone was holding a mirror or a shard of glass, trying to get his attention. Then it disappeared.

The message was clear. Someone in the COIL network needed assistance. No one else would signal him for anything. Not there.

The street wasn't empty, but Corban believed he was the only one who'd seen the signal. Broadway had always been a main thoroughfare for pedestrians moving up and down the island.

He stepped off the curb and crossed the street. The windows on the first floor had been covered by metal plates, wedged into place by forced laborers in an effort to discourage noncompliant squatters. Very few people found Midtown pleasant enough to live in, since it was mostly comprised of office buildings. The residential apartments in the area had long since been deemed off-limits; since during the first years after Pan-Day, the sewage and water system were too badly ruined and overwhelmed. Additionally, whole blocks had burned where hundreds had been killed or fled during the initial looting and rioting. Skeletons of buildings were all that remained for blocks in some areas.

Corban ignored a padlock on the front door, and used his cane to force one of the metal sheets aside in the window frame, which hadn't been a good fit anyway. A glance at the street told him that no one had noticed or cared what he was doing. Obrador had tried to encourage a police state where neighbors informed on noncompliant or suspicious citizens. But those efforts had just resulted in a paranoid society, everyone hiding what they still had or did. Socialism had never worked, Corban knew from his years as an agent during the Cold War, but he knew there were several recent generations in America who hadn't learned the lessons of the past, and the same mistakes of selfish people were being repeated.

After his eyes adjusted to the dimness, Corban walked across the broken glass of old showcases, and found the stairs. Ascending cautiously, he had to climb around a hole in the stairway where the carpeting had been peeled back, probably from scroungers searching for wood to burn or metal that could be shaped into weapons or tools.

At the top of the stairs, he witnessed a level that had been ransacked more than once in the last twenty years. The flooring had been torn up in huge sections, and the walls had been ripped open, exposing framing and trailing electrical wires. Over by the glassless windows that faced the street, behind up-ended metal shelving, three shadowy figures rose to their feet. The morning sun was at their backs, so their faces couldn't be identified immediately.

But Corban knew they were connected to him somehow, so he cautiously approached them. They moved away from the windows and met him in the middle of the destroyed room. Only someone in the COIL building across the street could've seen them, if there'd been anyone over there. So they were safe since Corban hadn't hosted any guests at COIL's old headquarters on account of the many secrets the building contained—namely, Jenna's unfolding operation, Corban's identification counterfeiting, and the occasional COIL underground visitors.

"Hello, Corban." The shortest of the three stepped forward first. "We've been waiting here for you. The basement under your building just has too much water in it, and more tunnels have collapsed."

"Scooter." Corban embraced him. They hadn't seen each other since Heather's death, two months earlier. "If you've been waiting here, who's taking care of the Bandit's responsibilities in the tunnels?"

"The Bandit is no more," the next man said. It was Luigi, who stepped forward to stand beside Corban and face the other two. Of all the COIL operatives, Corban had appreciated Luigi's familiarity, his constant coordinating, and his presence, just as they'd accompanied one another since the day they'd met. "Steelman was blamed for a death and identified as an ex-Enforcer, so we were run out of the tunnels."

"Blamed for a death?" Corban frowned at Brian, the third and tallest of the three. "I trust it wasn't an intentional death."

"A tunnel collapsed," Scooter said. "Brian brought the body back, but no one took it lightly. Then one of the Vags made an issue about Brian's past. The rest were incited, and, well, it was a mess. We barely escaped with our lives."

"That's not all." Luigi nudged Brian's arm. "Tell him. We've been hiding here for two days, waiting to talk to you, Corban. He has something to say."

"Well, I'm a believer now." Brian seemed shy about his confession. "I realized I wasn't ready to die and face the consequences of my sins. I'd learned just enough from Scooter to take a step of faith in the tunnel after it collapsed. Of course, I was almost killed right after that, but I'm told the Christian life is like that—one crisis after another, to refine us from this fallen world."

"Wise words from a recent convert." Corban shook the man's hand. "Glad the last two months haven't been a waste of time. So, you three are homeless? Don't assume I can bring you into the print shop. I'm still functioning, and I get Federation visitors most days and some nights."

"We were hoping we could help each other," Luigi said. "My papers are in order, but Scooter and Brian can't be seen anywhere. With Operation Esther still unfolding, if something goes wrong, you'll need a quick exit. We want to stick around for a couple weeks to see if we're needed, then we'll go to the mainland. Maybe you'll even want to go with us."

"You're going to stay here, just across the street?" Corban glanced at the windows. "It's risky, being so close."

"There's more to it," Scooter said. "When we left the tunnels, a man named Hedgehog, who's pushed for years toward a militant resistance, probably took charge of the Vags. The man who died was his best friend, and I don't trust Hedgehog to do anything honorable. I've spent years barely convincing him and some of the other Vags that we don't need firearms to harass the Federation. Anything could happen now."

"Luigi?" Corban called for his input.

"It's serious enough that we came here to tell you what happened. We're all that remains of COIL, at least outside of the Bowery complex, so we may as well all be in one place."

"Well, I suppose we can come up with a little system to use to communicate between buildings," Corban said, "as long as we aren't too obvious. No one's registered to be in my building except for me and Jenna, so you guys had better set up a more permanent station over here. I have some food and blankets I can put on the sidewalk after sundown. You can sneak across the street to get them, but this isn't a long-term solution."

"Let's pray Jenna works quickly in the Bowery," Luigi said. "This whole city is on the edge of tipping one way or the other. And like we said, if things don't happen quickly, we can cross into New Jersey and find more permanent housing."

"I'm not sure I'm ready to leave the city . . ." Corban looked down at the floor. "Or Jenna. But if things do take their time here, it would be better for me to be with friends. If I do end up leaving, I'll need to train a couple of apprentices right away for the shop here, rather than leave unexpectedly. That would look suspicious. Yeah, I see the wisdom in your proposal. I'll start the paperwork right away."

✝

Only three days had passed since Owen Travers had been publicly shamed by Corban Dowler, but he was already feeling better about himself. He knew this had everything to do with him heeding his sister's advice to stay in the hotel for a few days. Well, maybe it had something to do with the pageant and banquet that day, too. He couldn't help himself. The excitement at the Bowery was contagious!

Wearing his tux without the bowtie, which he would put on later, Owen drifted through the hotel lobby then into the banquet hall, which he'd seen used only once, years earlier for a state dance. Unlike Lena, Owen didn't mind the festivities. He could understand why Obrador was employing all kinds of citizens to plan the next week's events, which were beginning that very day. He even stood against the wall in the banquet hall to watch Chloe coach several pageant contestants in their duties that afternoon.

They'd been arriving the last few days—forty young, beautiful women who were flirting with the male soldiers, much to the disdain of the female soldiers. The contestants had been housed at the Bowery, which meant that some Federation officers had been temporarily relocated to accommodate the guests. But Chloe hadn't approached Owen to give up his room. That further substantiated that he really hadn't lost respect in the eyes of the Federation among those who really mattered. And whoever was still laughing at him would regret it, he guessed, as soon as it was uncovered as to what his sister was about to do on the island. Whatever she did, he knew she'd take him with her. And he'd find ways to be his own man, run his own way, and regain his respect from everyone, even if he needed to return to spontaneous executions on the street. It had been nice that everyone had bowed to him or showed him reverence for a while, but maybe he'd pushed it too far. Corban had ruined all his fun.

"Excuse me, Mr. Travers?" A junior officer with red hair walked into the banquet room and saluted him. "A message for you."

Owen straightened up and returned the salute, but eyed the man suspiciously. Just a few days earlier, he was sure this one had been among those laughing at him.

"Yes? What is it?"

"I tried your room first. I was told to give this to you immediately."

The man offered a mud-smeared envelope to Owen.

"What is it?" Owen didn't reach for the item. "Do you see what I'm wearing? I'm not touching that thing. What is it?"

The redhead glanced at the envelope.

"I haven't opened it, sir. I don't know what it is."

"Well, where'd you get it? It doesn't even have my name on it. Is this some sort of joke? A prank?"

"It's no prank, sir. Honest! It came from a civilian out at the gate. He just walked up and handed it to us, said you were expecting news about this, and to give it to you immediately."

"News about what?"

Carefully, Owen took the envelope in his fingertips and turned it over, avoiding the fresh mud. He thrust it back to the officer.

"Seems harmless. You open it."

"But sir, I'm just—"

"Open it!" Owen checked his voice, not wanting to attract the attention of those preparing the hall. "If it's not a prank, you open it."

The officer frowned, apparently oblivious to the dangers that Owen felt sure were out there wanting to catch him in a vulnerable position. It would be just like some of the clowns in the barracks to fill an envelope with glitter or something to cause a reason to laugh at him later.

The redhead split the seal open and looked inside. After a shake, a slip of paper slid into his other hand. Owen plucked the paper from the man's hand.

"I'll keep this. You keep the envelope. That'll be all. Thank you."

"Thank you, sir." The officer saluted and turned away, seemingly exasperated, taking the muddy envelope with him.

Owen didn't salute back. Instead, he curiously opened the paper to find a single page, folded once. The writing was sloppy but legible.

"To Owen Travers: You should know that Brian Steelman has been hiding in the tunnels with us, but he's no longer welcome with the resistance. He deceived and used us. The Bandit and Luigi Putelli have gone to the surface somewhere with him, definitely working with the Christians somehow in your city. Remember that I'm the one who told you this. I want more than what we've had down here. I'm expecting certain understanding from you in the future. We'll talk soon.—Hedgehog."

He read the letter twice, his eyes wide with wonder. Informants around the city weren't rare, but usually it was just a man reporting on his neighbor who had more canned food than he was supposed to have. The resistance never reported on themselves! Now they were ready to negotiate? Obviously, the absence of Radiant Shade was shaking things up in the resistance, even though Obrador had shared public statements that she would be released sometime that week. That was all a farce since she'd died two months earlier.

The Bandit and someone named Luigi Putelli? Owen didn't know what it all meant, but he knew Obrador would be happy to get his hands on Brian Steelman again. And the Christians? In Owen's opinion, they were the worst kind of noncompliant citizens who never pledged exclusive loyalty to the Federation, no matter how they were threatened or tortured. Their Bibles and morals—and Steelman was in their company now? How could they have even accepted him, after all the Christians he'd killed?

But Owen wasn't really thinking about how the Federation could prosper from this intel. He was wondering if he could advance himself—without Lena's help at all! Right now was the perfect time, too. The wedding was coming. Lena was making her plans, so why couldn't he help himself rise a few pegs in the Federation? Obrador no longer spoke down to him like he used to, so maybe the chancellor was beginning to understand he was valuable. He had, after all, caught Radiant Shade for him. Only his sister knew he hadn't, and she wasn't telling anyone.

After tucking the letter into his pocket, Owen walked across the hall, weaved through the banquet tables, and arrived below the stage where Chloe was rehearsing with contestants and a lieutenant named Isaacson. Owen had heard the tall, broad-shouldered supervisor was in charge of pageant security. Poor guy, tolerating Chloe and decorations and giggling girls. But he didn't seem to be too tortured, standing in his pressed uniform, with beautiful women all around him.

"Chloe?" Owen waved at her, interrupting her conversation with a Chinese-looking woman who was taping markers onto the stage floor. "Can I have a quick sec?"

Owen had always liked her professionalism, never seeming temperamental or moody like Obrador or his other staff members.

"Yes, Mr. Travers?" She took a knee on the stage above him. "Please tell me you're bringing me news about the napkins arriving?"

"Napkins?" He laughed. "No, I'm not here about napkins. Quick question: what's Obrador got planned for tomorrow night?"

"Nothing's on the state calendar after today until the wedding next week. What's on your mind?"

Owen looked around. No one seemed to be close enough to hear. He couldn't do this without Chloe, and he had to trust someone. Chloe had always been a Federation advocate, and had never been unkind to him.

"I just received this. Tell no one, you hear?" He drew out the letter. "Don't even tell Obrador. I want to surprise him. Sort of like a wedding gift."

He waited as she read the letter. Her brow furrowed.

"Do you think this is legit?" She studied the letter a little longer, then handed it back to him. "Who's this Hedgehog person?"

"I don't know. Obviously a resistance fighter. But do you see? The resistance is reaching out. It's slowly dissolving. We have a new enemy, now better defined. It's the Christians!"

"We've always known about the Christians. The forced labor crews are filled with Christians. You've executed hundreds of them yourself in the past decade, haven't you?"

"Sure, but we always sort of lumped the Christians in with the resistance, not really understanding that there was a distinction between the noncompliant people in the city. This letter is proof that the resistance isn't with the Christians, or the Christians aren't with the resistance. Opposition to the Federation is crumbling, and all we need to worry about is the lack of loyalty from these Christians. That's got to count for something."

"So, what do you want to do? Stop hunting the resistance and focus on Christians specifically?"

"Do you think Obrador will go for it? I mean, this is good news, right? With Steelman located, sort of?"

"Sure, it could be good news," she said, "depending on how you present it to him."

"How about a private dinner tomorrow night? Just a few of us, and Obrador's new woman. I'll break the news to everyone—that the resistance is crumbling. All of Obrador's strategies have been proven effective. It should be a hit, right? Can you set up the dinner?"

"I guess so." She nodded. "It won't be as elaborate as tonight's. Can we do it upstairs? How many guests?"

"No more than thirty. We'll connect a couple tables end to end, maybe?"

"Yeah, I can swing that. We're having veal tonight. We have beef steaks in the freezer. Will that work?"

"Perfect! Don't tell anyone what it's about, just that I'm presenting the chancellor and his bride-to-be a gift. Your lips are sealed?"

"You're quite the visionary, Owen." She smiled. "I'll make sure the surprise is all your own."

"Definitely don't bring my sister into it."

"You're not telling her? I thought you two were close."

"She can pout on the sidelines. She has her own plans for other things. I don't want her getting in the middle of this."

"Of course. But do you even want her at the private banquet tomorrow night?"

"You know what?" He scoffed, imagining Lena's response. "No, I don't want her there. For once, leave her out of the loop. A guy's got to break away from his family eventually, right? This is my thing, not hers."

"It's your call, Owen."

"Thanks, Chloe. How come we never became better friends? You know, privately?"

"For one, I'm old enough to be your mother. And two, both of us have usually put the Federation before everything else. Let's not lose sight of that. I'll have everything set up for tomorrow night, but I'll leave the presentation up to you, okay? Thirty place settings. No more. I'll get back to the rehearsal here while you work on your speech."

Owen backed away and watched the people on the stage without really focusing on them. Instead, his mind went to his breakout moment that would come the following night. He was doing this for Obrador, for the Federation. He would be the orchestrator of a whole new offensive. The resistance was no more. The opposition to the Federation was smaller now, hardly even a threat, just a nuisance to be tracked down and killed. With the Enforcers' full attention, the Federation could be void of Christians inside six months!

On his way out of the banquet hall, Owen paused to peek inside the gift bags that the several hundred guests and contestants would receive. There was candy, laminated Federation placemats, and several poetry books by Mora B. Leever. Good gifts, he thought to himself. He liked Leever's poetry, even though some people mocked it as simple-minded and corny.

But the laminated placemats? He growled to himself as he left the hall for the stairwell. There was only one person who did the Bowery laminating—Corban Dowler! But if Owen could spin it right, he guessed he could implicate Dowler with the Christians, and have the man permanently removed. Soon, no one would mock him, not even his sister!

Chapter Eleven

Colonel Milo Rotham crouched as he ran up the side of the street in Philadelphia, past disabled vehicles and dead men, and reached one of his trusted men, Sergeant Novak Ibojka. Sergeant Ibojka was the most brutal and crafty killers Rotham had ever known, so he wasn't surprised to see the man still alive when so many others had been killed by a number of mysterious soldiers in the distance. Together, they huddled behind a disabled, armored personnel carrier in the street. For a moment, Rotham gazed back at the courthouse and the city center of Philadelphia, just blocks away. There was a bunker back there, and a whole regiment of soldiers was preparing to join the fight. If he wanted to, he could wait for reinforcements, but he wasn't that kind of man. He hadn't become colonel by waiting on others to take the initiative.

After Rotham caught his breath from the sprint up the block, he tightened his gun belt around his waist. Lately, food had been scarce in the city and he'd lost some weight. He was in his mid-thirties now, only fifteen when Pan-Day had happened. Since playing video games throughout his youth, policing Philadelphia's wild streets had been the most thrilling adventure ever. But today, everything had gone wrong.

"Tell me what happened," he ordered his sergeant. "These were all of our transport vehicles needed for next week's New York invasion. This is disastrous!"

"I'm sorry, sir." Fear showed on Ibojka's face, which Rotham had never seen from the predator before. "It escalated too quickly to stop. I lost forty men in five minutes!"

"You said on the radio it's a force from the West?" Rotham rose slowly to peer past the turret of the personnel carrier. "I don't see them. Are they in the buildings? Or on the roofs? How'd they get the jump on you? Speak, Sergeant!"

"We got a radio call yesterday from upriver. Four travelers from out West refused to be processed as Federation citizens. Maybe it was them."

"It's the law that we process every person coming into Federation territory. Everyone coming here knows that ahead of time."

"I guess these people didn't know it."

"Well, what happened on this street today is from a lot more than just four drifters coming from out West, Sergeant!" Rotham checked his handgun, making sure it was ready to fire. He hadn't shot anyone for a couple years. "This is happening at the worst time. Lena Travers is going to leave us out of the new government if we can't get ourselves together!"

"I'm telling you, Colonel, the checkpoint upriver said it was just four travelers. They shot up the checkpoint and took out five of our men. When they came to, they radioed us and told us to be on the lookout."

"Wait. Did you just say they took out five at the checkpoint, and then they *came to?* What's that supposed to mean?"

"They said they were shot with some sort of tranquilizer. They weren't unconscious but for an hour or so, they figured, and the four travelers had moved on, coming deeper into Federation land. Apparently, they've arrived in Philly."

"Tranquilizers?" Rotham ducked behind cover to reach the nearest fallen soldier. He felt all over the soldier's uniform. "This one's not even bleeding, and he has a pulse!"

"It must be the same four, Colonel," Ibojka said. "I got a glimpse of one of them up on that overpass, and here we are."

"Overpass?" Rotham checked under the vehicle's track to study the street. "I don't see any overpass."

"Look farther."

"Farther? I don't see an overpass for a quarter-mile. You've got to be joking."

"I'm not joking."

"You said you lost forty men in five minutes. From four hundred yards away? You're not making any sense, man!"

"Have you ever seen me hide like this, Colonel?"

Rotham studied his sergeant's face.

"No. That's what's got me spooked. Look at these transports. Whatever they used on our vehicles, it wasn't a tranquilizer. What is this stuff? They've disabled our whole convoy!"

"Don't touch it, sir. It's some sort of acid. It ate right through the steel like butter on a hot skillet. The convoy was just at the wrong place at the wrong time, I guess."

"This seems planned, like the resistance has called in some mercenaries or something. There's no way this wasn't intentional. Somebody must've talked. A whole convoy doesn't just stumble across the kind of firepower necessary to take us out of the game like this."

"When I showed up here, the firefight was already raging. I think some of our boys tried to arrest the four again. Like I said, it escalated out of control."

"Okay, okay." Rotham sat down and took a deep breath. "What're we dealing with here? Resistance fighters? No, the Plains Zone doesn't have a clue what's going on out here in the Federation, unless they were told before they arrived and knew what to expect. They can't be just travelers, can they? What kind of weaponry do you think this is?"

"It sounded big. Some sort of heavy carbine."

"Okay, they're willing to disable our vehicles, but unwilling to kill us. That's assuming all our boys wake up soon. I don't see blood on any of our men. But who shoots like that? *Four hundred yards!* How're we supposed to invade New York on schedule next week? In six days! We can't march that far on foot."

"We can't repair all these vehicles, sir. We'll have to fuel up regular cars, if we're going to join the invasion now."

"We're an army, Ibojka! We don't ride into battle in Toyotas!"

"Well, what do you want to do?"

"I'm thinking."

Rotham wondered if he would've had a rifle instead of just a sidearm, if he could even hit the overpass with a bullet, let alone sight on a specific man-sized target. It was unlikely. What was happening out West that was turning out marksmen like this?

"We can't lose any more vehicles," Rotham finally said. "I want to talk to them, see who we're dealing with. Rip off that antenna from the roof."

"It's exposed, sir."

"You said they're firing tranquilizers, so what's to fear, a little nap? I'll put a pillow under your head. Get me that antenna, Sergeant!"

Ibojka had a heavy-set frame, not quite fat, but one of the heaviest men in Rotham's inner circle. He hesitated for a few seconds, as if gathering courage, then leaped onto the transport vehicle. It took two tugs to rip off the long radio antenna. Panting, Ibojka fell to the ground next to Rotham.

"Maybe they moved on, sir."

Yanking the antenna from his sergeant's hand, Rotham tied a stained, yellow bandana from his pocket onto the end of the antenna.

"I'm still not buying that there are just four of them."

"That was the report, Colonel. I wouldn't lie to you. And at least one of them's not even a man, but a woman."

"So? We have women on our force, too."

"Well, she shot some of our men."

Turning, Rotham watched several downed men in the street roll over and sit up. They shook their heads and reached for their rifles.

"There's got to be an explanation." Rotham rose to his feet, the flag of surrender held high. "Cover me."

"How? My rifle won't even shoot that far."

Rotham didn't take off his gun belt, but he holstered his sidearm so he could hold the bowing antenna with both hands.

This section of Philadelphia was nearly uninhabited, more like a forgotten warzone than a neighborhood. Battles and conflict had raged across the city when he'd still been a teenager, barely learning to shoulder a standard rifle. His early, loyal regard for Federation law had secured him a position when he'd been in his twenties. While others had fought for personal glory, Rotham had fought in the name of something greater than himself. The Federation was greater than any one individual, and therefore, the Federation became his cause for living.

Of course, that was a sentiment from his youth. Since then, the courthouse steps had run red with the blood of rebels, and Rotham had learned that he was no better than anyone else. They all fought to stay alive, and he no longer fought for the Federation alone. He used the Federation and the Federation used him. Clearly, his loyalties had swung back toward himself a few years earlier, but he would never let anyone know about such a shift in his socialist zeal.

Since he was serving himself now, Lena Travers hadn't needed to convince him of the benefits of joining her. Obrador's time was up. Lena would take over. For Rotham, it was just another step to stay alive, and he hoped he hadn't committed to something he couldn't uphold, especially now that he'd lost the greater part of his armored division!

He moved up the street cautiously, surveying the rooftops, dark windows, and shadowy doorways. *Four travelers?* Unlikely. Federation citizens were always inflating rumors about the Plains Zone. If they weren't whispering about feral packs of rabid dogs devouring every living thing across the Midwest, then they were crying about a ten-thousand-man army on the West Coast, rumored to be marching against the Federation.

Of course, nothing ever happened to the Federation. No one could attack it and hope to win. Philadelphia was on the Appalachian border, and she would meet invaders first—but there were no invaders. No one could hurt the army Rotham himself had built up. His Enforcers were the most ruthless south of New York City, and his troops were trained by him. Sure, he'd learned to kill from video games as a kid, but aiming and shooting was all the same, whether digitally or in reality.

But none of this was actually convincing Rotham that he was in control as he walked past men who were waking up all around him. Something had devastated his troops, something so superior and terrifying that he saw none of the enemy combatants lying in the streets—only his own men.

"Get off the street!" he ordered the men as they gained consciousness. "Find some cover and back me up!"

They obeyed, but groggily. Tranquilizers made so little sense. What kind of military force won battles when they didn't remove the enemy from the field of battle? His soldiers would simply wake up and keep fighting the same enemy, wouldn't they?

Then he saw one. Rotham halted in the middle of the street. Was that even a man? The person walked slowly out of an alley and leaned against the corner of the building. He was a bearded giant, larger than even

Sergeant Ibojka, with a monstrous backpack on his back. In his arms was a compact rifle that looked nearly like a toy gun. But Rotham wasn't about to laugh just yet, not when he'd seen the devastation the weapon had rained upon his convoy. Who fights an entire convoy of men armed with non-lethal weapons?

"Who am I speaking to?" Rotham asked the bearded one. He'd dealt with resistance groups before, meeting concessions until he could bring them to their knees. "Are you the one I should be talking to?"

The traveler pointed with his thumb to continue down the street. Rotham clenched his teeth. Why was he asking permission to walk down his own streets? As he passed the man, he noticed skis strapped to his backpack. *Skis!*

Rotham kept lifting his eyes and studying the overpass. Now that he was one hundred yards closer, he could see that someone was up there, maybe lying prone, aiming a rifle under the guardrail. He didn't care if they were shooting tranquilizers or not. Getting shot at all that day wasn't a welcoming thought. How could he invade New York and take over security for the Federation if he couldn't even hold his own city?

He moved past a burned-out charter bus, then a snowplow tipped over on its side. When he reached an intersection, someone behind him cleared a throat. Slowly, without making any sudden moves, he turned to see a tall, blond-haired man no older than forty, standing against the underside of the tipped-over snowplow.

"Are you the one I'm here to talk to?" Rotham asked.

The blond stranger had a thinner beard than the last man, but it appeared just as unruly. His backpack was piled with camping gear, and of course, the skis, as if they'd just arrived in the city by skiing through the winter months.

"It ain't easy underestimating new folks in town." The man grinned as he chewed on a piece of grass. His right hand steadied another compact rifle, loosely aimed in Rotham's direction. "What's that on your uniform? You a colonel?"

"I'm Colonel Rotham of Philadelphia's Citizen Army of the Appalachian Federation."

"That's a mouthful."

"You can't be this stupid." Rotham chuckled. "You just attacked an entire division of Citizen Army troopers."

"No, I'm not stupid enough to attack an entire division. I'm stupid enough to respond when an entire division attacks me."

Rotham scoffed and looked around, not lowering his flag. This joker could have trigger-happy friends near or far who were watching him, he considered.

"What are you supposed to be? Some sort of mountain man coming to the city for supplies or something?"

"No, I'm well-supplied. We took our time coming across Ohio. Some good folks helped us out along the way, taking care of us as we did a little hunting for them. I'd say whole parts of Ohio weathered the winter better than what I've seen of your crumbling city."

"So, what's all this about?" Rotham nodded with his head, trying to think past the Ohio comment. The facade of socialism was to convince the people that no one anywhere else could possibly be faring better than they were, but Rotham knew that couldn't be true. His city, and the rest of the Federation, was starving and corrupt and burdened with despondency. "Do you have any idea how much damage you've done to our vehicles?"

"I have a pretty good idea. You're not the first military I've gone head-to-head with. Probably won't be the last."

"You've made the Federation your enemy without provocation." Rotham rested the antenna over his shoulder. "Is that what you wanted? This is unforgivable, even if you didn't kill any of my men."

"The Federation was my enemy long before I came to town. Tell me, do you guys still arrest Christians?"

"Christians?" Rotham frowned. "What? We reeducate anyone who isn't devoted to the Federation. Some people call themselves Christians, sure. It's no big deal. But if you're talking about the radicals who once preached about heaven and hell, and judged people for living their own way—yeah, those people are long gone. It's a new era. We're not in the Middle Ages any longer. Those kinds of close-minded thinkers would never last, anyway. The world's changed in the last forty years. There's no more room for fairy tales these days."

"Your conscience isn't a fairy tale, is it, Colonel Rotham?" the man asked. "And neither is the God whose love for you is equally balanced with His justice against your sinfulness. You're a man in power who's clearly fallen prey to the Federation's dogma. It's time to repent. That's the age we're in. Remember the record of Jesus Christ, who died on the cross for your sins. You must've heard that truth at some point in your life. Jesus was killed, but He rose again the third day, according to the Scriptures. He's the Son of God, more powerful than death, Colonel, and that means He's worthy of your trust and devotion. We're all headed to the grave one day. Who do you trust with your eternal soul?"

"Not you!" Rotham swore. "Have you seriously lost your mind? I'm looking at you, hardly believing what I'm seeing and hearing. You're in enough trouble without preaching devotion to some made-up belief thousands of years old."

"So, you're not a believer?" The traveler tilted his rifle up, aiming directly at Rotham's chest. Then, he jerked it up and smiled. "I'm just kidding you, Colonel. I'd never shoot you for not believing in the God who made you. But seriously, you do need to get real about life after death. The way you're living, you'll be facing Him a lot sooner than you realize. You're living in darkness, and you need to come to the Light."

"And you're the light?" Rotham checked the street. Nearly all of his men were awake and out of sight now. "Why are you here?"

"You know this Chancellor Obrador character?"

"Of course. He's the chancellor. I run Philadelphia, so I've met him a couple times."

"He's in New York City?"

"Yeah. You think you're going there? It's a hundred miles in that direction."

"Sure, I think I'll take the grand tour. It's a free country."

"No, it— I mean, you're not going anywhere. You're going to answer for what you've done here today."

"Sure, take me to the chancellor. I'll answer to him." The man laughed, as if amused by a joke Rotham hadn't heard. "It ain't easy trying to convince someone of your authority when you really don't have any authority, is it?"

"You don't think I have any authority?"

"I'm not the one holding up a white flag."

Rotham felt his face redden. Even for a religious nut, this guy was no fool.

"Who are you? Give me a name. Who's the man who's so fearless that he's willing to take on the whole Federation Army, because that's what you've done here today. You'll be hunted down, wherever you go, no matter where you hide. This attack is an act of war, and we'll never stop coming after you until you and all your kind are put down. You will pay. All of you will pay."

"All of us? All of who?"

"You and all the people with you. All of you."

"Apparently, you think we're more than what we are. We're just a humble group of people, hardly worth noticing at all."

"How many are you?"

"I'd say we're more than enough, whatever we are. Is that the way you want it? You want to go to war with the Casperteins?"

"The Casperteins?" Rotham stared afar off, trying to recall the name. "Nope, never heard of you guys before."

"Well, now you have, and you've seen today that one of us is worth fifty of you. Of course, it helps that we have the favor of the Lord with us."

"The favor of—?"

"It ain't easy facing the fire of God's own ambassadors, is it? The Federation won't be the same when I'm done with it, Colonel Rotham. You just remember that I warned you about God, and when you're ready to come to your knees, He'll receive you just as you are."

"And you're a Caspertein? Is that some religious cult or something?"

"It's a family name. I'm Levi Caspertein. There's a few of us still sprinkled across this country."

"You're delusional, Levi Caspertein."

"So, you want to turn your city into more of a war zone, or are you going to let me move on to New York City? The chancellor and I have to talk."

"You're not reaching New York." Rotham glared at the mouthy stranger. Slowly, he let the antenna droop low, until the flag rested on the cracked pavement. "We're going to settle this here and now. You've destroyed more today than you can ever know. I had plans."

"It ain't easy losing to the Casperteins." The traveler stopped smiling. "But I guess you'll get used to it."

Rotham scratched for his sidearm. He would kill this idiot right now, and end this nonsense. But an instant later, he felt as if the snowplow had struck him on the shoulder. His feet left the pavement, and for a breathless second that seemed longer, his body was horizontal, floating, twisting through the air. Then, he landed on the street.

Gunfire erupted all around him, but he was left immobile, staring at a one-armed woman in the doorway of a house thirty feet away. In her one arm, she held a rifle with smoke drifting from its barrel. On her back, she carried a backpack, skis, and a long, metal staff.

As Rotham closed his eyes, he cursed the Casperteins, their God, and their disregard for Federation law. And he cursed them for ignoring his own authority. Whoever they were, whatever they were, he wouldn't rest until they were in the ground!

Nathan Isaacson stood at the corner of the banquet hall stage, facing hundreds of guests. Out of the corner of his eye to his right, the pageant unfolded according to plan, but not without a few hurdles. Two pageant contestants had been abducted by rogue militia fighters in New Hampshire, and their regional representatives were calling for the contest to be postponed until the abductees could be recovered. Of course, Obrador hadn't granted a postponement, only his condolences.

Additionally, a letter about a virus threat had been sent to the Bowery by an anonymous courier. Nathan had read the letter himself, and deemed it not credible, but not before several Enforcers had seen the letter and started a small panic among the guests. Three contestants had pulled out of the pageant and returned to their locales. For the pageant to go on, Nathan had had to take the stage himself and announce to everyone that there was no Meridia Virus outbreak. He'd explained it was merely a hoax meant to cause chaos and panic, instigated by someone who didn't want the pageant to take place.

Chloe acted as emcee of the event. She wore an elegant, blue gown that some of the contestants visibly envied. Chancellor Obrador sat at a central table at the front of the room below the stage, where he visited with both local and national Federation officials.

Since Nathan was old enough to have seen pageants before Pan-Day, he struggled to hold in his laughter when Chloe presented some young contestants to the audience. She read a short bio about each woman, most of whom were between eighteen and thirty, and then the contestant was given the microphone for two minutes.

Many of the women had been coached to embellish their successes at developing Federation soup kitchens or founding loyalty leagues within their communities. Others hadn't been coached, and it was these humble women who seemed to Nathan to be the most genuine. Some showed the audience the dresses they'd made by hand, others played an instrument, sang a song, or expressed themselves in interpretive dance.

Of course, the big moment came when Jenna, just shy of forty years old, stepped forward. Chloe read her brief bio, and as a final mention, said that Jenna had been completely blind since a young child. Before Jenna even spoke, the room was already whispering about her. Obrador was leaning forward, seemingly mesmerized by the gentle beauty of the slender woman on stage. Nathan knew Obrador himself had narrowed the selection days earlier to choose Jenna to be the pageant winner. But still, Nathan wanted to shout for victory already!

Except this wasn't a game. Nor was it just a contest. Their lives hung in the balance. Obrador's authority was still spiraling downward, and Jenna's years of planning was unfolding none-too-soon to deliver the countless Christians still in hiding, or already condemned to forced labor.

Nathan didn't know exactly how Jenna planned to reverse Obrador's laws against Christians. Especially since that very morning, Chloe had told him that Owen Travers was about to propose an aggressive, new campaign against the remnant of Christ-followers. They were the last noncompliant hold-outs in the Federation. The Lord was in control, however, and Nathan prayed privately as often as the matter made his heart tremble. Owen seemed to be Jenna's biggest obstacle, yet that night she seemed so poised and dignified in front of hundreds.

A piano from the back of the platform was rolled out to centerstage, and Chen Li, acting as contestant escort, guided Jenna to the piano bench. What followed mesmerized the room and brought tears to many eyes. Nathan had figured that Jenna would have some kind of bombshell in her holster to win over the audience—like revealing that she was really the beloved poet known as Mora B. Leever. But instead, she sang a sweet, simple song, accompanied by the piano she played softly:
"There was dark unleashed,
And hunger around.
A land without light,
A taming unbound.
Where pride once rode,
Tears came a'flooding.
Now heads hung low,
Hearts were a'fleeting.
But hope rose above,
And blue filled the sky.
A nation of dreamers,
With our heads held high.
Where justice prevailed,
And leaders stood low.
Where believers sighed,
With nary a foe.
A land of blessing,
And a land of song,
Mercy to the humble,
Always caring, forever strong."
The audience was on their feet. Nathan would never have imagined that Jenna could work some Christian themes into her song, all while ending it with the Appalachian Federation motto—*Always caring, forever strong.* Even he cheered for her, but he pitied the poor

contestants who would follow Jenna. There'd been no need to scheme for Jenna to be chosen. She'd truly won the hearts of everyone before the pageant was even concluded.

But it did go on, and the women who followed Jenna seemed daunted by the fact that she'd been the only one for whom the audience had given a standing ovation.

When all the contestants had been presented, Chloe announced a brief intermission while the chancellor discussed the performances with the honorary judges. Of course, Nathan had been in the room the night before when Obrador had insisted from Chloe's finalists that Jenna Dowler needed to be his top choice.

As hors d'oeuvres were served, Chloe went to Nathan and leaned close so no one else could hear.

"Did you know she was doing a song like that?" she gasped.

"I thought she was just playing the piano or something simple." Nathan shook his head. "She wrote that? The song mentioned believers!"

"Yeah, well, believers in what? But we know what she had in mind." Chloe laughed lightly. "Can you believe her? It'll probably become the Federation's anthem. She's planned this all along. Just like Corban—ten steps ahead of everyone."

"All while blind!"

Chloe walked away to conference with Chen Li. Nathan was still reeling from Jenna's bold performance when Owen Travers walked up and shook his hand. He had heard that Owen had gone through a phase expecting people to bow to him, and Nathan was happy the Twin hadn't tested him, because he wasn't bowing to anyone but his Savior.

"Very entertaining, huh?" Owen thrust his hands in his pockets and stood next to Nathan as they observed the room together. "We've come a long way. So have you, Lieutenant. I hear the chancellor has big plans for you."

"Forget about me." Nathan teasingly flicked Owen's bowtie. "Look at you. What's really going on here? You wife-hunting among the contestants? You can't wear the sharpest tux to these events and expect people to just look past you."

"Hey, a guy's got to look sharp once in a while." Owen laughed at the attention. "Say, I wanted to ask if you're free tomorrow night. Upstairs, I'm hosting a little dinner for the chancellor and some of the governors and mayors while they're in town. I'd like you to be there."

"I'm no governor, Owen," Nathan said lightheartedly. "Oh, you want me to serve the food or something? Wait on tables? I'd be glad to."

"No, no." Owen set his hand on Nathan's shoulder. "The more I get to know you, the more I like you, Nathan. You, Chloe, and your wife are all invited. I want you to be a part of what's happening next."

"Thank you, Owen." Nathan touched his chest, feigning surprise, although Chloe had already warned him that the chief Enforcer was introducing the new campaign right away. "I'm honored. You can count on me and my wife to be there—and to be as involved as we can be in whatever's happening next."

Beaming, Owen walked away and spoke to other Federation officials, definitely strategic figures for his campaign. Christians were far from safe yet, even with Jenna's position already made sure in the Bowery. There was so much to pray about, to shift into God's good hands, to entrust to Him all that Jenna was still putting into position.

Nathan wished Corban were there to witness what his daughter had achieved thus far. After all, he was the one who'd gotten her there.

Chapter Twelve

This was just what Corban needed—a night of stealth! It took his mind off the pageant taking place that evening. He'd find out how the event went in the paper in a couple days. Right now, while the Bowery was partying, there was other work to be done.

He was clothed entirely in black, like he was forty years old again, creeping along the Berlin Wall. But he was in his eighties, so there wasn't any actual creeping, only caution on the streets of New York City. He still had his cane and his pace was slow, but it was a warm night and his joints weren't hurting too badly.

At a cross-street, he saw Luigi and Brian dart across to another building. Luigi was no young buck, either, but he looked like he was keeping Brian winded. Meanwhile, Scooter patiently waited for Corban to get across the street where they could focus on the night's work.

"Company!" Corban warned Scooter. "Motorcycle coming from the south!"

Scooter grabbed Corban's arm and half-lifted him through the broken window of a hair salon. Together, they sat on the floor as the engine whined past.

"There's only one person who rides a bike like that," Corban said. "Lena Travers, Enforcer extraordinaire."

"That was her?" Scooter leaned out the window, making sure the machine was far away. "Why isn't she at the pageant?"

"Because she takes her job too seriously." Corban climbed back to his feet. "You don't find either of the Twins taking a break too often. She and her brother are probably skipping out on the pageant to see who's up to no good in the city."

"People like us?" Scooter chuckled. "Come on. The next entrance is right here."

Corban kept watch as Scooter collected materials to place on top of the homemade manhole cover inside the salon. This would ensure the cover couldn't be opened by anyone from below. Since the resistance now had no respectable leadership in the tunnels, Scooter thought it prudent to make it more difficult for them to come above ground. Of course, Hedgehog could have the Vags dig a new hole anywhere, but without having a network on the surface anymore, the Vags were at a disadvantage. And in that part of town, they'd find no easy access to the city. Luigi and Brian were doing the same thing on the next street over.

Scooter led Corban two avenues north to block the next hole, then they met up with Luigi and Brian.

"Did you guys see that?" Brian asked as the four men hid behind a garbage pile of rotting trash.

"It was just Lena," Scooter said. "Corban said this is her style, staying on patrol while everyone else is having a good time."

"No, not Lena." Brian pointed at the dark sky. *"That!"*

Corban's eyes were one of the few things that were just as sharp now as they had been in his youth. He had no trouble seeing the red shimmer in the sky to the southwest, a reflection off a few clouds on an otherwise clear night.

"We all know what that is," Luigi said, his voice low. "We haven't seen it for years, but that's a city on fire."

"Probably Trenton," Scooter said.

"Farther." Corban sighed. "I'd say Philadelphia. Philadelphia's on fire. Apparently, we're not the only ones up to some mischief tonight."

"There was nothing on the security reports two months ago," Brian said. "Has anyone heard who would be crazy enough to attack a Federation city?"

"I've read the recent reports." Corban rose to his feet to watch the sky from a better vantage point. "No one's been on the radar for years. That means that whoever Philly is dealing with was off the radar."

"Who do you think it is?" Brian asked.

"Do the math." Luigi joined Corban's side. "There's only one force of nature who's overdue to make his appearance. Who've we been expecting?"

"*The Serval?*" Brian asked. "Seriously? This is how he makes his entrance?"

"A Caspertein doesn't know any other way," Corban said. "Come on. Let's cover more of these tunnel entrances before dawn. I have a feeling it's going to be a busy week before the wedding."

Along with Obrador's announcement of the pageant winner, Chloe stood beside him as he also announced that Radiant Shade would be released due to her cooperation with the Enforcers. It was part of a strategic move by Obrador to further win any dissidents still in the corners of the Federation. But few in the room seemed to grasp the value of announcing anything about Radiant Shade, who wasn't even present, when Jenna Dowler was there in the flesh. The whole room applauded afresh for Jenna's acceptance of the honor, and some wept at the promise of prosperity that the betrothal signified.

But Chloe wasn't able to celebrate either announcement long, when Sergeant Sean Harris whispered the news in her ear—Philadelphia was under attack. The barracks had been placed on alert, in case whoever had struck Philadelphia was coming to New York City next.

"Congrats, Jenna!" Chloe kissed Jenna on the cheek. "It's truly a Cinderella story!"

It wasn't really a Cinderella story since Jenna was far from the downtrodden sister who'd risen to the arms of a prince, but no one in the room knew that. From everyone else's perspective, a simple blind girl with a voice like an angel had just been chosen to be the chancellor's wife. It was such a romantic moment that even the contestants who'd lost to Jenna were weeping for joy.

As planned and cleared by Obrador, Chen Li was at Jenna's side. She was one of the few that Obrador had trusted with the full plot to select him a wife who would strengthen the nation under him. With Chen Li beside her, he was further assured that Jenna would be the model citizen, a beacon of unity and devotion.

"Um, we have a situation," Chloe said privately to Obrador, even while he shook hands with people who streamed past the stage to congratulate him. "The radio was unclear of details, but Philadelphia is under some sort of attack. It was a small force from the West. We should send a recon team to find out more of what's happened. The whole sky southwest of us looks like it's on fire."

Obrador's face turned a shade paler.

"Send Lena," he said. "She has the fastest bike."

"I would, but she's not even here."

"She isn't?" He was taller than everyone in the room, and he turned to find her. "How dare she skip this moment!"

"Lena can't be trusted, sir. I suggest sending a small unit to patrol, but first send Lieutenant Isaacson on another route. He was a Marine for years. He can handle himself and he can be trusted. It's your call."

"Do it. Give it to Isaacson, but send another team just in case. I want a full report by morning. Who has the nerve to attack Philadelphia? Who do we have running the Citizen Army there?"

"Colonel Rotham, sir. He's young, but he rose up through the ranks."

"Rotham. Should we send reinforcements?"

"Not without knowing what's happening. It's not wise."

"Fine. Get back to me by morning. The mayor of Philly's here somewhere. I'll find and tell him. Go, Chloe, and try not to cause a fresh panic."

Chloe was far from panicked as she signaled Nathan away from the stage. He met her by the door. Briefly, she told him what she knew so far.

"Sergeant Harris will stay on the radio," she said, "but we need eyes on the ground, trustworthy eyes."

"Why would you volunteer me?" Nathan emphasized with his hands. "Operation Esther is unfolding, and you're sending me into a war zone? What if Jenna has plans for me tonight?"

"We'll have to cover for you, Nate, because it has to be you. There are only three of us who know Titus, and Chen Li and I can't leave."

"*Titus?* What does—?" He snorted. "You can't be serious! Why would he be fighting with Philadelphia? Better question: *how* would he?"

"We haven't seen him for twenty years, Nathan. Who knows what he's like now? Besides, it may not even be him. Remember, it could be his son, Levi. We were all together in San Diego that last week before Pan-Day. Corban even trained him alongside the KONs for the Korea operation, remember? I'm sure you'll recognize each other, even after all this time."

"If it *is* him, what do I tell him?"

"Tell him we appreciate his company, but he needs to stand down. We've got things under control here. And tell him about Operation Esther."

"The army probably tried to give him the *CEE*."

"Yeah, can you imagine a Caspertein taking the exam?" Chloe laughed, then hid her mouth behind her hand. "Sorry, but it's too funny to imagine. When he refused, they probably tried to arrest him and it sparked a fire."

"Then we might also be getting refugees from Philadelphia. I'm on it." He backed out through the door. "Tell Chen Li I love her."

Nathan took the liberty to break into a storage container in the underground parking below the Bowery to access four different street racing bikes, fully fueled. They were part of the chancellor's evacuation measures, which only his closest cabinet members like Chloe knew about. There were additional fuel barrels in the container, and three other motorcycles, so Nathan doubted Obrador would be too bothered if he found out he'd borrowed one. Besides, if he did have a problem with it, Chloe seemed to be the man's kryptonite. She had gradually molded him this far, and Nathan was confident that Jenna would take him to the finish line.

Just in case, Nathan strapped two extra fuel containers onto the back of the bike, then sped up Broadway. At the GW Bridge, he informed the checkpoint of what was happening, and to expect a recon unit to be close behind him.

Philadelphia was only one hundred miles southwest. Twenty years earlier, Nathan could've made the trip in under an hour with the same bike. However, only one lane had been cleared for traffic, since there were so few vehicles, and parts of the freeway were altogether impassable. Overpass collapses, erosion, or flooding had ruined whole sections. In those cases, he rode cross-country or pushed the bike through ditches for a hundred yards, then returned to the highway. All of this was complicated by the darkness, although Nathan used the headlight of the motorcycle where he thought it was safe, but sparingly. The closer he drew to Philadelphia, the less he needed the headlight at all. The city was indeed aflame, lighting up the landscape in a dull, orange shimmer.

Although it was nearly midnight as Nathan zoomed through the outskirts of northern Philadelphia, many citizens were standing outside on their lawns, considering the glow in the sky so near them. And as Nathan zipped past on his whining rocket, he drew their attention to himself. Since his engine was so loud, he didn't see the need to leave his headlight off any longer. Incognito he was not!

The first military checkpoint came at an off-ramp from the highway, and Nathan slowed to speak to the sentries on watch. Since he'd come straight from the pageant, he was in his finest military garb. When the soldiers saw his insignia, they saluted him. He stepped off the bike and saluted back.

"I was dispatched by the chancellor," he said to a black sergeant who carried two assault rifles on slings. None of the men at the checkpoint appeared to be new to conflict, since their faces were hard and their gear was weathered. "What's the situation, Sergeant? We saw you guys burning a hundred miles away, and the radio wasn't clear about what's happening."

"It's west of downtown." The sergeant pointed at the skyscrapers of the old city. "The radio is full of all kinds of military chatter. Colonel Rotham told us to hold the checkpoint and to stay off the air."

"Are they fighting an out-of-control barbeque fire," Nathan joked, "or is it an actual invader?"

"Maybe both?" The sergeant shrugged. "An hour ago, and earlier in the evening, there was a lot of gunfire. We heard some casualties were taken to the hospital, but then they were released."

"Does that make any sense, Sergeant?" Nathan frowned. "Casualties were released? How are dead people released? Is this a zombie invasion by fire or something?"

"Who knows what the Plains Zone is bringing to us these days? It could be anything."

"I was joking, Sarge." Nathan slapped the man's shoulder. "You're doing a good job. Pass the word that a recon unit from the Federation capital will be coming through here soon. Obrador wants to know what's going on."

Nathan continued on, arriving in the city amidst chaos and fear. Downtown, the streets were cordoned off. Philadelphia could've been mistaken for a sandbag city. White bags of sand were piled on nearly every street corner, with machine gun crews of three soldiers each stationed at the top. It had a formidable appearance, but Nathan knew that if the Casperteins had really shown up with their COIL battle rifles, there wasn't an armed defense in the world that would hold them back.

"Where's Colonel Rotham?" Nathan demanded from a passing corporal.

The man shifted a collection of papers in his arms to point down the street.

Gunfire sounded a couple blocks west, but Nathan knew he wasn't in too much danger. The only people with lethal bullets were the Federation soldiers, and they weren't shooting at lieutenants in Federation uniforms.

Finally, Nathan came upon an armored command vehicle—a steel-plated bus—which was accompanied by intimidating Humvees out front with men at the machine guns in the turrets. He parked his motorcycle and left his helmet on one handlebar.

"Where's Colonel Rotham?" he asked one of the turret gunners.

"Inside. Who're you?"

Nathan passed other loitering soldiers to enter the side door of the command vehicle. The bustling of personnel and gunfire outside was muffled as Nathan stood at the edge of a command briefing.

"And I want two units to get around their southern flank, here." A squinty-faced man in a colonel's uniform looked up from his spread map where several captains accompanied him at an elevated war table. "Who're you?"

"Lieutenant Isaacson with Bowery security." Nathan saluted. "The chancellor sent me as a forward scout."

"It's not a good time, Lieutenant!" the colonel barked. "Wait outside."

"No can do, Colonel. Chancellor Obrador's waiting for word from you on the HAM, or from me when I return. If this is an invasion, we can send reinforcements to repel attackers. If it's a rogue campfire, we can send a firefighting team."

"Firefighters?" The colonel stepped away from his table to belly up to Nathan. "Is that what you think we're dealing with here? You soft, party-goers from Manhattan, and your pathetic dreams for power! You think I want reinforcements from a pathetic force like New York? My men are the best the Federation has in boots. We'll deal with it before sunup, and I'll radio then, and not before. We've always handled our own affairs without anyone's help, and this'll be no different. Go back and tell the Bowery to keep their skirts and ties on, because here in Philly, we put down real troublemakers with an iron fist. You got that, Lieutenant Isaacson?"

"Your city's on fire, sir." Nathan cocked his head, not intimidated by a young colonel who was probably just a teen when Pan-Day had struck. "The whole eastern seaboard can see the sky."

"It's one neighborhood where no one even lived. It's under control! Besides, there's only about four of them."

"Four? Are they anarchists?"

"Tell Obrador it's just four travelers who came from the West looking to defy someone, and I'm dealing with it. Nothing of value has been lost. No one's even died, okay? The enemy is using *tranquilizers!*" The man cursed. "See? That's why we're not taking this too seriously, but we will put these dogs down by morning. You can expect my report by dawn. It's nothing. Everyone is excited over nothing. Now, get out of my city."

"Permission to see for myself, sir, the damage you consider as *nothing*. In and out, then I'll be on my way back to Manhattan within an hour."

"Fine, but if you get shot, you're on your own. Just stop interfering."

"Yes, sir!" Nathan saluted.

As he stepped out of the bus, he heard the colonel say to his men, "Now, there's a persistent soldier. Why can't you fools be more like that? He wouldn't let up until he got what he came for, which was really beginning to irk me!"

Nathan shook his head and chuckled as he returned to his bike. A line of soldiers marched past him going west, and two more lines moved past headed east. On one side of the street, an ammunition truck was unloading boxes of ammunition, and on the other side of the street, a pickup was loading ammunition to take somewhere else. Regardless of Colonel Rotham's zeal to put down four trouble-makers, his own men seemed ignorant as to how to proceed.

Once on his bike, Nathan left his helmet off and rode west slowly down the middle of the street. He'd aged a bit in the last twenty years, and he no longer wore his signature handlebar mustache, but they hadn't called him Eagle Eyes for nothing all those years. His eyebrows were angled, and he'd been told it sharpened the impact of his glare, although he guessed the few gray hairs creeping in weren't as intimidating as the dark brown had been. Nevertheless, whoever these COIL operatives were out there, he hoped they would recognize him, preferably before he was tranquilized.

"Get out of the street!" Soldiers yelled at him as he continued west, using no cover at all while they were hesitant to move along the sidewalks.

Armed units moved from green dumpsters to building corners, some advancing, others retreating.

Nathan figured these crack troops were as skilled as Manhattan's finest—experts at arresting, torturing, and executing Christians and other noncompliants. If four combatants had wreaked such havoc on their city, then they were learning that there were much better gunfighters out there than they were.

Nathan rode beyond where Federation troops held the streets, and stopped at the edge of where the fire had approached earlier in the evening. Gunfire sporadically blasted blocks away to the left and right, but Nathan guessed it was just overly-excited Federation soldiers. He had yet to hear the boom of a high-caliber battle rifle.

The fire burned high a few blocks away, though the heat could be felt even from where he was. The air seemed to push against him, but he didn't flee. The fire was indeed burning old residences and crumbling houses, either abandoned voluntarily due to lack of utilities, or abandoned by force as a population management measure by the government. New York had tried similar tactics to control or group civilians for resource purposes. From where Nathan sat, no one in sight was even fighting the fire.

He turned his bike around and started back the way he'd come when he saw a figure leap from one rooftop to the next, far above and to his right. Nathan parked at the curb and ran to the alley to see another person leap to the next building.

"Hey!" he yelled, then whistled.

A head reappeared four stories up on the roof, too far away for someone down the street to see. Nathan needed to think quickly, remembering Chloe's orders for him to pass on the message. To these people, he would appear to be only a uniformed Federation officer, so he needed to shout something that only a COIL-trained operative would know—and quickly, before he was tranqed. If these were Casperteins, then they were students of the Bible, even if the Bible was banned in that part of the continent.

"Hey! Who will give me rest if I'm weary and heavy-laden?" Nathan smiled and waved, hoping the silhouette of the head he could see above was indeed one of the four he was searching for, and not merely a looter leaping from roof to roof.

"Matthew eleven, twenty-eight!" a voice shouted back, but the voice came from above and behind Nathan.

He spun around to see two crouching figures on the opposite rooftop across the street. Of course, a shooting pair on one side of the street and a pair on the other was a sound cover strategy, which only experienced shooters would know to do. It was them.

"Who are you?" a loud voice thundered from above, but he still couldn't see more than a head.

Checking the distance to the nearest Federation soldier up the street, Nathan figured it was perhaps two blocks away. A safe distance to yell without being heard clearly.

"A Caspertein would know me as Eagle Eyes."

There was a pause, and Nathan thought he heard the squawk of a two-way radio. They had headsets!

"Come on up here!" the one across the street yelled.

Nathan jogged across the road and kicked in a door. Seconds later, inside the abandoned real estate office, he located the stairs and started climbing. Four stories later, he burst onto the flat rooftop that was high enough to see over most of the district to the east and all of the burned neighborhood to the west.

Pausing, Nathan acknowledged the two figures on the roof in front of him, spread out like they knew how to make themselves difficult targets. And across the street on the opposite rooftop were the other two, watching him.

"Just the four of you did all this?" he asked, trying to break the ice. He still hadn't received a confirming response that this was who he thought it was, or hoped it was.

"Walk closer," ordered the man directly in front of him.

Nathan licked his lips. Walking closer to that man would make it very difficult to keep his eye on his friend to the right. But realistically, Nathan had only a sidearm with lethal rounds, and he'd never actually used it on a person, nor would he do so with the intent to kill. He was at their mercy.

He walked forward. The man before him was a little taller and even broader than Nathan, which wasn't all that common. There seemed to be a heaping pack on the traveler's back, with all sorts of gear, including skis, sticking out over his head. Nathan stopped and glanced at the man's companion, now distinctly seen as a solid figure of a woman with wavy, dark hair in a ponytail.

"Hello, Nathan." The man grinned, his teeth shining white on the dark night.

Nathan could see his blond hair now, lit up by the fire behind him.

"It's good to see you, Levi. Is that your dad on the other roof?"

"Naw, Dad died last year. Poisoned in San Diego. Long story."

"Sorry to hear that. He was my friend. We heard you were coming." Nathan chuckled. "Didn't expect your arrival to be quite like this, but here you are, in Caspertein fashion."

"We're here for Jenna. Before our radios were taken in the Pacific States, she sent a message that things were bad for Christians."

"They have been for years, but Jenna's got it under control now. Chloe said to tell you everything."

"Chloe? Chloe's here?"

"In New York, with my wife. We've been holding down the fort, COIL style. Rumor has it that Scooter and Bruno are around, but I've only been in touch with Corban and Luigi on a semi-regular basis. Those of us who're still alive have been networking, supporting Jenna."

"Corban? Are you serious? He's still alive?"

"He's holding on. Pan-Day gave us the opportunity to reinvent ourselves. Jenna's nearly in charge of the Federation with Chloe, and I'm doing my part with Chen Li."

"Nearly in charge?" Levi scoffed. "They tried to arrest us, and when we resisted, they've been trying to kill us the last two days. We're light on sleep and growing lighter on patience."

"Well, Jenna is still working out a few kinks."

"More than a few. I tranqed a Colonel Rotham earlier today, and questioned him in holding. He was mobilizing a whole division against New York, and he was none too happy that I'd ruined his convoy. You have some internal strife even you apparently don't know about."

"None that—" Nathan hesitated, thinking of Lena Travers' distant attitude the last couple months. "There might be some power struggles going on. Like I said, Jenna's sorting it out."

"I'm here to get her out of harm's way."

"Levi, you're not listening. She's been working for years to get to this point—this very night. The Federation has chosen her to join the chancellor to run this messed-up country."

"And you're not listening to me, Nathan. I've just spent a year fighting my way across America. Now I'm here. No offense, but I'm not standing down until I hear it from her own lips."

"I'm her personal security in Manhattan, Levi. Please listen. She's safe. She's been undercover with me and Corban for years. She's about to make her big move to take control over everything."

"I know an army mobilization when I see it," Levi said, "and I'm telling you, this Colonel Rotham was about to take control of what you guys think you're building. We just disabled about forty armored transports, and they weren't on the move for our sake. Does that sound like a peace-time occurrence?"

"No, it doesn't." Nathan sighed, realizing there was more afoot in the Federation than they knew about in the Bowery. "That explains Colonel Rotham's attitude, I guess. He may have been mobilizing to take New York City, right in the middle of our coronation event next week. But burning down a neighborhood hasn't helped anything."

"It got carried away. The wind drove it until sundown. Truth be told, we were trying to figure out what our next move was. It ain't easy invading a country you know little about."

"I can fill in some of the blanks for you," Nathan said, thankful Levi was easing back, "including the location of about two thousand heavily armed troops about six city blocks that way."

"*Two thousand?*" Levi whistled. "I don't even have that many gel-tranqs."

"Who's that with you?" Nathan gestured toward the other building.

"Rex Caspertein, Rudy's boy."

"Doesn't look like a boy. He looks bigger than Rudy."

"He is, and he's with Alice Prine, a sister in the faith who's been with me since California."

"And I'm Lyla Caspertein," the woman on the roof said, shifting her battle rifle aside, "which my husband so politely remembered to disclose."

Nathan shook her hand. She had a firm grip and a kind yet bold face.

"Hey, it ain't easy burning down a city *and* being polite!" Levi laughed and came forward, his arms wide. He embraced Nathan and slapped him heartily on the back. "It's good to see you, old friend, as Dad always called you. I'm sorry to make a mess of things for Jenna and you guys.

I've had a one-track mind for so many months, I've met any resistance with my own stubbornness."

"Chloe didn't sound like she was expecting an apology from you," Nathan said. "She just asked if you'd stand down, at least temporarily, and that I fill you in on Operation Esther, to protect Jenna's interests."

"What's Operation Esther?"

"I'm sure there's a place for you in all of this, Levi, but it's going to take some time to explain. Colonel Rotham is planning an assault on your position as we speak, flanking from the south. How about we head north, which is closer to New York City, anyway?"

"Sounds good to me." Levi lowered his head to his chest where a small black transmitter was fastened. "You guys good, Rex? Head north, stay in sight."

"Roger that," a deep voice responded on the radio. "Lead out, we'll cover."

Chapter Thirteen

The next morning, Chloe was feeling somewhat overwhelmed. In the past, when COIL had been operating internationally, she'd best directed Corban's operatives when she herself was in a safe place. But there was nothing safe about Operation Esther or the Bowery. Jenna had elevated the level of risk by moving herself straight into the Bowery. Of course, Obrador thought he was running things, but it was Jenna, with the help and direction of God, who'd arranged everything down to the Federation's anthem—and Chloe couldn't stop trembling because of it.

Since the wedding wasn't for another week, Jenna had moved into a hotel room two stories below the chancellor's suite, where she could be closest to Chen Li, her unofficial personal assistant. Chloe would've preferred her to be one floor up with herself, but Jenna had insisted, since Chloe had far too much to coordinate already.

"Chloe, are you ill?" the chancellor asked from his desk. "You're holding your stomach. Some bad veal last night?"

"No, no." She smiled from where she sat on the divan in the middle of the room. "It's nothing. You were saying?"

"I was saying, we don't need Lena anymore. I'm not offended that she didn't stay for the whole pageant. It just gives me further reason to push her out of my affairs. Maybe I should just get rid of her completely."

"You can reassign her, Kendrick," Chloe said, and raised her fingers for air quotes, "without getting rid of her. I wouldn't even know who you could call on to get rid of someone like her."

She usually only called him Kendrick in private, when they were alone in his office. Even the bodyguards were out in the hall this time.

"Lieutenant Isaacson could handle her." He set his elbows on his desk and sipped hard booze even though it wasn't yet noon. "The way he moves, even with that leg brace—you can tell he was a killer in his prime. He's still in his prime. What is he, not even sixty yet?"

There was a knock on the door, and an aide stuck her head in to announce Sergeant Harris.

"Send him in," Chloe said, and rose to her feet, not to welcome Harris but to hide her trembling. Nathan should've been back from Philadelphia by then! "Sergeant Harris has been covering Bowery security while Isaacson is gone."

"Oh, good!" Obrador smiled broadly, far too jovial, Chloe thought, for the tense situation taking place around the state. "What's the latest, Sergeant?"

Harris' old face, wrinkled and frowning, spoke volumes before he opened his mouth. He was nervous. It was more bad news. Obrador had a reputation for blasting messengers who brought bad news, although he hadn't done so recently.

"There's chatter, sir—all kinds of it. I can't fully make it out, since they're speaking in codes, but something big is happening."

"Of course something big is happening, Sergeant." Obrador chuckled. "You were there last night. The Federation is engaged to be married—the people to its ruler. There should be chatter. It should be all about Jenna, in my opinion."

"No, this is on military channels." Harris wiped his brow and glanced at Chloe. "Where's Lieutenant Isaacson? This is way over my head."

"Speak plainly, Sergeant." Chloe gestured to the chancellor. "We've been in here all morning broadcasting farm production demands for next quarter. Maybe it's just that?"

"No. It's Boston, Hartford, and Baltimore who are talking. They keep referring to Rendezvous New Castle. Then they talk in code about dates, times, and I think military units."

"Where's New Castle?" Obrador asked Chloe. "Is that in Vermont?"

"It's probably another code." Chloe went to the map to identify Boston, Hartford, and Baltimore. "Nothing from Philadelphia, Sergeant? They were all fired up last night, and now nothing?"

"Just smoke. We can see it smoldering." Harris stepped to the wall map. I'll tell you what's in the middle of those three cities, ma'am. It's us. New York City."

"New Castle is Manhattan?" Obrador leaped from his seat. "What are you saying?"

"I'm sure it's nothing," Chloe said. "Just some late maneuvers or war games they didn't want to bother us about."

"Now you're making me nervous." Obrador crossed his arms. "Unless it really *is* harmless. Maybe a surprise tribute to me for the wedding? The nation's really behind this, right?"

"The buzz on the street is all thumbs-up, Mr. Chancellor." Harris raised his thumbs. "Everyone I know is excited about last night. There wasn't a prettier girl there who stole our hearts more than Jenna Dowler. Everyone knows her name now."

"There. See?" Obrador raised his arms. "Everything is fine. The people approve. I'll tell you what I need to do is get Isaacson a new commission to run my military intelligence. Lena isn't being too helpful about this. We need her here to answer questions, and no one's even seen her."

"Unless that's her." Harris pointed out the window to the north. "She's riding her bike in on Broadway right there."

Chloe snatched up binoculars they sometimes used to observe Uptown.

"No, it's Nathan. I mean Lieutenant Isaacson. He borrowed a bike from the garage. It looks like he's finally back from Philly." She set the glasses down. "Sergeant, thank you for your report. Keep it to yourself until we know more. No need to create false rumors about things that could be perfectly harmless. I'm sure the lieutenant will keep you apprised. On your way out, would you please make sure Isaacson comes straight here?"

"Yes, ma'am, certainly." Harris saluted Obrador. "Mr. Chancellor."

The instant Harris was gone, Chloe expected Obrador to share what he really thought about the radio chatter. Instead, he sat down at his desk and poured himself another drink.

"You know, I bet with morale so high right now," he said, "planting season will be richer than ever. Which means we'll have extra to put away from the harvest this fall. We can get back to thinking about expanding to the West, where the real fields are probably ripe for cultivating after lying dormant for twenty years. Imagine wheat fields as far as the eye can see, Chloe. That could all be ours."

"If Pacific States doesn't get there first," Chloe reminded. "We haven't had reports back for weeks from scouts telling us what's really going on in the Plains Zone. We can't function without consistent, dependable reporting."

"All that's changing. I can feel it. The Federation has turned a new leaf. My wife will be honored with the anthem she wrote for the country, and the country will in turn sing songs about her."

Following a knock on the door, Nathan walked in and saluted. Chloe wanted to run over and embrace him—*he was alive!* His formal uniform was dirt-smeared and wrinkled. Dark circles under his eyes betrayed his weariness, but Chloe knew he was a man of discipline. He could continue to function at a high level of alertness even after being up for a day and a half.

"Philadelphia was attacked," Nathan briefed, "but it seems to have passed. Colonel Rotham responded in force against a small band of travelers who set a number of fires, which in turn got out of control from the wind. But no casualties have been reported. All that burned was a neighborhood where utilities had collapsed and it had been vacated, anyway. Now, it's ready for rebuilding."

"See?" Obrador raised his glass to Nathan. "You're my kind of guy, Lieutenant. You see the glass half full. There was nothing to even worry about, Chloe."

"Why haven't they reported in?" Chloe asked. "We nearly mobilized reinforcements to repel an invasion. This isn't how we run a country! This Colonel Rotham should be called in for a formal demotion."

"I think he was just embarrassed that a few strangers came into his back yard and caused so much damage before he could respond." Nathan shrugged, but Chloe knew him better than that. Something else was going on. "By the time I left the city, the problem was resolved."

"He'd better hang those fire-starters." Obrador's words were starting to slur. "The country's on the rise. Instigators need to be quickly punished to make an example."

Chloe glared at Nathan, knowing he had more intel to share. He was holding back, and she could barely contain herself.

"Well," she said, "I'm glad it all worked out, Lieutenant. Go get cleaned up and we'll see you tonight at the banquet that Owen is throwing for the newly engaged couple. Chancellor, I'll call the aides in. I need to go to my room for a while."

"Fine, fine." Obrador waved, fully drunk now. "Tell them I want turkey on rye today. Turkey on rye."

Chloe held the door open for Nathan to leave and the aides to enter. Then, she hustled after Nathan and caught him one flight down where he was waiting on the landing.

"It was Levi Caspertein!" he whispered, clutching her shoulders. "The crazy kid burned down half of Philly and destroyed most of whatever mobile unit Colonel Rotham was knocking the dust off!"

"Slow down, slow down." Chloe held up her hand. "Explain, Nathan, because we're getting reports that Boston, Hartford, and Baltimore are suddenly mobilizing for something called Rendezvous New Castle."

"Oh." Nathan leaned against the wall. "Oh, now it's making more sense. Levi stumbled onto this. Rotham didn't have anything good to say about Obrador or New York City. I suspected he was up to no good, but this is on a whole other scale."

"This is terrible timing!" Chloe wrung her hands. "We're less than a week away!"

"It's gotta be a coup." Nathan shook his head. "How in the world do we tell Jenna about this?"

"Obrador thinks the nation is just fine, Nathan, and you just told him Philly is no big deal!"

"I thought Operation Esther took precedence over everything."

"Yeah, everything except being overrun by an army! Use your head, Nathan! There's no Bowery to run the country from if we're all killed in a coup!"

Nathan looked down the stairwell, not meeting her eyes for a moment. The stairwell was still clear, and his silence forced her to reflect on her words.

"Look, Nathan," she said, her words softer. "We've both been up all night and day. I shouldn't have spoken to you like that. I'm sorry. I have to go tell Jenna everything we now know. Chen Li is with her, so you and I can both go and tell them together. But before we go, tell me about Levi. Did Titus raise him well?"

"The kid's an animal, even spiritually. We prayed together, and he's got passion, I'm telling you. He's married, too. A nice, Christian woman named Lyla. She bosses him around like Annette use to do with Titus. But I think Lyla keeps him in check."

Chloe muffled her laughter with her hand.

"You said there was a band of travelers. He's with others?"

"I'd say the others are with him. He's a natural leader, like his dad. He's got two more with him. Remember Rudy Caspertein? Well, Rudy had a son just as monstrous as he is. He's bigger than Levi, and Levi's taller than me!"

"Seriously?" Chloe sighed. "If Operation Esther is falling apart on us, the Casperteins arrived just in time."

"And there's a black woman named Alice. She has one arm. Real quiet—maybe late fifties. While we talked north of the city, she scouted around for danger like she knew what she was doing. Those four devastated that city, Chloe, and Rotham couldn't keep his men conscious long enough to stage an offensive. Levi kept tranqing his soldiers."

"Well, he's COIL-trained, so what else would we expect?"

"I expect nothing less from a Caspertein." Nathan yawned. "It's too bad Titus didn't live to see what his son has become."

"Oh, you didn't say." Chloe nodded slowly. "Titus is gone?"

"Meridia got him last year, then Levi headed east to rescue Jenna, just like she figured he would."

"Can you imagine Titus dealing with this mess? We're probably facing a coup now. He'd probably start cracking jokes in the middle of a government uprising about how it ain't easy being a Caspertein!"

"Oh, just wait until you meet Levi again. That kid's taken over just fine in the wisecrack department!"

Jenna listened carefully to Chloe's report. From where Jenna sat on her hotel bed, she could tell Chloe was standing against the wall near the bathroom door, and Chen Li sat quietly on the other end of the bed. Chloe spoke softly, her years of operative debriefings revealing her efficiency and objectivity. It was sometimes daunting for Jenna to work with Chloe since the older woman had so much more world experience, but in those moments, Jenna remembered her own training from her father. Chloe had served Corban faithfully for many years, so there didn't need to be any awkwardness in seeing her as an intelligence proxy for her father.

"So, Levi's really arrived." Jenna kept her hands folded on her lap, and spoke just as softly back to Chloe, even though the walls were nearly soundproof. Nathan and Chen Li's room was next to her own, so no one was near them on the floor to listen, but caution had kept them alive this long. "And he's married."

"That isn't our main concern right now, Jenna," Chloe said. "A coup seems to be in the works."

"It's to be expected." Jenna sighed as she reached out for God's counsel. What should she do now? So many were relying on her. "We knew to watch for something like this."

"Excuse me?" Chloe snorted. "We did? When did you say to expect a coup? I mean, besides the thing our own team is doing."

"Satan's aware of our intentions to set up a stable government here, which would enable the gospel of Jesus Christ to be shared more openly once again. This has never been a fight between flesh and blood, Chloe. As Christians, if not intelligence operatives, we knew to expect this exact kind of opposition coming from left field."

"But an invasion or a hostile takeover of the Bowery ends this operation," Chloe stated. "I mean, besides getting us all killed. We're part of Obrador's cabinet. You'll be part of his family. Medieval rules will apply in this case, I think, which means we all get executed."

"So, we need to figure out who's behind it," Chen Li said in almost a whisper. "If we can figure out what they're after, then we can strike a deal or something."

"We already know who's behind it," Jenna said, "and we already know what she wants."

"Sure, we know Philly was involved," Chloe stated, "and now we know Boston, Hartford, and Baltimore are up to something similar. We can assume it has to do with power, control, and calling the shots from here. Wait, did you just say *she?*"

"Lena Travers." Jenna turned her head, sensing Chloe and Chen Li's surprise even without seeing them. "Ever since Operation Esther was initiated, she's been acting peculiar. It was in one of your reports to me, Chloe. She opposed the pageant proposal from the beginning. She said it made the Federation seem weak. But Obrador sided with you and Nathan, Chloe. We took it as a win, sure, since we persuaded the chancellor with the idea, but we didn't realize we'd created a monster at the same time."

"Yeah, but Lena Travers?" Chen Li asked. "That woman's just an Enforcer. Sure, she's cold-hearted and argumentative, but hardly the mastermind behind a coup."

"Would you believe me if I told you she's the one who really killed Heather?" Jenna said. "It wasn't Owen at all. He just took the credit."

"*What?*" Chloe's clothes rustled as she knelt on the carpet in front of Jenna. "How do you know that? How do you figure these things out? I can see everything with my eyes, but even I'm not able to figure these things out!"

"Heather was coming to meet me two months ago. I know from Luigi exactly where she went above ground to find another route to make it to me. And also, Nathan read to me the daily Bowery logs on Enforcer arrivals and departures."

"I wondered why you wanted those," Nathan said as he entered the room. Jenna could smell the steam coming from the bathroom revealing that he'd just showered.

"Owen was here when Lena called him for something," Jenna continued. "He left with a truck, and twenty minutes later, he came back with Heather. Lena was logged as coming through the front gate soon after."

"Why would she do that?" Chen Li asked. "She allowed her brother to get credit for catching who they thought was Radiant Shade?"

"She used him as a pawn," Jenna said, "to hide her true intentions, it seems. Owen gained the favor of Obrador, but meanwhile, she was staying off the radar while she formulated this whole other situation."

"And now she's using us as pawns!" Chloe's voice was low, almost a growl. "I swear—"

"Chloe." Jenna reached out and cupped the woman's chin. "Lena's in no more control than we are. It may seem like people or rulers or chancellors get away with evil, but even a blind woman can see through it all, if we look intently. A coup from a woman on the inside wasn't in our plans, but God isn't surprised or caught off guard. We serve the God who knows all things."

"But we've spent years on Operation Esther." Chloe's voice was back to a softer tone, almost pleading. "This undoes everything."

"No, it doesn't. Until God closes that door completely, we still see Operation Esther through. We gather intel, and move by truth and faith, not by rumors and fear." She suddenly laughed. "And the one thing we do know for sure now is that a year ago, when things seemed particularly bleak in the Federation, I called Levi Caspertein to come help us. Twenty-four hours ago, I couldn't have told you why or how he fit into our plans, but God knew all along. Now we have someone local who can withstand an invading army. There are only two ways into Manhattan—across the GW Bridge, or from the north, coming through the Bronx and across the Harlem River. Either place creates a bottleneck for a large force, but not for a small one. Levi could be very instrumental in the coming days!"

"So, we keep going?" Chen Li asked. "Just like we don't know anything? What if Lena shows up and does something?"

"Change nothing we do," Jenna said, "but we need to shift our prayers to include what we now know about this three-fold invading force. It sounds like Levi removed Philadelphia's division from the equation. Maybe the Lord has something similar in mind to deal with the other three divisions."

"That's thousands of soldiers." Chloe sighed. "It won't be a fight. It'll be a flood of people. And artillery."

"Such threats haven't intimidated COIL Christians before," Jenna reminded. "All of you have faced off against superior forces, like North Korea just twenty years ago, and you're still standing. Even if this is our end, has it been so bad that we should grow discouraged? Operation Esther gave us something to fight for. We've saved thousands over the years, and the ones we couldn't save, we comforted them in their moments of death. You three are more responsible for that than even me. So what if we have to abandon ship right now? Or be publicly executed by Lena? As Dad has said, *just die well*. Die for Christ. Don't die for justice or the Federation or for your own self-pity. Die for Christ, and do it with a song in your heart, because in the following instant, you'll be with Him!"

"Well, when you put it like that . . ." Chen Li laughed.

"But I want to win!" Chloe said. "We can't allow darkness to win this battle. Think of all the forced laborers outside in the cages right now. We still have people to save!"

"We can only do what we can do, Chloe," Jenna said. "Ultimately, we can't expect any earthly government to be set right for too long, since one of God's lessons throughout history has been to show that human governments fail miserably—to make way for the only King's government that won't ever fall. This world is passing away, so we don't need to cling too tightly to winning or controlling, or even to the freedoms or rights of this world. Let's look toward heaven."

"Invasion could come at any time," Chen Li mentioned. "Are we ready at least for that?"

"We'll get ready." Jenna held out her hands to the women, who each took a hand in their own. "And we'll pray more desperately now, since we see more clearly."

Once Jenna was alone, she remained on the bed contemplating before God all that was now apparent. She even talked to the Lord about her feelings regarding Levi being married. *How could he?* Didn't he remember their connection? But an instant later, she realized she was no one to talk! In a week, she'd be ceremonially married to a tyrant she'd spent years planning to defeat. No, she couldn't feel too distressed about Levi finding a wife besides herself. After all, he'd still come for her. He'd actually come all the way from San Diego for her—like a whirlwind, too, it sounded like!

She laughed at herself and wiped at her tears. Corban had told her all about Titus Caspertein's reckless life, and the supernatural hand of God over the witty man's spontaneity. If Levi had even half the favor of God that his father once had, Lena Travers had better watch out!

The door to the hallway clicked, and Jenna rose to her feet to greet whomever seemed to have a key to her room— but the person hadn't even knocked! Jenna instinctively smoothed down her summer dress, still adjusting to being in public again after have lived alone with Corban for so long. Her only visitors had been Heather and Luigi, or the occasional Federation citizen who'd come by the office to pick up ID papers.

A hint of salty air wafted in from the hallway as the door opened, then swung closed. Jenna felt it on her face, and smelled the hallway in the air before it was cut off. It was a scent that Jenna knew that no one with eyes could probably decipher. Someone had entered her room. And that someone was now standing there in front of the door.

She swallowed with difficulty, fear rippling across her skin. After all of her brave talk to the experienced COIL people, she was now the one who licked her lips and prepared to scream for Chen Li in the adjoining room.

But as the seconds ticked past, Jenna began to read the intruder differently. He was trespassing, yes, but for what reason? Assault? Curiosity? She imagined that some men would like the control they would feel over a blind woman—defenseless, completely vulnerable to an attacker . . .

Her heart thudded with adrenalin, but she didn't call out. She resisted the urge to turn and run into the bathroom. There were two steps to the corner of the bed, then it was a straight shot for nine steps to the bathroom door. Four paces, if she were running. It would take an extra second to turn and shut the bathroom door once she was inside. From there, she could scream, if her trespasser's hands weren't already around her throat. Maybe she wouldn't even make it to the bathroom. Maybe he would step forward and punch her hard enough without warning that she'd lose consciousness, or be stunned to silence.

It was indeed a man. She could smell his sweat. And his boot polish. He was perfectly quiet, his breathing not even reaching her ears. Yes, he was a predator, someone who knew how to wait, when to act, how to remain in hiding until the perfect opportunity to pounce on unsuspecting prey. This man was dangerous.

"So, here we are," she said, but not loud enough for Chen Li to hear. Slowly, she sat back down on the edge of the bed, her hands at her sides. By sitting down, she'd abandoned any chance of successfully reaching the bathroom without being caught. "You're standing there, maybe conflicted about why you're here. Maybe you're even wondering why I'm not calling for help. Chen Li from Citizen Processing is on the other side of that door, and she would handle you quite smartly, you probably know. And if you got past her, you'd need to deal with her husband, the notorious Lieutenant Isaacson. I hear he's one of the largest men in the whole hotel—Lieutenant Leather.

"Don't be mistaken," she said, raising one hand, then lowered it to the bed again, "I'm not threatening you. I'm just letting you know that I'm willing to show you mercy to let us get to know one another. Already, I know quite a bit about you, but I'm good at keeping things to myself. Being blind, I'm often underestimated, so I use that to my advantage. I listen. I hear. I contemplate. For instance, I know already who has access to the master key cards in the Bowery. And I know you're an official, not someone who's merely stolen the master key card. Your boots are polished, and your clothes were laundered recently. You've showered in the last couple days, because I can smell the soap. But you have the scent of a man. It's not covered by deodorant or aftershave. You have nerve. You know what you want. Now, let me tell you what I can give you, since that's what you've come to find out. If you were here to take me, you would've done so already. Yes, we understand one another. Water?"

Jenna gestured to her left toward the dresser where she remembered Chen Li had left a pitcher and glass cups. Rising slowly so as not to alarm her trespasser, she felt for the pitcher. She poured water into one glass, then turned and cleared her throat. By echolocation off the bare walls and door, she identified where he was standing. Then she took three steps and stopped in front of him.

Now, she could smell his breath and hear him breathe. He was breathing deeply, smoothly, trying to remain absolutely silent, but even a slight breath through the back of the throat made sound.

She sipped her water and focused her eyes straight ahead, level, about where his face would be. He wasn't a tall man.

"I'm about to marry the chancellor. I'm going to need good men near me, men I can trust with sensitive matters, personal matters, and sometimes matters of state. But you're also a man who has ambitions of his own. You're a man who would like someone near the chancellor, someone who may help you with a sensitive matter when it's time. We all need friends. You're a man who knows where to find those friends, and you're a man who knows such friends are rare. You're a man who knows how to hold an opportunity like this in your heart—until it's truly time to call upon that friend. When you do that, when you're ready, I'll be that friend. Will you be that man?"

Taking a full gulp from the glass, she then offered it to him. The gesture, she hoped, was clear, like an ancient truce between warring parties, to drink from the same chalice, for peace that could be bought no other way.

He gently took the glass. She did her best not to grimace when the tips of his fingers brushed over hers. She heard him suck in a mouthful of water, then swallow noisily. Her hand was still extended, and he pushed the glass back into her palm.

"Very well," she said. "We drank from the same cup. That will be our code phrase. It's ours and ours alone. *We drank from the same cup.* When you repeat that phrase to me, I'll know it's you, and our friendship will be acted upon, no matter the circumstances, unconditionally. Go now, before we have company. Check the hallway before stepping out. Make sure it's clear. Goodbye."

She took a giant step backward and stood expectantly, the glass still in her hand. For a moment, there was no sound or shift in the air, and she began to doubt that her words had made any effect. But then, the door handle clicked. The air brushed over her face and hair as the door opened, then it closed. After clearing her throat, she sensed she was indeed alone again.

With more control than she felt she had, she set down the glass on the dresser and went into the bathroom, where she closed the door. In the solitude of the bathroom, she buried her face in a scratchy towel and cried softly. She had been afraid, but she'd sensed the Lord giving her the very words to speak to the intruder. Though she'd meant every word, she had only half-expected a trespasser to agree to what she'd proposed.

"Give me strength, my Father," she whispered as she dried her eyes, knowing she was a blind lamb among crafty wolves. Evil—some of it known and some of it unknown—was all around. The intruder was a healthy reminder that she wasn't under her father's protection any longer. For the first time in her life, she was on her own, and if she gave way to the terror of it, she would be paralyzed, useless, and defenseless.

Anyone could attack her at any time, and she was in the business of making enemies, regardless of her desire to reconcile people to the Lord. She needed to secure herself better. The completion of Operation Esther demanded it!

Owen Travers was thrilled that his hosted dinner was going so smoothly. He saw his whole life climaxing that very night! Thirty of the most influential people in the capital city, including governors and mayors from elsewhere, were all there for him, and to honor the chancellor.

In the midst of the various conversations over dinner, Owen raised his glass across the table to Chloe. She'd come through for him, giving him this moment to make an even bigger splash in the chancellor's eyes. Lena wasn't there, and the embarrassing incident from days earlier with Corban Dowler was in the past, though not forgotten. Of course, he might need to adjust his plans for the old man, since the man's own daughter was now due to be the chancellor's wife!

Chloe nodded her head in return, rather than her wine glass. He realized he'd never seen her drink alcohol. She had a glass of iced tea next to her plate. Owen vowed in his heart never to forget that Chloe had made this possible for him. It had been a lot to ask of the busy woman in the midst of a hectic week. But because of it, he could add his contribution to the Federation's might across the land!

As he waited for the right moment to make his speech, he acknowledged the discussions up and down the table. Jenna was at one end, and the chancellor at the other. Obrador had taken a special liking to Lieutenant Isaacson, who was seated to his right. They were engaged in a conversation about water management and the snowfall that winter in the Catskills and the Delaware Water Gap. The mayor of Dover was there, since his granddaughter had entered the pageant. He was in a discussion with the governor of Rhode Island about expanding the forced labor laws to include more of society in general, requiring all citizens to work for the good of the Federation.

Owen watched Jenna, though guardedly and with cautious glances. The night before, he'd seen his chance to finally get back at Corban Dowler. Jenna had been left alone—Corban's own daughter completely vulnerable! He'd seen his chance to pay the old man a devastating blow by taking his blind daughter's life. It would've been so easy. Even as personal as his past injuries had been by

Corban's hand, Owen hadn't been able to follow through. After he'd entered her room, prepared to kill her then and there, he'd looked into the face of a mature woman who knew exactly how to appeal to his ambitions. As much as he wanted to hurt Corban, he wanted even more to rise in the hierarchy of the Federation, right up to Obrador's side. The chancellor would've never known who had killed his fiancée, and Owen might've even found a way to lead the investigation to find the killer. But all of that had changed when Jenna had spoken to him.

She reminded him of Chloe, just younger, knowing exactly how to touch his desire. He was going places, and he did indeed need people at the top who would also look out for his best interests. Her proposal to help him as a friend, at any moment he revealed himself, gave him such power! But he realized she'd done so by reserving power for herself. Yet, he trusted her to follow through. Such an agreement threw off his entire plan to avenge himself against Corban, her father. Perhaps he really could move past Corban's slights if it meant he could advance in other ways. After all, Corban didn't seem to actually be targeting him personally. The man had only responded to humiliate him when Owen had tried to do so first to Corban. It seemed possible that to hold the daughter's promise close, Owen would need to tolerate the father.

Finally, Owen could wait no longer. He stood over the table and tapped his glass, bringing all eyes to rest on himself. Taking a deep breath, he savored the moment. If Lena had been seated there with them, she would've criticized him, or ruined the moment with her scowling. But he was his own man now. Her schemes were her own. These were his people. They loved him, and he loved them.

"Chancellor Obrador, Bride-to-be Jenna Dowler, distinguished guests, thank you for being here this evening. I've asked you all here to witness and celebrate an announcement I've chosen to make to the chancellor himself. It's an announcement and a proposal, from the humble mind of a mere Enforcer, I know, but I hope that together we can turn it into something more, for the good of the Federation."

He paused and drew out the note he'd been given not two days earlier. As he unfolded it, he noticed Chloe watching and waiting with as much anticipation as everyone else. Even though she already knew the content of his announcement, she was allowing him to bask in his glory. What a woman! No wonder Obrador had kept her close all those years.

"Here in my hand I have what amounts to be a treaty from the resistance here in the city!" He waited as the exclamations and words of awe lingered a few seconds. "Someone who calls himself Hedgehog has gathered the resistance behind him, and the infamous Bandit has been ousted. With the Bandit's departure, the resistance has designs to cooperate with us in exchange for the help of the Federation to hunt down three criminals. The names of the three are the Bandit, Brian Steelman, and a man named Luigi Putelli. These three have been taken in by a sect of noncompliant citizens somewhere in the Christian underground.

"The Christians are the last holdouts, my friends. The Federation is so close to exclusively owning the hearts and minds of its populace. The Christians are running scared, and they'll be rooted out by what I propose next. But first, I salute the leadership at this table, which has brought the resistance to its knees—and better yet, has brought the resistance to the negotiating table with us!"

"Here, here!" Applause erupted. Faces were bright. Even Obrador leaned over to Isaacson and said something, their smiles broad and approving.

"The wedding is Sunday," Owen continued, emboldened by the support thus far. "I propose a decree be enacted across the Federation for one day, and one day only—the day after the wedding. This day will be for the complete cleansing of nonconformist Christians from our land, once and for all! If approved, the announcement could be made immediately, Federation-wide. Every conforming citizen will be permitted for one day only to destroy the nonconforming Christians. Neighbors always know. Now, it's time for neighbors to act!

"For the citizens who respond to this Day of Cleansing, the possessions of the Christians they publicly execute in the streets will transfer immediately to those faithful, loyal citizens of this fine country. *The spoils go to every loyal citizen!* We can rid this country of this cancer once and for all—and no official Enforcer needs to lift their finger. In one day, we become a nation of Enforcers! Let's all support our new Day of Cleansing!"

With his fist held high, Owen was breathless as the applause and shouts of approval went on and on. Owen thanked the people through the cheering by looking them each in the face and mouthing his thanks. He felt their approval and he couldn't imagine life getting any better than that moment.

Suddenly, Jenna rose from her chair. She wore a simple but beautiful gown that seemed to shimmer in the candlelight glowing from the windowsills. The room grew quiet as they gazed expectantly at the blind woman. Owen sighed, completely satisfied, and seated himself. These were his equals now. They would remember him as a policy-maker, a Federation leader, a first-generation visionary. And to think he'd recently been obsessed over whether or not people bowed their heads to him!

"I have a passion for the Federation as well," Jenna said, her voice sweet, her sightless eyes moving as if meant to express the care she felt. "Mr. Travers' announcement and proposal brings the Federation to a crossroads. This week will be forever remembered by all citizens, so I say we make it even more remarkable. In honor of this important juncture, I propose we hold three more banquets—one each on Wednesday, Thursday, and Friday night. These will be in regard to Mr. Travers' proposal against the Christians, and as a salute to the man who has brought us to this point, Chancellor Obrador!"

"Maybe we should ask the one woman on whose shoulders such banquets would fall," Obrador said. "Chloe, can you swing three more dinners this week?"

"We all have to eat." Chloe threw up her hands. "So, we may as well eat together. The kitchen staff may need a ration raise, but—let's do it!"

Applauding this latest announcement, Owen was thrilled that his boldness was already paying back dividends. One meal had turned into three more! If he wasn't mistaken, the additional three banquets were for him and what he'd directed the Federation to do next about noncompliant citizens—the Christians!

"It's a stroke of brilliance," Obrador said to Owen later that night as the guests departed. He squeezed Owen's shoulder. "I like it so much, I'm going to write it into law tomorrow and have it broadcasted across the Federation before Monday. The citizenry will take care of the rest. Faithful citizens get the spoils of executed Christians? Brilliant, Owen! They'll be racing to eradicate the vermin from this land. There's a future for you in politics, my boy. Brilliant!"

Owen beamed. Obrador had never praised him so. It made him feel almost like . . . like family!

Chapter Fourteen

Chancellor Obrador knocked on the hotel door of the room assigned to Jenna Dowler. He'd seen her the night before at Owen's groundbreaking dinner, but he hadn't spoken to her much at all—*ever!* Although he'd been satisfied by many women over the years, he'd seen in Jenna's sightless face the promise of a companion in his old age. She wasn't a cheap, young passion who would last but for a moment; she was a citizen who valued greatness and glory. She'd written the nation's national anthem, after all!

"Stay out here," Obrador ordered his two body-guards—young men who'd built up their muscles from working out, but hadn't the brains for government affairs. "I won't be needing you inside."

The door opened, and he looked down into the face of his future wife. It was Tuesday morning, and she wore a t-shirt, jeans, and no socks on her bare feet.

"It's Kendrick . . . um, the chancellor." He shook his head at himself. "May I come in? I come bearing gifts."

He held up a pillowcase packed full of papers, then realized she couldn't see them. Suddenly, he grasped that having a blind wife was going to require a lot more foresight in conversation.

"Of course, Mr. Chancellor. Come in." Jenna opened the door wide. "Are they coming in as well?"

"Uh, no." Obrador stepped inside, then considered her question. His bodyguards hadn't made a sound, yet she had known they were there. She was more perceptive than he'd presumed. "Call me Kendrick, please. Even Ken will do."

She closed the door and walked to the dresser, hardly seeming to be blind at all.

"Would you like some water?"

"No, I—" He studied her slender hands on the pitcher, her head slightly tilted, as if to angle her little ears to take in every word he spoke. "Sure. Yes, please. Just half is fine."

He didn't mind that she poured with her finger inside the glass, measuring the amount to stop at the halfway mark. She handed the glass to him, then poured one for herself.

"I would've dressed up if I'd known you were coming."

"Oh, no, that's not necessary." He sipped his water, reflecting on how much he communicated with gestures and facial expressions, which she wouldn't be able to see at all. "This isn't an official visit. Uh, the gifts. I'm holding a bag, a pillowcase full of letters from citizens. They're mostly for you, of course. But I don't know how you'll be able to read them. Well, I guess—"

"You could read them to me," Jenna offered. Her face was so innocent, so honest. "Maybe not now, but later. We'll have time together."

"Of course. I'll set them here on your bed. Is that okay? They're on the lower, right-hand corner. There'll be a lot more letters, I think. These are just from people in the city. Citizens from all over the country will be writing, once the full report of the pageant reaches them. Everyone is very excited about this upcoming Sunday."

"As am I." She smiled so warmly, he wanted to hold her in his arms that very minute. "As you know, I've never been married. I've waited for this my whole life, for it to be special and meaningful. The Federation and its people are important to me, so the ceremonial marriage will carry special significance for me."

Obrador couldn't contain himself any longer. He roughly set down his glass and went to her, taking her empty hand in his own. She didn't recoil or make a face.

"Oh, Jenna, you've opened my eyes to a vision of what this nation needs. I don't want it to be just a ceremony. I've seen who you can be for a room full of people. You emit hope. You're radiant with inspiration. I don't want the old, dark Federation of demands and shades of gray. I want your purity, your picture, everywhere. Marry me for real—your heart, not just your body for the Federation. Maybe you've heard that I'm no good, or that I'm a drunk, or a womanizer. But I can change. I will. For you."

She set down her glass and lifted her hand to his face. Her touch melted his heart and made him want to weep.

"It's okay, Kendrick." Her fingers brushed over his nose, his eyes, his mouth, seeming to read him fully. "Yes, I've heard things. But I believe you, that you want to change. Will you let me help you? And you can help me. Can we do that, together?"

"Yes. Oh, yes, Jenna!" He pulled her into an awkward embrace, awkward because he didn't feel her arms around him at first, and he was so much taller than she. "I'll be a good husband to you, I promise. You're just what I need right now. You're just what the Federation needs. You've won our hearts. Now, we need to unite all the compliant people as one, and we'll be unstoppable!"

"Can we sit down?"

"Of course, yes." He backed away. "I'm not usually like this. I'm not myself. I didn't mean to smother you. Is this better?"

He sat down next to the bag of letters, but she remained standing in front of him, her hands in his. Since he was such a tall man, their heads were now nearly level with one another.

"Change will happen, Kendrick," she said softly, "but it won't happen overnight. We'll need to settle into steady, cautious growth, and that's not something that happens automatically because we put rings on our fingers. Our whole lives, we've lived moving in our own directions. I think for me, what I need most from you right now, to help me transition to being the best wife I can be for the Federation—"

"Yes? Anything."

"You know my father, Corban Dowler."

"The master printer? Of course."

"His whole life, he's worked hard. Let him retire and live here with us, as soon as he's able to train a couple of apprentices. He's a wise, old man with supernatural insight into matters of life and society. You and he should become friends."

"Your father?" Obrador frowned, glad she couldn't see his face. Of course, he should've realized before that marrying her would mean joining with the in-laws. "I think that would be okay. Dowler is someone we've worked with for years. I'll talk to Chloe Azmaveth about it, and we'll work something out. That's it? That's all you wanted? You want your father to live here?"

"Kendrick?"

"Yes?"

"My own father wasn't even at the pageant. I won, but he wasn't invited. What if people find out? He'd be so embarrassed. I'm embarrassed for him."

"Of course. I'm sorry." Kendrick sighed. This marriage business was full of landmines! "I didn't think of that. I'll make it up to him. And to you. We'll move him in right away. Some of the pageant contestants are leaving today, so there'll be rooms available. And he can come to the banquets you're hosting starting tomorrow night. You'll want him there, I presume?"

"That would be wonderful. I know it's all going to work out. But this needs to go both ways." She sat down next to him, still holding one of his hands. Kendrick felt like a teenager again, his heart racing, his palms sweating. "You're the chancellor of a struggling country. We've all been through a lot. We mustn't pretend in front of one another. I know you're overwhelmed. You have worries and concerns. People place unreasonable expectations upon you. Others can't be trusted. The ones who can be trusted are held back by selfish and ignorant hearts."

"You understand so much already, Jenna. Your words are like poetry. How could I be so lucky to have such an understanding woman?"

"I want to be your right hand. I want to help this country regain its dignity. I want to see you do that, as I witness it all from beside you."

"Yes, I want that, too. Chloe hasn't shown any concern about bringing you fully on board. My new security officer, Lieutenant Isaacson, has already expressed support for you as well. My staff all loves you. You'll be my private advisor, giving me perspective I've never had before."

"Oh, I would like that, even if I'm just sitting quietly in the corner, listening in on meetings."

"I can't imagine that anyone would object. You've shown everyone your heart, Jenna. It's for the Federation—its people. No one would doubt that."

"Let's be patient with one another." She patted his hand. "Now, you'd better get back to work, or they're liable to start rumors that I'm distracting you."

"You are distracting me. You're distracting every-one—in a good way, of course."

"I'll see you tomorrow night for dinner. It's a big week."

She rose and kissed him on the cheek.

Obrador stood and gazed into her innocent face. He'd known many women, but never one with such grace and honor for herself and for others. The closest he could think of was Chloe, who had an inner poise, but she was nothing like Jenna!

Lena Travers leaned into a sharp corner as she zoomed off the bridge from the Bronx into Manhattan. Her dog, Death, pointed her nose into the wind, seeming to enjoy the speed as well.

Owner and pet had been gone for two days, coordinating the invasion to unseat Obrador once and for all. Rendezvous New Castle was going forward, even without Philadelphia's manpower. With Boston, Hartford, and Baltimore on board, the chancellor's forces on the island would be overwhelmed. Along with her own sway over New York City's Citizen Army, Lena believed she might even take the Bowery without a shot fired! It all had to do with timing. The soldiers would do what they were told, as long as she told them what to do at the precise moment of the takeover.

She was anxious to get back to the Bowery. Her trip to visit the invading armies would've been faster, but Hartford had been stingy with their fuel, and she'd needed to refuel there twice, going out of her way on the return trip from Boston. Although her absence probably wasn't all that important in Manhattan, she did want to return to make everything seem normal before the invasion. Besides, she needed to be in place to assassinate Obrador and kill Chloe Azmaveth in the first few minutes of the coup. Anyone else who stood in her way, she guessed she could deal with them during the invasion, with her dog's jaws leading the way.

Changing gears, Lena sped down Madison Avenue, formulating a story to tell the chancellor to justify her absence, when someone ran across the street in front of her. The person wore dark, drab clothing . . . *and a rifle on a sling?* She immediately identified the person as a resistance fighter—but since when did the resistance fighters in Manhattan carry firearms?

She tapped her brakes to slow down, hoping to send Death after the man. The pavement ahead appeared matted and oddly lined. Death barked, and fear gripped

Lena's heart. As she coasted her bike, her attention was drawn to her right by the distinct squeak of a pulley, and in the next breath, the matting that stretched across the road rose abruptly from in front of her. *It was a net!*

Her motorcycle slid sideways a few feet before it was yanked skyward. From the sudden stop, Lena was flung over her handlebars into the coarse netting. She heard Death yelp. Then, the netting collapsed on them both. The motorcycle's handlebars were immediately entangled, and a moment later, Lena was lying on her side, completely wrapped in the scratchy netting.

With one hand, she reached for her knife, and with her other hand, she drew her sidearm. She guessed if she could cut just one or two strands of the net, she could fit through the loops and stand up. Death wasn't barking or struggling, and she knew what that probably meant. Rage ignited Lena's limbs to thrash and tear at the net. Cursing and yelling, she wrestled her way free and stood upright. Her bike seemed undamaged a few feet away, but Death lay at an awkward angle, her head twisted backwards.

Then she saw them—three tunnel rats, two young and one older. The older one held a submachine gun aimed at her. He wore a long-sleeved sweatshirt, the emblem on the front long faded, and his wavy, blond hair was so greasy from lack of washing that it shined.

"Holster your gun," the man said, his voice steady. Though the two teens at his side appeared nervous, he wasn't. "We know you're Lena Travers. We're not here to hurt you. Put your gun away so we can talk."

Lena wondered if there were more than just the three of them. Maybe there were, and maybe there weren't. Just in case, she slid her gun into her holster and sheathed her knife on her hip. It was a good sign that they were letting her keep her sidearm. A good sign, but a careless idea. They'd killed Death, and that meant she'd kill them, no matter how they treated her now!

"Speak!" she demanded. "If you know who I am, then you know I'm not interested in courting. What do you want?"

He slowly lowered his machine gun.

"My name is Hedgehog. I'm leading the resistance group in the tunnels now. I sent your brother a message. He didn't tell you?"

"I left town during the pageant. What happened to the Bandit?"

"He deceived us and ran off to join the Christian underground. We want to come back to the surface. I have information you need to know. It's a trade for us to become legalized citizens."

"I'm listening." She walked carefully across the net so as not to tangle her boots further. "What do I need to know, Hedgehog?"

She glanced about. These three seemed to be alone. And stupid, if they thought they could buy off her fury with information.

"Brian Steelman and the Bandit left the tunnels. They're up here somewhere."

"So what? Why's that important to me?"

"For years, the Bandit has been working with people on the surface."

"We've always suspected that."

"But we know who it is now."

"So? Who is it?"

"It's bigger than you've ever imagined. They've completely infiltrated the Federation leadership."

"Let me decide that reality. Get to the point."

Lena studied the one who called himself Hedgehog. Besides his greasy hair, his cheeks were smudged with dirt, and his fingernails, which poked through fingerless gloves, were chipped and filthy. He probably hadn't bathed in years. The weapon he'd aimed at her had been held away from his body, like someone unfamiliar with a firearm. That made sense to her, since she'd never heard a confirmed report of any resistance fighter inside the city actually killing anyone, let alone carrying guns. Sabotage and harassment, yes, but not murder. These three were amateurs, and she knew that before she left them she would kill them.

"The Bandit used us for years, spray-painting secret messages on the walls of certain buildings. The messages were codes in braille."

"Braille?" Lena had seen the graffiti all over the city, but braille was a surprise. "Why braille?"

"They're covering it up all over the city right now, wiping out any trace of the codes. They're trying to distance themselves from the resistance, but I remember everything. The Bandit taught everyone in the tunnels braille years ago. These two learned braille before they could read and write. You understand what I'm saying?"

"So they used braille for codes in the dark tunnels." She rested her hand on the butt of her sidearm. They would pay for killing Death! "I don't care. It means nothing to me."

"Jenna Dowler won the pageant, and she's blind."

"She won?" Lena frowned. "I've been traveling. I hadn't heard."

"Her dad is Corban Dowler. And there's a guy named Luigi Putelli who's been real close to the Bandit for years. He lived with us down in the tunnels. How do you think the resistance moved around so well without getting caught? Someone was making sure we had identifications when we needed them, working with people at the Bowery. But that's not all."

Lena stared at the tunnel rat. *Corban Dowler!* Owen had been right all along!

"You're not really connecting the dots for me," she said. "Just because the woman's blind doesn't mean she's part of the resistance with you. There are other blind people in the city who use braille. It doesn't mean they're anything for or against the Federation. Jenna was fully vetted by Obrador's staff. Only compliant citizens were contestants in the pageant."

"But listen to this: two months ago, you guys killed Heather Putelli. We read the paper, which said she was alive. But she's been dead this whole time. We knew it in the tunnels. How'd we know it?"

"I don't know any Heather Putelli."

"You thought she was Radiant Shade, but Heather was taking a bunch of hearing aids to Radiant Shade that day. She lived in the tunnel with us. I heard things over the years. All those people knew each other before Pan-Day—Corban Dowler, Jenna Dowler, Luigi and Heather Putelli, the Bandit, and someone named Scooter, but no one's sure who that is. Scooter was just a name that came up now and then."

"No. What you're saying is impossible. Radiant Shade is dead. We caught her and she died in custody. That much you have right. There hasn't been a whisper about Radiant Shade from anyone since we killed her."

"That's because we were told to stand down. The whole resistance was supposed to convince the Federation that we believed she really was gone. But all you did was kill Heather. All of this was about the pageant and the wedding, to get the right people into the Bowery."

"This weekend?" Lena frowned. "What do you know?"

"Something big is supposed to happen. It has to involve Jenna Dowler marrying the chancellor."

"That's it? She's blind. She's hardly a threat."

"She's Radiant Shade. They're all Christians. Aren't you listening?"

Lena didn't like being spoken to as if she were an idiot, but she was too shocked to respond for a moment. *Radiant Shade?* Suddenly, she put it all together. Hearing aids had been used for recordings because Jenna couldn't write. Her father was in the perfect position to create false identifications, but it would require someone in the

Bowery or Citizen Processing to alter the compliant lists, someone high up, but who? She knew all those people, and they'd all passed multiple *CEE* tests.

"You're saying the woman who Chancellor Obrador picked out of all those contestants just happens to be Radiant Shade, who is still alive?"

"That's what I've been telling you. She's a Christian, and so is the Bandit, who's friends with Luigi Putelli, the husband of Heather who you guys thought was Radiant Shade. Now you understand why we had to stop you this way."

"I understand," Lena said, even though she didn't believe it all quite yet. "Anything else?"

"No, that's every—"

She shot him in the chest, then turned on the younger resistance fighters.

A moment later, she cut the net away from her motorcycle and climbed onto it. Death was under several layers of netting, and freeing her would've been too difficult. She would miss her companion, but she needed to get to the Bowery now. If Obrador had indeed been compromised, she needed to find out by whom. Or maybe she didn't need to find out at all. Maybe all she needed to do was wait for Rendezvous New Castle to happen on Saturday—then she could kill anyone who defended Obrador.

One way or another, she would take over the Bowery, whether it had been infiltrated or not.

Nathan escorted Corban Dowler through the Bowery checkpoint into the lobby, then to the stairwell. At that ground level, there were too many people moving past them for the two old friends to speak openly. As much as Nathan wanted to update Corban on the latest happenings, he would have to wait until they were safely up in Jenna's room.

But he realized the update for Corban would be delayed even longer when the man in his eighties stopped to rest on only the third-story landing.

"Nearly the top floor, you say?" Corban sat on the lowest step of the landing. "It seems with power in the building, you'd get the elevator working for men like me who need special treatment."

"It would take up too much power," Nathan said, leaning against the wall. "Besides, with all the erosion in this city over the past twenty years, I'm not trusting an enclosed metal box to carry me two hundred feet up a vertical shaft."

"Well, when you put it that way . . ." Corban doubled over and coughed. "Sorry. My new body in glory can't come soon enough."

"No need to apologize, Boss," Nathan said, using an old reference from years earlier. Now, he used it as a term of endearment, rather than the term of authority reserved for the intelligence agent who'd taught him espionage techniques. "Would you let me carry you? Jenna and Chloe are waiting. I know you've been with Jenna until recently, but Chloe hasn't seen you in years, and she's about to lose her cover by running down here."

"I'm not too proud to be carried, but you're no specimen of perfect fitness yourself these days, are you? How's the leg?"

"Good enough."

Nathan crouched for Corban to climb onto his back, then they continued up at a slow but steady pace.

"Hey, Lieutenant." A junior officer who was descending the stairs stopped and saluted as Nathan trudged past him. "Maybe you'll carry me up to my room later?"

"Sure," Nathan joked back, "then you can carry me up tomorrow."

After two brief rests, they finally reached two floors shy of the chancellor's suite. Nathan held the door open for Corban as they entered Jenna's room. With one last check for spies in the hallway, Nathan closed the door and faced Jenna, Chloe, Chen Li, and Corban. Corban and Jenna embraced like they'd been apart for years, though it had only been a few days. Then it was Chloe's turn. She was all tears, but didn't hesitate to point out a few new lines on Corban's aged face. Chen Li elbowed Nathan and smiled, reminding him of their private conversations over the years when they'd anticipated a COIL reunion exactly like this one.

"If anyone asks," Nathan said once they'd gathered in close proximity on the bed, "we're here to coordinate the wedding ceremony on Sunday. What a blessing to have Corban finally join us for these brainstorming sessions! It's been years in the waiting, Boss. There are others nearby still missing from our number with whom we hope to reunite soon. With that said, Corban, would you pray for us all in this special moment?"

Corban prayed, and as he finished, Nathan reflected on the five of them in that room. Everything they were doing for Christ was illegal, and had been illegal for years. If someone happened into the room to hear them praying, although the door was locked, they'd all be arrested.

Nathan started the meeting by sharing with Corban the latest rumors of the armies from various cities about to invade Manhattan any day. They talked about the wedding going forward as planned, and that Obrador was in the dark about the true threats—both Rendezvous New Castle and Operation Esther.

"We have a decision to make today about that," Chloe said. "We've reached a tipping point. We could advise the chancellor of all we suspect in regards to a violent coup by Lena Travers, so he can defend himself, or we could allow him to fall and we all get out of the city before that happens."

"We've come this far," Chen Li said. "How can we just run off and abandon everyone we've been protecting, even Obrador?"

"If we stay," Nathan said, "we'll be fighting for our lives. But if we say something to Obrador, the cat's out of the bag. Lena's back, and she's intent on taking over in some fashion, like Chloe said. Lena will get wind of Obrador being aware of her intentions, and all the military support she's gained will clash with the few loyalists Obrador still has."

"How much support does Lena have?" Corban asked. "Can we undermine her?"

"She has about half the officers of the Citizen Army, and all but a couple of the Enforcers."

"Where does Owen stand with his sister right now?" Corban's questions showed Nathan he was still mentally sharp, even if his body wasn't in peak condition.

"Interestingly," Chloe said, "he's endeared himself to Obrador lately, and he's been confiding in me more, sharing his ambitions to please the chancellor with Monday's Day of Cleansing. We still need to find a way to reverse that terrible decree, since every city's now been ordered to implement the public executions of Christians everywhere."

"So," Nathan said, "the question is posed—do we risk it all by trying to go through with the wedding, or do we do what we can to save the ones we can?"

Each person was in silent reflection for a few moments, then they gradually turned to Jenna who hadn't weighed in yet.

"We've spent years infiltrating the Federation," she said softly. "And we've rescued many from the gallows, and helped thousands more stay fed or equipped with God's Word. But all of it would be a waste if I married Obrador on the eve of a coup, which we're certain will lead to our demise under Lena, or whoever she has in mind to head up the government."

"She hates me," Chloe said. "She'll probably execute me right after Obrador."

"It seems, then, that our final act as COIL operatives inside the Federation is this . . ." Jenna bowed her head a few seconds, as if regretting what she was about to say. Yet, when she raised her head, Nathan saw resolve. "I'll convince Obrador to reverse the Day of Cleansing order that he gave, so the Christians are safe for at least another day. And then we run with every person we can save. It goes without saying that we're not willing to stand toe to toe with Lena and fight against a hostile takeover of the Bowery. Though we could kill and probably destroy all of her assets, we won't do that. We care too much for even our enemies to hurt them like that."

"Where do we run?" Chen Li asked. "These other armies that are coming probably have vehicles. Obrador has hardly any vehicles the resistance hasn't sabotaged. We'll be on foot."

"Yes, we'll be on foot," Corban said, "but we have what the Federation and Lena don't have. We have the Lord on our side—and we have Luigi and Scooter, and even Bruno somewhere across the river."

"It's the old Flash and Bang team back together again," Chloe said, grinning. "We can dust off our battle rifles and get busy. While retreating."

"We do have assets," Jenna said, "but let me add two more thoughts. First, we need to offer an escape for all the forced labor workers. Many of them are Christians under sentence for their first offense of failing the *CEE* or having a Bible."

"I already have about one hundred Christian's files pulled," Chen Li said. "It won't be hard to gather them, but it'll be another story to get them from the cages to a safe place outside the city."

"We'll need Scooter and Luigi," Corban said. "They're on standby but they know the tunnels. We can go underground most of the way to the GW Bridge."

"Then we go to Colorado," Chloe said. "It'll be an exodus, fighting and retreating the whole way, if Lena comes after us. And I think she will."

"Especially when we take Obrador with us," Jenna said, which drew the surprised looks of everyone in the room. "Lena thinks this is about power and politics, so she won't stop until she kills him, and those of us who've tried to take over the Federation will be just as threatened. She may already be aware of what we've been doing, in which case, we're on borrowed time."

"Yeah, but taking Obrador?" Chloe sighed. "It'll be against his will. He'll be in shock that he has to leave at all. I know he'll want to stay and fight."

"It won't be a fight," Nathan said. "He'll be out-numbered ten to one. If he fights, he dies. If he joins us, he lives. Those are his choices. We've basically unseated him already, we just haven't told him yet."

"The Chancellor of the Federation joining our group of Christians?" Chen Li asked with a chuckle. "That'll be a sight!"

"It may be what God has intended all along," Jenna said. "Nebuchadnezzar is being brought to his knees. We've been focused on a non-hostile takeover, when we could've been focused on his salvation."

"Well, he may be ready." Chloe shrugged. "He's pretty smitten with you, Jenna. You can use that, especially to reverse the order about the Day of Cleansing."

"You said there were two things, Jenna," Corban said. "The first was saving the Christians among the forced labor prisoners. What's the second?"

"We're a band of disabled, aging operatives. I'm blind, Dad's body is giving out, and let's face it, Chloe and Chen Li—neither of you are able to march fifty miles a day with a heavy pack, anymore. I'm just pointing out the obvious. You'll all need to shoot straight, all while leading one hundred unhealthy prisoners west. But God has provided us with someone who isn't crippled, old, or aware of these seemingly insurmountable odds.

"We have someone who's been trained by who my dad says was the most careless and courageous Christian operative who ever worked inside COIL. That was Titus Caspertein. Now, we have his son, and from what I understand from Nathan, Levi and his cousin Rex, along with two others, have already devastated Philadelphia's ability to participate in the invasion. The Casperteins are faithful Christians, and they don't know the meaning of backing down or being intimidated. They aren't viewing this fight by numbers or what's physically possible. With God on their side, they've traveled thousands of miles to get here, and they aren't going to give up even as we're retreating. Yes, we may be outnumbered. But with what God has provided us, our enemy is facing a formidable foe who's never lost a fight."

"I guess we don't have to wonder if you're counting on Levi Caspertein or not," Chen Li said with a wink at her husband.

"Counting on him? No." Jenna laughed. "I believe God has sent him to us for this very moment—*for such a time as this*. Our Lord has provided salvation as a free gift, and He continues to show us His grace through these worldly dangers. But we need to keep our eternal perspective. It's a spiritual battle. Our mission must be about saving the lost, like Obrador, and strengthening the believers to defy darkness, for Christ's sake. This is God's eternal purpose for the church, and as the church, it's our purpose, even in this unique and strange situation. Whether we live or die through what's about to happen, we prevail because we trust and wait on God Almighty!"

It was Wednesday night, and Jenna was secretly praying through her nervousness. Their escape from the city was scheduled for Saturday, the day before the wedding, since that was the earliest they could gather all their moveable pieces. Nathan needed Luigi to fetch two crates of COIL gear from two different hidden locations, and Chen Li needed to figure out how to smuggle one hundred prisoners several city blocks north where Luigi and Scooter could take them underground.

And there were all kinds of variables that threatened their plans, things they simply had to entrust into God's hands. For one, they knew the invading armies could arrive soon, but they didn't know when. Also, the resistance was an unknown factor. How dangerous were the Vags these days, without Scooter down there as the Bandit, guiding and limiting their aggression? And there was Owen, who was unpredictable. And his sister, Lena, who could snap at any moment, in an attempt to take over the government using the forces already in the city who were loyal to her.

Jenna waited as dinner guests filed into the room for the first of three banquets meant to honor the chancellor and the latest Federation successes. The guests first greeted Obrador, then moved to the other end of the table where Jenna stood with Chen Li. They each greeted Jenna there, before they found their assigned seats. Several Federation diplomats were still in the city, so they were dispersed along the table's two sides, but Jenna had advised Chloe to seat a COIL operative next to Owen and Lena, both of whom had been invited.

"Congratulations, Jenna," Lena said quietly, her hand like ice on Jenna's arm. "You've made it to exactly where you wanted to be."

Jenna just smiled politely, hoping that she was able to hide any other visible reaction.

"It's nice to have you here, Lena, and to finally meet you. I've heard so much about you."

Then Lena had passed her, and Jenna was greeting the next guest.

"She knows!" Chen Li whispered as she leaned close to Jenna's ear.

But Jenna simply continued to smile. She'd already surmised the same from Lena's simple statement. Someone must've told Lena of Operation Esther. But where was the leak? Jenna guessed that people had somehow connected some old COIL operatives to each other—Scooter to Corban, or Nathan to Luigi. If Scooter and Luigi's covers were blown, everyone else's covers were possibly beginning to collapse as well.

Once the guests were seated, the meal was served, this time chicken parmesan. Jenna bowed her head and prayed privately to God in thanks for the food. She guessed the others at the table may have thought she was smelling the food, or pausing for someone to indicate it was time to eat, or maybe to describe to her what was on her plate, and where. Regardless, she knew her Lord was honored by her secret prayer. No doubt, Chloe, Nathan, and Chen Li had been secretly praying for years, disguising their faith, waiting for precise moments to smuggle arrested Christians whatever message or gift Jenna could send them. Remaining faithful in secret didn't make them any less courageous. They had maintained their faith without compromise because they were courageous.

Almost immediately, Owen began to share with the chancellor the good response the city was having about the wedding day and the Day of Cleansing to come in a few days.

"What do you guys think about the Day of Cleansing?" Lena suddenly asked at Jenna's end of the table. "Finally rid the Federation of all the noncompliant Christians, huh?"

"To whom are you speaking?" Jenna asked.

"You, Jenna," Lena said, the bite in her voice needing no interpretation. "This should be interesting."

Jenna felt everyone within earshot turn to look at her. Silverware at that end of the table stopped clinking, and she suspected Chloe and Chen Li were nearly frozen, not even chewing, until she responded. But this wasn't Jenna's first experience at being on the spot.

"I think the Day of Cleansing will be an opportunity for the Christians to reveal who they really are. Do they exclusively love their Savior, whom they claim died and rose again for their sins? If they do, then the Federation's compliant citizens will kill them."

"You sound like you admire them," Lena said accusingly.

"I admire devotion."

"But their devotion isn't to the Federation." Lena's words snapped like a whip from her mouth, even though they were only having a casual conversation. "Their devotion hurts the Federation! You admire that?"

"When the Romans took the last fortress of the Jews, a place called Masada, two thousand years ago, they found that the rebels had chosen to kill themselves rather than be taken prisoner. They chose death over captivity. The Romans admired that kind of courage, even though they hadn't agreed with the rebels in principle. Do you have no respect for people with whom you disagree, Lena?"

"How can I respect them if they're wrong?" She sneered. "Only a fool would acknowledge another fool."

"Lena!" shouted Obrador, who had obviously heard. "You are a guest here!"

"To become wise, Lena," Jenna said to a quiet table, "we must realize we are foolish and ignorant, since only a person who admits he or she doesn't have knowledge will receive knowledge. That means we were all foolish and base at one time, but someone wiser than we were showed us mercy. If someone wise hadn't shown us mercy, we'd still be foolish. So, we can be generous to others who are foolish as well."

"This is ridiculous!" Lena shouted. "You're standing up for Christians! Are you hearing this, Owen?"

"I'm speaking from the Federation's perspective," Jenna said. "Surely, your brother isn't blinded by hatred for Christians who trust exclusively in their God. Owen is just zealous for the Federation. Isn't that true, Owen?"

"I think the Federation would be, uh, a better place without citizens who undermined our authority," Owen said. "But no, I'm not blinded by hatred. There are people I once hated whom I now like, so I guess I need to be open-minded about some things."

"I've heard, "Chen Li said, "the Christians believe that obedience to the authorities is one of the marks of faithfulness to their God, so is that really undermining?"

"Where did you hear that's what they believe?" Obrador asked from the other end. "I've never heard that."

"As a Citizen Processing Supervisor, I meet many of these Christians we arrest, processing them through their *CEE* answers before they're sentenced. We should all understand their stand for their God, even if we may not agree with their stand."

"I can't believe what I'm hearing!" Lena growled. "Have we lost our minds? Christians are the epitome of everything this Federation stands against! They serve an unseen, imaginary God, but the Federation demands— nay, *requires*—service that can be seen and expressed here, now, today, in this city! Sympathizing over brainwashed fantasizers only makes us seem weak. People notice, and we're the worse for it."

"Young lady?" Corban called from his seat two places to Jenna's left, "what if I could prove to you that faith in the unseen is more powerful than the faith you have in what you can see and feel?"

"Go for it," Lena said. "Prove it."

"Oh, this should be good." Obrador laughed. "I love a good philosophical puzzle. Careful, Lena, Mr. Dowler's been around twice as long as you've been alive."

"It's simple, really," Corban said. "From an ancient Greek text, we need to consider the definition of faith. You could say faith, young lady, is the assurance of things hoped for, or the conviction of things not seen. Can you see and feel what you hope for? Of course not. Faith is the evidence of hope, or simple confidence in the unseen. The things that are unseen are made convincing by the faith we have in them, as long as the things hoped for are real."

"So?" Lena scoffed. "You've proven nothing."

"Young lady, you are trusting in the Federation, which can be seen and touched. Yes, it's grand, but it's material, so you need no faith to obtain it. The Federation requires no faith, since it is discernible with the five senses. But the God of these Christians can't be seen. Therefore, faith is required to experience Him. So, I've shown that you not only have weak faith in the Federation, but that you have no faith at all, since faith is only necessary when something is unseen. These Christians, who are destined to die soon, won't be defeated by our lack of faith when they have so much faith. Why? Because they believe in what can't be seen, while we here may believe in what can be seen. What can be seen may be destroyed, but that which can't be seen, will last forever. That's why a government who fights against an idea will never win. It's the heart of the people that must be won."

"You're saying the Christians are more powerful than my gun and bullets?" Lena asked. "You sure you want to put that theory to the test?"

"I'm merely pointing out that guns and bullets, and your faith in them, can't destroy an idea, which their faith is in. I'm just a lowly printer, but I suspect the more the Enforcers have executed Christians, the more resistant they seem to become."

"We've suspected that," Owen admitted, "but they've gotten so tricky. They're mostly underground, but not necessarily in the tunnels. The city could be more infected than we think. Somehow, they're still able to traffic their ideas around to one another."

"Tell us, Mr. Dowler," Obrador said, "you've been around for a long time. How would you defeat these Christians once and for all?"

"I believe there's only one way to remove the influence of a Christian," Corban said. "Remove their God, and you remove their influence."

The whole table laughed at the absurdity of such an idea as removing God. Even Jenna laughed, hoping the tension at the table would be diminished for the rest of the dinner. She and her father were both unwilling to give Lena an edge against God's truth or His people, but their defense needed to remain subtle. Their escape from the city wasn't yet secure!

Jenna couldn't wait to get alone with Chen Li to find out what kind of look had been on Lena's face. She'd been shut up, at least, but surely not for long.

Chapter Fifteen

Thursday morning, Lena Travers was still fuming about the banquet the night before. She was in the presence of idiots, she thought as she emerged from the Bowery's front entrance. Trying to calm herself, she climbed onto her street bike but sat there a moment appreciating the dawn sunlight on her face. Two more days was all she needed to tolerate their insolence. The wedding plans, banquets, and weak grip on the Federation would disappear with Obrador and his dinner friends who had so corrupted him.

As she sat there, Corban Dowler and Lieutenant Isaacson emerged from the hotel and walked toward the parking lot where only a handful of vehicles were still parked. Corban's mind tricks from the night before still caused her blood to boil. In the past, she had executed noncompliant citizens for such rantings about faith and God. And Obrador had sat there amused! But it was all about to end. Her careful planning to bring in the Citizen Armies of Boston, Hartford, and Baltimore would crush the final dissidents in Manhattan once and for all. Systematically, everyone would be given the Citizen's Entrance Exam under her supervision. It would take weeks, but it had to be done. There were too many people in the Federation's administration she simply didn't trust.

Lena frowned as Isaacson held a Jeep door open for Corban to climb into the passenger seat. Isaacson was rounding the front of the vehicle when Lena jogged up to him.

"I'm not used to seeing you without Death on a leash, Ms. Travers," Isaacson said. "Where's your dog?"

"Where are you two going?" she asked instead, ignoring his question. Although she'd tried to sound casual, her inquiry came out as a demand. She couldn't shake her Enforcer heart, suspicious of everyone after the night before. "Don't tell me you're going on patrol with the old man."

"He's not that old." Isaacson chuckled. "I'm taking Mr. Dowler back to the print shop where he'll be training a couple replacements. He's retiring."

Lena tried to read Isaacson's face, but he was a veteran soldier. If he were up to something contrary, his face wasn't revealing it. And if she was catching them at something, she doubted she could physically wrestle the large man to the ground. She'd need to shoot to kill, or invite a half-dozen other men over to pin him down long enough to handcuff him.

Instead, she glanced into the cab where Corban sat. The elderly man didn't look at her, but she knew he wasn't really as old as he tried to portray. He set an envelope on the dash, held a satchel on his lap, then with one hand, clutched his chest, like he was winded. But Lena wasn't buying it.

"Why are you taking him?" she asked Isaacson. "It's a babysitting job, right? Don't you have something to secure for the wedding?"

His eyes narrowed at her, and she knew then that he was trying to read her, to figure out how much she knew. It wasn't important that she reveal that she knew they were all Christians infiltrating the Federation. She'd have them all executed on Saturday, alongside Obrador, who seemed too caught up in the wedding festivities to realize what she now knew. Isaacson was too tight with Chloe not to be involved.

"Are you volunteering?" Isaacson offered her the keys. "We just need to make sure he passes the baton to adequate apprentices."

"I was going that way." She snatched the keys from his hand, not intending to make the Christians' subversive activities any easier for them than they already were. "Go plan for the big day. Sunday's the day, right?"

"That's right." He backed away. "You two have fun."

Lena climbed into the driver's seat as Corban gave Isaacson a thumbs-up. Although Lena preferred the motorcycle, she'd driven a few of the vehicles around the city over the years. She shifted the Jeep into gear and roared out of the lot. Guards at the front gate saw her coming and raised the arm an instant before she careened onto Broadway.

"How long do you need to be at the ID office?" she asked as they raced north.

"All day." He looked at her. "You can leave me there if you have errands to run."

"And leave you all alone?" She scoffed.

"The two apprentices will be there."

"I'll be with you every minute today." She leaned forward to better see the envelope on the dash. "You don't mind me spending the day with you, do you? After all, you'll be living in the Bowery from now on. You're the chancellor's future wife's father."

"It's been an exciting couple of months."

Lena didn't respond. She really wanted to search the man's satchel and thumb through the contents of that envelope, but she couldn't risk revealing her own hand or causing a scene that would disrupt her own plans for Saturday. Yet, she did want to limit the damage these Christians were still apparently trying to cause the Federation.

They reached the print office and parked directly in front at the curb where one camera could keep watch over the Jeep. Lena climbed out and stared at the fortress-like, glass building. She'd been inside a few times over the years, but never beyond the front desk.

Corban carried his satchel to the front door where he shook hands with two young men in their thirties. Lena recognized one of them as a ration distributor from the East Side. They glanced suspiciously at her, but she didn't offer a greeting. Most people in the city knew her by sight, and she'd worked hard to build up a reputation for people to steer clear of her.

As she entered the front door behind them, she looked back at the Jeep. Corban's envelope was still on the dash! Had he had a senile moment and forgotten it? Then, she smiled. If Corban really was a Christian, then it was probable that he and Isaacson had emerged from the Bowery's security to make contact with the Christian underground. The envelope was a hand-off!

She desperately wanted to run back to the Jeep and open the envelope, but she wanted to keep her eye on Corban as well. Maybe the two apprentices weren't really printers in training, but Christians in mid-scheme! After checking the street for any movement and finding none, she bounded up the stairs and into the next room where Corban was holding up several finished prints for the men to study.

Lena wandered through the printing room, searching for anything amiss, while listening to Corban's every word. Was he talking in code to the men? Was he including braille writing on anything? Was he passing messages on to the apprentices?

Corban moved to a computer scanner and explained the resolution requirements for formatting the photos for Federation IDs. Lena listened for a few minutes, then drifted away, back to the front room, where she could see the Jeep. The envelope was still on the dash. It was fat, too, with several pages inside it. It was teasing her, testing her patience. Who was it for? Since Isaacson wasn't there, maybe whoever the envelope was for wouldn't reach its target.

When Lena turned around, she spotted the stairs on the right. She leaned around the corner and heard Corban droning on about cropping ID photographs just so. Quietly, she ascended the stairs. As an Enforcer, she could go where she wanted, but she didn't want to set Corban off and warn anyone that she was onto them by needlessly revealing her suspicions. If she were careful, she might just catch someone in the act of sedition, which would save her administration a headache down the road.

Upstairs, she walked through the living quarters neatly styled by Corban, she guessed, and where Jenna had lived. There was a bookshelf with several poetry volumes and braille books. She pulled out a few books, checking for Bibles, but realized since she didn't know braille, the contents of the books couldn't be confirmed, even if the covers indicated they were about geography or history.

The rest of the room was so neat that Lena guessed it had been specially prepared by Corban to be shared by the next printers. Lena moved to the street window and tapped her chipped fingernails on the double-plated glass. The Federation capital needed its own ID office, but she wasn't trusting anyone Corban trained, unless she polygraphed both new apprentices. Maybe she'd keep the apprentices on staff, and maybe they'd be loyal subjects to her.

Peering out the window and straight down, she acknowledged a few pedestrians. None of them seemed concerned that a Federation vehicle was parked there, and no one approached it. In two days, an army would rumble up Broadway, and the city would forever change, but on this day, the populace seemed content with the way things were. And Lena hated the way things were.

From her vantage point, she could see through the windshield of the Jeep. The envelope was still on the dash. Maybe she was being too paranoid. Maybe Corban wasn't up to anything. Of course, he wouldn't try to smuggle anyone a message with her there with him. Her presence alone would surely discourage his Christian zeal!

She continued up the stairs to the third floor and found herself in a long and wide storeroom of office desks and chairs. Emblems on some of the sheet-covered furniture signified they belonged to an organization called COIL. On one wall opposite an inoperable elevator a map of the world was hanging. The map was color-coded, but not in any code that she could discern by studying it. Many of the Middle Eastern countries were highlighted in orange or red, as were China, North Korea, and most of Africa. Cuba and Southern Mexico were orange and red, but the rest of the countries in the Western Hemisphere were blue or green.

At the bottom of the map, "Closed countries in red and orange" was printed in small letters.

"Closed to what?" Lena asked aloud, and drew her flashlight to inspect the map closer. Little pins had been stuck into the map, some on the borders of the orange and red-colored countries, and some inside the orange and red-colored countries. But no pins were stuck into the blue and green-colored countries. "What are they closed to?"

"Maybe we should stop playing games, Ms. Travers."

Lena dropped her flashlight and spun around. As she turned, she reached for her sidearm. Yet at that instant, she recognized Corban's voice. There the old man stood, leaning uneasily against the wall above the stairs, his cane in one hand. She sure missed having Death around to alert her when people were sneaking up on her.

"I didn't hear you come up." She picked up her flashlight. "Are you already done downstairs?"

"No, the two young men are practicing with the laminator. I'll go back downstairs in a minute."

"What did you mean that we should stop playing games?"

Corban used his cane to walk closer to where she stood. He paused as he approached, stopping to gaze at the desks and chairs as if remembering who once filled them.

"I was in the CIA for decades, Ms. Travers. May I call you Lena?" He drew a sheet off an office chair and sat down. "Long before you were born, I traveled to those countries, especially to the orange and red ones. In those days, all of the Soviet Union was red as well, but they've eased their policies since then."

"What are the pins for?" Lena crossed her arms, realizing she was on edge for no reason. Corban was an old man. He was harmless, even if he was more of an intellectual than she felt she was.

"Every time I lost a COIL operative, I put a pin in the map."

"Lost?"

"They were killed."

"COIL? So, COIL was CIA?"

"No, I started COIL after I left the Agency. We were a relief organization, but with a secret and specific agenda. Those red and orange countries were closed to our purpose inside their borders, and that's why my agents died. Sometimes, they gave their lives in secret, with no one but me knowing their names or their missions. The least I could do was remember them. And put a pin on the map. A single pin isn't much, but it's something. Every pin you see up there represents a whole life lived, sacrificed, and offered for a cause that I couldn't talk about with anyone back then."

"You couldn't talk about it then, but you can talk about it now?"

"Can I, Lena? Can I truly and freely speak openly with you? We both know why you came with me today, why you insisted coming instead of Lieutenant Isaacson."

"You mean, you think you do."

"Of course." He chuckled and held his cane across his knees. "I'm not as sharp as I once was, but I still have my moments. You're easy enough to read, though. You're too suspicious to let anything slip by you. You're a hunter. You have good instincts, just a bad purpose."

"My purpose for living is the Federation. You're saying that's bad?"

"Federations, countries, empires—they come and go. And at my age, I've seen many rise and fall, including America."

"So, why do you think I came here today?"

Lena sat on the edge of a desk.

"You've reached a point of critical mass."

"What?" She snorted. "What's critical mass?"

"Uncontrolled radioactivity can build up and reach what's called critical mass. It's a stage where all that can happen now is an explosion. Because certain events have transpired that have brought you here, you're vulnerable. That's why we can talk plainly today."

"I'm not vulnerable, I assure you." She rolled her eyes. "I could shoot you right here and drag you out to lay in the street. No one would say anything about it. I'm not vulnerable. I'm invincible."

"You're vulnerable, because if you step wrong now, things will explode. Your plans will go awry if you don't tolerate the way things are right now. As you wait."

"What plans do you think I'm waiting on?"

"Would you be surprised to know that I know what went wrong in Philadelphia for what you had planned with Colonel Rotham?"

Lena's breathing paused, and she had to intentionally tell her body to take another breath after a few seconds. *He couldn't possibly know such intel!*

"Who've you been talking to?"

"Do you even understand why Colonel Rotham won't be joining the invasion?"

Now, Lena couldn't stop her gasps. She was panting. Never had anyone made her react with such physical emotion. She meant to be stronger than this, and smarter, more secretive. How could someone like this old fool know everything—even more than she knew?

"There's no way you can know that." She blinked at him through her anger. "Who else knows?"

"Like I said, it's time we lay everything out and stop playing games." He smiled so gently, and for an instant, Lena was tempted to trust herself with this strange man. "Are you ready for that kind of conversation?"

"Fine. Here's one for you: you're a Christian."

"The fact that you know that doesn't bother me, Lena. What should bother you is that I already knew that you knew that I'm a Christian, but you didn't know I knew all about Philadelphia."

"You're diabolical."

"Steady now, Lena. Don't get emotional when you need to keep functioning with discipline. I know about Boston as well."

"You're guessing."

"And Hartford, and Baltimore. More guesses?"

"You're listening to the radio transmissions?" She cackled with forced laughter, trying to hide her fear. "There's a harmless exercise going on in those cities. It's not what you think. You're the one who's vulnerable. You're a Christian. I could have you executed before sundown. Or just have my brother do it. He hates you already."

"But you won't, not the father of the chancellor's fiancée. It would set off too much upheaval before you see your plans unfold. Critical mass, remember? You're probably even trying to coordinate a surprise execution at the Bowery with the invasion of the three armies, all perfectly scripted, which means you can't upset the timeline. I'm guessing the three armies are already on the road? Yeah, that's what I figured. That's why we're talking.

I know you're at a moment of critical mass, so I can say what you need to hear."

"I don't know how you know all—" She thought about drawing her sidearm right then and killing him, but he was right. Anything she did now would set off a chain of reactions that could undo everything, or make things more difficult on Saturday. "Obrador doesn't know what you know, or I'd be in chains. You haven't told him."

"We haven't told him what you're doing, and you haven't told him what we're doing."

"And what do you think you're doing? I already know Jenna is Radiant Shade. Very clever, getting Obrador to choose her from all the women. But the pageant nonsense is the whole reason I'm turning on the chancellor. Your influence, whatever you're attempting, is what turned me off. You're the reason I'm taking over, and all of you will be destroyed in the process. I loathe Christianity."

"I've seen dictators try to eradicate Christianity before. You won't kill all of us, even if you kill some of us. God Almighty always preserves and protects a remnant for a purpose. People who love you, Lena, and pray for what's best for you, will always be maintained by God, no matter what cruelty you devise for them. God makes sure that happens, just to prove that love triumphs over evil."

"I could have you shot right now. There is no God. The Federation is the only entity that deserves your complete loyalty and gratitude!"

"We established that last night, didn't we? Your earthly Federation is weaker than my heavenly faith. No, Lena, I'm not the one who needs to adjust perspectives. Let me challenge you with this: call off the invasion. Help us help Obrador establish a caring, just government. The pace of executions the Federation has continued all these years—it's unsustainable. How can you not wipe out everyone within five years at this rate? It's over, Lena. Work with me. Meet me halfway."

"It's not over. You're about to lose, and you know it. You wouldn't be begging me to call off the invasion if you weren't scared."

"I'm scared for you, not for myself." He shrugged, and she believed he was being sincere. "What do I have to lose? My life? I've lived a full one, content that my soul is safe in the hands of God, in whom I've trusted. I know what eternity holds for me, and I'm excited to meet face to face the Savior who bought and paid for my sins."

"You'll lose Jenna. I'll kill her myself, slowly, after all the problems she's caused us for years! There's no escape off this island. Baltimore from the south, Hartford's coming from the west, and Boston from the north. Jenna's the third person I'm executing, just so you know—after Obrador and Chloe. You can be number four."

"I'm flattered."

"Just telling you the way things are. They're already in motion. You can't escape. Even if you run now, I'll still hunt you down—you and your daughter. I'd like to see you run, actually. It wouldn't be a challenge for me, though— a blind brat and an invalid who can barely walk up the stairs? I heard Lieutenant Isaacson had to carry you up the Bowery stairs. You really think you can escape what I have planned? You can't be that naïve, to trust your God for all that."

"All that and more." Corban chuckled. "You haven't read the Bible, so you don't know the historical record of God's interventions on behalf of His people. But even if God, in His wisdom, should choose to allow me to suffer death for Him, He is no less impressive in my eyes, and one day, you'll see Him in all His glory for yourself. He's already shown me what He can do to one of your armies in Philadelphia."

Corban held up four fingers.

"What's that supposed to mean? Four? What's four have to do with Philadelphia?"

"It's the number of my people who devastated Colonel Rothams' entire army in Philly."

"Your people?"

"COIL-trained and equipped. You've been playing checkers, Lena, for a few months. Radiant Shade has been playing chess for decades."

"So, she's behind it all? You and her?" She felt her ambitions sinking, her pride attacked. "You're going to tell Obrador?"

"If you tell him what we're up to, you'll expose yourself. And if we tell him what you're doing, we're exposed. It's a tricky situation."

"So, we're both at critical mass."

"No, you're the only one at critical mass. We're going to express Christian mercy. If you come on strong against us with your invasion, then we'll bow out. We won't fight you, Lena. But you'll still lose."

"I'll be chancellor. That's not losing."

"For a period of time, you'll be chancellor, perhaps, but you'll remember this conversation. That's why I'm risking everything on this moment, because you're that precious to God, Lena. I'm a father, and when I look at you, I see someone's daughter. I don't want anything but what is dearest and best for you. Hold these ideas in your heart: receive by faith that God loves you in a personal way, that He sent His Son Jesus Christ to die in payment for your sins, and that by Him alone you may receive eternal life. Don't live another day in bondage to your hatred, strife, and guilt. Let Him clean your conscience and set you free. That's my message for you today. That's the message you've hated for no valid reason. You are deeply loved."

For an instant, while she considered him in the light from the window, she indeed wondered why a message of love and mercy was such a danger to her. But then she recalled the Federation's charter. No deity could coexist within a country, for a people chose either the divine or the government to follow, never both.

"The Federation is my god. I'll die before I give up on her and its people."

"If you do it God's way, your devotion to the Federation and its people will be pure and prioritized. That's all that Radiant Shade has been trying to support all these years—justice and order."

She looked back at the map and sighed.

"You're persistent, I'll tell you that." She stood and adjusted her sidearm in its holster. "So, what now? Everything's on the table, just like you wanted. The invasion can't be stopped. You said you'll back down, and I'll be chancellor. I'll hunt down all you Christians and your infiltration into the administration. Eventually, I'll find you all."

"We're not sticking around, it looks like, remember?" Corban tilted his head. "I thought I was the senile one."

"There's nowhere for you to hide. I'll smoke you out of the tunnels if you go down there. You think I'm amused by what you and Chloe have done to Obrador, using your blind daughter? He was once a visionary. Now he's Jenna's lap dog. The games are over. Critical mass or not, I won't stand for any more secret agenda."

"Well, in the days and weeks to come, Lena," Corban said, adjusting the cane on his lap, "just remember what I told you about Jesus Christ. You need a Savior from sin. We all do. Let Him give you a new life. If you remember that, my people will help you, even if there's just a few of us left."

"Your last conscious vision, old man, will be of me standing before the gallows that my brother rebuilt. Have you forgotten the Day of Cleansing on Monday? Of course, according to my calendar, it happens two days earlier. But you already know that."

"Two days earlier than Monday? I didn't know that, but you've certainly helped narrow down the timeline we can expect the invasion. Thank you."

"You smug—"

She started toward him, not to shoot or kill him, but to punch that look off his face. After all the threats she'd voiced, he'd remained obstinate.

Instead, she felt a hard blow to her solar plexus. The force made her back up two steps. When she touched her chest, she expected to find blood on her fingers, but instead she felt only a spongy, sticky gelatin. Corban's cane was still aimed at her. *He'd shot her!*

Before she could reach him or draw her sidearm, she slumped unconscious to the floor. Her last glimpse was of Corban catching her head and easing her gently to the floor.

Owen Travers was in the Bowery lobby that Thursday afternoon when his sister stomped through the front door. He'd been in the middle of assigning patrol orders for a squad venturing into Queens, but the look on Lena's face told him he was finished with his duties as an Enforcer for the moment. The other Citizen Army officers in the lobby backed off, then walked away, their heads down. No one seemed interested in Lena's company.

But there was no backing away for Owen. He braced himself for the confrontation that had been building for years between himself and his older sibling.

"Where's Corban?" she demanded, her voice barely under control. "How long's he been back?"

"I thought you were out on patrol."

He acted like he was scanning a clipboard until she slapped it out of his hands. It clattered to the floor, drawing glances from army clerks and porters across the room.

"Don't play games with me, Owen!" She held up her index finger like a dagger. "How long has Corban been back? I went up to the ID office with him, and then I just woke up outside in the parking lot in the Jeep we left in. There's about three hours missing from my memory!"

"Well, well, well." Owen chuckled and picked up the clipboard. "So, you finally had a brush with the old man. I told you I didn't faint at the sight of my own blood. Maybe now you'll believe me that there's more to that old geezer than meets the eye."

"Yeah, if you only knew." She fanned her face with an envelope. "I'm telling you, Owen, you'd better be ready for what's about to happen. I don't want any hesitation from you when I tell you to jump!"

"Oh, yeah?" Owen moved over to the old check-in counter and browsed a list of overdue delivery trucks from Boston. He acted disinterested intentionally to annoy her. "When you say jump, I just jump, huh? What's in the envelope?"

"Nothing. That's the problem." She scowled, wrinkled up the envelope, and threw it into the corner of the room. "Corban was in Times Square making a drop to the underground. I'm pretty sure there was a message in this envelope. But when I woke up, it was just empty, laying on the dash."

"You're not making much sense, sis." Owen signed a driver's shift slip, then the man hustled away from the infamous brother and sister duo. "The underground is no more. The Bandit and all those people—they've run off."

"Not the under-underground in the tunnels, Owen! I'm talking about the Christian underground. Corban's been with them from the beginning."

"Oh, yeah?" Owen cursed as he picked up a cup of instant coffee that had gone cold. "This was one of my last coffee packets. Now I can't even drink it."

He poured the contents into an empty planter that had been near the counter for as many years as he'd been there.

"I swear, Owen!" Lena punched his shoulder, and not playfully. "If you don't start listening to me, you and everything that's important to you will—"

"Will what? I'll get held back by you a little longer? Look around you, Lena. The chancellor is giving me a real shot here. I'm more than just an Enforcer now, doing what you tell me to do. Nobody even wants to be around me when you're around. What'd I ever get from listening to you all those years? Blood on my hands, that's what!"

"You wouldn't be where you are without me!" Lena charged toward him, but he shoved her back by her shoulders. "I gave you Radiant Shade. But you don't even know what the Christians are doing in this building right now, Owen!"

"The Christians will be dealt with on Monday. You'll see. The Day of Cleansing can't come soon enough for us all. Just get out of my face."

"Are you shutting me out?" Her voice was cold and high-pitched, and he'd only heard her get that way with noncompliant citizens, when she was torturing them in the interrogation room, but getting no results. "If you're shutting me out, Owen, then there won't be a Monday for you!"

Owen couldn't remember ever striking his sister, but he did right then. Using his left hand, he backhanded her across the mouth. She twisted and fell to the ground. He'd seen her take punches from wild prisoners before, so he guessed her fall was more of a surprise than from the force. Nevertheless, with his right hand, he drew his sidearm. Sure enough, she reached for her own sidearm, then froze when she saw him aiming his gun at her head.

"Get out, Lena. I'm not yours anymore. You don't tell me what to do any longer. I loved you and followed you once, but that child is gone. I don't care what you do now.

I'm with Chancellor Obrador. He's actually taking me places."

She touched her jaw where he'd struck her, then climbed to her feet. The look she gave him made him cringe on the inside, but he hoped it didn't show on the outside. His own sister had become his enemy.

For the rest of the afternoon, he worked in the lobby, signing orders and receiving deliveries for the capital. He tried to shake his sister's threat and words, but he'd been at her side for forty years. It was only natural that their falling out would sting him a little.

But everyone else in the lobby suddenly seemed more pleasant towards him, and he immediately knew why. He'd stood up to the hurricane that Lena had always been. Sure, they would follow her on a raid before they followed him, but no one joked around or enjoyed themselves back at the Bowery when she was near. Then he realized the fuller meaning of it all. *They were taking his side against her!* And they liked him more than they feared her. It was her own fault, he decided. She didn't want friends and honor, only power and control.

That night, Owen sat at the banquet table among all the honored guests. His sister's place was taken by one of Obrador's cabinet members. Lena didn't even show up that night, and Owen's happiness rose two more notches because of it.

"I'm so glad all of you could be here for this second dinner," Jenna Dowler said, raising a glass. "This dinner is for my husband-to-be, to honor him once again for what he's made himself and made for this new country. I hope this weekend will be as meaningful to you all as it will be to me."

Owen nodded, then smiled at Chloe across from him. Yes, a marriage in the Bowery was a good idea, and he was on the inside now, one of them, a noble, a prince of the Bowery. His name would be remembered alongside the chancellors.

"I want us to remember this night," Jenna continued. "Although I can't see you with my eyes, I can see you with my heart. And I hear your voices and your laughter. As I've met you, our hearts have touched, and I shall never forget any of you. Each of you is special in your own way. What is happening is bigger than us as individuals, but that doesn't mean you are insignificant. To changes worth making!"

"To changes!" the table echoed, and then drank the toast.

Owen gulped the fizzing alcohol, then coughed into his hand. He wasn't a drinker like Obrador was, but he hoped no one thought he was weak because of it.

"Wow." He shook his head, fighting tears as the fluid burned all the way down.

"You okay, Owen?" It was Corban, his voice low under the conversation and clinking of plates as the servers dished food onto plates. Corban was seated next to Chloe across the table. "Did it go down the wrong pipe? You good?"

Owen remembered his sister's words about Corban, and he remembered his own sentiments toward the man. For weeks, hatred mixed with embarrassment had been associated with the name Corban Dowler. If he was really so evil, then how was he concerned like a father about him? Of course, Owen didn't know what to think about the two times he'd been rendered unconscious when Corban was present, but his own heart yearned for acceptance and reconciliation with the common people. Maybe Corban and the others had been his adversaries because of his sister's bad attitude. Maybe Corban wasn't really his enemy at all!

"Yeah, I'm good." He smiled and jutted a thumb toward the end of the table. "That was some toast, huh?"

"Jenna's always had a gift for words, probably because she speaks from the heart."

"The world might be a better place if we all could, right?" Owen heard what he said and was fascinated by the depth of it. "I never used to say things like that."

"What's changed in you?" Corban used a fork to point at Owen. "Something's different. Your eyes are even a little brighter."

"My eyes?" Owen chuckled self-consciously and glanced around, but no one was listening. They were all having their own warm and interesting conversations. "Actually, I think it was my sister."

"Your sister opened your eyes for you?"

"Sort of. We had a falling out. I never realized how much she was weighing me down. It's like some . . . force is moving me toward greatness, and one step at a time, I'm walking toward it. One of those steps was walking away from her. She has her own agenda. It isn't mine."

"That's good to hear." Corban's face became serious, then he leaned closer over his plate. "You're not with her this weekend, then? Saturday?"

"You know about that?" Owen looked in Obrador's direction, but the chancellor was discussing something about rebuilding the Queensboro Bridge with Lieutenant Isaacson. "She didn't even tell me what's going on! See what I mean? She's a snake, manipulating me by keeping me in the dark while everyone else knows everything."

"She thinks a fist of fury is stronger than a word of kindness." Corban shook his head and took a bite of Pennsylvanian pheasant. "Look around you, Owen. These people care about you. They want what's best for you. Greatness comes by freedom and grace, not by demands and threats."

"So, things really are changing in this administration?" Owen nibbled on baby carrots, contemplating. "So, it's all just a power struggle my sister is involved in? The chancellor is going for a gentler approach to win the people? The wedding and all?"

"Oh, not just to win the people," Corban said. "There's less personal motive in it than you realize. This administration is learning to *care* for its people. We're all molded on a personal level, so it's to be expected that it takes time for a government to be molded in turn. It's all in hands much bigger than mine or yours, so we need to wait and trust that all will be well in the end, and that our own hearts are ready for the changes."

"Yes, I see." But Owen didn't see or understand. His face suddenly felt hot as he thought of the Day of Cleansing. Maybe he wasn't moving with them like he thought he was! What if he was still trying to be severe like his sister had trained him to be, while the administration was growing more compassionate? "Can I get your personal opinion?"

"Of course." Corban wiped his mouth on a napkin and set down his fork. "Anything at all, Owen."

"This Day of Cleansing—is it too much? I mean, your daughter applauded it last night, and Obrador issued it as law, but maybe it's, you know—the old, gruesome way. The fist of fury and all that."

"Help me understand, Owen." Corban folded his hands, his elbows on the table. "The Day of Cleansing is about killing off the Christians, right?"

"Yeah. They're a nuisance to the Federation. They defy the authority of this administration. At least they were, when Radiant Shade was around."

"Try looking at it from another perspective, Owen. Judge for yourself between these two things."

"Okay."

"A king who makes his people do what he wants them to do, and a king who protects his people after he instructs them to live in harmony and obedience. Which king is more loved?"

"Obviously, the king who protects and instructs."

"And to which king will the people offer more of their service?"

"Again, to the king who protects and instructs them. But how will he get what he wants if he doesn't make them do what he requires?"

"Ah, good question! That's all in the relationship the king has with the people. A good king gives his life for the people, and the people are so drawn to the king's love that he has to help them where they can't help themselves. They naturally obey what is right and good, because they see that the king loves them. They love the king in return. No control is necessary. The people are compelled by love to obey and do all the king would want, and he doesn't even need to make them do it. He simply loves, protects, and instructs them."

"I've never been taught this." Owen looked about the table to see it was now silent. Everyone was listening. "We've never done it that way."

"Don't feel too shocked, Owen." Obrador raised his glass. "We all seem to be learning lately. It's a welcome attitude. It feels . . . hopeful, somehow."

"But won't people think we're weak?" Owen looked from Obrador to Jenna, remembering her promise to him. "What about rebel uprisings and nonconformists? We just let them run wild? We just love and protect them as well?"

"Freedom isn't weak," Corban said. "The demands upon the populace are kept to a minimum to preserve the peace and safety in society. Naturally, the contentment strengthens the arm of the law of a benevolent administration. Instead of wrath, discipline is administered only where appropriate and always in proportion."

"But what about the Christians?" Owen asked the table. "They're the last known nonconformists in the Federation. This is where we discipline, right?"

"It's already law," Chloe said, and Owen thought he sensed sorrow in her voice. "Every Christian will die by the hand of their neighbor, and their possessions will pass to their executioner."

"Well, it'll all be done on Monday." Owen nodded resolutely at Obrador, hoping he continued to receive the chancellor's approval. "We can make more of the changes after the Day of Cleansing. We'll be free of the Christians, at least."

But Obrador continued eating, and other conversations started up, almost as if everyone was eager to discuss something other than a few thousand deaths about to occur Monday. Owen felt queasy inside, as if all he'd gained in the last week wasn't real at all, since he'd been too zealous and harsh, even against nonconformists. He realized he'd made a mistake by pushing for the Day of Cleansing, but there was no way to save face except to push it through and hope people remembered his patriotism more than his fist of fury.

Chapter Sixteen

Lieutenant Nathan Isaacson was up praying before the sun rose on Friday morning. The threat of evil was in the air. Greater oppression against God's people almost suffocated him as he wept before the Lord. He felt a heaviness of the soul, which exhibited itself upon his very body. Every breath was labored. Every inhale took physical effort. It was easier to exhale than inhale.

From where he prayed on the floor beside their bed, he could see that Chen Li was finally sleeping peacefully. She'd cried into the night as they'd both prayed. Their emotions were raw. The inner tension was palpable. But they lived by faith, so they had fallen asleep late into the night, praying for God's strength for the days ahead. They desperately needed sleep and physical strength, but they needed the Holy Spirit's presence and stamina even more.

Both operatives had originally met one another under the strain of violence and oppression, so they were under no delusion of what they now sensed in the air. Their years of quiet living, private struggling, secret staging—it all came down to these few days they were now facing.

The evening before, Corban had called them all to meet in Jenna's room one more time. He'd told them that he'd made one last effort to draw Lena from her wicked intentions, but she'd acted adversely. The stakes were higher now. Each side knew what the other intended. While Lena had been prowling and planning, she was merely a threat. Now, her plans were about to unfold, and her plans were on a collision course with COIL's plans, which were heaven-borne.

"Sweetie?" Nathan whispered to Chen Li. "It's time."

She stirred and sat up.

"Please tell me I slept through the weekend," she mumbled, "and everything turned out just fine."

"I can tranquilize you over and over again, if you'd prefer." He chuckled. "God didn't promise us a *just fine* life, babe, but He did promise that eternal life would be better than fine."

"Yeah?" She rolled out of bed. "When does that start?"

"You can't tell? It's already started."

"I forgot how comical you tend to be when you're staging for a mission." She scowled playfully as she stumbled groggily toward the bathroom. "Well, I don't have the same sentiments as you and Scooter do for times like these."

"Scooter's not here, so I guess you'll just have to embrace my comic relief."

She closed the bathroom door, and Nathan stretched his aching limbs. He thought of Corban, who was twenty years older and had been shot up and wounded twice as much as Nathan had been. Somehow, Corban's broken and crippled body was still hobbling along. It gave Nathan encouragement that he could also endure his own few aches and pains.

From a cup of pens and pencils on the corner desktop, Nathan selected two tranq-pens, disguised with regular ink pens. He'd tested one of the tranquilizers on himself a week earlier, so he knew the shelf life of the non-lethal toxin was stable. It was the only COIL weaponry he and Chen Li had around, but they would need much more if they were to survive as well as guard the hundred Christians under their charge.

Chen Li emerged from the bathroom a few minutes later, appearing weary but refreshed. He gave her a tranq pen.

"I'll try not to tranq myself," she said, and tucked it into her pants pocket. "Let's do this."

In full uniforms, husband and wife descended the Bowery's stairs, exited the guarded lobby, then crossed the empty parking lot to the Citizen Processing building. Nathan gazed to his right as the sun rose enough to illuminate a few buildings in golden-red. He could see the side of the prisoner cages behind the building. Razor wire and stainless steel had been the home for first-time offenders of the Federation compliance laws—but all that ended now.

Since Chen Li was a Citizen Processing Supervisor, none of the remaining night-watch staff questioned her or Nathan as they signed in and went to the back room, closest to the cages outside. In the room, Sergeant Sean Harris rose to his feet and stood at attention.

"You beat us here." Nathan patted the shoulder of his right-hand man. "We've got a job to do today. You ready?"

"When my commanding officer tells me to meet him at dawn, I don't get up for nothing."

"Well, today is definitely not about nothing." Nathan gestured to the bench where they could both sit. Chen Li went to the cabinet and began pulling out files. "Today, you're Sean and I'm Nathan, instead of Sergeant Harris and Lieutenant Isaacson. You're at a crossroads, Sean, and I need to bring you in or throw you out right now. It's up to you, and it's a matter of life and death."

"What?" Sean's graying, bushy eyebrows quivered as he frowned and eyed Chen Li. "What's happening? Is this about those dinners you've been having up with the chancellor? And the radio traffic I've been picking up from the other cities?"

"This has everything to do with all that." Nathan took a deep breath, remembering that God was present no matter what happened. He held the tranq pen in his left hand in case he needed it.

"A coup has been uncovered."

"*A coup?*" Sean sat up straighter. "Well, where do we stand?"

"How do you know we stand together?" Nathan asked. "You need to decide for yourself where you stand, Sean. Chen Li and I have already made our decision, and we're ready to face the consequences of our stand, because we believe it's the right stand."

"You really think so little of my loyalty?" Sean shook his head. "You're the most conflicting guy I know, Lieutenant—I mean, Nathan. You can execute a woman one minute, and include me in an unexpected honor the next minute. How many years have we been together? I have no problem, no hesitation, no reservation, staying right beside you through whatever cursed thing is about to happen. But I want to know everything."

"Lena Travers is staging a coup against Obrador. Three different armies are about to invade Manhattan in an effort to squash any resistance. She's planning to kill everyone who stands with Obrador."

"Please tell me we're not siding with that nightmare," he said with a cringe, "even if the odds are against us. By nightmare, I mean Lena. We're not, are we?"

"No, we're sticking with Obrador, but it means acting in his best interests without him knowing right now. Lena intends to execute him, Chloe Azmaveth, and the rest of us, including Jenna and Corban Dowler."

"She's crazy."

"And she has a crazy military backing her."

"What do you want me to do?"

"We're getting out of the city. We're running for our lives, and since people like Jenna and Obrador aren't soldiers, that means you and I put ourselves in harm's way for them, to escort them to safety."

"I always wondered if you had a little hero in you, Nathan." Sean's eyes brightened. "Can you imagine the two of us old war dogs dying of old age? Trying to rise in rank in the Federation? That just doesn't compute. So now, we'll die for something that matters, huh? The chancellor's in the dark about this?"

"He's in the dark, and we can't risk telling him without this thing exploding and costing a lot of innocent lives. But listen, we have a whole coalition that we're pulling out with. Elements of the disbanded resistance are willing to assist us, old friends of mine."

"Friends of yours? In the resistance? Things aren't as they seem, Nathan."

"We're taking everyone out of the city who's in danger of Lena's wrath. We'll use the tunnels to travel as far north as we can, then swing west to cross the GW Bridge."

"What do you mean by *everyone?*" Sean frowned. "Wait. Why are we here in Citizen Processing discussing this?"

"You're aware that Monday is scheduled to be the Day of Cleansing?"

"Yeah. Noncompliants will be executed without trial. It's civil justice."

"Well, we're undermining that order today. That's why we're here. We're going to take all of the professing Christians out of here."

"*What?*" Sean stared at the outer door that led to the cages. "But that's most of our forced labor crews. We've been working them to death. Now we're helping them?"

"I was always helping them, behind the scenes."

"You helped them? I saw you execute them! I saw it with my own eyes, just two months ago. They aren't going to accept your help!"

"Two months ago, you saw me throw a woman into the tunnels. Those old friends of mine—they recovered her from the water. She was too old to be working for us through the winter, so I rescued her before she actually died. It was a mock execution. I've done them before. The Christians aren't our enemies, Sean. That's an idea that socialism has instigated. Christians support the authorities in power, and uphold the cause of Jesus Christ every step of the way. I should know—I'm a Christian. Chen Li and I are both believers in Christ's love and God's eternal judgement against nonbelievers who reject His gift."

Sean stood and walked across the room, his hands on his hips. When he turned around, he was shaking his head but grinning.

"That woman's still alive? I knew there was another layer to you, Lieutenant! So, what now? The Federation ceases to be? What are we going to do with Obrador? He can't join with Christians, can he?"

"Later tonight, we'll brief him on what he needs to know, and everyone in the Bowery we're taking out will leave as one group. But we're getting these Christians out of their cages today. Otherwise, Lena will kill them the first day. As for what happens to Obrador afterwards, that's up to him. We're going to Colorado. We have people there who can stand against the Federation."

"You mean Meeker, Colorado?" Sean asked. "The place that caravan of noncompliant people went? Where Colonel Tentmaker disappeared? I've heard stories from the men who returned."

"Well, then you have an idea of how far and how hard this is going to be."

"Yeah, too far to be traveling with Lena Travers on our tails." Sean paced across the room. "You have a plan? We're fighting men, we're not retreating men, Nathan. We're really gonna run away?"

"Yes, we're running for the sake of the ones we're protecting. We can't fight well until they're safe. And yes, we have a plan. Once out of the city, we can break into a couple of parties—a fleeing band and a fighting band. The fighting band will hold off Lena's pursuing troops until the fleeing band is safely out of Federation territory. We have the artillery to do that effectively. But we'll also have the Plains Zone to deal with. I hear it's wild out there. If you have any designs on a comfortable Manhattan riverside retirement, this won't be your kind of mission."

"Do I look like the retirement type to you? Just give me my orders and let me worry about where I retire."

"Look here." Nathan pulled a hand-drawn map of Manhattan from his pocket. Simultaneously, he tucked the tranq-pen away. "We have to evacuate the island in stages. The tunnels this far south are flooded and impassible, but we can temporarily hide the prisoners safely there, on 20th Street. The man you've known as the Bandit received instructions to meet us there and help hide the Christians until tonight, when we can move them through the city in the dark to the next tunnel opening."

"You're giving the Bandit orders?" Sean asked, shaking his head.

"No, just instructions. We're old friends. He loves this kind of work."

"Do you have any idea of how angry I am with you that you're bringing me on board about all this right now?" He growled through clenched teeth. "I knew there was something different about you!"

"I couldn't risk telling you until right now, Sean. But look. I want you here, at this 20th Street tunnel opening, to prep for tonight."

"The Bandit?" Sean slapped his knee. "This should be good. If he used to know you, then I'm going to ask him who the *real* Nathan Isaacson is!"

"You'll have time to visit," Nathan said, "but he goes by Scooter now. He'll give you a weapon when you reach that tunnel, and from there, you do what he says as if I'm telling you myself. I'll be coming with the Bowery crowd tomorrow sometime, and meet up with you under the Upper West Side. Be rested, because it'll be a long couple of nights."

"And this whole time, you've been a Christian? Right under my nose? All that Jesus stuff?"

"I'll have to tell you more about it on the road." Nathan stood and approached Chen Li. "Right now, we need to start pulling all the Christian prisoners out, and then you and I will march them north a few blocks, just like a normal work detail."

"Except this time," Chen Li said, a stack of files in her arms, "we won't be returning them to the cages at the end of the day."

"This is amazing." Sean shook his head, his eyes watering. "Thank you, Nathan. You've done it again—you've included me. I won't let you down."

Luigi had been waiting inside a gutted bank on 20th Street all night and all morning. His eyes were on the alley to the south, when he finally saw movement, and he sighed a prayer of relief. A forced labor detail was walking toward the intersection. God had prevailed. One night had been short notice from Corban to be in place to receive the one hundred Christian prisoners. Corban's handwritten instructions were all they were able to rely on. Since they'd watched Lena herself accompany Corban to the print office, Luigi had been forced to sneak the instructions from the dashboard of the Jeep.

Retreating deeper into the bank, Luigi fetched his pack and an NL-X2 battle rifle from the vault, then returned to the front door. Nathan was in the street, harshly directing the workers to apply their shovels, brooms, and picks to the rubble on the sidewalk. Cautiously, Luigi studied the uniformed guards, in case it wasn't safe to reveal himself. Chen Li was one of the guards, as was an older sergeant with bushy eyebrows. Three other guards were there, but by their postures, he was sure they were Christians clothed in Federation uniforms, since their bodies were thin and bowed from abuse and starvation. From a distance, however, the labor crew would've seemed like any other detail in the city, cleaning up the streets in preparation for the wedding and scheduled parade.

Since the door had been removed years earlier, Luigi stepped through the opening of the bank. Nathan noticed him and waved him into the street. Warily, Luigi walked out among the labor workers. The workers' heads were bowed as they pretended to work, but their eyes were alert, their faces full of excitement. It was obvious to see they were ready to leave, even if they weren't in the best of physical condition.

"Okay, you ready for this?" Nathan smiled and shook Luigi's hand. "How many years I've prayed to see you again, openly like this!"

"Maybe we shouldn't celebrate too much right now." Luigi checked the other streets. There were a few pedestrians, but none were paying attention to the work detail. "We can take the prisoners in here and move them about two blocks west where we can emerge tonight to find a tunnel that leads at least to Central Park."

"Scooter's around? I haven't seen him in years."

"There." Luigi gestured to the manhole cover in the middle of the intersection. Scooter's head appeared. "Five more battle rifles are back in the bank vault, the ones you told me to get. You and Chen Li have it from here? I'll go to the Bowery if I need to. I'm worried about Corban."

"No. We've got it." Nathan signaled to the sergeant at his side. "This is Sean. He'll help you with the Christians. You have quite a few who can barely walk."

"I'll carry two of them at a time if I have to," Sean said, and shook Luigi's hand.

Luigi instantly liked the hearty man.

"We'll siphon one at a time into the hole here," Nathan said for Sean's sake. "Let's get this done and move out."

"No one'll notice them missing?" Luigi asked. "One hundred men, women, and children?"

"That's something I need to ask you to help us with, Luigi. There's enough prisoners, mostly men, left in those cages, so the hundred we've taken won't be noticed, at least before sundown. Regardless, I don't like leaving those other prisoners behind just because they're not Christians. Once it's dark, can you sneak up on the backside of those cages and cut them free?"

"I've been behind the Bowery before. Those cages are just chain-link fences." Luigi nodded. "I can cut through that with the wire cutters in my pack."

"Good. Those people won't receive justice under Lena, and besides, their freedom will cause the new regime a bit of a hassle."

"Consider it done."

Scooter risked exposure by climbing from the hole and embracing Nathan. Luigi watched as the two old friends laughed and teased one another. It had been years since they could rejoice together, but it would be longer still before they could do so safely.

"Nathan!" Chen Li called from across the street, where she pretended to supervise the prisoners. "Reunion later! Let's move it!"

Moving back under the awning of the bank, Luigi stood with the rifle at his shoulder to cover the evacuation.

Scooter ducked into the hole, where Luigi knew Brian Steelman was waiting as well, and Nathan numbered the workers as he walking among them. Then, he returned to the front and called the first number. A woman dropped her broom in the street and walked straight to the hole. Hands received her as she climbed down.

Luigi listened as more numbers were called, but he was now focused on the nearby streets. An ambush from Federation troops at that moment would've meant death for them all. The tunnel there led nowhere, so there would be no escape. It was merely a hiding place, and Luigi wouldn't feel safe until darkness fell and he could lead them all to a passage that ran northward. He alone would remain above ground hiding in the bank until it was time to cut open the cages at the Bowery, then return and move the Christians out. Scooter had expressed his relief that Luigi was willing to take lead for a change.

Nearly half of the Christians were in the hole when a personnel transport rumbled up the street toward them. Luigi moved into the shadows of the bank, and sighted through the battle rifle's scope at the thirty armed soldiers in the back of the truck.

Out in the street, Nathan ceased calling numbers, and he stood in front of the manhole with Sean, since there had been no opportunity to replace the cover.

The truck slowed as it arrived at the intersection. Chen Li waved the truck through as she shouted sharply at workers to move aside. Luigi watched Nathan touch his brow in a brief salute to the driver of the truck, maybe someone he recognized, then the truck continued on.

"Too close!" Luigi gasped and lowered his rifle.

Nathan continued to call numbers, until all that remained were the three phony guards. Then they, too, disappeared into the hole.

Finally, Nathan and Sean shook hands, and Sean descended into the tunnel. With a grinding sound of metal against pavement, Nathan shifted the cover over the hole. Together, Nathan and Chen Li gathered the workers' tools and entered the bank where they dumped the tools against a wall. Nothing remained in the street that signaled the presence of the Christians underground.

"I nearly had a heart attack when that truck drove through!" Chen Li clung to her husband's side. "I thought we were gonners!"

"They have enough for themselves down there?" Nathan asked Luigi. "It'll be a long day, and some of them are unhealthy."

"Food, water, and blankets." Luigi shrugged. "But not enough to go around. Tonight will be no better, and then we'll be on the road to Colorado."

"Jenna says Bruno is in New Jersey at some warehouse getting ready for us and others," Nathan said. "He might be able to harbor some who can't travel west with us, but we'll need to move out with those who can. The Federation will rapidly become inhospitable to us after tonight."

"I thought it was this whole world in general that was becoming inhospitable," Luigi said, thinking of Heather. "Lord willing, I'll see both of you tomorrow. Don't forget your rifles."

"Be safe, brother," Nathan said.

"I'm safer out here than where you're going." Luigi waited until Nathan and Chen Li emerged from the vault with rifle slings over their shoulders. "Now don't let Corban make a martyr of himself. I want to see him on the mainland."

"Like Sean said about others a minute ago—I'll carry him if I have to."

They walked away, and Luigi was left alone in the bank. From his pocket, he drew a single piece of bubble gum. He'd been saving it for months for a special day. This was the day, he decided, and unwrapped it.

When Lena entered the chancellor's suite that night, she almost laughed at the looks on everyone's faces. Obrador raised his head, like a ground squirrel who'd spotted a soaring hawk. Owen turned red-faced. Chen Li whispered to Jenna. And Chloe turned her head away. Of the thirty people at the dinner table, only Corban Dowler smiled and raised a hand in greeting toward her. She respected him a little for his friendliness, but only a little. If he hadn't been so opposed to her vision, she would've been tempted to like him. She did like him. But his Christianity was incompatible with her fight for control over the Federation and its people.

"There's no room for me?" Lena asked, realizing they must've just started the first course. "I'm not welcome here? All I did was miss one night."

"We weren't expecting you." Chloe rose from her chair. "Scoot down, everyone. Lena, come sit next to me. Another plate here, please?"

Lena walked around the table, then adjusted her sidearm on her hip as she sat down. She was served a plate of pasta with white sauce that smelled like clams. But she wasn't there to eat; she was there to gloat. Leaning forward, she counted the people who would be dead before dinner was finished. There was Obrador, Jenna, Chloe, Isaacson, Corban, Chen Li, and Owen, whose face was still red from embarrassment. His words of betrayal still rang in her ears. No one drew a gun on her and lived!

Killing Obrador was just business. For the administration to truly change hands, he had to be permanently removed. Otherwise, the people who loved him would never move on. A public execution would've been preferable, but any kind of death would suffice at this point, as long as she had his body on display by midnight in Foley Square for the army to notice.

The army was early, thankfully, so her own business in the Bowery needed to be dealt with early as well—that evening. And even though Philadelphia's forces had been immobilized by Corban Dowler's friends, Colonel Rotham was still on his way with a few men. Lena wanted him close to her, especially because he shared her hatred for the Christians who'd thought they'd bested them recently.

However, Lena couldn't remember hating anyone as much as she hated Owen, so killing her little brother wasn't business but personal pleasure. His ungratefulness and disloyalty would cost him his life, and she intended his death to be on full display, right there at the table. After all, she knew how much he cared about the opinion of others. She wanted him to cry in shame in front of the very people he'd tried to impress.

With one hand, she picked up her fork, but she placed her other hand on her lap where she could draw her sidearm with ease. Again, she counted the shots she'd need to aim and fire as rapidly as possible. Isaacson was armed, so she'd shoot him first. Obrador's bodyguards were excellent marksmen, and they could shoot her from their positions against the wall. But she'd bought them both off and convinced them to join her in the next administration. No one else in the room seemed to be armed or a threat. Thanks to Jenna's redundant dinners, everyone was at ease, totally complacent.

The small talk around the table remained superficial, and no one engaged her, which allowed her to focus on the deed she needed to do. The politicians seated among her enemies shared their excitement about the wedding in two days, and Obrador was once again locked in discussion with Isaacson about city expansion, but no one realized there was about to be bloodshed.

"I'm guessing you came for the announcement?" Chloe suddenly asked her, touching Lena's arm, as if to let Lena know her hidden hand wasn't unseen. "Jenna should be making it any minute."

"What announcement?"

"Oh, you'll see. I don't want to spoil the surprise. It's going to be wonderful. The chancellor is expecting to hear something from Jenna for all these banquets, but he doesn't know yet what it'll be."

"And do you know what she'll be saying?"

"I've heard about it. I'm glad you came. It'll be something to witness."

Frowning at her dinner plate, Lena tasted nothing in her mouth as she chewed. Chloe was glad she'd come? None of these people were acting like they knew they were about to die. Hadn't Corban warned them? They'd had all day to try to run away, she thought, but now they were trapped on the island. One army was already in Newark, pausing only until the other two armies radioed that they were ready to cross the bridge, staging at Union City. Lena had only to do her part: remove Chancellor Obrador and secure the Bowery.

But now she was concerned about Chloe, who was seated so close to her that if Chloe responded adversely to the first couple of shots, the woman could interfere with her plans altogether! True, the chancellor's bodyguards would back her up, but only if she drew first blood to assure them of a decisive win with Obrador permanently removed.

Lena tried to recall what she knew about Chloe and her past. The woman had been only a public liaison in her past life, so how harmful could she be now? But then she remembered that Chloe had known Corban Dowler back then, and that meant she'd been connected to COIL. She'd been a COIL operative, of course! No wonder the woman had so expertly coaxed Obrador into accepting her. Chloe had been trained in subterfuge and clandestine techniques. Chen Li must've been as well. And obviously, Lieutenant Isaacson was a threat, since he'd been some sort of Special Forces soldier, but with clandestine training as well, maybe all the way back to when he'd been in the Marines.

None of this was good, she realized. Instead of sitting at a table of weak citizens, she realized removing Obrador and Chloe wouldn't be so easy. She needed distance. Maybe she could find a shooting position behind Chloe. Or she could move around and use Jenna as a human shield, and pick off her targets while they ate their last meal.

Jenna rose from her chair. Without tapping her glass, the table went silent. They all watched the magnificent blind woman. So plain, yet so beautiful. Dignity and poise emanated from her, Lena thought, even though she was wearing the same gown as she had two dinners earlier.

"Here we are again," Jenna said softly, maybe a little sadly. "This is our last dinner together, and I'm sorry that I won't see any of you again, because something dreadful has arisen from within our midst."

Lena tensed. *This was it.* She'd waited too long! Looking at Corban's face, she wondered if this was the way he'd planned it, to expose her through Jenna in front of everyone and hope for the best.

"The man I'm meant to marry," Jenna continued, awkwardly gazing in Obrador's direction, "has been so patient with me these few days. Thank you, Chancellor."

"Uh, it's been my pleasure." Obrador glanced at his bodyguards. "What's so dreadful, Jenna? What are you talking about?"

"These dinners have built up to this final night. Ever since Monday's dinner, I realized I needed to prepare us all for what I must ask of you, Mr. Chancellor. A favor to spare my life from someone at this very table who wishes to kill me."

Lena barely breathed as she slowly eased her hand back to the butt of her gun.

The table stirred. Obrador himself rose partially to hush his guests, perhaps suspecting each one of them.

"Please, everyone!" Obrador raised his arms. "Quiet! Be silent! Let my fiancée speak! Jenna, who would dare to kill you? This is preposterous. Everyone loves you. We're not even married yet, and people are ecstatic about having you here at the Bowery."

"An entire plot has been hatched to kill me, Mr. Chancellor. And not just me, but what's left of my family. Father? Where are you?"

"I'm here, Jenna," Corban said from Lena's right, two chairs farther down than Chloe. "Explain what you're talking about, daughter."

"My killer is at this very table," Jenna said. "Full of passion and blind zeal. I can't bear it any longer. In my blindness, I must ask for your help, Mr. Chancellor."

"Anything, Jenna." Obrador stood tall at his place, taller than anyone at the table, if they were to stand. "Anything! All of you hear me? There's nothing I won't do for this woman. She already has our hearts, and we've only begun to know her. Who is it, Jenna?"

Licking her lips, Lena slowly drew her weapon halfway out of the holster—when Chloe's own hand clamped down on her hand, forcing the weapon back down!

"Not yet," Chloe whispered through her teeth and frozen smile. "Just wait. Wait."

Lena's eyes widened, and panic was setting in. *This was all wrong!* Chloe had set this up, seating her beside her. This ruined everything!

"If I tell you," Jenna said loudly, "will you reverse the order to kill me, Mr. Chancellor?"

"Of course!"

"Will you reverse the order to kill my loved ones?"

"I won't hesitate! I'll execute the criminal this very night, and his order to kill you will die with him! Tell us! Tell us who it is who wishes to kill you!"

"It's *him.*"

Jenna paused, pointing to no one. Lena, like the others, searched up and down the table for the culprit. If not her, then who? Who was being exposed and for what? What game was this? She no longer fought Chloe's strong grip on her hand. She couldn't wait to see how this unfolded!

"Him *who?*" Obrador shouted.

"It's Owen. Owen Travers."

Her words were like thunder, and Lena watched her brother's face turn from red to white in two seconds.

"What? No!" Owen gasped. He rose from his chair, his hands held out to defend himself, but Obrador's signal to his bodyguards was decisively faster than Owen's ability to fight them off. "No, it wasn't me! I love you, Jenna! I swear it, Chancellor! I've never tried to kill her!"

"Hold him!" Obrador commanded. "Owen, what have you done now?"

"Nothing! She's wrong. She's confused. I would never turn against you!" Tears flowed down his cheeks. "I serve you. I'd give my life for you, for either of you. Please, Jenna! Don't do this!"

"Jenna, can you prove it?" Obrador asked.

Lena waited breathlessly, and with everyone else, turned to stare at Jenna who stood stoically at the other end of the table.

"You'll reverse the order?" she asked.

"I said I would, my love," Obrador said, a sensitivity in his voice that Lena had never heard before. "Tell us."

"Since I was a child," Jenna said, "I was raised as a Christian. I love the Federation and its people, but I'm a Christian. And on Monday, the order was made by Owen Travers to kill me and all whom I know and love, many of us Christians at this very table."

Lena's mouth fell open. It was perfect. She didn't need to destroy them. They were destroying themselves!

"*What?*" Obrador's face drew long, his eyes seemed sightless, focusing on nothing. "You're a Christian?"

"As am I," Corban said from his chair.

"Me, too," Chen Li said as she rose to stand next to Jenna.

"I'm a Christian as well, and devoted to Jesus Christ." Isaacson stood tall next to Obrador. "If you kill her, you'll have to try to kill me as well, sir."

"If you kill her," Chloe said, "you'll need to kill me, too, Kendrick, because I've been a Christian for decades, faithfully reading the Bible and serving those around me, especially you."

"I'm a Christian as well," said the chubby mayor from Hackensack, as he rose to his feet. He used his table napkin to dab his brow. "I've been hiding it for years, but I'd rather die than keep silent any longer. If all of you are revealing yourselves, then I will, too. I didn't know so many in the Bowery were Christ-followers! I love my Savior, and death holds no fear over me."

Lena looked up and down the table, not believing her ears. Was that all? Were there no more revelations? Why was Obrador hesitating?

"Arrest them!" she shouted to the two bodyguards who were still holding Owen. "Now! Arrest them all! They're Christians!"

"Wait." Obrador held up one hand, and the bodyguards were torn between their obligation to the chancellor and their loyalty to Lena. "Chloe, you're really a Christian?"

"Yes."

Lena tried to jerk her hand free, but Chloe's grip was immovable.

"Lieutenant? You, too?"

Isaacson nodded.

"People who care for you, Kendrick," Jenna said, "and people who care for this Federation have always looked out for what is best according to God's Word. We've been here for you. Now, on this dark eve of death, will you be here for us? For your wife-to-be?"

Obrador slumped into his chair, a hand on his brow.

"I've relied on all of you," he mumbled. "The whole nation knows your names, your reputations, and your glory . . ."

"*No!*" Lena blurted. "Arrest them! Don't be weak at this moment, Kendrick Obrador! Arrest them! Let me kill them right now!"

"Quiet!" Chloe growled. "Or else!"

"Yes, Lena," Obrador said, his face showing defeat, but his voice steady. "Be quiet. Think about it. I can't have Jenna executed. She's my own fiancée. The whole country loves her more than they love even me. She wrote the Federation's anthem. It's already being sung by school children!"

"They've used you!" Lena yelled. "Chloe, let me go!"

Lena wiggled away from Chloe and jumped to her feet. She raised her sidearm, but at that very instant, a sting in her thigh pulsed from where Chloe stabbed her with something. Chloe withdrew a pen from her thigh, and Lena could make no sense of the pen or its debilitating effects. Her arm and handgun hung limply. Her shoulders sagged. Her mind became cloudy. She fell back into her chair, and the world went dark.

Chapter Seventeen

Scooter appreciated the feel of a COIL battle rifle in his arms as he walked up the side of Amsterdam Avenue. Being alone on the streets of Manhattan gave him an eerie expectation of trouble. There weren't any patrols out, as if they'd been cancelled or recalled by the Twins. And Scooter knew why. The invasion must've already begun, and Lena and Owen had locked down the city. Probably within hours, they'd take command of the New York Citizen Army and tell them to stand down against the invaders.

For this reason, since the city was already so ghostly, Scooter had chosen to remain above ground as the one hundred Christians were escorted below ground, through the old subway tunnels. But now he wondered if they could've all crept through the streets together, since no one was around.

At the next intersection, Scooter paused against a building and checked the streets and avenues for movement. It was almost midnight, but he'd never seen Manhattan this still. Only a few rats and stray dogs were lurking about. He would've been less nervous if there would've been normal Enforcer patrols marching along the sidewalks, screening identifications, enforcing the curfew, and checking the locks on doors.

Jogging across the street, Scooter kept moving north, guessing he was ahead of the subway group by now. Ten of the hundred were so unhealthy, they'd be a burden to the others, so Scooter guessed Luigi would slow their pace up the tunnel. This worked for Scooter since it gave him a chance to scout ahead and determine where the Christians could emerge from the tunnels to cross the bridge.

Near Harlem an hour later, Scooter saw traffic lights on the George Washington Bridge. A stream of armored vehicles rolled across the bridge. He lifted his rifle scope to his eye to see better. Infantry soldiers walked beside convoy vehicles. There were hundreds of soldiers, far more than Obrador could deploy against an invader and hope to defend the Bowery for long, even if he did control all of his own troops on the island.

"We're too late," Scooter mumbled, glancing left and right. If he was witnessing the main body of the invaders on the bridge, then there were certainly some scouts out ahead, probably already on the streets of the city. He had to warn the sleeping city. He had to make some noise to warn Corban and Jenna!

From years of living under the city and raiding the Federation's warehouses above ground, Scooter knew the city streets. He guessed the invading show of force would want to press all the way down to the Bowery as directly as possible. That probably meant they'd been instructed to get on Broadway once off the GW Bridge, and stay on Broadway the whole way to the hotel.

Running to the west for one block, Scooter reconnected with the avenue, then dropped to one knee and looked through the scope of his rifle. Two SUVs, one red and one black, were cruising slowly up the avenue, side by side. Only one headlight on each vehicle was working, but even with only one, the whole avenue was lit up on the dark night. The main force was surely not far behind.

Ducking behind a building corner, he ejected his thirty-round, gel-tranq magazine and quickly rummaged through his pack for two phosphorus rounds, which were capable of quickly corroding metal.

He took two rapid gasps of air, then held his breath. When he emerged from the building's cover and leveled his rifle, he felt the familiarity of a weapon he'd fired in dozens of conflicts worldwide. The headlight of the farthest vehicle filled his scope. He traced his view down to the SUV's bumper and the front tire. The first round he fired made a sound that echoed off the buildings around him, but he knew he would need to make much more noise than one or two gunshots to get the Bowery's attention.

Shifting his aim to the other SUV, he fired at that front tire as well. Fifty yards away, both vehicles stopped, and inside two seconds, men emerged from the doors, laying down cover fire in every direction. They hadn't located him yet, and he took advantage of those few seconds to reload with non-lethal shells and target the four riflemen from each SUV. He tranquilized two before the other six moved behind their vehicles for safety.

Scooter dropped to his belly as bullets pummeled the building behind him and the sidewalk in front of him. As quickly as he could squeeze the trigger, he raked the ground under the SUVs, skipping gel-tranqs into the feet and legs of the remaining men.

Confident the eight were neutralized, he spent two more rounds taking out the headlights, then reloaded. Only the drivers of each vehicle were left, and they weren't going far since the sizzling acid on their front tires was doing its destructive work even as Scooter approached on their left.

"Get out and walk away!" he yelled, moving up to the nearest driver's window.

The driver inside had his hands raised, and chose not to battle it out against the gaping rifle barrel aimed at his head. The door opened, and a young soldier in Federation fatigues exited the SUV, his sidearm held in his fingertips. A patch on his shoulder indicated he was from a Baltimore division.

Moving to the front of the first vehicle, Scooter threatened the second vehicle's driver. He guessed they were assuming he wasn't alone, since no sane, lone shooter would assault two heavily-armed patrol vehicles. The second driver emerged as the first.

"Drop your weapons and run away," Scooter ordered. "Go ahead. I'm not a back-shooter. Return to your unit and tell your commander that we will defend our city to our dying breath. Go!"

They ran, and Scooter lowered his rifle. Of course, he wasn't speaking for the actual Federation Army on the island, since Lena had probably told most of the commanders to stand down no matter what they saw coming down the street, but by threatening the drivers with misinformation, it might cause the invaders to halt long enough to buy the Bowery a little more time.

It took Scooter only a few minutes to search the vehicles for explosives. He found one single-shot grenade launcher, and a handful of grenades. From the street level, he looked upward, gauging which building was nearest and tallest. He selected an office building one block south, and jogged over to it. After several heel kicks, he broke loose the metal plating over the old entrance, then he charged inside.

Twenty-seven floors later, he reached the roof of the building and took a breath of the night wind, its coolness a relief after the muggy staircase. He gazed in the direction of the Bowery, and because of the darkness, he could see the glow of the capital building above the skyline.

Two blocks away, an even taller building rose into twilight, and it was at this skyscraper that Scooter aimed the grenade launcher. He fired the tube, then watched the rocket stream in a high arc. It exploded one floor below the domed roof. Even from that far away, the fire illuminated Scooter's face. The ignited blaze acted like a torch for blocks around, lighting up the streets in shimmering brightness.

He used the light to throw five grenades at the opposite corner of his own building's roof. They each created deafening explosions, but didn't ignite anything on fire on the roof. Scooter hoped the noise and the RPG he'd fired were enough to warn the Bowery. Finally, he descended the stairs to street level again.

Since the invading army had arrived in the city early, Scooter didn't know how COIL would smuggle the one hundred off the island. Their food supplies were low with so many people, and by daylight, Scooter figured the new troops that Lena had brought in would have an impenetrable perimeter established. Escaping across the GW Bridge was out of the question now.

Satisfied that he'd alerted Corban and Jenna of the early danger, Scooter opened a manhole cover to enter the tunnels. They'd been so close to getting off the island. Now, he was reminded of the first days of the Federation, when Jenna had given him charge over the so-called resistance in the tunnels. Again, he was going below ground as the military swarmed down the streets.

Uncertain of his future, he dragged the manhole cover closed. In the darkness and familiar odor of sewage, he climbed down the ladder to the tunnel floor. Sadly, it was time to find Luigi and the hundred to tell them they that were trapped on the island. There was no way out.

Nathan stood guard over the chancellor's suite, making sure all dinner guests kept their hands flat on the table as instructed. Over Nathan's left shoulder were two more battle rifles, and another was in his hands aimed at the table. Corban held a fourth rifle, and Chloe carried the last of the five that Luigi had secured for them.

From a small office off the main room, Obrador, Chen Li, and Jenna emerged.

"It's finished," Chen Li announced. "He transmitted the message. The Christians up and down the Appalachian Federation won't be attacked on Monday. Everyone with a radio heard the broadcast. A couple cities down south even radioed back and expressed relief. They didn't want to kill the Christians, either. What we've done tonight, no matter what Lena tried to do, has permanently reversed the Federation's view of Christians down at the local level."

Obrador slumped into a chair away from the table. He had the appearance of defeat, but Nathan wasn't willing to gloat, and neither was Jenna. It wasn't time for celebration. Jenna kneeled next to the man who suddenly seemed very old.

"For once, Kendrick, you've saved lives. Because you've done this, your life will be spared."

"What's that supposed to mean?" Obrador lifted his head to her. "You were going to kill me? You've used me this whole time? I'm an old fool."

"It's time to get out of here," Chloe said from her position, standing over the still-unconscious Lena, who'd been laid on the carpeted floor against the window. "The Day of Cleansing has been reversed, so we can leave now. We'll need a vehicle to make it to the bridge in time."

Owen fidgeted in his chair at the table, his head low, as if he was afraid of what Nathan might do if he opened his mouth. Nathan had never seen a man caught in such an ambush as Jenna had laid for him, all to reverse the order for the Day of Cleansing.

"Chen Li," Nathan said, "get Jenna moving down the stairs. Mr. Chancellor, Lena was planning a coup for tomorrow morning. We're offering you a ride out of the city with us. That's how we're sparing your life. Are you coming?"

"I'll take my chances here." He turned his head and looked at the unconscious woman. "I never did trust her, but she was the most vicious Enforcer I ever had, besides Steelman."

"You won't be able to stop her, Kendrick," Chloe said to him. "She's gained too much support on the island. Look, she's starting to wake up."

"Chancellor," Nathan said, "she has three divisions of the Citizen Army invading your city within a few hours. Most of your own troops are waiting for instructions from her. You won't survive here. No one who is her enemy will survive."

Lena sat up and rubbed her head, and Chloe used her knee to nudge the woman, letting her know she was well guarded.

Chen Li led Jenna to the door. Nathan knew both women would pick up their small packs on the way past their floor two stories below.

"Wait, Jenna." Owen shifted in his chair at the table. He glanced at Nathan, and Nathan was tempted to tranq the man then and there. "I can't stay here, either. She'll kill me. *My own sister.* You've got to let me come with you. Please!"

Jenna stopped and reentered the room.

"Go ahead, Jenna," Nathan urged, now assuming operational control. Jenna was a great strategist, but now they were in flight mode, and that was his specialty. "We've got it from here. You know we can't take him. He can't be trusted. Besides, he's killed as many Christians as his sister, maybe more."

"You would try to run away!" Lena hissed at her brother. Weakly, she climbed back into her chair at the table. Chloe still hovered over her. "You've always been a coward, Owen, so why wouldn't you leave with the other cowards?"

"We need to go," Corban stressed to Nathan. "Is he going or staying?"

"Jenna?" Owen turned in his seat to face the blind woman. He appeared to be on the verge of tears. "I didn't know all of you were Christians. I thought I was just pleasing the chancellor. I thought it would make me popular. Please! You once promised me that you'd help me. I can't stay here. Everything has changed now. Nothing worked for me."

"You're such a whiner!" Lena growled.

"Quiet!" Chloe jabbed her rifle against Lena's shoulder. "Not another word from you!"

"Owen," Corban said, "you've had your heart set on killing all of us. Now you want to escape with us?"

"I've never promised you any help, Owen," Jenna said. "You've been a confused man for many years, chasing only what seemed best for you. You can't be trusted with us. It's too late to change sides. Much of what's happened this past week was your doing."

Nathan adjusted his rifle to tranquilize Owen. They wouldn't get far, he guessed, unless they tranqed Lena once more as well. Otherwise, she'd take command of the troops downstairs.

"No!" Owen held out a hand, as if reaching for Jenna across the room. "We drank from the same cup, remember? You promised!"

Nathan glanced at Jenna and saw her otherwise blank face alter to one of surprise and then concession.

"Jenna?" Nathan asked. "We don't have time for this! What's he talking about?"

"I did make someone such a promise." Jenna struggled with her words. "I didn't know it was him, but it makes sense. He just invoked the pass-phrase. Owen?"

"Yes?" He rose halfway from his chair. "Please. You have to let me come. I'm finished here."

"If I'm to grant you passage with us, you have to agree to do what I say."

"I will. I promise."

"That's typical of him," Lena said, "doing what everyone else tells him to do."

"Don't make me regret this!" Nathan slid one of the battle rifles off his shoulder and held it out to Owen. "You go with Jenna now. Guard her with your life, or you'll deal with me!"

Nathan was pleased to see the man shudder, but grab up the rifle, and hustle out of the room after Jenna and Chen Li.

Suddenly, a mushroom cloud of fire lit the skyline many blocks to the north. Nathan moved around Corban and Obrador to reach the window. One of the taller buildings on the West Side was on fire. Then, lower and on another building, several more flashes of light shot into the sky.

"So, it's begun," he said softly. "They're early, but the invasion's begun."

"You're all going to die!" Lena snarled. "They're already here!"

Nathan turned from the window to tranq her himself. Instead, he saw her rise from her chair, a small handgun drawn from a hidden holster, probably on her ankle. She leveled the gun across the table and aimed at Obrador.

Chloe fired her rifle point blank at Lena, and Nathan was an instant behind her, but both operatives were too late. Lena had gotten off one shot toward Obrador.

"No!" Nathan screamed as he rushed around the table to catch Corban as he started to fall to the carpet. "Boss? *Why?* You stepped in front of him!"

Next to Nathan, Obrador knelt over Corban, whose shirt front blossomed with blood.

"He saved my life." Obrador's lips trembled, his voice a whisper. "A Christian just saved my life!"

"Lena's down!" Chloe shouted from the other side of the table. "She had a hidden ankle holster! What happened? Nathan?"

"Corban . . ." Nathan gripped the older man's hand. "We were seconds away from leaving. This isn't how—"

"Quiet." Corban panted through the pain and struggled to breathe, then he looked at Obrador. "You've been a fool, Chancellor, but I couldn't let her kill you. God has plans for you still. Nothing . . . would bring . . . Him more glory . . . than if you trusted . . . in His Son . . . for your forgiveness . . . of sins."

"What?" Obrador gasped and tore open Corban's shirt. "Do something, Lieutenant! I order you to do something! No one is dying for me today! Corban Dowler, you hang on!"

Nathan stared at the bullet wound in Corban's exposed chest. It pulsed out blood with every heartbeat. Obrador pressed his hand flat on the wound, bloodying himself, but Nathan knew the blood would still flow into the chest cavity.

"I know . . . it's a mortal wound." Corban's face was full of resignation. "Forgive her . . . and get out of here."

Clenching his teeth, Nathan checked on Lena. She lay face down on the table where she'd been tranqed. Her clothes were soaking up the evening's meal. Chloe's face was a mask of shock and dread.

"If I could choose . . . one way to die," Corban whispered, "this is it, with the ones . . . I love. Tell Jenna I love her . . . and I'm proud of her. I'm going . . . to see my Savior. And I'm seeing . . . Janice soon . . ."

"Chloe!" Nathan shouted. "Get over here!"

Chloe was there in seconds.

"Corban?" she wept. "Corban, look at me. You're going to make it. Fight it. Come on! *God, help us!*"

"I'm finished . . . fighting." He smiled, tears streaming from the corners of his eyes. "Don't . . . be . . . angry. I'm not angry. Say goodbye to Luigi for me. Nathan?"

"I'm here, Boss." Nathan gripped Corban's hand, while Obrador still held the other.

"Don't . . . give up on Lena." Corban drifted, then fought back. "Tell Levi . . ."

"Tell Levi?" Nathan shook Corban. "What, Corban? Tell Levi? Tell Levi what?"

"Tell Levi," Corban said again, then closed his eyes. He didn't open them again.

Chloe wailed and bowed her head onto his chest. Nathan rose to his feet and glared at the rest of the guests still seated like stones at the table, too afraid to move. His eyes settled on Lena. She'd killed Corban Dowler. No one had checked her for another firearm, Nathan realized, and it had had fatal consequences. Of course, Lena had wanted to kill Obrador, the one on whom all her anger had been focused, but Corban had interceded. With Obrador still alive, none of Lena's plans could really be sealed.

"You." Nathan pointed at the mayor from Hackensack. "You revealed yourself as a Christian. When Lena wakes up, she'll be on a rampage, killing everyone who stood with us. It's your choice—do you want to go with us or stay behind?"

"You shot her twice," the chubby man said. "I doubt she'll be doing much of anything."

"We shot her with tranquilizers. In an hour, she'll be angrier than a hornet's nest."

The mayor rose from his chair and looked at the faces of the other dignitaries.

"I'll pray for you all," he said to them, "that you find your way in this sad time. Lieutenant, tell me what to do."

"You ever fire a rifle?" Nathan offered him the last spare battle rifle.

"No." The man accepted the weapon, hefting its weight in his small hands. "Aim and pull the trigger?"

"Why don't you just carry it for me?" Nathan rested his hand on the short mayor's shoulder, reassuring him. "And stay on my heels. Chloe, it's time to go. Obrador, you too, if you're coming."

Obrador drew Chloe to her feet with him, then picked up Corban's fallen rifle and ammo vest. The chancellor hooked one arm of the vest over his shoulder and checked the rifle like he knew how to use it. The man's hands were bloodied and his face was grim.

"Get us out alive, Lieutenant. I don't want anyone else to die for me tonight."

Nathan took Chloe, who seemed to be in shock, and guided her by the arm toward the door.

"Follow me."

Chen Li reached the lobby of the Bowery with Jenna on her elbow and Owen Travers trailing close behind. On her back, Chen Li carried a small pack of necessities, as did Jenna. Owen carried nothing but the COIL rifle, but he didn't seem too concerned over fleeing with nothing but his life.

In the lobby, Chen Li could see that something was clearly happening, since soldiers ran to and fro outside, and officers with flashlights were asking each other what they should do.

"Owen," Chen Li said to the man standing annoyingly close to her elbow, his face full of fear, "go out there and find us a vehicle. There's got to be one left. It's our only hope."

"What if they try to kill me?" Owen moved even closer to Chen Li, like a foal trying to hide behind its mother. "I'm not with them any longer. None of us are."

"They don't know that." Chen Li held Jenna back with her right arm and used her other to coax Owen toward the door. "Go ahead. See if you can find us a car. They don't know what just happened upstairs. All they know is that you're Enforcer Owen Travers. Go, Owen! The others will be down any minute. Do it for Jenna!"

He stepped hesitantly away from her side, then walked outside and to the left toward the motor pool.

"How are you doing?" Chen Li asked Jenna. "I'd tell you what's going on out here if I knew anything myself."

"I'm just praying." Jenna had wrapped both arms around Chen Li's right arm. "You can probably feel me shaking."

"We're all scared."

"Oh, I'm not scared." Jenna barely kept her feet under her as an officer from upstairs barged past them. "I'm excited. God has gone before us. I can't wait to see what He does next!"

"I don't know what God will do next," Chen Li said, "but I can tell you that the way everyone is acting seems like they're aware that an army is on its way down here."

"The ones who were loyal to Lena won't know what to do without her." Jenna turned her head, angling her ears as officers across the lobby rallied. "They're unprepared. They were expecting orders from Lena already. Upstairs isn't responding. They'll desert unless some sort of leadership steps in. If the invasion has begun, we need these troops to buy us more time."

"If you say so. Come with me." Chen Li walked across the lobby to the officers. In her formal Citizen Army uniform, she hoped they recognized her, even if she didn't outrank all of them. "What are you doing standing around? Follow your orders! Set up defenses to protect the Bowery! No one gets through! The rest of you, take a stand out on Broadway. Get out there and organize the men! Fight for Obrador! Fight for Jenna Dowler! Fight for the Federation! Go! Go!"

The men scattered, along with a few women, nearly trampling each other on their way out the front entrance.

Owen returned after the stampede of officers had fled.

"There're no vehicles left." He was panting, and Chen Li was glad Jenna couldn't see the terror on the man's face. "The skyline is on fire. Someone's attacking the city! What do we do?"

"We get out of Manhattan," Jenna said, the calmest one of them all. "If we can get into New Jersey, Bruno will find us. He's been preparing for another wave of Christians heading west ever since the first wave went to Colorado."

"There's no way out of Manhattan if the fighting has started." Chen Li glanced back at the staircase. "Where's Corban and Chloe? Nathan should've been down here by now!"

Just then, Nathan emerged from the stairway door, a battle rifle in his hands. Chen Li wanted to run to her husband, but both her hands were full. Chloe, Obrador, and the mayor who'd revealed his faith were following Nathan. But there was no Corban yet.

"It's begun." Nathan stopped and placed his hand on the back of Chen Li's neck, which was about the closest thing to an embrace she'd get at that moment, she guessed. "Our only hope is to get into the tunnels near Columbus Circle, before the northern army intercepts us. It'll be close."

"We're not ready for this!" Obrador gasped. "We'll be slaughtered in the streets!"

"You may not be ready," Jenna said to the ex-chancellor, "but we've been preparing for something like this for years."

"Stay close on my heels," Nathan instructed everyone. "If anyone tries to hold us back, shoot them. Mayor? You ready? Chancellor?"

Chen Li thought both men appeared skeptical about what was happening, but they both nodded.

"I'm ready," Obrador said.

Owen elbowed his way past Obrador to be first behind Nathan as he led the way outside. Chen Li almost called out to Nathan to slow down, but he was already outside, and she didn't want to hold anyone up.

"Come on," she said to Jenna. "We need to try to move faster, or we'll be left behind."

But outside, they were immediately bombarded by racing soldiers, many who were carrying ammunition boxes, sandbags, and rifles. Some didn't even have their boots tied, as if they'd just run from the barracks. It was midnight, so many had certainly been in their bunks.

"This is it." Chen Li glimpsed the backpack of Chloe ahead, and led Jenna after her as they jogged away from the Bowery. "We're finally leaving it all behind!"

"Where are the others?" Jenna asked, the first sign of concern in her voice. "Do you see them? I didn't hear Dad. Do you see him ahead?"

"They're all in front of us a little ways, moving past the front gate onto Broadway."

"We need to stay off Broadway," Jenna said. "The invaders will definitely be coming down Broadway."

"I'm sure my husband knows that. Whatever you do, don't let go of me!"

The flow of soldiers surrounded them, and they were carried up the middle of the broad avenue toward the north. Though Chen Li lost sight of Nathan and the others, she knew where they were going. Columbus Circle was on the southwest corner of Central Park. She suddenly doubted what she knew about the tunnel entrances, but hoped Jenna had an idea where to go if they lost the others. Chen Li had never needed to learn the tunnels, not since her assignment had been inside the Bowery and Citizen Processing.

"Nathan will wait for us at some point," Chen Li said.

"You lost them?"

"There are hundreds of people around us, all running to set up a defensive line, I think."

"Yeah, those were your orders," Jenna reminded.

"Well, I didn't want them standing around and getting suspicious of why we're taking you and the chancellor outside for a midnight stroll."

Chen Li flinched to a stop with Jenna as they heard gunfire far ahead. Others around them found their courage checked as machine gunfire rattled on the streets from the direction of the Empire State Building.

"This is total chaos," Chen Li said to Jenna. "No one's in their unit. They're all just streaming together."

"Do you see Nathan or Dad?"

"No, but they've got to be ahead. I really don't think we passed them."

"Regardless, we should get off Broadway. We can parallel Broadway by going up a side street that won't be as busy or dangerous."

"The blind leading the blind here," Chen Li said as a joke, but realized it was an accurate statement. "Okay, stay with me."

"You don't have an NL weapon?" Jenna asked.

"No, everyone but you and I are armed." Chen Li touched her pocket. "All I have is a tranq-pen. We'll have to be way too close for comfort to the enemy for me to use this thing."

Chen Li forced her way to the left and out of the flow of foot traffic. Once off Broadway, the flashlights were no longer there to light the street, and she studied the dark pavement ahead with uncertainty. Only the tops of the buildings high above glowed red from a fire's reflection, indicating where the street was. Not even starlight reached the ground level. Jenna seemed to sense her hesitation to move forward.

"Go over two or three blocks," Jenna directed, her voice low, "then we can turn north again. We'll be out of the fighting, but still in line to find Nathan and Chloe."

The gunfire to the north intensified, somewhere on Broadway. The cries of the dying and wounded mixed with the screams of rocket propelled grenades and the concussion of heavy artillery. Even disorganized, it sounded like Manhattan's ragged Citizen Army was putting up a fight. Of course, if Lena had been there, she would've told everyone to surrender so her plans could proceed.

"Steady, Chen Li," Jenna urged as they turned the corner to march north.

"How are you not more terrified than me? It's so dark out here!"

"You still think if you could see, you'd be safer?" Jenna asked. "I haven't seen anything for years, and God has protected me. Here, let me lead. We can do this."

Jenna pulled ahead with only Chen Li's hand clinging to Jenna's. After whistling a long, steady note, Jenna then silently moved forward. A few seconds later, she whistled again and clicked her tongue. Chen Li heard the small sound echo and bounce off the buildings around them. She didn't want to make a sound to throw off Jenna's sense of echolocation.

The noise of the battle grew louder to the right several blocks away, but also ahead to the north, as if the invading army was fighting the Bowery infantry troops head-on.

"Nathan will be looking for us by now," Chen Li said.

"Actually, he should go straight ahead without us." Jenna tugged her forward. "He knows that we know where to go: Columbus Circle."

"Jenna, stop. Stop!" Chen Li pulled Jenna closer to a standstill, but she was gazing far ahead. "I can see all the way to Midtown. It's on fire! We can't go that way. Nathan won't be going that way, either. He'll find another way. Now we're really separated!"

"Where's the nearest tunnel entrance to us?" Jenna asked. "We could go underground on 10th Avenue somewhere, right?"

"I don't know where any of the tunnel entrances are, Jenna. Nathan, Chloe, and I have been in the Bowery for years. We've never known where the tunnels were."

"We have to get underground," Jenna insisted. "That's what Nathan will do. The instructions my dad gave to Luigi and Scooter were to meet up with us in the tunnels, so they'll find us. Luigi will find us. Let's just get below."

Chen Li couldn't hold back her sobs and shaking.

"I'm sorry, Jenna. I can't see. I don't know where to go. Lena is behind us, and there's an army fighting in front of us all the way down Broadway. Tell me what to do!"

"Don't cry."

Jenna embraced Chen Li, and Chen Li thought how ridiculous their situation was—a blind woman was more sensibly collected than she was!

Several minutes passed as the two women clung to one another in what Chen Li thought was the middle of the street. She heard Jenna whispering, and knew she was praying, but Chen Li's nerves were too rattled to pray, to focus, to trust. Every explosion and battle cry in the distance made her melt inside, making her knees weak. Being captured was unthinkable!

"Okay." Jenna held Chen Li by her shoulders. "We're going to take charge. I'm making an executive decision for both of us. You ready?"

"I'm ready."

"You and I can't be taken prisoner. Our priority right now is to get off this island, one way or another. We have to do it in the dark, or we'll be caught in the daylight trying to escape. With me so far?"

"Get off the island. I'm with you."

"Nathan knows you don't know where the tunnels are, and he'll know we definitely won't be able to cross the GW Bridge without him. Besides, they're fighting every-where to the north of us. So, what will he guess we're going to do? Since Nathan knows me, he knows I won't let us sit still or stay on the island."

"He knows me, too," Chen Li argued. "He'll think I'm in hiding somewhere until he comes to find me."

"But he knows we're together, and he knows I wouldn't let you do that, to just stop and wait for him. He has other people to take care of, Chen Li, and we can't expect him to abandon everyone else for little ol' us, right? Besides, if he comes back here for us, he'll be in greater danger of being caught himself, and he knows we wouldn't want that for him. There's only one place for us to go: the Hudson River."

"No way. It's too cold to swim, Jenna. I'm in no shape for that, even if the water was warm."

"It's not too cold to float across. We're two light women. We can find something that floats and paddle across. Problem solved."

"We're doing all this in the dark?" Chen Li groaned. "I'm out of my element. I'm sorry, Jenna. I guess I've just become conditioned to the dangers inside Citizen Processing."

"It'll be brighter, too, out on the shoreline. We'll find tires or something to float on. Let's get started. How many blocks are we away from the shore? Come on, Chen Li. Stay with me. We need to work together."

"Three, maybe four blocks."

"All right. Let's get to the Hudson."

Brian Steelman adjusted the battle rifle in his hands as he stood against the wall of the tunnel. He was one of the few who had a headlamp, and he was careful to keep it shining over the one hundred Christians under his charge, along with Scooter, Luigi, and Sergeant Sean Harris. The battle above ground had shifted to the southern half of Manhattan, closer to the Bowery, but still, Scooter had told Brian to hold tight.

The tunnel spanned to the south before Brian, and it was packed with praying, whispering, and coughing Christians. Men, women, and children, some barely able to walk, had hiked dozens of city blocks, all the way to the end of that tunnel branch. Behind Brian, the tunnel was completely caved-in, and overhead was a makeshift manhole that Luigi had said was only a few blocks from GW Bridge.

As the refugees waited and rested, a shadow moved closer to Brian's side. He shifted his light to see it was Sergeant Sean Harris.

"I never thought I'd find you with these kinds of people," Sean said. His green Federation uniform was still soaked from where he'd leaped into sewage drainage after a refugee who'd fallen into the pool. "How'd this happen?"

"Probably the same way it happened to you." Brian leveled his light on an elderly woman whose coughing had worsened. There was nothing to do for these poor people, but try to take them to safety. Treatment, warmth, and comfort was unlikely until they got across the bridge. "It seemed like I stumbled upon all this by accident or coincidence, but then I realized there was a divine plan behind it all, moving me in this direction. God was trying to get my attention."

"So, you buy in to all this God stuff?" Sean sighed. "I've been next to Lieutenant Isaacson for years, and I never realized what he was doing. It all makes sense now, though. We were just trying to stay alive, I guess."

"Not me." Brian knelt down as a boy of about ten walked up to him. "I was thinking only of myself, and I wasn't concerned with who I hurt along the way."

"I guess you're right." Sean leaned his rifle over his shoulder. "If we weren't helping these people, then I guess we were hurting them by looking the other way."

"She died." The boy pointed at the crowd of people. "Now I have no one."

Brian hugged the boy, though he couldn't remember the last time he'd hugged anyone. He could feel the boy's ribs through the blanket wrapped around his slender shoulders. The blanket was wet, like most of their clothing, since they'd walked through a gushing spray where a water pipe had burst.

"You stay here with Sean," Brian said as he took off his coat. The coat was many sizes too large for the boy, but it was drier than the blanket. "Sean, watch him."

Although Brian knew Sean wasn't yet a Christ-follower, he'd already seen Sean shed his own coat for a woman in the crowd. He knew the boy would be safe with the gruff sergeant.

Leaving the wall, Brian waded through the sea of refugees. He excused himself as he moved among them, accidently disturbing them to reach the woman who'd been coughing. People were shivering around him, and he could hear their whispers clearer now that he was so close. They were trusting him, praying that God would guide their protectors.

When he reached the woman, he felt her neck for a pulse. There was nothing. She'd coughed herself to death, certainly from a previous condition, but the hard march hadn't helped. He remembered that the woman had held the boy's hand, comforting him along much of the uncomfortable trek. She and the boy probably weren't even related, Brian guessed. They'd met in the labor force cages, and their faith had made them family.

Brian found himself weeping over the woman. She'd died helping the boy, caring less for herself. And these who prayed for him now—he'd sent many of their kind to the gallows and into hard labor. And they were praying for him?

"She'd been sick for weeks," a nearby man about Brian's age said. "It's a shame, being so close to freedom. We are close, aren't we?"

"Yes, we're close." Brian knelt lower, moved his rifle onto his shoulder on the sling, then lifted the woman in his arms. "But she's the one who's free now. At least that's what I've read in the Bible."

"You've seen a Bible? You've read from an actual Bible?"

Brian didn't feel qualified to encourage these brave souls with the little he knew from reading the Scriptures in the tunnels. But he couldn't help it, now that he knew a few certain truths.

He carried her gently back down the tunnel, and set her against a cold wall in the darkness, where she would be out of the way when the refugees were ready to move out.

"You can leave her there," a voice nearby said. Brian turned to see it was Luigi, a quiet but stoic man he'd learned to admire more by working beside him the last week. "I'll keep the rats off her."

"Scooter's not back yet?" Brian folded the woman's hands in her lap, then touched her still-warm head. He wouldn't forget her. He wouldn't forget any of them. "It's nearly dawn. We need to move soon."

"Listen!"

Shutting off his headlamp, Brian aimed his rifle down the tunnel. If a unit of Enforcers had followed them, or even if some of the Vags had turned militant and were coming to rob them, Brian wasn't about to go quietly. The rifle in his hand was compact, nothing like his old Bushmaster, but Scooter had assured him it would do the job.

Two flashlights wobbled toward them as a small party drew closer, their boots splashing through puddles. Then, they were face to face. Luigi recognized them sooner than Brian did, and turned on his headlamp.

"Where's Corban?" Luigi asked Lieutenant Nathan Isaacson, a man who Brian was still shocked to learn had been a covert Christian all these years, helping the people he now cared and cried over. "And Jenna? Where are they? Tell me!"

"We got separated." Nathan wiped his brow, having traveled through the same wet obstacles as had the refugees. "My wife and Jenna never showed, though we waited as long as we could. They'll either hole up for a little while, or find another way over the river. Either way, we won't find them today."

Scooter moved up next to Luigi.

"I'm sorry, Luigi, but Corban died," the man said softly. "He died back at the Bowery."

Luigi looked away, and Brian felt the man's pain. These few old friends had known each other for decades, and their loss was beyond anything Brian had known in his life. He envied their closeness and care for one another.

"If Jenna is out there alone," Luigi said, readying his gear and turning to face them again, "then I have to go back for her. I need to—"

"No." Nathan gripped Luigi's forearm. "She's not alone. She's with my wife. Think about it, Luigi. It's Jenna. They've entrusted us with these people. It'll take everyone we have to get across that bridge in the daylight. I need you here, Luigi. Once we get across the river, we can come back. We'll come back, if necessary. Do you hear me, brother?"

Brian turned his headlamp on to see who else was in the small party that Scooter had brought through the tunnels from the Bowery. He saw a plump man in a soiled suit, Chloe Azmaveth, and to his shock, Chancellor Obrador and Owen Travers!

"What are they doing here?" Brian backed away two steps and squeezed the grip on his rifle. "They can't be here! Think of the people we're—"

"There's no time for arguing or reunions," Nathan said. "Let's get ourselves together, if we're moving forward. We have a fight ahead of us. Scooter, Brian, Luigi, and Chloe, you're with me. The rest of you move the refugees across the bridge. No one gets left behind."

"I can fight." Owen stepped forward, the battle rifle already held firmly against his shoulder. "And I know what's out there."

"Yes, I know you can fight, but this isn't about that." Nathan tightened his ammo vest. "Are you a born-again follower of Jesus Christ?"

"Of course not!" Owen snapped. "I mean, no. I don't believe in that stuff."

"Exactly," Nathan said. "If you die out there, you won't be going to anything pleasant in eternity. I'd rather one of us died for you, because we know who we are and where we're going."

Brian wanted to laugh at the surprised look on Owen's face, but Nathan's words were an example of the kind of selflessness he'd witnessed for weeks from Scooter and Luigi.

Luigi, Chloe, and Nathan moved through the refugees, but Brian lingered in the back another moment. He studied Obrador—a giant of a man reduced to a downcast hulk, his tuxedo sopping wet, and mud on his nose. The chancellor raised his eyes.

"Steelman, I'm not here by choice," the man said in a raspy, weak voice. Obrador was finished, and he seemed to know it. "I'm ruined. It's all Lena's fault."

"Most of what we're in the middle of right now is actually your fault, Kendrick." Brian wanted the words coming out of his mouth to sound like words spoken from a heart where Christ now resided. "But if it wasn't you, it would've been someone else. I hope you find the peace I've found through all of this happening."

"You've been living down here since I sent you out?" Obrador moved closer to look past Brian at the refugees. "I imagined it to be different down here. It's horrible."

"Some of the other tunnels are habitable," Brian said, "but not this one."

"I don't know how I can be one of these people, Steelman. Yesterday, I was eating caviar. If they realize who I am, they'll kill me."

Brian grunted, realizing he'd gone through something similar with the Vags.

"Help them," Brian said, "and they'll see who you really are."

"Who I really am?" Obrador's voice cracked, and his shoulders shook with a sob. "I was changing, Steelman. Honestly, I was. Chloe and Jenna had me thinking so differently. I thought I could become something . . . good. Even Corban Dowler was helping me see how I could lead differently. But Lena has ruined it all. Even Jenna is gone. Now, what do I have?"

Taking a deep breath, Brian knew in his heart that he was still shedding his own past grievances against the man.

"You have an opportunity for a new start, Kendrick." Awkwardly, since they both carried rifles, Brian embraced the larger man and held him a few seconds, long enough to feel him relax. "Find out about what Jesus Christ did for you, and you'll really have a fresh start. It's real. Don't miss out on it any longer."

Brian pulled away from the chancellor.

"I don't know anything about the Man," Obrador said. "I've just . . . ridiculed Him. Everyone in society has for so long. But I know you, Steelman. You wouldn't cave in to something so fake, so passive. I mean, *Jesus? You?*"

"Being a Christ-follower isn't just about being passive." Brian took his pack off and unzipped it. "There's a strength in living for God that transcends death itself. Read this, and you'll see."

"A poetry book?" Owen moved into their conversation. "I've read that one. It's one of my favorites. There's nothing about Jesus in there."

"It's a coded book printed by Radiant Shade. All of her poetry books are coded with portions of the Bible. People all over the Federation have been reading the Bible for years this way. Count every third and seventh word on each line of poetry. When we made Bibles illegal, Chancellor, the Christians came up with these."

"Jenna?" Obrador shook his head and touched the cover of the book. "Chloe explained to me on the way. She was actually Radiant Shade? All this time?"

"Let's pray she's safe, wherever she is," Brian said. "You two bring up all the stragglers. I need to get in the front with Luigi and Isaacson. Owen? Can you make sure no one is left behind?"

"You guys didn't leave me behind." Owen nodded. "I'll bring everyone else."

Brian left the two men, their faces reflecting their stunning situation.

As he moved back through the people, his stomach trembled from nerves. And excitement. He'd returned to the Federation for one purpose, and he hoped from the bottom of his being that he was finally about to meet that purpose. The Serval was somewhere across the river, and Brian owed the man his life.

Now, if only they could get across the bridge safely.

Chapter Eighteen

Nathan slid the plywood cover away from the manhole, and climbed into an old arcade room. The blank screens of the machines were dusty, and the old-fashioned token machine had cobwebs across its colorful front. The glass windows of the arcade had been covered like the first floor windows of most of the stores in the city. But he guessed the resistance had been using the tunnel entrance and exit enough to have fashioned some sort of door to the outside.

Behind him, Chloe ascended from the tunnel exit, followed by Scooter, Luigi, and Brian. He pushed against the metal plating on the windows and door until he found one window from which the rivets had been removed, except for one, allowing the metal sheet to be hinged aside. Crouching, he peered through a crack between the window frame and the plating.

"I can see the bridge!" he whispered. "We're about five blocks short."

He moved aside so the others could see the challenge for themselves.

"It's daylight." Chloe took her turn at the window, then stepped away. "I can't see our end of the bridge, but they must have it guarded."

"There were machine guns and a mortar tube when I was last there," Brian said. "I can hear gunfire. They're still fighting south of us."

"Luigi?" Nathan nodded at the old spook. "You have only eight phosphorus rounds, right? Split them up between me and Scooter. Brian and Chloe, you two are with me. We'll cover left. Scooter and Luigi, use the phos rounds to take out any vehicles. As soon as we clear this end of the bridge, Scooter and I will move to the rear and cover your retreat. Luigi, Chloe, and Brian will lead the people across the bridge. Brian, what can they expect on the other end?"

"A minimum? A checkpoint and another machine gun. Who knows what the invaders have left in place after they came across last night."

"So, we have lots of unknowns, and maybe more enemies to face than we have ammunition. Great."

"Seems like a good time to pray," Scooter said, and immediately lifted his voice to God, dedicating their actions and lives in a fresh way to their Lord's care, whether they survived or not.

As Scooter concluded his prayer, the refugees emerged from the hole and slowly filled the dim arcade room. They clutched blankets and blinked their worried eyes at Nathan. He clenched his fist to his chest, a sign he hoped they understood, even though they'd known him only as Lieutenant Leather for so many years. They could all die in the next ten minutes, or they might live another ten years. Regardless, these people were in his heart. Nathan knew he'd been harsh, working them hard as prisoners, but now he hoped they understood that their endurance had brought him and them together at this very point.

Chloe gave Nathan a half-hug, and he first thought she meant to encourage him, but then she mouthed words, clearly intending to communicate privately. He lowered his head, his arm across her shoulders. She was the closest thing to a sister he'd had.

"Jenna and Chen Li are still back there," she said. "We can't leave them, Nathan."

Nathan stiffened.

"Don't you think I know that?" he whispered back. "But these people come first over Jenna and Chen Li. Do you know how much trouble I'd be in with them if I sacrificed these people to go find them?"

"Well? What're we gonna do about it?"

"We're going to get these people across the river, which has been the plan all along. Once they're safe—hopefully in Bruno's hands—then I can work out a plan, even if I have to swim the Hudson to come back here!"

"Lena will kill them. She knows everything now. She knows Jenna was Radiant Shade."

"One thing at a time, Chloe."

He smiled to reassure her, but inside, he was barely holding himself together. Along with his lack of sleep, his attention was distracted when he imagined Chen Li and Jenna in Lena's hands. The Lord had to preserve those two. Even with Obrador, Owen, and Mayor Nick, he was short-handed. Reaching Colorado with such a parade hardly seemed likely.

Owen finally climbed as the last man from the tunnel. Nathan gestured to the wide-eyed ex-Enforcer. At least he knew he could speak to the Twin as an experienced soldier, even if most of the man's experience was preying on innocent, unarmed people.

"Give us about thirty yards, Owen, then you start the people after us. Tell them to stay on the left side of the street, so they don't need to cross the street later. Got it?"

"Got it. Can I have another magazine? I only have this one."

"It's all we have," Nathan said. "One for each of us. Let's hope you don't even need the rounds you do have. I'll see you on the other side."

Nathan surveyed his five-person fighting team, including himself. He and Chloe were still in their banquet clothes, but Scooter, Luigi, and Brian had been living underground for at least a week, and their drab clothing and unshaven faces made them appear more like refugees than elite soldiers.

"There's no retreating," Nathan said to the whole room. "Keep moving forward. If someone falls, pick them up and carry them. But there's no going back. Lena already said she'd gut these tunnels as a top priority."

Scooter held back the metal sheeting, and Nathan climbed through the window frame. He checked the street to the left and right, then walked along the sidewalk, his shoulder against the wall to his left. In seconds, he was better oriented and was thankful the tunnel exit was one street off Broadway. Residential apartment buildings choked the street. Trash and litter was everywhere.

At the next intersection, he judged they were four blocks from the suspension bridge. He could see parts of its length ahead—thirty-five-hundred feet of total exposure to artillery from either shoreline. The battle rifle could cover only eighteen hundred feet, or six hundred yards, about half the distance of the bridge. Under most circumstances, the battle rifle had made COIL a superior force, but not this time. The distance was too great.

At Broadway, Nathan knelt and held up his fist to signal Chloe and Brian behind him. He glanced back, past his two gunners, and saw Luigi and Scooter working steadily up the right side of the street. Farther back, the refugees hustled forward, crouching, shuffling, completely out of their element. In that moment, Nathan remembered all that COIL had ever been, and he was filled with God's joy. He was a COIL operative, and he had dedicated his life to the well-being of God's precious people. Gladly, he would die for one or all of them.

"What's the holdup?" Chloe asked as she caught up. "Danger?"

"Just postponing the inevitable," he said. "When we cross Broadway here, that's it. We'll be fighting it out all the way to Colorado. And we have no food, no clothing, no other provisions. This is it."

"Well, what about Levi?" Chloe asked. "Or maybe we can find Bruno even without Jenna?"

"We might have to. Okay, the street's clear. Let's do this."

Darting across the wide avenue, he reached the other side with a grunt. Six blocks south, Broadway twisted around a thirty-degree corner, so he couldn't see beyond that. He waved the others across, then checked the street again. There was no ignoring the dwindling battle sounds somewhere to the south. It was unlikely that Lena's invading forces had lost. The sun hadn't even visibly risen yet, and the fight around Columbus Circle or farther was on its last breath.

Nathan charged ahead, back in the shadowy streets lined with apartment buildings. One block, then two, he paused at the last building corner. The on and off-ramps to the bridge curled around what he believed was Riverside Drive only a block away. The bridge was manned by three vehicles—two SUVs and one armored personnel carrier, military grade. Using his rifle scope, he counted twelve men, maybe more inside the vehicles.

"Mop-up crew," Nathan said to Chloe and Brian as they each scoped ahead as well. "They were probably left behind to kill anyone who tried to escape the island."

"Lena's orders." Chloe nodded. "They're here for us. There's only two ways off this rock, and she knows this is our most likely route."

"No point in disappointing them," Nathan said. "Let's just hope our weapons are a bit of a surprise."

"What do you have in mind?" Chloe asked.

Nathan used one hand to signal Scooter to advance on the right. They needed those vehicles!

"You know how far we could get with a couple vehicles?"

"We have over a hundred people," Chloe said. "It'll be a tight fit."

"It's still better than the cages they were used to," Brian said. "Let's do it. I'm anxious to see how these tranquilizers really work!"

"You COIL men are all alike." Chloe rolled her eyes.

"I'm not COIL," Brian said.

"Well, you are now." Nathan chuckled, then moved forward.

The two parties advanced in cover formation as close as Nathan dared. The troops on the bridge weren't on high alert, or the refuges would've been noticed right away. But they were staying on the left side of the street, in the shade of the buildings.

Between Scooter's position and Nathan's advance, the twelve at the head of the bridge were nearly sandwiched in the middle, sure to be caught in the crossfire as soon as the shooting started. Aiming ahead, Nathan targeted an officer near the bumper of one SUV. He waited a few more seconds, then signaled Scooter. Scooter nodded back.

Nathan shot the officer first, then shifted his aim to the next soldier, an assault rifle slung across his back. Chloe crouched and fired as well, like the expert markswoman she'd always been. The gunfire was deafening, and it was over in less than a minute. With Scooter and Luigi shooting from the other side, the troops had had no cover.

"Oh, yeah!" Brian exclaimed louder than necessary, probably because his ears were ringing. He admired his rifle. "I need to get me one of these babies!"

"Go! Go!" Nathan directed, and they charged up to the vehicles.

Barely had he cleared the vehicles, checking for sleepers just in case, when he heard gunfire from the rear of their group. He ran out in the street and used his scope to see Owen and Obrador frantically engaging two vehicles with troops that had come up Broadway. The refugees broke rank and charged up the on-ramp toward the bridge.

"Scooter!" Nathan called to his friend, who'd been a Marine sniper many years earlier. "Deal with it."

"Already on it." Scooter sat down on the pavement and rested his elbow on one knee. From the elevated ground of the bridge on-ramp, he fired over the heads of the approaching refugees. Although Scooter was one hundred yards farther away than Owen and Obrador, Scooter's three shots hit two targets, and the vehicles retreated out of sight.

"Let's go!" Nathan yelled to the refugees. "Let's go!"

"I've got keys!" Brian announced. "But we're on empty tanks here."

"We just need them to get across the river," Nathan said. "If we can get to the top of the bridge, we can coast down the other side."

The refugees arrived, breathless and frightened. Several had fallen and were being helped along by their companions. Scooter and Luigi stood like guardians a few yards away, scoping the street and avenues to the east. The sun was in their eyes, but Nathan knew they'd hold the line, even though all the wrath of Lena's army was about to pour down upon them.

"Women and kids into the vehicles!" Chloe instructed.

The people packed into the vehicles. Then Nathan and Brian started lifting them onto the roofs. Twenty-five fit into the personnel carrier, and about eighteen apiece fit into or on top of the SUVs, but that still left nearly forty on foot, mostly men.

"Drive slowly!" Nathan told Owen, Chloe, and Brian, who'd hopped into the drivers' seats. "Give us cover if something starts. Roll 'em out!"

"Nate!" Scooter called, and pointed to the east.

Nathan swung around and froze. An armored vehicle with a turret cannon was driving up the street toward them.

"Take it out, Luigi!" Nathan ordered as he jogged backwards to keep pace with the vehicles. Around him, refugees were weeping and gasping, limping and dragging their feet. "Scooter, push them back!"

But Nathan saw what an impossibility that would be. They were nearly out of gel-tranq ammo, and they'd had only eight phosphorus rounds between the three of them. Together, they stopped and fired all they had, allowing the three vehicles to roll ahead without them. Six Federation vehicles now in sight were disabled, but another dozen rounded the corner of Broadway, and a hundred foot soldiers were marching with them.

"Lena's sent everyone after us!" Nathan growled. "I'm out!"

"Me, too." Scooter clicked his rifle trigger and swung the weapon onto his back. "We won't be able to stay ahead of them, Nathan. What do you want to do? They're coming faster than we're going."

Nathan wanted to weep. New Jersey was right there! *So close!* He turned to see the vehicles moving farther away, but they weren't even halfway up the bridge yet. The Federation troops below weren't even firing, as if they knew the fleeing party was out of ammunition.

"Let's run as far as we can," Nathan said. "No point in going easy. Come on!"

He turned and walked after their three vehicles. As he walked, he drew a tranq-pen from his pocket, remembering Chen Li had the other one. Chen Li—he loved her as much as a man could love his wife. They'd had more than twenty good years together, even living secret lives as Christians. Somehow, he hoped she'd helped Jenna get off the island. It was a lot to hope for, but Jenna was a master strategist, and Chen Li was resourceful. It could happen, with God's help.

"We should throw our rifles over the side," Luigi suggested as he walked on the other side of Scooter. "There's no sense in giving the Federation the finest rifles in the world. They'll only use them for evil."

"Yeah." Nathan frowned, then took a deep breath. "Hey, we could be with the Lord soon, huh?"

"Depending on how long Lena wants to torture us," Scooter said, but in a joking tone rather than a depressed one. "We almost won. Now, we can die well."

"I'm honored to die with you two," Luigi said. "I'd rather live, but I'm not disappointed to go with you both."

Nathan stopped walking. There was no use continuing. The enemy convoy behind them was moving rapidly to overtake them, men jogging alongside the vehicles. The three embraced, realizing their end was near.

"Will you do the honors, Scooter?" Nathan passed his rifle to Scooter, who took Luigi's as well. "It sure was fun firing those again."

Scooter laughed sadly, and walked to the edge of the bridge.

Up the bridge, someone was honking the horn of one of the SUVs.

"What's that?" Nathan put his hands on his hips and peered ahead. "They've stopped."

The horns of both SUVs were now honking.

"I think they want us," Scooter said, and handed the rifles back to Nathan and Luigi.

Together, they ran up to the vehicles. Chloe climbed out of the driver's seat of one SUV. *She was grinning!*

"Jenna was right! God is good, huh?" She clapped her hands together. "I mean, He would've been good even if we would've gotten caught, but you know what I mean."

"Chloe?" Nathan looked back at the Federation troops, steadily advancing, holding their fire, but clearly ready for a fight, with turrets manned and soldiers armed. "What am I missing? We have nowhere to go. I think we've reached the end; we're caught."

"You're looking in the wrong direction, Nate," Scooter said, and pointed west.

Nathan turned and gazed past the three vehicles they'd commandeered. One man walked toward them up the middle of the bridge. It was only one man, Nathan realized, but it wasn't about how many men there were, but *who* the man was.

"Caspertein. *Thank You, Lord.*" Nathan wiped at his teary eyes. "And where there's one, there's usually more. Get back in, Chloe. Keep driving. Get everyone off the bridge. If I know Levi, I'd say he's got it from here."

✝

Lena raced up Broadway on her street bike. The radio had confirmed what she'd hoped for all along—that Chloe and Obrador would try to get off the island. She'd killed Corban already, and now she would kill the rest of them. Obrador *would* try to get off the island! Not only had her new forces taken the Bowery after a hard fight that had lasted until dawn, she was now able to chop the head off the old administration once and for all. She would execute Obrador publicly, that very day, in front of her new troops. The Federation was born again. The *New* Federation!

She reached the bridge in time to see several of her armored vehicles and foot soldiers move steadily up the bridge's length toward a motley crew of escaped prisoners. Many of the prisoners were on foot, and those in the three vehicles didn't seem willing to drive away and leave behind those on foot. Furthermore, Lena had already spoken to a colonel from Baltimore who'd said he'd left behind vehicles at the bridge that were out of fuel. Whatever Chloe and Obrador had carjacked for themselves, they were running on fumes. They had nowhere to go. Now, she would make them all suffer!

Though she could've waited for her new troops to capture the enemy, Lena wanted to be there herself to see Obrador's face. Colonel Rotham was back at the Bowery, holding the capital building for her inauguration later that day. She knew she'd have time to deal with the previous administration.

The troopers in front parted for her to ride her bike onto the bridge, and accelerate up to the assault team about to capture the escaped prisoners. When she'd nearly caught them, she parked her bike on the left walkway and jogged ahead to catch up to the several armored trucks and dozens of soldiers.

Suddenly, the vehicle brakes squeaked slightly as they came to a stop in front of her.

"Victory tastes so, so sweet," she said to the soldiers within earshot. "Everybody out! Take them into custody! There's no point in being gentle. I'm just going to hang them later."

She half-expected the soldiers to high-five her as she moved through them to the front. Where was Obrador? This was her moment, the conclusion of her two months of planning. Now, Obrador would die, and the New Federation would function under a stricter, stronger head. The country would thrive under her developing ideas. And there would be no more Christians to bring their ideas of morality and weakness into her social reformation!

But when she reached the front of the convoy, she found one man standing in the way, blocking the whole Federation. The escaped prisoners were a hundred yards ahead, distancing themselves more by the second!

Lena stepped in front of the lead armored truck and set her hand on her sidearm. It had been a long, bloody night of fighting. She didn't have time for martyrs, heroes, or lone wolves.

"Who're you supposed to be?" Lena asked the man.

Even with his untrimmed, blondish beard, he was tall and handsome. His winter coat was faded and his blue eyes squinted at the bright sunlight. In his hands, he lightly held one of the snub, compact rifles she'd been shot with the night before. She still felt the bruise. It had been some sort of non-lethal ammunition, which left her scoffing at this single man who faced her whole formation.

"Who? Me?" He playfully glanced about, and Lena hated him instantly for wasting her time. "Oh, I'm just coming to close the bridge. You could say I'm the bridge keeper today."

He smiled so casually, so confidently. Lena looked back at the armored truck, wondering why they hadn't already shot this nuisance. Clearly, he was a tunnel rat. Nobody above ground in the city would wear such a beard and worn-out coat.

"I'm taking you into custody," Lena said. She'd arrested hundreds of people over the years. What was one more? "Put down your weapon, get on your knees, and lace your fingers behind your head. There's no point in shooting us with your little toy. I already know it won't hurt me."

"Oh, you're familiar with the gel-tranqs?" He held up the rifle, its stock against his ribs. "I didn't load this with tranquilizers this morning. It's loaded with high-grade phosphorus. Are you familiar? Just a nasty little surprise for you. Tell your people not to fire. I'll show you what it can do. A little demo."

Lena checked behind this distraction. Obrador and Chloe were getting farther away, but it would still take them a few minutes to get off the bridge. They'd be easy to catch.

"Hold your fire!" Lena raised an arm to the convoy. "Hold your fire! Go ahead. Show me what you've got."

The stranger aimed his rifle at a thick suspension cable and fired. The rifle was loud and made Lena's ears ring. But that wasn't what she focused on. She gazed at the suspension cable, comprised of hundreds of individual steel strands. Some sort of acid ate rapidly away at the cable. The substance hissed as globs of the cable dripped away!

The bridge itself groaned, and the surface of the road shifted, as if an earthquake shook the ground.

"Like I said," the gunman stated, "I'm here to close the bridge."

Lena held out her arms to keep her balance against the shifting bridge, and she heard others behind her cry out. In a flash, she raised her handgun and aimed it at the stranger.

"Put down your weapon! Now!"

"If you shoot me, they'll open fire."

Two more people emerged from behind bridge structures, one on each side of the bridge. One was a woman with flowing, dark hair and gray eyes that seemed to bore into Lena. And the other was another bearded man, larger than the one in front of her, in a winter coat that appeared to be partially made of animal skins.

The bridge groaned loudly, then settled.

"Easy, now!" Lena glanced at the other bridge cables, now under serious strain. Her mind flashed back to the reports from Rotham she'd heard about four people taking out his whole convoy. "Don't shoot! I'm putting my weapon away. This bridge is more important to me than you know. You're not even from the city, are you?"

"Do I look like I'm from the city?" The man pivoted and aimed at the cable on the other side. "It ain't easy retreating, lady, but this is one battle you ain't winning. My friends and I are leaving the area. Let them go, and I'll let you go."

"You'll *let* me go?" Lena clenched her teeth. "You'll *let* me? Nobody *let's* me do anything! They never have."

The man moved forward. Lena understood now that he was a traveler, not at all a local who was familiar with her reputation. He wasn't afraid of her and knew nothing of what she'd done to reach her fearsome status. Before she could react, he was within arm's length from her. No one could even shoot him now, unless they shot her first.

"Look into my face," he said softly so that only she was able to hear. All humor had disappeared from his eyes. "Maybe you're used to giving orders instead of taking them, but today, I'm ordering you to back off, or you'll go down with this bridge. I came for my friends, and now we're leaving. Whatever you're playing at in this city no longer concerns me. You don't control me and I don't control you, of course. But you're up against an immovable object right now, and seeing that you have more to lose, and I'm willing to give whatever it takes to win this little standoff, you're taking orders. Walk away."

"You will never—"

"Be quiet. Whatever threats or comments you have to mutter, lady, I'm not interested. I'm Levi Caspertein. Over the years, I've looked into the faces of countless commanders—from the Pacific all the way to this coast—and you're all the same. You're afraid. You don't know who God is so you don't know who you are. So keep your words to yourself, because I already know they'll be spoken to cover up for your fear. If you want to say something, turn around and tell your men the bridge is too unstable to cross. From what I witnessed overnight, you don't need to be wasting any more time with me up here. Go back to the city and carry on with whatever it is you're trying to accomplish. No, don't speak to me. Just turn around and go."

Lena stared up into his face. No one but Obrador had ever spoken to her with such humiliating words, but even Obrador hadn't had this man's . . . authority. He looked like a bum, homeless and impoverished, but what power! And although all humor had left his face, he wasn't snarling. She definitely wanted to shoot him, but she was chancellor now, and she needed to start making decisions for her country, not just for herself. The New Federation needed her.

She lowered her eyes, glad that no one else had heard his insulting words, and turned toward the convoy.

"The bridge is too unstable!" She waved both arms. "Back it up! Off the bridge. Let's go! We're done here. Everyone back to the Bowery Hotel!"

As an afterthought, too proud to leave without having the last word, she looked back at the stranger.

"We'll meet again one day. I'm coming after you."

He smiled. The humor was back.

"I don't care."

She walked after her men. The vehicles made tight U-turns, and they crawled away from the center mass on the bridge.

The bulk of the convoy was off the bridge when Lena heard more gunfire behind her. Over and over, the rifles blasted.

Lena reached her motorcycle and climbed on. She heard the tremendous noise and the shock of her people as the bridge collapsed, but she didn't look back. Levi Caspertein? Whoever he was, she'd make him pay. That bridge had been the capital's primary access to the mainland. Now, they were limited to traveling through the Bronx, the long way.

It wouldn't be possible, she knew, to hide such a defeat from her new commanders, who wanted to see her invincibility. She wasn't even formally chancellor yet, and already she was losing ground!

Obrador, Chloe, and Levi Caspertein would pay. Yes, Owen would die, but she'd make the rest suffer!

✝

Chloe was the last person to walk through a doorway that opened into a dim, expansive, compartmentalized warehouse. Dozens of army cots were already filled with family members, but there were over one hundred cots still available for those arriving. Food stores and water containers were stacked in the center of the warehouse around a distribution desk where familiar faces were gathered.

The vehicles hadn't had enough fuel to drive more than a mile west of the bridge, so they'd walked all that afternoon, following a one-armed woman carrying a staff in her hand, and a rifle and pack on her back. Chloe was so overwhelmed and thankful that they had such a place set up for their arrival that she collapsed to her knees a few feet inside the door, and wept. Through her tears, she saw Luigi at the center desk, packing a bag of provisions as if he was preparing to leave that very minute. And Nathan was slapping the back of a tall, broad-shouldered black man—Bruno. The rest of the refugees, including Obrador and Owen, were welcomed by the families who'd already taken up residence in the warehouse.

Though Chloe was crying for joy, she was also crying for Jenna and Chen Li, who were still missing. If she had any energy left, she would've found Levi Caspertein and seen if he had more gel-tranqs to spare, so she could return for the two COIL operatives who'd been left behind.

One of the two women Chloe had seen accompanying Levi on the bridge walked up to her and offered a bottle of water.

"Do you need help getting to a cot?" the woman asked. Her hair was dark, her eyes a flinty gray. "We've got enough for everyone. Come on. I'll help you."

Chloe accepted the younger woman's arm.

"My legs aren't working too well," Chloe said. "How is this place even possible, right in the middle of New Jersey? I thought we'd be camping in the cold woods of Pennsylvania tonight."

"As I understand it, that man named Bruno over there has been preparing this place for a long time. It was used by the first wave of Christian travelers last year."

"Yes, Bruno." Chloe sobbed, her physical and emotional stamina exhausted. "Of course, Jenna has been taking care of everything with Bruno."

The woman helped her sit on a cot, and Chloe immediately lay on her back. In the middle of the warehouse, the laughter of men seemed so strange. How could they even have energy to laugh? One of them was Levi, a couple inches taller than Nathan. And an even larger man than Levi stood nearby with the one-armed woman who'd shed her rifle but still held her iron staff. Chloe wanted to meet them all, and visit with and comfort the refugees, but she needed to rest first.

"Let me take these off for you." The gray-eyed woman untied Chloe's boots and slid them off her feet. "You're safe here, so you just rest now. This is a COIL safe house. Have you ever heard of COIL?"

"Ever heard of COIL?" Chloe chuckled through her tears. "At the beginning of COIL, I was— Oh, never mind."

"I'm just kidding." The woman smiled and unfolded a blanket over Chloe. "I know who you are, Chloe. My husband, Levi, pointed you out to me when we were waiting on the bridge. I'm Lyla Caspertein."

"Well, I'm not sure I'm in the mood for kidding." Chloe struggled to keep her eyes open. "But I'm glad to hear the Caspertein wit is alive and well after all these years."

If more was said, Chloe didn't hear it, because the next thing she realized, she was waking up to a dark warehouse. She sat up and tugged on her boots. Two lanterns hung from beams in the floor's center space where a dozen tables had been unfolded and set up. Bruno had been busy for some time, but certainly Jenna was to be credited with the preparations. Once again, the blind woman had thought of everything for everyone. Except for herself.

People were sleeping on cots all around Chloe, snoring, mumbling, hardly stirring. She stood upright on legs that desperately needed stretching after the miles marched the day before. Slowly, she walked to the center counter where Bruno stood with Levi who had shaved off his beard. Now he looked even more like his father.

"Do you two ever sleep?" she said in greeting.

Bruno was a baldheaded, black man who'd served with Nathan in the original COIL Special Forces team, and Chloe had also been part of that squad. So it was with compassion, after so long, that he embraced her like the bear-sized man he was.

"Chloe, I've waited years to have us all together again."

"Not all together," she corrected. "Corban's not here."

She shook Levi's hand, remembering him as just a skinny teenager at his father's side before Pan-Day.

"This place is amazing, Bruno," she admired as Bruno served her a mug of steaming oatmeal. "How long can we stay here?"

"The Federation could find us any minute," Levi said, "but it looks like everyone needs a couple days at least. You'll leave in two days."

"You're not coming?"

"I can't. No offense, but I came for Jenna. And I can't leave without her."

"Even if it means your capture?" she asked.

"Even then." He raised his own mug. "It ain't easy walking into the jaws of death, but I've looked into the eyes of this Lena Travers lady, and she's just another lost soul who needs the Lord's love and the gospel."

"Funny you should say that," Chloe said. "Corban's last words to Nathan were to tell you that she's not a lost cause."

"I'll remember that, if we stick around long enough to cross her path again."

"We?" Chloe looked at Bruno. "Are you staying behind, too? You're expecting more refugees? More Christians?"

"Oh, no. I'm pulling out with all of you in a couple days." Bruno yawned and stretched. "It's time this old bear was put out to pasture in Colorado."

"Only Nathan and I will stay behind," Levi said, "that is, if I can keep up with the guy. He still looks like he's in his prime."

"It could take an army to get Jenna and Chen Li back," Chloe said, "if they were caught. But you two together? I'd say that's an army."

"Three, including me." Brian Steelman walked in from the direction of the cots. He shook Levi's hand. "You may have come to find Jenna, but I came to find you. Do you remember me? Brian Steelman?"

"It was a long time ago." Levi crossed his arms. "Arizona? Yes, you had a leg injury."

"You asked me some questions about the Federation, so I knew you were headed this way. I returned and got caught up with your friends here. God used it to teach me the gospel."

"Glad to see the leg's doing better."

"If you're staying back here, I am, too. No one knows this area better than me, and you'll need someone who knows New Jersey and New York to navigate around whatever Lena is about to do."

"I'll have Nathan for that." Levi set his hand on the older man's shoulder. "This caravan that's headed west will need you more, Brian. I need to ask you to help Rex get these others back to Meeker, Colorado. Since you've been out West before, you'll know how to guide them. As you're aware, the Plains Zone is some pretty rough territory."

Chloe watched disappointment shadow Brian's face, but then the man took a breath.

"Okay. I'd be honored to help them. Just don't make me return to break you two out of prison back here."

"Don't worry. I'll request immediate execution, since I don't think I'd favor prison too much."

"You're just like your father." Chloe shook her head. "Never serious."

In the morning, Chloe walked to the door with Nathan. His pack had fresh provisions from Bruno's stores, and his ammo vest contained enough gel-tranqs and phosphorus rounds for a small war.

"I don't like going one way while you go another," Chloe said, "but if you're able to find those two right away, you'll get a quick start after us. We'll all be in Meeker before it snows.

"Nothing would please me more." Nathan embraced her. "Did you know Luigi left without a word earlier this morning?"

"*What?*" Chloe turned and gazed across the warehouse floor. "He didn't even say goodbye."

"Does he ever? He's been pretty broken up about Heather. And now Corban. He's always been quiet, but now he's more of a shadow."

"Well, Luigi's doing what Luigi does." Chloe smiled sadly. "It's actually comforting to know that he'll be staying back, watching over you and Levi."

Levi crossed the floor and kissed his wife, then playfully shoved Rex as a goodbye.

"Maybe it's better this way," Chloe said to Nathan. "I can't imagine hiking the road with those two clowns. It's like having two Tituses."

"It ain't easy," said Alice, Levi's one-armed companion, who stood next to the door. She was a few years younger than Chloe, but gray hair had colored her temples over her ebony skin. "They've tried my patience the last few months, but I'd trust Levi over anyone else on earth to get the job done. We'll see them again soon."

Lyla walked her husband to the door. Bruno put a giant arm over the shoulders of each of the two departing men, and spoke a brief prayer to God about their mission, and Jenna and Chen Li. Above all, he prayed that God would receive the glory from their lives, whether they succeeded or failed at what they sought to accomplish.

Wiping at tears, Chloe watched as Levi and Nathan left the warehouse and jogged out of sight across a parking lot. But Lyla and Scooter were there to hold her close. Already, she felt Lyla's womanly presence was one that was easy to warm to. It seemed she didn't take anything too seriously, but knew how to handle her responsibilities.

Chloe thought of all the loss she'd suffered since Pan-Day. Even after everything that had happened, God had still made sure that she had ended up with family. Yet, she wasn't going to rest until she heard that Jenna and Chen Li were free from this terrible land of oppression.

Thanks for reading *Dawn of Oppression!* I pray it was a blessing to you. I look forward to bringing you Book Three! Please leave me a comment wherever you bought this book so I know if it hit the mark. Thank you for taking the time. It would be a great help to me! —*David Telbat*

What's Next?

Dawn of Subjection

Enjoy this teaser for Book 3 of the *Last Dawn Series.*

The New Federation has been born under Chancellor Lena Travers, but she has spawned an evil she can't contain. His name is Colonel Milo Rotham, and he lives for war, death, and destruction in America's Last Days.

As Chloe Azmaveth leads the COIL survivors from New York City, Levi Caspertein and Nathan Isaacson return to the carnage in hope of finding Jenna Dowler and Nathan's wife, Chen Li. Amidst the power struggle following Operation Esther, the New Federation is more dangerous than ever, but Levi has come too far to give up his rescue mission now. He won't abandon Jenna in her own blindness, or to the persecution of her tormentors. Nor will he leave other victims behind who are in desperate need of the love of Christ. From God, he has learned that even his enemies need compassion.

As if the COIL operatives don't have enough to face, a bounty hunter and skillful tracker from the West has arrived to cure the New Federation of its Christian problem. The bounty hunter's name is . . . Andy Radner, the adopted son of *Eric Radner. And though Andy is only a young man, he already has a reputation for being cold-blooded, always catching his prey, if the bargain is to his liking. He also has his sights set on Levi Caspertein, who is wanted dead or alive.

The country is burdened by increasing woe, and weighed down by heightened suffering. The New Federation has an appetite to see its enemies defeated and begging for mercy. Unless COIL keeps the faith and clings to their eternal hope in Jesus Christ, they, too, will be defeated in this new . . . Dawn of Subjection!

Only the steadfast will survive in America's last days!

*Eric and Andy Radner are main characters in *The Steadfast Series*.

About the Author

D.I. (David) Telbat is a Christian author best known for his **clean, Suspenseful Fiction with a Faith Focus**. This includes his bestselling and award-winning *COIL Series, Steadfast Series, Last Dawn Series,* and other Christian Suspense and End Times novels. He wrote his first book at age 14, and he hasn't stopped since!

David studied writing in school and worked for a time in the newspaper field. Getting into serious trouble with the law as a young man became a turning point in his life. The Lord used that experience to draw David into a personal relationship with Him. Re-focusing his life for Christ, he now seeks to honor God with his life and writing by doing what he loves most—writing and Christian ministry.

Subscribe to receive David Telbat's FREE, bi-weekly **D.I. Telbat Newsletter** with one of his Christian short stories, or an Author Reflection, or his Novel News Update. You'll also receive **exclusive subscriber gifts**, such as his ***Three For Free***—three-novels-in-one eBook! You can join the adventure by visiting his site at books2read.com/DITelbat/ and click on the "**Follow this Author**" button.